D1799612

Relativity

Relativity

Justice Keepers Saga Book IV

R.S. Penney

Prologue

Harry leaned against the wall with his arms folded, frowning at Jack. "You cannot be serious," he said, shaking his head in disbelief. "You think we should give weapon's tech to Earth's governments?"

This meeting had gone on for the better part of an hour while Harry filled them in on the latest political quagmire. The poor guy was stuck trying to force several different law-enforcement agencies into playing nice. It had been a simple suggestion – nothing more – but he could already tell this wasn't going to go over well.

Jack winced, pressing a knuckle to his forehead. "I'm dead serious," he insisted, backing away from the other man. "Look, I'm not suggesting that we give them guns or death spheres, but some of the defensive tech like force-field generators…"

Anna stood beside him with hands clasped behind her back, tilting her head up to stare at the ceiling. "I'd like to note that I'm against this plan," she said. "Defensive tech can very easily be turned into offensive weaponry."

"Yeah, but-"

"Children," Jena cut in. "No fighting."

The leader of their little group sat on the edge of her desk with hands resting on her knees, directing a scowl into her own lap. "Every suggestion is worth considering," she added. "That said, I think Anna has a point about-"

She was cut off by the door chime.

"Open," Jena shouted.

The double doors slid apart to allow Harry's daughter Melissa to stumble into the room. The girl was hunched over with a hand pressed to her stomach, gasping as if she had just run a marathon. "Bleakness take me, girl," Jena said. "You look like you've just seen a ghost. What is it?"

"I know…" Melissa gasped. "I know. I understand."

"You know what?"

A wince twisted the girl's face into something painful to look at, and she stood up straight with some effort. "I know what Grecken Slade is planning."

Jack spun around to face her.

Those words made him feel like someone had just flicked him right between the eyes. How could a high school student possibly know that? But the sincerity in her voice made it clear that she believed it.

He shuffled over to the girl with hands shoved into his pockets, keeping his eyes downcast. "Okay, Melissa, let's just take it slow," he began. "How exactly do you know what Slade is planning?"

Melissa looked up at him with sweat glistening on her face, blinking slowly as if she'd never seen a grown man before. "Raynar showed me," she whispered. "The other day when I visited him in his cell."

Chewing on his lower lip, Jack shut his eyes tight. "Yeah, that makes all kinds of sense," he said, nodding to her. "Melissa, I know you believe it, but that boy could have put any fantasy into your head."

"It's true, Missy," Harry added. "Anything he imagines he can force into your mind with very little effort."

"My name is Melissa!"

The girl bared her teeth like a feral beast, hissing and seething. She backed up until she was standing in the doorway. "I know how telepathy works, but I'm telling you this is real! I felt it!"

With a heavy sigh, Jena got off her desk and paced across the room with her head down. "Okay," she said with more patience in her voice than Jack would have expected. "Let's hear her out."

"Really?" Harry asked.

"All suggestions are worth considering."

They took a few minutes to get Melissa settled, offered her a chair and a glass of water. She seemed grateful for it, and Jack couldn't help but feel a little guilty for the way they had so casually dismissed her. Whatever the girl had seen, it had left enough of an impression on her to make her scramble through the hallways of the station in a frenzy. That alone made it worth giving her their undivided attention.

Anna was down on one knee next to Melissa's chair, smiling up at the girl. "You okay, kiddo?" she asked with surprising gentleness in her voice. "Would you like a few more minutes to collect yourself?"

"No," Melissa insisted.

Jena leaned against the opposite wall with hands on her thighs, refusing to look up. "Let's get started then," she murmured. "What did Raynar show you, Melissa? And how would he know Slade's plans?"

Melissa scowled into her drink. "Slade would visit that station on Ganymede." She took a sip of her water, slurping as she tried to force it down. "While he was there, Raynar probed his thoughts."

"And what did he see?"

The girl heaved out a shuddering breath, trembling as she tried to find the words. Clearly, she was nervous, but Jack couldn't say why. Maybe she thought they wouldn't believe her.

"Slade is looking for something called the Key," she said at last. "It's some kind of Overseer technology."

Tossing his head back, Jack felt his brow furrow. "Well, at least it's not anything original," he said. "I find it reassuring to know that the bad guys are sticking to the classics."

Anna glanced over her shoulder with a glare that told him he should shut the fuck up right now. "So what is this Key?" she asked, turning her attention back to Melissa. "A device of some kind?"

"No, the Key isn't a thing; it's a place."

"Do you know where?"

Closing her eyes, Melissa let her head hang. She brushed a lock of dark hair away from her face. "I don't," she mumbled. "Somewhere on Earth, but I can't be any more specific than that."

Harry squeezed his eyes shut, shaking his head. "Well, that makes things difficult, doesn't it?" he asked, moving forward to join them. "So have we decided how credible the young telepath is?"

Jack noted that he didn't say how credible his daughter was. Poor Melissa looked so shaken; her father seemed more skeptical than anyone else here. *Fathers…Doubting you is what they do best.*

"The Overseers have left remnants of their technology behind," Jena said softly. "Places where the ancient Leyrian tribes could speak with the 'spirits of the great ones.' We later realized these were holograms."

"But no such places exist on Earth," Harry said.

Jack paced over to the door with his arms folded, heaving out a deep breath. "We don't know that," he countered. "Just because we haven't found them doesn't mean they aren't there."

Melissa looked up at him with admiration in her big dark eyes. She blinked a few times, then turned her attention back to the others. "I believe Raynar," she said. "I know that I can't offer you anything more than my word, but I trust him."

"And I trust you," Jena said.

She stepped away from the wall with a groan, shaking her head as she made her way across the room. "I trust everyone on my team," she added. "So, from now on, we make this a priority. Anna, you and I are going to go through every Leyrian religious text we can find and search for any reference to something that might fit the description of this Key. Jack, Harry, do the same for your own people. It's likely that some of Earth's creation myths are at least partially inspired by the Overseers. Melissa, I want you to meet with me regularly and describe everything that Raynar showed you in exquisite detail. Any questions?"

"Yeah, I've got one," Anna said. She turned to stare up at Jena with apprehension on her face. "Doesn't anyone else want to know what this thing does?"

"It doesn't matter what it does," Jena said. "If Slade wants it, it can't do anything good. So what do you say we find it first and have ourselves a little game of keep-away? Sound fun to you? Good, let's get started."

(Three months later)

At the very bottom of a stairwell, she found a door bathed in the flickering light of a fluorescent bulb on the wall. An electric buzz filled the air to the point where it almost seemed like sparks would crackle.

She pushed through the door and stepped into a parking garage where concrete pillars supported the ceiling and bright lights shone down on the yellow lines of dozens of empty parking spaces. There were few cars here, and she couldn't detect a sign of any other living soul. Nevertheless, she was apprehensive. She hated parking garages. Every time she stepped into one, she heard the gunfire in the back of her head, remembered the hulking metal giant ripping her people to shreds.

Aamani Patel let out a sigh.

As usual, she wore a black pantsuit with a gray blouse and kept her black hair tied up in a clip. It took some effort to make herself move forward, but she managed to do it without any visible delay. Projecting confidence was crucial.

Closing her eyes, Aamani took a deep breath. *It happened almost four years ago,* she thought with a nod. *You must put such fears behind you. There are much larger concerns in the here and now.*

Her car – a blue Honda Civic – was parked alone in a row of empty spaces, facing the wall to her left. The paint job still glistened after two years, but that was the result of conscientious care. What was the point of owning a thing if you wouldn't take care of it?

She deactivated the alarm.

Pulling the driver's side door open, she slipped into the car with a soft sigh and let her body relax. After the day she'd just endured, it was tempting to let herself fall asleep right here. Her car made her feel safe.

Then she noticed it.

In the rearview mirror she saw the silhouette of a man in the back seat, a man who sat poised and calm like a wolf waiting to gobble up some poor defenseless little bunny. The only thing she could say for certain was that he had long hair. "Don't be alarmed," he said when he realized that she had noticed him.

Aamani drew her pistol from its underarm holster.

She twisted around, pointing the gun in his face, and used the dome light to reveal her unwelcome guest. He was a tall man with Asian features and black hair that fell over his shoulders. "Grecken Slade," she said.

He smiled, bowing his head to her. "I didn't know if you would remember me," he said, leaning back against the seat cushion. "We have much to discuss, Ms. Patel. I think we could be of great use to each other."

She shoved the tip of her gun in his face, and he didn't flinch. Not even a bit. "The only thing we have to discuss is whether you can use one of your Keeper tricks before I pull this trigger. I'm thinking no."

"Look to your left."

She did so and found a metal briefcase that he had left in the space underneath the glove box. "What's this?" she asked with disdain in her voice. "Some attempt to win me over with a bribe?"

"Open it."

Keeping the gun on him, she reached over and set the briefcase on the passenger seat. She undid the snaps and pulled it open to reveal…pistols. Six of them stacked side by side. These were weapons identical to the one she had once seen Anna Lenai use.

Aamani frowned as she stared down at this treasure trove. "Leyrian weapons," she said softly. "Your people have always been adamant that you would not share defensive technology. Why the change of heart?"

Grinning like the devil himself, Slade closed his eyes and tilted his head back. "It's called an exchange, Aamani," he teased. "I thought someone raised on this planet would be familiar with the concept."

"And what do you want in exchange?"

"Information."

The tip of her gun was just an inch away from his nose, and yet he didn't seem to mind. Should she pull the trigger? Aamani had been briefed on the incident with Slade some months ago. He was persona non grata among the Justice Keepers now.

She could end his miserable existence here and now and still take the weapons. Her people could analyze them and learn how to make more. An alliance with this man would not end well; she was sure of that.

The grin on Slade's face only widened as he sank into the cushion. "I can see the calculations in your head," he said, staring up at the roof. "Should you kill me and just take the weapons? You're welcome to try."

Meaning she would fail.

Worst of all, she believed him. There was no doubt in her mind that if she tried to kill him, they would find her bloody corpse somewhere in this garage tomorrow morning. That left her with very few options.

Aamani turned her back on him.

Closing her eyes, she thumped her head against the seat cushion. "So what kind of information do you want?" she asked in a breathy whisper. "I am no longer in contact with your former compatriots."

"Nothing so prosaic."

He leaned forward between the driver and passenger's seat, smiling like a madman. "I want you to keep me up to date on the political climate in your country," he said softly. "Do that, and I will see that you are well-compensated."

"Why would you want such information?"

His burst of soft laughter made her feel as if she had just amused Satan himself with a very stupid question. "Let's be blunt with each other, Aamani," he said. "You don't approve of my people's presence on your planet, and most of us don't want to be here. It should be clear to the galaxy by now that there is no Overseer tech on this benighted little world. We can leave."

"And you believe you can help me achieve this goal?"

"With your cooperation, yes."

"Very well," Aamani hissed. "Tell me what you want to know, and I will see what I can do."

The cargo hold of the tiny ship that had carried him across the galaxy was cramped and packed with empty crates pressed up against the walls. There was just enough space in the middle of the room for a SlipGate.

The seven-foot-tall metal triangle stood silent and ominous, the sinuous grooves on its surface beginning to glow with eerie luminescence. Even though he fully understood the technology, anything of the Old Ones always left him a little uneasy.

Wesley spun around, turning his back on the thing.

The bubble formed around him, making every crate and box in this room seem to ripple as though caught in the heat of an August afternoon. Half a second later, he was yanked forward, pulled through an endless tunnel.

The bubble slid to a stop, and he found himself in a spacious room with hardwood floors and cream-coloured walls that had been decked out with African tribal masks. A single man stood demurely with hands folded over his waist, head bowed in respect. Of course, he was blurry to Wesley's eyes.

The bubble popped.

"Mr. Pennfield," Gilbert said. "It's good to see you."

Wesley felt his lips curl, then nodded to the other man. "I've been away too long," he said, making his way across the room. "After four years, I'd imagine that things have fallen apart around here."

Gilbert blushed, hanging his head as if it were a matter of personal shame. "Your company was dismantled after your departure," he murmured. "However, most of your wealth was spread through the accounts of numerous aliases. We can resume our work at your convenience."

"Excellent."

"Are you well, sir?"

Pressing his lips together, Wesley stared up at the ceiling. He blinked through the lenses of his glasses. "Four years, Gilbert," he said softly. "Four years exiled from this world and forced to witness Slade's bumbling incompetence."

"The Key, sir?"

Wesley turned on his heel, making his way toward a door in the wall with his hands shoved into his pockets. "We will find it first," he replied. "And when we do, we will be favoured by the Old Ones."

He pushed the door open to reveal a large balcony ringed by an ornate stone railing. In the distance, he saw palm trees standing like shadows under the starry sky and heard waves crashing on the beach. Oahu was a truly beautiful at any time of year. This place would do until he could find a more permanent residence.

After four long years, Wesley Pennfield had come back to Earth.

The sun was high in the clear blue sky, shining down upon a field of yellow grass that stretched on for several dozen feet before ending in a chain-link fence. Beyond that, the back parking lot of James Polk High School stood in the shade of the towering three-story building.

Lifting a cigarette to his lips, Kevin Harmon closed his eyes and took a puff. "Bad enough I had to waste three days on this stupid project," he muttered. "Why do I have to be the one to dig the hole?"

He turned around.

Amanda Simmons stood in front of him with her hands folded over her belly, her head bowed in respect. She was a pretty girl in a white, short-sleeved sundress with flowers on the skirt.

Her face was a perfect oval of pale skin framed by curly dark hair that fell to her shoulders. "Miss Sutherland said it was extra credit," she mumbled. "She said burying the time capsule was a privilege."

Kevin shut his eyes, turning his face up to the morning sun. He felt sweat prickle on his skin. "You want the credit even more than I do," he muttered. "How 'bout you go dig the damn hole?"

Of course, the question left her flustered, and she backed away from him to show her discomfort. The answer was pretty straight forward when you took a minute to think about it: Amanda wouldn't be digging the hole because she was a girl. This was a very conservative school in a very conservative neighbourhood. Some things never changed.

He didn't bother saying as much.

A tall boy in ripped jeans and a t-shirt that seemed to hang off his body, Kevin was considered good looking by most of the girls at this school. He'd even seen Amanda cast the odd glance in his direction when she thought he wasn't looking. A few days working side by side with her made him realize that he actually enjoyed the attention. Only one problem: he was black, she was white, and this was a very conservative school.

The day was getting warmer with every passing second, and he very much wanted to get back to the cool, air-conditioned building. Miss Sutherland said that she would be along any moment now, but he saw no reason not to get started. He picked up the shovel.

Kevin had been the one to suggest burying the time capsule here. This small field behind the school was a hot spot for social activity. There was always someone sneaking back here for a cigarette or few minutes alone, and come lunch time, this area would be teeming with bodies until some teacher came along to make them all disperse.

There had even been cases of couples sneaking out here to have sex. Why anybody would do something so stupid was beyond him; this little patch of grass was in full view of anyone who came out the school's back entrance. People just seemed to gravitate to this spot. Even now, with most of the student body in class, he had been forced to chase away a couple preppies who had come out here to make out.

Digging the trowel of his shovel the ground, he uprooted a chunk of dirt and grass and tossed it aside. Already he could feel fatigue, but he kept digging. If he finished before Miss Sutherland returned, they could skip to the part where she said her little speech and then head back inside.

Amanda stood just a few feet away with fingers laced behind herself, refusing to look up at him. "We should probably wait," she said softly. "Miss Sutherland would want to be here for this."

Next to her, the large metal box that contained a few non-functioning iPods, some teen magazines and a poster of Holly Bop sat untouched in the grass. He couldn't wait to leave the thing buried under three feet of dirt.

Wincing hard, Kevin wiped sweat off his brow with his fist. "You could help," he said with a little more venom than he had intended. "Go back to the Janitor's Room. You should be able to get another shovel."

Amanda wilted.

He shoved the trowel of his shovel into the dirt and deepened the pit by a few more inches. His muscles were starting to ache, but the damn thing was almost large enough to hold the box. Just a few more minutes.

His shovel hit something squishy.

Scooping a bit of dirt up with the blade, he flung it aside to reveal…something. It looked like a thin layer of skin with pulsing veins. What in god's name was it? He should have been frightened, but instead, he was curious.

Dropping to his knees in front of the hole, Kevin let his head hang. "Holy crap," he said, scrubbing a hand through his short dark hair. "Amanda, go get a teacher. Someone should take a look at this."

She turned and ran.

Kevin touched the sheet of skin with his fingertips, marveling at the soft, smooth texture. He would have expected something rough or slimy, but it wasn't like that at all. On some level that he couldn't understand, it felt like it belonged to him.

The skin began to rise, curling up on itself until it formed a sphere about the size of a tennis ball. When he picked it up, he realized that it was solid all the way through. This thing was…alive.

The ball lit up with soft white light, growing brighter and brighter until it seemed as if he held a small star in his palm. It flared once, then went dim again. Something about it tugged at him. This thing was *his;* he knew it. He had to get it away from here, had to put it someplace safe. He took off at a run before anyone could spot him.

Part 1

Chapter 1

Morning sunlight came in through the window along with a breeze that made the curtains billow, leaving a square of radiance at the foot of the bed. The sweet scents of spring filled the room.

Anna pressed her cheek into the pillow, squeezing her eyes shut. "Not yet," she grumbled, rubbing her nose with the palm of her hand. "I was having the nicest dream I've had in months."

Bradley was lying next to her.

Her boyfriend was a handsome man with dark stubble on his jawline and black hair that he wore cut short. "What were you dreaming about?" he murmured, staring up at the ceiling. "Kicking terrorist ass?"

Anna sat up.

Hunching over, she scrubbed both hands over her face and ran fingers through her cherry-red hair. "You, of course," she said, hoping that he didn't notice her hesitation. "I was dreaming about taking you to Leyria."

She got up and stood on the carpeted floor of her bedroom in white shorts and a red tank top. "I wanted to show you the Calassarin Cliffs," she added, stretching to work out the kink in her back.

In her mind's eye, she saw him sit up and glance out the window. "So what's on the agenda for today?" he asked. "It's been a few weeks since you've gone on a mission."

"I know," she said. "It's making my skin itch."

He got up and made his way to the window in nothing but a pair of old track pants. "Does that mean you're going to be working on that special project of yours?" he asked. "Are you ever gonna tell me what it is?"

A sigh escaped her when she considered the question. He was talking about their search for the Key. In the last three months, she had been called up to Station Twelve for any number of secret meetings. It was hard for Bradley not to notice. She could sense his curiosity every time he did.

Closing her eyes, Anna let out a breath. "I wish I could," she said, spinning around to face him. "Sorry, hon, but secrets are a part of the package when you date somebody like me. I'm not trying to keep you in the dark."

He turned and stood before the window with hands in his pockets, smiling down at the floor. "No big deal," he said with a shrug of his shoulders. "Guess you'll be going to the park for your morning workout?"

"You know me so well."

She loved him for that, his unconditional trust. He wanted to know the truth, but he wouldn't push. Very few people were lucky enough to find a partner like this. "Yeah," she added. "I'm craving a little fresh air. I think I'll see if Jack's up for a little sparring."

"Have fun."

The jungle gym in the small park behind their apartment complex was a tall metal monstrosity with two towers connected by a bridge. A slide emerged from one, and the other had a slanted roof.

The air was warm on this April morning with only a few gray clouds in the bright blue sky. Thankfully, there were no children about – most would be in school at this time – and they could use the equipment freely.

A sloping hillside ran up to the back of their apartment building, and there were already spectators gathered there to watch the show. These regular sparring sessions had become a source of entertainment to the other tenants.

Anna stood with fists on her hips in gray track pants and a black tank top, staring up at the playground equipment. "The game is 'don't touch the ground'," she said with a nod. "First one to touch the ground loses."

Next to her, Jack wore a similar outfit.

He smiled, then wiped his mouth with the back of his hand. "If you insist," he said, shuffling over to the base of one tower. "But I've gotta warn you I was playing on these things when I was a kid. Ever heard the phrase 'home court advantage?'"

"Ever heard the phrase 'cocky boy meets girl's shoe?'"

Anna paced through the dirt with her arms crossed, sighing softly. "I'm pretty sure I can keep up," she said. "You just worry about me scuffing up those pants with my inevitable victory."

Anna jumped.

She somersaulted through the air, then uncurled to land on one of the railings that surrounded the bridge. Perched like a cat, she took a moment to inspect her surroundings. The roofed structure would do nicely.

She jumped, hopping across to the opposite railing, then leaped again. Flipping in midair, she landed on the slanted roof with a loud grunt. In her mind's eye, she saw Jack coming up behind her.

He sailed right over her head – propelled by a light Bending – and landed crouched at the peak of the roof. "All right, let's do this," he said, standing up straight. "Those folks came to see a show."

He spun around to face her.

Anna kicked at his stomach.

Jack flung one hand out to strike her ankle and knock her off balance. He stepped forward, then delivered a mean right hook to the face. Silver flecks danced in her field of vision. Anna fell backward off the roof.

Flipping upside down in midair, she grabbed the bridge railing and rose into a handstand. She flipped upright to land on the bridge, and focused on Seth's attempts to heal the damage. With Slade and those who followed him possessing symbionts of their own, she would have to be ready to fight enemies who could match her strength and skill. These sparring sessions were designed to be full-on training. She had insisted that Jack treat it like a real fight, which meant real injuries.

He landed on the bridge beside her, spinning around to face her with his fists up in a boxer's stance. "You doing all right," he asked, striding toward her. "I really don't want to hurt you."

He threw a punch.

Anna ducked, allowing the blow to pass right over her. She slipped past him on the left, then flung her elbow into the soft spot over Jack's shoulder blades. That earned her a grunt and made him stumble.

Spinning around, she seized his shirt in both hands. A light Bending made her skin tingle, but she was able to warp the fabric of space-time around him. Jack flew upwards and sideways, over the bridge railing.

He changed direction in midair, yanked as if by a tether toward the set of monkey bars a few paces away. He landed down on one knee, head bowed as if in prayer. Through her connection with Seth, Anna could sense the Bending he had crafted.

She hopped up onto the railing.

Anna leaped and used a Bending of her own to carry herself across the wide gap to the monkey bars. "I'm doing quite well," she said, landing perched on a metal bar. "How about you?"

Jack stood on one bar with his feet apart, arms hanging casually at his side. "I'm a little thirsty," he said, nodding to her. "But I'm thinking it won't be long until I can take a quick breather."

He came at her.

Anna jumped, spinning in midair for a hook kick.

When her foot hit nothing, she knew she was in trouble. She dropped onto the bar just in time to see Jack rise up in front of her. He seized the front of her shirt and gave a hard shove, throwing her off the structure.

Anna fell backward with a squeak. The only way to save herself at this point was a Bending, and she wasn't of a mind to stress Seth any further. When her ass hit the ground, she let out a groan of pain. Damn him! When exactly had Jack become so good at this? It must have happened while she was away.

He dropped to the ground in front of her, landing in a crouch with his head down. "Looks like I win," he said. "Don't worry, Anna. You're still way ahead by the numbers."

Clenching her teeth, Anna winced. "Yes, I am," she said, turning her face up to the open sky. "But I've got to give you some credit: you're getting really good at this. I guess my training really paid off, huh?"

"Somehow you still make it about you."

"Naturally."

Jack stood up with a groan. He shuffled over to her, muttering under his breath the whole way. "Come on," he said, offering his hand. "Let's go get cleaned up. I think we've both had enough for one day."

She let him pull her to her feet.

Turning away from him, Anna reached up to brush a few strands of hair out of her face. "I have to run a few errands," she said softly. "You want to meet me this afternoon, and we can go over the research?"

He shuffled backward with hands shoved into his pockets, clearing his throat with some force. "Sure." Though she didn't draw attention to it, she knew that Jack felt a little uneasy about the idea of full-contact sparring. It wasn't because she was a woman – he had outgrown such antiquated attitudes – but she was his friend, and punches were reserved for enemies. "I've got to head out to Winnipeg to see my mom anyway."

"Cool," she said. "See you later."

"Okay."

Anna turned partway, glancing over her shoulder with a warm smile. "Hey, Jack," she said, eyebrows rising. "Good match."

The dark waters of the Ottawa River stretched on before her, flowing underneath a bridge that connected the city with Gatineau. On the shore, a path of black asphalt ran parallel to the river, and joggers kept running past.

She spotted Gabi sitting on a bench and staring out at the water, her long dark hair falling to the small of her back. The sight of her left Anna feeling a little uneasy. Why did the woman have to choose this spot of all places for their lunch date? Was this the same bench where she and Jack had shared their first kiss?

Anna approached with hands clasped behind her back, keeping her eyes fixed on the ground. "Hello there," she said, taking a seat next to her friend. "So you finally came out for a little fresh air."

A warm smile bloomed on Gabi's face as she stared out at the water. "The weather has finally become tolerable," she said with a nod. "Something that a civilized person might actually want to experience."

"What's your grievance with winter?"

"It exists."

Tossing her head back, Anna rolled her eyes in frustration. "Well your fear of snow made you miss out on the skating," she said, slouching down on the bench with her arms crossed. "I think Jack would have liked it if you'd joined us for that."

Gabi chuckled, hunching over with elbows on her thighs. She covered her mouth with one hand. "He probably would have," she admitted. "But I maintain that if a place gets cold enough for water to freeze, humans have no business living there. So how are things with Bradley?"

"Pretty good."

"I see," Gabi murmured, "and note the lack of detail."

Anna closed her eyes, hanging her head in chagrin. She touched two fingers to her forehead. "He's starting to get curious about my work," she replied. "Things I can't really tell him about."

In the distance, a seagull swooped low over the river, then changed direction and took off toward the shoreline with wings flapping. It really was a beautiful day; winter could be fun – and she did like to bundle up – but it was nice to go outside without shivering. "How do you handle it?" Anna asked. "You must have had partners who asked about things you can't discuss."

"Many times." Gabi said. "My ex-girlfriend Elana was notorious for her avid curiosity. She was a fashion designer that I met when I was working on Salus."

"What did you do?"

"I find it's best to get creative," Gabi explained. "The next time he asks a question you can't answer, try casually changing the subject to something that you know he'll find interesting; he'll probably be quite eager to talk about that instead."

It made her feel a little odd, thinking that she had to keep things from her partner; she had always imagined a relationship based on total openness, but what could she do? Knowledge of the Key wasn't something she could share with just anyone. Perhaps this was why so few Keepers ever settled down.

She was about to say as much when her multi-tool beeped. Lifting her forearm, she slid one finger across the screen on her gauntlet, answering the call. Jena's face filled the window. "Get up here now," she said. "We have a situation."

"On my way," she said. "I'm sorry, Gabs. It seems we're going to have to do lunch another time."

The other woman glanced over her shoulder with a bright smile, her eyes twinkling in the bright sunlight. "Quite all right," she said. "Whatever it is…good luck. Sounds like you're going to need it."

Chapter 2

The gray light of an overcast morning came in through the large window above the kitchen sink, leaving a slight sheen on the linoleum floor. Dark cupboards lined all four walls, and the fridge rumbled like it might start coughing up smoke at any moment.

Dressed in jeans and a black polo shirt, Jack leaned against the cupboards with his arms folded. "So you like the place?" he asked, surveying the little apartment. "Must be weird living like this again after twenty years."

His mother stepped into the kitchen with a cardboard box held in both hands, her honey-coloured hair in a state of disarray. "The peace and quiet makes it all worthwhile," she said, setting the box on the table. "Honestly, this is the first time in years that I haven't felt like I had to walk on eggshells."

"I can't argue with you there." Just thinking about it made his chest tighten. "So how's Dad taking the separation?"

"Well enough."

"That bad, huh?"

Crystal let her head hang, slapping an open palm over her nose. She ran her fingers through her hair. "He keeps going on about the degradation of family values," she said. "Apparently women having the right to leave a bad marriage is a sin in the eyes of God or something like that."

It made anger bubble in Jack's chest, white hot rage that burned through his veins like acid. The man pushed everyone away with his scathing criticisms, then complained when he ended up alone. Twenty damn years of never feeling adequate in that man's eyes was enough to relieve him of any urge to earn his father's approval.

Summer offered comfort.

Jack hopped up on the counter and sat with his hands on his thighs, hunched over as he let out a sigh. "You know you're going about this all wrong," he said. "Most TV moms would have guilted me into helping by now."

Crystal turned her back on him. "I can handle a few heavy boxes, my dear," she said, marching over to the open doorway that led to the living room. "Just stay and keep me company."

She stood there with fists on her hips, surveying the mess of unpacked knickknacks she had left on the living room floor. "Having somebody to talk to eases my stress," she said absently. "Every time I call Lauren, she asks me why your father and I can't just sit down and work it out."

"Lauren's an idiot."

"Nathaniel Jack Hunter!"

Jack felt his face grow warm, but he found the will to keep talking. "I'm sorry, but it's true," he insisted. "She was always more concerned with looking like a happy family than with being one."

Crystal's shoulders slumped, and she leaned against the doorframe like a wilting flower. It saddened him to realize that he had just upset his mother, and it made him angry to realize that the source of her frustration was the fact that she agreed with him. It had always been that way in his family: Jack and his mother vs Lauren and his father. Not that Lauren didn't occasionally have her own spats with the old man, but more often than not, she wanted to smooth things over, which suited Arthur just fine.

Jack decided to let the conversation die and watched as his mother went into the living room to resume her work. One thing he had learned over the years was that when Crystal was upset, she needed a few moments to work things out on her own.

He had left a tablet on the counter beside him. A Leyrian tablet: which was to say a large piece of SmartGlass that had been synced to his multi-tool. Picking it up, he tapped the surface to pull up the page he had been reading.

The dossier of a professor appeared in white text, complete with a picture of a man with dark olive skin and gray hair in the upper right-hand corner. Dr. Aldin Nareo was an academic who had dedicated his life to studying the Overseers. He had authored fifteen peer-reviewed papers on the subject. It was safe to say he was Leyria's foremost expert on the Overseers. If anyone knew how to find this Key, it was him.

Three months of searching, and they had come up empty. Anna had scanned the Earth four times in a fly-by with her shuttle; there was no sign of Overseer tech anywhere. Not anything large enough to be detected from orbit, anyway. It occurred to him that Slade must have tried the exact same thing on numerous occasions, and too many scans would be conspicuous. That left them with no option but to comb through ancient texts, and that was getting them nowhere.

His mother returned a moment later, carrying yet another box. "So when do I get to meet this new girlfriend of yours?" she asked, setting it down on the table next to the first one. "I hear she's quite the woman."

"As soon as I can get her to come down here."

Crystal looked up at him with lips pursed, blinking as if confused by his response. "You realize that's not a good sign, right?" she inquired. "That your girlfriend isn't eager to meet your family."

"I'm not sure Gabi would call herself my girlfriend."

"I see."

Their conversation was cut short by a beep from his multi-tool. "Transfer call to tablet," Jack said with a little more roughness in his voice than he would have liked. Why did everyone always want to talk about his personal life?

The screen lit up with a close-up of Jena as she sat behind her desk. "I need you up here now," she said, leaning closer to the camera. "We have a situation on our hands, and it's gonna be ugly."

He stepped through the door to Jena's office to find Anna already there, facing the desk with her arms folded. Something in the atmosphere radiated tension. Jack began to worry that Slade might have done something.

Jena sat behind the desk with her chair turned so he saw her in profile, frowning at the wall. "That's two out of three," she said, swiveling around to face him. "Now we just have to wait for-"

Harry came through the door behind him with hands shoved into his jacket pockets, an angry scowl upon his face. "Sorry I'm late," he muttered. "I was driving Melissa to school when you called."

Which meant that he was arguing with Melissa. The two of them had been at each other's throats lately, ever since she had become more involved in their search to find the Key. Leave it to the Overseers to screw up everything right down to the love between a father and daughter.

"It's fine," Jena said.

"Still…"

Crossing her arms, Jena leaned back in her chair to stare up at the ceiling. "About an hour ago, we picked up a signal from a small town in Tennessee." The low grunt that passed through her lips made it clear that she was feeling pretty stressed right now. "Only one thing gives off that kind of signal: Overseer tech."

Closing his eyes, Jack let his head hang. He touched two fingers to his forehead. "Which means Slade will have picked up the signal too," he said. "The bastard probably has someone on the way already."

"Spot on."

"All right, you might have to spell this out for me," Harry said. "I thought we scanned the planet multiple times and found nothing."

"Overseer tech can remain dormant for centuries," Jena explained. "But when it's unearthed, it sends out a signal to broadcast its location. Presumably this is a fail-safe of some kind, a way for the Overseers to recover whatever they had lost. Sunlight is one of the things that can trigger reactivation."

Anna stood by the desk with arms folded, her face tight with anxiety. "My people have developed the technology to detect these signals," she added. "Which means Slade will have detected it as well."

"Do we know what this thing does?"

Jena leaned forward, setting her elbows on the desk's surface. She buried her face in her hands. "No we don't," she muttered. "And we won't find out until we locate it, which means this is our number one priority."

Something occurred to Jack, something that had been tickling his brain for the last few minutes and only now jumped to the forefront of his consciousness. "Why are we the ones being assigned to this case?" he asked. "Our division handles eastern Canada. Why isn't someone from Station Eleven taking this?"

Jena threw herself back in her chair, pressing the heels of her hands to her eye-sockets. "Larani Tal gave this one to us," she said. "We got this assignment because she knows for certain that we aren't working with Slade."

Jack puckered his lips and blew out a deep breath. "And anyone else might be," he said, shaking his head. "What a glorious world we live in. Is now the appropriate time to reaffirm my faith in the glory of Almighty God?"

"All right," Jena murmured. "Let's get-"

"Wait," Jack cut in. "There's something else."

He swiped a finger across the touchscreen of his multi-tool, bringing up the main menu. Then a few quick taps accessed the holographic imaging software. "I've done a little research on my own."

The dossier of Professor Aldin Nareo appeared above his out-stretched hand, crafted from transparent light. "This man's an expert on the Overseers," he explained. "So far, we haven't had any luck finding the Key. Maybe it's time we brought in a little outside help."

Spinning around, Harry paced over to the wall with hands thrown up in frustration. "How far are we going to take this?" he snapped. "We've been searching for this Key for three months with *zero* results. Am I the only one who wonders if that's be-cause it's not there to be found?"

Gritting his teeth, Jack squinted at the other man. "Yeah, because this is all about the logic," he said, stepping forward. "This couldn't possibly have anything to do with your need to smother your daughter."

Harry turned halfway around, glancing over his shoulder with a snarl that belonged on a wounded lion. "Don't you talk to me like that!" he growled. "What the hell would you know about what I'm-"

"Enough! Both of you!"

Jena was on her feet in half a second, casting thorny glares at both of them. "If this keeps up, I'm going to put you both in the med-bay," she said. "Seems like you've got a severe case of testosterone poisoning."

A heavy sigh exploded from her, one that made her deflate like a balloon that had lost its air. "Jack, do you really think this professor could give us some insight on how to find the Key?"

"I do."

"Then congratulations, you just earned yourself more work." Jena dropped into her chair and began trailing her fingertips across the surface of her desk, bringing up various menus. "You think this man knows something about the Overseers? I want you to make contact. Get a sense of who he is and decide if we can trust him before you give him any crucial information."

"Got it. I'll make the call."

"No," she said. "I'm booking passage for you on a starliner. You'll go to Leyria and make contact yourself. Slade got away because he rigged up our computer systems with a bunch of back-door commands. I don't trust any call to be secure."

Pressing a fist to her mouth, Anna squeezed her eyes shut. She cleared her throat quite audibly. "If someone has to go to Leyria, it should be me," she said. "Jack doesn't know the culture as well as I do."

A frown put creases in Jena's forehead. "Maybe," she said with a quick bob of her head. "But he's a little less trusting than you, and I want him to put those keen instincts to good use. You're going to Tennessee."

"Where *I* get to be the fish out of water."

Planting her elbows on the desk, Jena laced her fingers and rested her chin on top of them. "You're the one with a mind for technology," she replied. "If anyone can track down whatever they unearthed, it's you."

Jack backed away from the desk with his arms crossed, his eyes downcast. "Just a thought," he said with a shrug of his shoulders. "But if I have to go to Leyria, it might be better if I don't go alone."

The bright smile on Jena's face could have melted the permafrost. "Good point," she said. "So I guess it's your lucky day. You and your girlfriend just won an extended vacation to the Capitol."

Chapter 3

A dirt path cut through a forest where trees stood tall on either side, their branches providing shade from the fierce afternoon sun. The sound of birds chirping filled the air, and every now and then, she caught sight of a squirrel.

Anna stood on the path in jeans and a dark blue t-shirt with white sleeves, her face shielded by the bill of a baseball cap. "Can't imagine why they sent me down here," she said for Seth's benefit. "The girl who's likely to piss everyone off with her big mouth."

He responded with amusement.

The path stretched on for several dozen paces, but she saw light at the end, a place where the forest gave way to a field of yellow grass. Her multi-tool directed her to move onward, toward the coordinates where the Overseer device had sent its signal.

Anna closed her eyes, tilting her head back. She took a deep breath through her nose. "At least we'll get a little fresh air," she muttered. "Better than a day spent filling out forms at my desk."

A few minutes later, the path ended in a wide open field that stretched on to a chain link fence, and beyond that, she saw the back wall of what appeared to be a school. The small group of teenagers who hid in the shade, sharing cigarettes, were her first clue. So, the device had been unearthed by high-school students; that might pose a problem.

About ten feet from the fence, she found a hole where the ground had been recently disturbed and a shovel that had been abandoned. Whoever dug up the device must have taken it and ran.

Anna approached the hole.

Dropping to her knees in front of it, she inspected it carefully before scanning it with her multi-tool. You could never tell how Overseer tech might react. "How long do you think it was down there?" she asked her symbiont. "How many centuries passed before someone decided to dig here of all places?"

Inside the hole, she found nothing but dirt. There was no sign that anything out of the ordinary had ever been buried here, nothing that she could detect with her naked eye, anyway. Seth, however, was quite apprehensive. Some Nassai preferred to have a more open relationship with their partners, but her symbiont was something of an introvert. For her to feel his concern so strongly…It didn't bode well.

Thrusting her left fist into the hole, she said, "Multi-tool active!" The metal disk on her gauntlet responded with a soft chirp. "Run a level three scan. Highlight any biological or technological anomalies."

The tool began its work.

Anna winced, rubbing her nose with the back of her fist. "Whoever took this thing could be anywhere by now," she said, leaning forward to peer into the hole. "Assuming they're still alive, of course."

Her multi-tool beeped, and the screen on her gauntlet lit up with bright text. It was as she had suspected; the scan had detected cellular residue consistent with that found in Overseer devices. Well, that settled it then. Not that she had expected any other results – the signal given off by Overseer tech was unique – but it was best to be thorough. A few years as Jack's best friend had left her with a propensity to assume that nothing was quite what it appeared to be on the surface. She had yet to decide whether that was a good thing.

With the presence of Overseer tech confirmed, the next step was to figure out who had dug up that hole. Not an easy task in a school with several hundred students, but she had an idea of where to start.

Sunlight through a pair of rectangular windows was split into thin bands by blinds that were left half open, silver rays falling upon a rectangular table that took up most of the space in the staff room. The sweet scents of spring filled the air, and Anna picked up the sound of birds chirping in the distance.

Miss Sutherland was a tall woman in a black pantsuit who sat at the table with her head down: a truly beautiful creature with dark hair that spilled over her shoulders in thin ringlets. "I'm sorry," she said. "Who did you say you were again?"

Anna leaned against the wall with arms folded, sucking on her lower lip. "Special Agent Leana Lenai," she said, pacing across the room. "With the Justice Keepers. Your principal told me to speak with you about Kevin Harmon."

The title was still new: granted to her less than two months ago in recognition of her success in recovering the telepath Keli Armana. Anna wasn't sure she would call it a success; the incident had almost resulted in an interstellar war.

Miss Sutherland looked up with a tight frown, creases lining her forehead. "I told them not to start digging until I got out there," she said. "I would have been there sooner if I hadn't caught Paul Rutherford dealing pot."

Anna lifted her chin to stare down her nose at the woman. "Are you assuming that I'm trying to place blame?" she asked, eyebrows rising. "'Cause I can assure you that I'm not. I just want to know where those kids might have gone."

The teacher shook her head in dismay. "I honestly don't know. Kevin's a good kid, but he's got a history of truancy."

"And he took off?"

"He was gone by the time we got out there."

Well, of course he was. Overseer tech was something of a wild card. Sometimes it did nothing – nothing they could detect, anyway – and sometimes it had a strange effect on the minds of anyone who got near it. The SlipGates were relatively safe; researchers on her world had studied them extensively before implementing them as a mass transit system. There was no evidence that traveling through SlipSpace had any influence on human behaviour, and every paper claiming otherwise had been discredited.

SlipGates, however, were something of an anomaly. For one thing, they were made of metal when most Overseer technology was organic in nature. It was almost as though they had been designed for human use.

Shutting her eyes, Anna tilted her head back. "We need to find him right away," she said, nodding once. "There's no way to know what he dug up or what it might do to him if he holds on to it for too long."

"It can't be that bad, can it?"

Anna dropped into a chair near the table, crossing one leg over the other. She stared into her lap for a long moment before saying anything. "We've seen Overseer technology produce serious health defects in people who were exposed to it."

The other woman studied her with a scowl that could crack rocks, shaking her head as she considered Anna's words. "Can't you do something?" she snapped. "You have all this technology to watch us from orbit."

"We don't watch you from orbit."

"But-"

"No sensors are so precise that they can find a single individual among tens of thousands." She let out a soft sigh, trying to contain her frustration. "We can scan for thermal signatures, electrical signatures, radio signals, but we are *not* omniscient."

A low groan escaped the other woman, and she hung her head, grabbing two fistfuls of her own hair. "I understand," she said with forced emotional composure. "Do whatever you can. If Kevin shows up here, we'll call you."

It wasn't very hard to figure out what Miss Sutherland was thinking; no doubt she blamed herself for not being there when Kevin dug up the device. Anna felt nothing but sympathy, but she had no time to indulge the woman's guilt. "What about the girl?" she asked. "Principal Jensen said there was a girl working on the project. I believe her name is Amanda."

"She went home."

"Why?"

Miss Sutherland looked up with sweat glistening on her face. "Amanda was a little frightened," she explained. "She didn't get a good look at whatever Kevin had dug up, but his reaction scared her. We called her father, and he insisted that she be excused for the rest of the day."

Anna got out of her chair, folding her arms as she stood over the other woman. "All right then," she said with a quick bob of her head. "I'd like to talk with Amanda. Can you give me her address?"

"I'd advise against it."

"Why's that?"

"The girl's father is a school board trustee with some very conservative opinions. He dislikes Leyrians; he sees you as foreigners interfering in Earth's affairs. I doubt he'll let you speak to Amanda." And there were no legal grounds for Anna to enter the man's house. Brilliant. Finding out what Amanda knew, even if it was very little, was crucial, but if the girl's father stood in the way…Perhaps it would be best to wait until tomorrow. Amanda would be back at school, and Anna could speak to her without fear of any parental obstructions.

"I recommend talking to the other students," Miss Sutherland went on. "Some of them are friends with Kevin. They may have some insights."

Taking the woman's suggestion proved to be a fruitless enterprise. She interviewed several students who were often seen with Kevin Harmon, but none of them were able to tell her anything specific, and one young man who couldn't be more than two months shy of graduation decided to try his luck by hitting on her. There were days when a Keeper's youthful face was more curse than blessing.

After finding nothing of value at the school, she decided her next move would be to check in with the local police department. If there was a piece of Overseer tech wreaking havoc in this town, the authorities deserved to know. Anna wondered how the citizens of Manchester Tennessee would react to that tidbit of news. Hopefully they would display a little more sense than Miss Sutherland had.

A long hallway with doors in the wall to her left stretched through the police station to the front lobby, and one of the fluorescent lights in the ceiling flickered. The scent of floor cleanser was quite strong.

Officer Bruce Smith was a tall, broad-shouldered man in a dark blue uniform, a handsome fellow who wore a cap over his dark hair. "Who did you say this kid was?" he asked, pausing in the middle of the hallway. "We see a lot of teenagers around here."

He rounded on her.

Lifting her forearm, Anna tapped a button on her multi-tool to reload the image of Kevin's yearbook picture. The hologram rippled into existence between them, oriented so that the cop could see him clearly.

"Yeah I've seen him," Smith said, tucking both thumbs into his pants as he backed away from her. "The kid hangs out with a bad crowd. I've arrested a couple of his friends for petty theft."

"Does Kevin himself have any priors?"

"No. But it's only a matter of time."

Anna held his gaze for a moment, then narrowed her eyes to slits. "That sounds like a bad attitude," she said, shaking her head. "Tell me, Officer, have you ever heard the term 'self-fulfilling prophecy?'"

"Look, Agent Lenai, you can play Little Miss Idealist all you want." The disdain in his tone made his feelings on that issue perfectly clear. "But those of us who live here have to accept certain realities."

"Do you know where Kevin is? Yes or no?"

The officer crossed his arms and spun to face the corridor wall. He let out a growl of frustration. "There's a skate park on Emerson Street," he said at last. "Kevin and his friends like to hang out there."

"Thank you."

The bowl of vegetable soup that sat upon a red tablecloth, sending waves of steam into the air, looked positively delicious, but Anna had no desire to consume even a single spoonful of it. Her stomach was tied in knots by worry and frustration, and it had killed her appetite. Somewhere in the back of her mind, Seth scolded her.

Across from her, Bradley sat in an ornate chair, looking positively dapper in a dark button-up shirt with short sleeves. His jaw was lined with dark stubble, and his black hair was gelled into spikes.

She paused for a moment, scanning the periphery for something to talk about that would take her mind off this latest case. Their small table was located at the edge of a patio with a wooden railing, and to her right, she saw a four-lane road with cars rushing in both directions under a starry sky. What kind of a name was US-41? It was like the town had never gotten around to naming this street.

Bradley shut his eyes, breathing deeply through his nose. "You're not even going to finish your soup?" he asked, sliding closer to the table. "I know you like to play Super-Girl, but I'm pretty sure you need sustenance."

Anna felt her lips curl, thin strands of hair framing her face. She tossed her head to send one flying back over her ear. "I'm just not very hungry. But thank you for coming all the way down here to see me!"

"And if I point out that I paid for the meal?"

She took a spoonful of soup and popped it in her mouth, savouring the taste. They used a little too much spice in her opinion, but it was still good. That seemed to appease him for the moment.

Bradley sat forward, leaning in close to smile at her. "So, you gonna tell me what you're doing all the way down here in Tennessee? Or do I have to guess."

Dabbing her mouth with a napkin, Anna closed her eyes. "Sorry. You know how it goes," she said, scooching closer. "I'm down here on Keeper business. I can't be any more specific than that."

"It's all right."

Anna slouched in her chair with a grunt, looking up at the sky. "No it's not," she muttered. "I know it's hard, me keeping you in the dark, but trust me, I want to tell you."

His grin was infectious, and he bowed his head to stare into his lap. "We're good," he said with a curt nod. "I get it. This is the price of admission for dating Secret Agent Girl. So, are you coming home tonight?"

"No. I need to stay here and get an early start tomorrow." A thought occurred to her, one that filled her with mischievous glee. "You could stay with me. We could have crazy hotel sex."

Pressing a fist to his mouth, Bradley cleared his throat. The slight flush in his face only made her want to press the point. He was just so damn cute when he was dying of embarrassment. "I love how you're not afraid to say it out loud."

Anna rolled her eyes at the starry sky. "No point in hiding it," she muttered with a touch of exasperation. "Seriously. Take me up on this. Otherwise I'm gonna have to convince the waiter to have crazy hotel sex, and I am not willing to do any more work today."

"Well…So long as it prevents you from doing work."

It was the Anna Lenai guarantee; stick with her long enough, and she'd eventually say something that left you flustered and embarrassed in a public setting. Perhaps she should have been sorry, but she liked her candor, and she suspected that Bradley liked it too. Right then, the only thing she felt was exhaustion and a desire to take her mind off the wretched day she had experienced.

Trees rose up like shadows all around him, black against the darkness of a clear night with a crescent moon in the starry sky. The soft chirping of crickets should have been soothing, but every noise seemed to put him on edge.

Kevin sat with his knees drawn up against his chest, his back pressed to a tall tree in the small patch of woodland behind his school. He'd been on the move all day, unable to stay still. On some level he couldn't fully understand, he knew that if anybody found him, they would take it away from him. He couldn't let that happen; so he turned off his phone and kept moving.

Squeezing his eyes shut, Kevin thumped the back of his head against the tree trunk. "This is nuts," he whispered to himself. "You can't be on the run forever. Sooner or later, you gotta eat."

He'd stopped at a sandwich shop for five minutes to grab some supper and use the restroom. The whole time, he had been afraid that someone would notice the ball in his jacket pocket.

No one had paid him any mind, thank god, but that didn't stop him from getting the hell out of there as soon as he could. He could keep this up for a few days, but eventually he would run out of money.

He held the ball in the palm of his hand, marveling at the warmth. This thing was alive; he could feel it. It hadn't done anything out of the ordinary since that brief flash of light when he first held it, but somehow he knew it was special. Ancient and powerful. Most importantly, it was *his.*

The ball unfolded, becoming a flat sheet again and then conforming to the shape of his hand. Kevin felt the soft prickle of a million tiny barbs digging into his skin, setting his nerve endings ablaze with new sensations.

It was like a second layer of skin.

Breathing deeply through his gaping mouth, Kevin closed his eyes. "No…" he said, scraping a fist across his forehead. "What the hell are you? What are you doing to me?"

The…thing – whatever it was – made its presence known to him. It was like a new limb that he could control as easily as he could move his arms and legs. The knowledge of what to do was there in his mind.

Kevin thrust his hand out.

The air before his open palm began to ripple and shimmer like heat rising up from black pavement on a hot July day. Then it sped forward and hit a tree with enough force to crack the trunk and send the whole thing toppling over.

The noise it kicked up was awful. Anyone within half a mile would have heard that as surely as they would have heard a lightning strike. He had to leave! If they found him, they would try to take it from him.

Kevin got up and ran.

Chapter 4

Harry stepped through his front door to find his eldest daughter at the far end of their galley-style kitchen, sitting at the table with headphones on while she typed on her laptop. The instant he saw her, a surge of anxiety flared up inside him. The two of them had been fighting a lot lately, and though he tried to avoid any confrontations, somehow the tension just kept building. Every conversation was a minefield.

Melissa grimaced, rubbing her eyes with the back of one fist. "You had a meeting with Jena," she said, sliding the headphones back to let them rest on her neck. "And you didn't tell me even though she asked me to be a part of this."

Harry closed his eyes, breathing deeply through his nose. "No, I didn't," he said, striding through the kitchen. "Because I'm not going to call you every time my boss asks me to stop by her office."

The girl looked up at him with dark eyes that smoldered, trying to burn a hole in his head with her stare. She must have learned that particular trick from her mother. "I'm the one who told you about the Key."

"You mean the Key that doesn't exist?"

Melissa went beet red, hanging her head to avoid looking at him. Tears glistened on her cheeks. "Of course you don't think it exists," she whispered. "If I'm the one who says it, it must be wrong."

Harry looked up at the ceiling with his mouth agape, blinking several times. "We really don't have time for this," he said, approaching the table. "Melissa, I just talked to your guidance counselor. She says you haven't responded to any of the schools that have accepted your application."

"Because I'm not going."

He sat down across from her, leaning back in his chair with his arms crossed. The look of fatherly disapproval he tried to project was probably no match for her stare, but he tried. "You could have a great future."

She met his gaze with an expression that he could only call regal, and somehow, the tears only made her seem stronger. "The future I want is up on Station Twelve," she said. "You just won't let me go."

"I can't stop you."

"Good. I'm glad you realize that."

"But I'd be lying if I said that I approved of your decision. Melissa, if you become a Justice Keeper, it will cut your life in half."

"I can accept that."

Harry looked up at her, blinking tears out of his eyes. "*I* cannot accept it!" he all but shouted. "I'm not thrilled about the idea of outliving my own child, and you're too young to make such a permanent decision."

Melissa got up with a sigh.

Turning away from him, she stomped into the dining room and then up the stairs to her bedroom. Well, it seemed that was the end of their discussion for the time being. On some level, Harry knew the girl had a point – much as it pained him to admit it – and he was willing to concede that Melissa had a right to make her own choice.

This particular choice, however, was one that she could never take back. At times he wondered how the Leyrians could force such a decision on people who were barely old enough to vote. Anna was *sixteen* when she Bonded her Nassai. Most people changed careers several times before they found the right fit, and the Leyrians expected children to make a lifelong decision.

He'd read about Keepers who had left the profession to pursue other opportunities. The Nassai were willing to experience human life in all its forms, but that didn't change the fact that once you bonded a Nassai, twenty-five became middle-aged.

What was wrong with him?

He had always insisted that he would be the kind of dad who respected his kids' choices regardless of what they were – the ones that weren't classified as stupid teenage stunts, anyway – but here he was, lecturing his daughter. Twenty years of progressive attitudes down the drain because he couldn't let go. He sat their chastising himself for the better part of half an hour.

The front door swung open to admit the very last person he wanted to see. His ex-wife stepped into the foyer, dressed in black pants and a white shirt that she left untucked. Della was still beautiful to him even after everything she had put him through.

Long blonde hair fell over her shoulders in waves, framing a pretty face with just a few fine lines. "Harry," she said with a nod. "I get the impression that you're not exactly pleased to see me."

Baring his teeth in an ugly snarl, Harry lowered his eyes to stare into his lap. "Don't you ever knock before entering someone's home."

"Not when I'm invited."

"Invited?"

Half a moment later, he heard footsteps on the stairs, and then Melissa came into the kitchen with a gym-bag slung over her shoulder. "I'm staying with Mom for a couple days," she said, pacing through the narrow aisle between the cupboards.

Harry opened his mouth to protest but decided against it. Convincing his daughter that he didn't intend to micromanage her life would require him to let her make decisions he didn't like. "All right," he said. "Have a good time."

Melissa left without another word.

When she was gone, his ex stood there with arms folded, frowning at him. "You still haven't learned, have you?" she asked in frosty tones. "You still have to be the white knight even when no one wants you to be."

"I don't need a lecture from you," Harry said, sinking into his chair. "In fact, I'm willing to bet you don't even understand the first thing about this situation."

Della wore a tight expression that he had seen far too many times when they were married. "Melissa wants to be a Justice Keeper," she said, stepping into the kitchen. "You don't like it."

"It'll cut her life in half."

Tossing her head back, Della grinned up at the ceiling with such malicious glee. "Oh, poor Harry!" she mocked. "Did it ever occur to you that how someone lives their life might be more important than how many years they have?"

"Spoken like a-"

"Middle-aged woman?" she asked, cutting him off. "Believe me, I'm well aware of the limited time I have remaining, and my position is the same. Harry, you could die in a car wreck tomorrow. No one knows how much time they have. So if it turns out that you only have three years left, wouldn't you rather spend them doing something meaningful?"

She left him to chew on that.

His faint reflection in a mug of black coffee rippled as he blew on its surface, steam rising up to fill his nostrils with a delicious scent. Sadly, he couldn't bring himself to take a sip. Alcohol wasn't the only thing that Nassai disliked; caffeine was an issue as well. He could drink it – and sometimes he did – but too much would irritate Summer.

Jack remembered what it was like to enjoy a cup of coffee. In the past few years, he had consumed many, trying to recapture that feeling. It never worked. It wasn't as though Summer protested his dietary choices – she was quite content to let him live his own life in his own body – but his taste buds had changed. His body craved different food. More fresh vegetables, less sugary crap. He figured that was a good thing.

Perched on a bar stool, he watched a man in a white shirt move through the space behind the counter and select a bottle of whiskey from a shelf that was lined with every type of liquor he could imagine.

In his mind's eye, he saw the rest of this little pub, a moderately sized room with wooden tables spaced out on the floor and booths along the back wall. The *clack-clack* of billiard balls colliding filled his ears.

"Are you just going to sit here?"

Jack looked up with lips pursed, blinking several times. "Is there something else I should be doing?" he asked with more exasperation than he intended. "You two have had your heads together all night."

Ben stood beside him with elbows planted on the counter, his forehead pressed to the knuckles of laced fingers. "Darrel's just worried," he said. "He's not comfortable with the idea of me accompanying you on this trip."

A yawn stretched Jack's mouth, one that he stifled with his fist. "You'll be gone for a couple weeks at most," he said, swiveling on his stool. "Seems to me that your boyfriend is a little clingy."

Ben looked over his shoulder with a hard frown. "Maybe," he conceded with a nod. "But Darrel's got a lot on his mind right now, and he really needs my support."

"What's bothering him?"

The other man stood up straight and folded his arms, directing a fierce scowl into the mirror behind the counter. "Darrel's family," he said softly. "They've stopped talking to him now that he's openly dating me."

Jack winced, slapping a palm against his forehead. "Dude, I'm so sorry," he managed at last. "I need to learn to keep my big mouth shut."

"It's fine."

"No, it's not."

Before he could say another word, the front door swung open to admit one very distraught-looking Darrel. The man shuffled back into the bar with his hands shaking, refusing to look up.

Ben was on his feet in an instant and rushing across the room to meet his boyfriend. Faster than you could blink, they were wrapped in a tight hug. Jack still felt a little guilty about his comment.

How easy it was for him to forget the struggles that men like Darrel would have to endure. No one ever snubbed him for his relationship choices. Oh his mother might get a little overprotective, but Jack could date the most horrid, abusive bitch on the planet, and his family would always accept him. Even his ultra-conservative father wouldn't kick up a fuss. But Darrel? The loneliness must be awful.

A wave of sadness crashed over him, and it took a moment for him to recognize it as one of Summer's emotions. Nassai shared everything with each other. Loneliness was the most terrifying concept they had ever encountered. In fact, they had not known that such a thing could exist until their first encounter with humanity. At the moment, Darrel was probably as frightened of loneliness as any Nassai.

No, Jack thought. *If the guy needs a friend, he'll have one. Hell, he'll have a whole freaking lot of them.*

The hug was warm and gentle, and for a very long moment, Ben was tempted to just collapse against his boyfriend's chest and let all his concerns drain away. But this wasn't about him. Tonight, he had to be the strong one. "You're gonna be all right," he whispered over and over.

The other man smiled, his cheeks flushed to a deep crimson. He bowed his head. "I know," Darrel whispered. "And I'm sorry I've been such a mess. Dad actually unfriended me on Facebook."

Ben looked up at his boyfriend with resolve on his face. "You've been nothing of the sort," he said, backing away. "It disgusts me that your family would turn their backs on you for something so trivial."

"Yeah."

Crossing his arms with a huff, Ben hung his head to avoid eye contact. "I know we talked about this before," he said. "But maybe it's a good time to think about leaving all this behind."

"You mean moving to Leyria?"

Lifting his chin, Ben squinted at the other man. "Can you think of one good reason to stay?" he asked, shaking his head. "If the people who are supposed to love see you as some kind of outcast, then what's the point?"

"It's not that simple, hon," Darrel muttered. "I mean... What would I do if we moved to Leyria?"

"Whatever you want."

"Just like that?"

"Just like-"

He cut off at the sound of footsteps approaching. You didn't have to be a Justice Keeper to know when someone was coming up behind you; you only had to develop an attention to detail.

Jack approached with hands in his pockets, head bowed as if he was afraid to make eye contact. "Hey, Darrel," he said softly. "I was just thinking. We don't get to see you all that much. You should come out with us more often."

The flush painting Darrel's cheeks intensified until it seemed as though he might catch fire. "Thank you," he said. "I really appreciate the offer."

"I'm gonna turn in, guys," Jack said. "Long day tomorrow."

They exchanged their good-byes, and then Jack went through the door, leaving Ben to sort out this latest bout of relationship drama. Right then, he couldn't have been more thankful for his friend's sensitivity.

Closing his eyes, Ben took a deep breath. "Just promise me you'll consider it," he said, turning away from the other man. "I think you'd live a much better life on a world where you aren't treated as a degenerate."

When he opened the door to his apartment, Jack found only darkness waiting on the other side. Every wall and surface was visible to him despite the lack of illumination, and spatial awareness allowed him to perceive Spock waiting just inside the front door.

The big orange tabby sat with his tail curled around his legs, his front paws together as he stared up at Jack. Of course, he didn't make a sound; he only waited patiently with that imperious stare cats inevitably mastered.

Turning his face up to the ceiling, Jack squeezed his eyes shut. "Hey, buddy," he said, stepping into the apartment and shutting the door behind him. "Have you been a grumpy boy? All by yourself with no one to lavish attention on you?"

He dropped to one knee.

Spock approached to slam his forehead into the palm of Jack's hand, nuzzling him over and over. Cats…From what Jack had read, this was actually an attempt to mark him as property by rubbing scent glands all over him. Maybe. He had a feeling that the people who wrote those articles had a distinct canine bias.

After all, the biological purpose of sex was the exchange of genetic information for procreation, but that didn't mean the emotions involved weren't legitimate. Spock adored the humans in his life; you only had to spend two minutes with the little guy to realize it.

He got to his feet.

Jack shuffled through the long hallway with his arms hanging limp, frowning down at himself. "You're gonna miss me," he said, glancing back at his feline companion. "I'm gonna be gone for a little while."

He approached the first door on his left only to find it open. Odd…he always kept it shut to prevent Spock from napping on his bed and leaving fur all over the place. So why was it open now?

He peeked inside.

The darkness was no impediment to a man who had Bonded a Nassai, and he could easily make out the lump lying under the covers of his bed. A moment later, his would-be girlfriend sat up with a grunt. "You're here," she said, touching a hand to her forehead. "I had intended to wait for you, but it seemed as though you were going to stay out all night."

She held the covers to her chest with one hand and shook her head as if trying to clear her mind of haziness. Was she naked under there? It occurred to him that he might have ruined what could have been a very nice surprise.

"Ben's having some troubles with his boyfriend," Jack explained. "Seems the guy descends from a long line of bigots."

"Is there anything we can do?"

With a sigh, Jack shook his head. "Doubtful." He strode past the foot of the bed to the window, pausing there for a long moment. "We can be there for Darrel when he needs a friend, but nothing really makes family drama any easier."

In his mind's eye, his partner was bent over with long dark hair framing her lovely face. "It's a sad thing," she murmured. "And difficult to wrap my head around. I've read about such prejudices."

"But never lived them?"

"No."

Jack spun around to stand before the window with hands clasped behind himself. Cold rage pushed the bile right to the tip of his tongue. "Funny thing about living on this planet," he said. "When you're a bit of a freak, you learn to sympathize with all the other freaks. Even the ones who aren't like you."

Gabi looked over her shoulder with a sad expression. "And is that how you see yourself?" she asked with obvious sympathy in her voice. "You really think of yourself as a freak?"

"Well, a freak of the super variety."

He dropped his jacket to the floor and watched as Gabrina settled back against the pillows, a soft sigh escaping her. It occurred to him that he should stop thinking of her as his girlfriend – she hadn't ever agreed to any such thing – but they'd been growing closer for three months, and it was hard to resist the temptation.

Crawling onto the bed, Jack smiled down at her. "Well then," he said, shaking his head. "What can we do to relax before the long, annoying flight tomorrow. I can think of a few ideas."

Chapter 5

A black asphalt driveway cut through a lush green lawn to a small house with blue aluminum siding and black shingles on the roof. Sheltered in the shade of a tall oak tree, it was a quaint little residence.

A man in blue jeans and a gray flannel shirt stood at the foot of the driveway with his head poked into the back door of his car. From this angle, it was impossible to see his face, but Anna sensed tension.

She walked along the roadside in jeans and a white shirt with a frilly neckline, her hair done up in its customary ponytail. "Trevor Harmon!" she called out. "Mr. Harmon! I was hoping I could speak with you!"

The man stood up straight.

When he turned to face her, she saw that he was a handsome fellow in his middle years with a dark complexion and black hair that was only starting to turn gray. "And who might you be?"

Anna grinned, bowing her head to him. "Special Agent Lenai," she said, stepping onto the driveway. "I'm with the Justice Keepers, and I was hoping I could ask you a few questions about your son."

She used her multi-tool to project a hologram of her badge, a four-pointed silver star on a field of blue. It rippled in the air before her, and by the expression on his face, she could tell that

Trevor Harmon was impressed. "We need to talk about your son, Mr. Harmon," she said. "He's in trouble."

The man lifted his chin to squint at her. "Is that a fact?" he asked, coming closer. "I don't know where the boy went. He didn't come home last night, but when he does, the word grounded won't begin to cover it."

"You're aware that he skipped school yesterday?"

"I am."

Anna closed her eyes, sweat prickling on her forehead. The days here got very hot very quickly. "Are you also aware that he's in possession of one very dangerous piece of alien technology?"

The man pursed his lips, staring at her. "No, I wasn't aware of that," he muttered, leaning his shoulder against the side of his car. "What exactly can this thing do? Is Kevin going to be all right?"

Crossing her arms with a heavy sigh, Anna frowned down at herself. "We honestly don't know," she admitted. "Overseer technology is highly volatile. It could be harmless, or it could be killing him right now."

Trevor Harmon shut his eyes, fat tears rolling over his cheeks. "God Almighty…" He trembled as sobs ripped through his body. "Can you do anything? Can you help him?"

"We'll try. I promise."

She tapped at her multi-tool, opening the app that forwarded contact information. Then she sent out a pulse. A soft buzz from the man's pocket indicated that his phone had received the data. "If he comes home, contact me right away," she said. "We're going to want to run some tests to make sure he's all right."

"I will," Harmon replied. "And thank you."

Her attempts to find Kevin were less than fruitful. After talking to his father, Anna went back to the school with some faint hope that maybe, just maybe, she would find him in his first-period science class. Reality had a frustrating propensity for crushing dreams. Kevin hadn't come back to school, and worse yet, Amanda Simmons – the only person who might have caught a glimpse of whatever he had unearthed – was still absent.

Something felt off there.

School officials insisted that Amanda's father had kept the girl home to help her get over the ordeal, but did anyone really need *two* days to get past the sight of a hole in the ground? Maybe some people really were that fragile, but four years as Jack Hunter's best friend had trained Anna to assume there was more going on beneath the surface.

She went back to the skate park, hoping to find Kevin or his friends. Sadly, there was no sign of them. That left her with only one option, and she was pretty damn sure that pursuing it would make waves.

Amanda Simmons lived in a small house with white aluminum siding and black shingles on its slanted roof. A large porch with a rocking chair and a love-seat completed the picturesque setting.

Knocking on the blue front door with her fist, Anna waited patiently for someone to answer. Nothing about this house raised any red flags, but she reminded herself that she wasn't all that familiar with Earth culture.

The door swung open.

A tall man in gray pants and a blue polo shirt loomed over her. He had a stern face with wrinkles in his forehead and curly gray hair. "Who are you?" he asked in tones that conveyed his hostility.

Anna stood upon the porch with hands clasped behind her back, bowing her head respectfully. "Mr. Vic Simmons, I presume," she said. "I'm Special Agent Anna Lenai with the Justice Keepers. I was hoping I could talk to your daughter."

The man's face hardened until it seemed like he could stop bullets with his skull. "We've got nothing to say to you," he muttered, backing away. "Amanda wasn't involved with whatever that delinquent dug up."

Anna looked up at him. "I wasn't accusing her of anything." The teachers she had spoken to were right; this man was going to make himself an obstacle in her path. "I want to know what she saw."

Mr. Simmons thrust his chin out and studied her with hard gray eyes. "I won't have you filling her head with nonsense," he barked. "She gets enough of that from the school. Sinful ideas breed sinful behaviour."

"What exactly do you think I'll tell her?"

In response, he spun around and turned his back on her. "Follow me," he growled, moving deeper into the house. "Keep your questions short and to the point, and we can get this over with."

The front hallway led to a kitchen with a sliding glass door that looked out on the patio. A yard with lush green grass stretched on to a wooden fence, and she could see a bed of dirt that would no doubt be used to grow flowers.

Simmons opened the door.

Anna stepped through with arms folded, pausing to inspect her surroundings. "You have a lovely home," she said, trying to sound cordial. "My mother keeps a garden in our backyard. I've got no talent for it myself."

In her mind's eye, she saw the man standing in the doorway behind her, watching her like a hawk. "The garden was my wife's," he grumbled. "She died several years ago, and we haven't used it since."

"Why's that?"

Before he could answer, a young woman in a blue dress with short sleeves came around the side of the house. She was taller than Anna – not that there was much chance of her being shorter – with dark curls that fell to her shoulders.

"Amanda?" Simmons barked.

The girl jumped at the sound of his voice, placing a hand over her heart. She froze in place, then turned her head to look at him. "I'm sorry. Timmy was here, and I tried to shoo him off before he made a mess."

"Timmy?"

"Mrs. Hammond's cat."

An icy lump settled into the pit of Anna's stomach. The girl's reaction... Amanda was genuinely afraid of her father, and that was never a good sign. Very few things could elicit that kind of response in a child, and none of them were pleasant.

"Amanda, this is-"

"A Justice Keeper." The girl stood with a hand pressed to her chest, refusing to look up. "She probably wants to talk to me about what I saw yesterday. I'm guessing they still haven't found Kevin."

Tilting her head to one side, Anna replied with the warmest grin she could manage. "Hey, look at you go!" she said, her eyebrows rising. "With deductive skills like that, you might want to consider a career in law enforcement."

"She'll do no such thing." The silhouette of Mr. Simmons stepped through the door with a harsh growl, directing most of his anger her way. "Amanda will grow up to find a good husband, and take her place at his side as God intended."

Anna glanced over her shoulder, squinting at the man. "Silly me," she said. "Here I am trying to corrupt her with my evil feminist ways. I should have realized that you have divine intervention on her side."

"You won't influence my daughter."

Grinning ferociously, Anna let her head hang. She brushed a strand of hair off her cheek. "I don't know. Have you seen our pamphlets? Two or three of those and she'll be a full-fledged lesbian socialist who can't wait to swear herself to the goddess Athena."

Only then did she notice the expression on Amanda's face. The girl was very obviously upset. "I'm sorry, Amanda."

"It's okay."

"What can you tell me about Kevin? Did you see whatever it was he dug up?

"No," Anna said, shaking her head. "I only saw the hole. He told me to get help, and I ran inside."

"Any guess as to where he went?"

"No."

The misogynistic piece of shit who dared to call himself this girl's father was now standing on the patio and watching them intently. "She answered your questions, Agent Lenai," he said. "I think it's time for you to go."

"There's a lot of ground we could cover."

He stiffened, shaking his head in disgust. "I'm asking you to leave my property," he said, coming up behind her. "My daughter didn't have anything to do with what that boy did, and there's nothing she can tell you."

For half a moment, Anna considered protesting, but it dawned on her that Amanda might suffer the consequences for anything she did to piss off the girl's father. Abusive pigs like him tended to channel their frustration into a weapon they used to keep their victims in line. "All right," she said. "Thank you for your time."

When she pushed open the door to her small motel room, Anna found that the staff had done their jobs. The blankets on the single bed were pulled up and tucked in neatly with pillows arranged for that perfect aesthetic charm.

Jena stood in the wan light that came in through the blind-covered window, dressed in jeans and her long brown coat. The woman had her arms folded, her posture stiff and tense like a riled cat.

Anna closed her eyes, hissing softly to herself. "Come to check up on me?" she asked, slamming the door shut. "I haven't had much luck finding the kid."

A frown compressed Jena's mouth into a thin line, and she grunted as she peered through the window. "Yeah, I figured as much," she said. "But I'll take any excuse to get some fresh air. What can you report?"

"I just spoke with Amanda Simmons."

"And?"

"The poor girl is being abused," Anna said. "I'm making it a priority to get her out of that situation."

Jena glanced over her shoulder with an expression as cold as ice. "Are you now?" she asked, raising an eyebrow. "Do I need to remind you that isn't even remotely related to your assignment?"

"Witness my lack of caring."

"Anna…"

Crossing her arms, Anna leaned against the wall with a deep breath. "We're Justice Keepers," she said, ignoring the bile churning in her stomach. "See evil, punch evil? I'm pretty sure there's a whole chapter about it in the handbook."

The other woman spun to face her, bracing one hand against the window pane. "That's true, but at the moment you have much larger concerns to deal with."

"I'll deal with both."

"Oh? And have you thought about how you plan to accomplish this? You don't have the authority to remove a child from her home; so you're going to have to work within the system. That means you'll have to produce solid evidence of the abuse taking place. Do you have that? Or is it just a hunch?"

"I can tell."

"The courts won't accept that."

Anna felt her face heat up. "I don't care!" she spat. "If I have to, I'll tear this wretched little town apart, but I am *not* leaving that child in the hands of that monster."

"I see," Jena replied. "And if rescuing this girl costs you your career?"

In that brief moment of tense silence, the only thing Anna could do was stare into the other woman's pleading brown eyes. This wasn't the sort of argument she would have expected from Jena; in truth, it sounded more like the kind of slimy politicking that put people like Slade into positions of power.

These past few months, she had often chastised Jack for his tendency to buck the system, but here she was doing the exact same thing. Her best friend's defiance suddenly made all kinds of sense. "If that's what it takes," she said. "So be it."

Jena's smile was positively beatific, the kind of smile a mother wore when her child won first prize in a contest. "I knew taking you on was a good idea," she replied. "You're right; we're not gonna leave that girl to suffer."

"Then what-"

Jena paced back to the wall. "Focus on locating Kevin," she said, glancing back over her shoulder. "I'll start the paperwork to have Child Services look into Amanda's situation."

"Thank you."

"Oh don't thank me," Jena said.

Chapter 6

Banks of lights in a very high ceiling cast a kind of golden radiance down on a field of lush green grass with elm trees dotting the landscape. A cobblestone path slithered its way around flowerbeds and the odd boulder. That a place like this could exist *inside* a starship… Two days ago, he would have never imagined it.

Dressed in beige pants and a dark blue t-shirt, Jack stood with arms crossed behind the railing of a small balcony. "You weren't kidding," he muttered. "When you say a ship is designed for comfort, you mean it."

Gabi stepped up beside him in a pair of black pants and a matching blouse, her long dark hair tied in a ponytail. "Some people spend much of their career on ships," she said. "So we try to make them as hospitable as possible. The lights are designed to match the natural frequency of sunlight and to wax and wane in a twenty-four-hour schedule."

"I've always wanted to go to space," he replied. "But I'm not sure I could live most of my life on a ship. I need fresh air."

Of course, the air in here *did* feel fresh. It was even a little muggy. Summer found the experience quite pleasant. From what he had been told, the Leyrians were prone to constructing environments like this on all their space stations.

"Come on," Jack said.

He descended a set of steps two at a time, keeping his head down. "I want to get a good look at this place," he added as he stepped onto the path. "It's not every day you see a whole ecosystem inside."

They walked in silence for a little while as he marveled at this indoor… park. There were even bees floating about over the flowers. It was truly remarkable, and he couldn't help but cringe at the insane amount of maintenance something like this would require.

Then he saw it.

A small, cylindrical robot about the size of a footstool went rumbling through the grass, and where it passed, the blades were shorter. Not far ahead, human-shaped bots stood over flowerbeds, spraying them with some kind of solution.

It wouldn't be water – he understood Leyrian thinking well enough to know *that* would be handled by an automated sprinkler system – but perhaps it was a fertilizer of some kind. One robot glanced in his direction, its camera lens focusing on him, and then it went back to work.

Jack stopped under a tree.

He slipped his hands into his back pockets, then spun to face his companion. "So we meet with the professor the day after we arrive," he said softly. "You have any plans in the meantime?

Gabi shut her eyes, breathing deeply and then letting it out again. "I was hoping to visit my mother," she replied. "I haven't been home in nearly two years. She'll want to know what's going on in my life."

Chewing on his lower lip, Jack bowed his head to her. "Is that an invitation to join you?" he asked. "Because my mom keeps nagging me to make you come to dinner."

"I didn't mean-"

Jack turned away from her, starting up the path. "It's fine," he said with a shrug of his shoulders. "I really didn't want to push…I just thought we won't get another chance to visit for a while."

In his mind's eye, he saw her walking with a hand pressed to her stomach, her eyes downcast. "I didn't mean it like that…" she murmured. "It's just…We haven't even defined what this is or how long it'll last."

Jack felt his face burn, tension flaring up in his chest. "Well, it's not for any lack of trying!" he snapped. "At this point, I'm honestly thinking of cracking open the Big Book of Rom-Com Clichés."

"Jack…"

"Oh, don't worry; you'll love it," he pressed on. "It features such stock dialogue as 'what is this to you?' and 'where do you see this relationship going?'"

His voice had more bite than he would have preferred, but it was hard to keep the bitterness from creeping in. Summer urged caution – relationship advice from a Nassai; now there was a new one – but he couldn't help himself.

It had been three months, for fuck's sake! He was beginning to think of Gabi as the Queen of Mixed Signals. Every time he started to wonder if maybe it was time to call it quits, she did something that made it abundantly clear she *really* liked him. But ask her what she wanted, and she froze up.

He turned.

Gabi stood on the path with hands folded over her stomach, her face stern but not angry. "Are you finished?" she asked, raising a dark eyebrow. "Because I'd like to make sure I've heard the *entire* adolescent rant before I respond."

Jack felt the heat of anger that wasn't his. Apparently Summer was pissed off on his behalf. Not that it surprised him much. His symbiont would gladly bitch-slap anyone who did him wrong. "Yeah," Jack said. "I'd say this conversation is pretty much over."

A railing overlooked a dance floor in a night club where the walls lit up with fierce blue light, bathing everything in a cobalt glow. Down below, people shuffled about, some grinding up against one another.

Jack gripped the metal bar in both hands, leaning over to watch the crowd. "Well, Summer," he said. "The results are in. Just three short months, and I'm back to awkward wallflower. What do you think? New record?"

The spatial awareness that came with his Bond had its perks. Without even looking, he could sense half a dozen single people spaced out on this balcony and also the couples who clung to the wall, making out or talking quietly.

Ben approached in a pair of gray pants and a black t-shirt, his dark hair now falling to the nape of his neck. "So here you are," he said over the music. "Gabi's been trying to get a hold of you."

"I'm sure she has."

"Everything okay?"

"I'm fine," Jack answered with a curt nod. "Just reviving my grand tradition of avoiding all things fun and sociable. It's important not to lose touch with your roots."

His friend stepped up to the railing, frowning down at the crowd below. "She was saying something about dancing with you," Ben said. "I think maybe she wants to make up for…whatever's going on."

Jack paused for a moment.

There were times when he forgot his friend had a knack for reading emotions. He hadn't said anything to Ben about the fight, and it was *very* unlikely that Gabi would have confided in the other man. But the ability to read a situation was the most useful skill in a spy's toolkit; Ben had told him more than once that he would fit right in at LIS.

"I can't dance," Jack said.

"And you can't talk either."

Clamping a hand over his mouth, Jack shut his eyes and trembled with laughter. "I think I'm gonna have to stop you right there. Any more, and Phil Collins will be forced to sue for copyright infringement."

"What?"

"Never mind."

Jack spun around to lean against the railing with fingers laced over the back of his head. "So, she wants to dance with me," he said. "You really think my spastic gyrating is going to improve the situation?"

"We're gonna be stuck on this ship for another two days," Ben answered. "Do you really want to spend them fighting with your girlfriend?"

There was some truth in that, though Jack had to resist the urge to point out the fact that Gabi was not his girlfriend. Not yet anyway. He still held out some small hope that might change, but he was beginning to suspect that it wouldn't.

A set of stairs led from the balcony to the first floor of the night club, bathed in the soft light that radiated from the walls. Jack made his way downward with a grunt. At the very least, he could have some fun this evening; from what he'd read on the subject, it was a truly pleasant experience.

At the foot of the stairs, a hologram appeared under the overhang of the balcony. The image was that of a tall man with fair skin and dark hair that he wore parted in the middle. "Good evening, sir," he said. "Can I be of some assistance?"

"Who picks the music here?"

The hologram flickered for a moment, then reappeared, standing straight and tall with a vacant expression. "The music is selected by software that measures the mood of the crowd," he said. "Would you care to make a request?"

"Got any Dexys Midnight Runners?"

"I'm afraid not, sir."

Jack shuffled passed the hologram, making his way out to the dance floor where he could feel uncomfortable in time to the music. If you were going to make a complete ass of yourself, it was best to do so with rhythm.

It wasn't hard to spot her.

Gabi was still dressed in her black pants and matching shirt, and she swayed to the music while snapping her fingers. A young man with copper skin and black hair that he wore in a long ponytail danced in front of her. The pair of them seemed to be having a good time.

Odd…Jack would have expected himself to feel jealous, but while he did have his concerns about the future of this relationship – if you could even call it that – the sight of Gabi with another man didn't provoke them. Was that a bad thing? *Should* he feel a little more jealous?

Someone tapped his shoulder.

He whirled around find a woman in a pink halter-top dancing in front of him. She was a gorgeous young twenty-something with tanned skin and dark hair that fell well past her shoulders. "Come on," she said with enough volume to overpower the music.

Jack closed his eyes, exhaling softly. "You probably don't want to do this," he said, shaking his head. "I'm not a very good dancer. When the whole thing's over, you'll have nothing but sore feet and a bruised ego."

She didn't hear him, of course – the music was much too loud for that – and before he could say one more word, she took his hands and pulled him close. It occurred to him that his instinct to shrink away from a woman like this was the product of a bad habit he'd been trying to break. On some level, Jack still saw himself as utterly undesirable, but it was time to do away with such nonsense.

The woman smiled up at him, her green eyes sparkling as she held his gaze. *Well, this is nice,* he thought as she lifted his hand to twirl underneath it. *It's not so bad. I pretty much just stand here while she-*

The woman turned, pressing her back into him, then reached up to clamp one hand on the back of his neck. She writhed against him, and suddenly he felt very much like a boy at a sixth-grade dance.

Blushing hard, Jack closed his eyes. He tried to ignore his own rising anxiety. *No, this won't be awkward at all,* he assured himself. *Just stand here and try your best to look like you're having a good time.*

Up on the balcony, Ben watched his friends enjoy themselves. It would have been nice if Darrel were here with him, but this kind of mission was best handled by a smaller team, and his boyfriend wasn't exactly well-versed in Leyrian culture. At the very least, he could take some pleasure in seeing his friends happy.

Jack seemed to have found some companionship, though it was clear that he wasn't quite sure what to make of the woman who pressed her body up against him. The irony would have been delicious if it wasn't so tragic; here was a man who could jump several times higher than a normal person, react several times faster than a normal person and call on years of martial arts training…and he had no clue what to do with himself when put on a dance floor with a beautiful partner.

On the other side of the room, Gabi watched him with one hand over her mouth, trembling as if she found the whole thing very funny. Well, it was. Though Ben wasn't sure how Jack would react to the idea that the woman he was seeing wasn't the least bit jealous. Problems, problems, problems.

Ben closed his eyes, taking a deep breath through his nose. "And you can't solve any of them," he said to himself. "Focus on your own concerns. Let them sort this out on their own."

He tapped at the screen of his multi-tool, logging in to the e-mail application. One particular message had been sitting there for three days, vexing him. With a few quick taps, he read it for the hundredth time.

Ex-militia operatives still in possession of stolen weapons captured on Palissa. Serial numbers match those of the missing shipments. Interrogations have proved fruitful. The prisoners have confirmed that the weapons were delivered by a rogue LIS agent, but they are unaware of his identity.
- Agent Marc Tarens
LIS field ops, Palissa.

Ben had asked his superiors to keep him up to date on the investigation that would eventually result in his arrest. That e-mail had come three days ago. He wasn't willing to interfere with that investigation – his willingness to ignore his conscience in the service of some greater good only went so far – but if they had come this far, it was only a matter of time before they learned the identity of the culprit.

Ben felt a single tear rolling over his cheek. He drew in a rasping breath. *You may have to say good-bye after all, Darrel,* he thought to himself. *I know I promised to come back for you, but…*

In the meantime, he had a mission to complete. He would do his duty for as long as he could, and when the hammer fell, he would accept his fate. That was all anyone could expect from a man.

A long rectangular window behind the couch in his sitting room looked out on an endless void. There were no stars – they would be invisible so long as the ship remained at FTL speeds – but just the same, he found the view sufficient for a little introspection.

Jack stood by the window with his head down, his chin touching his chest. His face twisted into a grimace. *So, you're finally going to visit Leyria,* he thought. *With a woman who hates the thought of dating you.*

The door chime rang.

"Come in."

The door slid open to reveal Gabi standing in the corridor. Somehow, he'd known it would be her; Keepers couldn't see through walls, but something in his gut told him this conversation was inevitable.

Gabi strode into the room with her arms swinging, refusing to look up at him. "Nice to see you having a good time," she said. "I was worried you'd spend the whole night moping."

"It was fun."

"Was it?"

He turned on her with his arms crossed, blowing out a deep breath. "Let's cut to it, Gabs," he said, forcing down a wave of anxiety. "I like you a lot, but if it's really this hard for you to commit to something permanent, maybe we should call it quits."

She just stood there like a statue with her eyes glued to the floor, her lips twitching as she tried to find the words. "I like you quite a bit as well," she murmured. "But I have to be honest; I want kids one day."

Lifting his chin to stare down his nose at her, Jack narrowed his eyes. "Well, now *that's* out in the open," he said softly. "Gabs, I'm not gonna stand here and give you the 'we can make it work' speech."

"I wouldn't expect you to," she said. "But you mean a lot to me."

He set his hands on her shoulders.

Gabi fell forward, touching her nose to his chest. He gently laid a hand on the back of her head. "I know," Jack whispered. "I'd like to find a partner that I could live with one day; if you don't think that's you…"

She looked up at him with tears glistening on her cheeks, blinking as if to clear her vision. "Maybe it could be," she said. "I don't…There are Keepers who have made great parents to adopted kids."

"That, there are."

"So…"

Tilting her chin up, he leaned in to press a soft kiss to her lips. "Maybe we don't have to decide it tonight," he whispered. "I don't expect you to marry me tomorrow, but I would like it if you stopped trying to downplay our relationship."

The fierce hug she gave in response to that told him she was amenable. Well, that was good at least. He wanted to believe there was *some* hope they might have a future together. Sadly, he wasn't feeling very reassured by her hesitation. Jack didn't consider himself to be an expert on relationships, but he did have a very simple outlook. Either you were in, or you were out. And if you kept trying to straddle the line, if you weren't willing to say "yeah, let's do this…" it probably meant you wanted out.

The windows in this penthouse apartment looked out on the city of Beijing under a starry sky, tall buildings rising up with hundreds of lights in their windows. Bright, silver moonlight spilled through the glass, leaving a soft sheen on hardwood floors that stretched from wall to wall.

Lounging on a gray couch with his feet propped up on an ottoman, Grecken Slade held a tablet in front of his face. *Interesting*, he thought to himself. *It seems the boy has been doing a little digging.*

With a casual flick of his finger, he scrolled through a list of Jack Hunter's recent search history. Links to database entries on the Overseers appeared in a list on the tablet's screen along with web-searches for cat-food and something called Buffy-Con: Toronto. Most of it was fluff, but Hunter's fascination with the Inzari caught his attention.

As the former head of the Justice Keepers, Slade had taken a hands-on approach to the construction of the twenty-four space stations that now floated in orbit of this planet. The back-doors he had left in each station's mainframe allowed him to periodically check on his former subordinates. Provided he didn't do it too often, of course.

Cyber-security teams had located and shut down many of the programs that would allow him to take direct control of each station's core computer functions – he had to give them credit for being able to oust several Trojan horses that he would have expected to go unnoticed for years – but there were still a few weak points he could exploit.

Hunter's recent searches included data on a professor Aldin Nareo, one of Leyria's foremost experts on the Inzari. Slade was vaguely familiar with the man's work. In all likelihood, Jack intended to contact this professor.

If that was the case, Slade would have to remove Nareo from the game before he could divulge anything useful. Assassinations were always regrettable – they tended to draw unwelcome attention, and Hunter would almost certainly realize that Slade had deduced his intentions – but he could think of no other recourse at this point. Analyzing the comm logs revealed that Hunter had not placed a call to Nareo's office, which meant one of two things: either the log had been deleted or young Jack intended to go in person. Slade was willing to bet on the latter.

His multi-tool beeped.

Slade felt his mouth tighten. *Is it time already?* He pinched the bridge of his nose with thumb and forefinger, groaning under his breath. *That fool woman will drive me to insanity if I let her.*

He stood.

The sitting room in this apartment was vast and decorated with gorgeous paintings hung on the cream-coloured walls. Behind the couch, an elevator led down to the ground floor, but he seldom went out that way.

This apartment was not really his, after all, but the small cabal of men and women who served the Inzari on this planet maintained several safe spaces they could make use of at need. It would do for the moment.

In the wall to his right, a hallway branched off and led to the three bedrooms that had been vacated upon his arrival. He started down the corridor with a sigh. So much to do and so little time.

Pushing open the second door on his left, he found a Slip-Gate in the middle of an empty bedroom, its surface gleaming when he flicked the light switch. The metal triangle stood tall and proud, its top corner nearly brushing the ceiling. Most of the time, *that* was how he left the apartment.

At the moment, the Gate was dormant, undetectable by anyone else on the network. It wouldn't do to allow Justice Keepers to come waltzing into his home at their leisure. A little privacy was one of the most treasured commodities a man could possess. Slade only activated the Gate when he intended to use it, and visitors had to request his permission before they made an appearance.

Rolling up his sleeve, he tapped at the screen of his multi-tool and brought up an app that would let him interface with the Gate. He keyed in his passcode and cleared the Gate to receive incoming travelers.

A moment later, the grooves on the triangle's surface lit up with a fierce white glow, accompanied by a soft humming noise. A bubble appeared from out of nowhere, seeming to expand from a single point to something large enough to contain a full-grown man.

Inside, he saw a cloaked figure with her hooded head bowed, her body rippling in the distorted light. In truth, she looked almost like a physical manifestation of Death himself. Isara did have a flare for the dramatic.

The bubble popped.

Quickly, he deactivated the gate.

Isara flung her cloak open, exposing a low-cut black dress that displayed milky-white cleavage. "They sent Lenai to Tennessee," she said. "Locating the boy will be extremely difficult if I have to avoid crossing paths with her."

Thrusting his chin out, Slade squinted at her. "Is the costume really necessary?" he asked, shaking his head. "I've seen your face, Isara. One might start to think that you are growing paranoid."

She huddled in on herself, head bent so that he could only see the top of her hood. "You are not the only one who has seen my face," she reminded him. "I would hate to be recognized by the wrong people."

Well…she had a point.

He spun on his heel and left the room, strolling through the long hallway with his hands clasped behind his back. "So the boy is still missing," he said. "And I take it he is still in possession of the Inzari device."

"So far as I can tell."

Contact with his symbiont allowed him to perceive Isara like a silhouette of wispy smoke in his mind's eye. She walked behind him with fists clenched, grumbling to herself. Not long ago he had warned her that if she ever came to Earth without his permission, he would kill her, but the Inzari had decided to return Pennfield to the world of his birth, and Isara was to oversee his transition. One did not argue with a god, but it seemed as though his masters were growing desperate.

He stepped into the living room.

"How is our dearest friend Wesley?" Slade asked, turning around to face her. "More importantly, has he made any progress in finding the Key?"

The woman leaned one shoulder against the corridor wall, her eyes downcast so that he could not look into the hood. A habit, he assumed. "Pennfield no longer answers when I call."

"Really?"

"I believe he might be playing his own game." It came out as a growl. Something about Isara made him think of a feral lioness. "The humiliation he suffered at the hands of Hunter and Lenai seems to have affected him."

Slade felt his lips peel back from clenched teeth, a soft hiss escaping him. He let his head drop. "Of course the man would choose now to come unbalanced. We have another problem on our hands."

Isara perked up.

A surge of heat burned in Slade's face, and he growled, shaking his head in disgust. "Jack Hunter is trying to contact a professor on Leyria," he explained. "A man who built his career on studying the Inzari."

Hearing that set off Isara. She strode past him, into the living room, and paused by the couch with her fists on her hips. "Does it really matter? What can this professor tell him that would be of any threat to us?"

"An unusually casual response from you."

She whirled around to face him, instinctively smoothing the fabric of her dress with one hand. "The only alternative is to kill the scholar," she said. "Is it worth drawing that much attention?"

"Hunter is very resourceful."

With a sigh, Isara sat on the couch and folded her hands in her lap. It was odd, the sight of a hooded figure relaxing on his sofa as if they were about to share a friendly cup of tea. "How soon before the boy makes contact?"

"In all likelihood, he has already departed for Leyria."

Isara was still for a moment, then she sat forward with elbows on her thighs and her chin resting on her laced fingers. "You realize we're already too late," she snapped at him. "Neither one of us could get to Leyria before he makes contact."

Pressing his lips together, Slade narrowed his eyes to slits. "The thought did cross my mind," he said, nodding once. "Which is why I ordered you to remain on Leyria in the first place."

The woman remained doubled over with her hooded head bowed, refusing to show even a spec of irritation. "I have agents on Leyria," she said. "If the good professor has to die, it can be arranged."

She picked up the tablet that he had left on the couch cushion and began tapping at the screen with no regard for his privacy. "I will need to access the SlipGate to make an off-world call."

Slade nodded.

A hundred years ago, when he first brought this woman into the fold, he expected her to grow into a grateful subordinate, but Isara had a dogged sense of independence, and she would accept no human as her superior. Only the Inzari could expect obedience from her. A pity.

She was the most skilled warrior that Slade had ever encountered, but a valued servant must possess more than the ability to physically dominate her opponents. For a moment, Slade wondered if she saw the irony in her complaints about Pennfield's refusal to take direction.

Lifting the tablet up in front of her face, Isara stared into the screen as though she expected to find the secret of immortality therein. "He's not answering," she murmured a moment later. "I wonder…"

Had she meant for Slade to hear that? Though not as crafty as Pennfield, she could maneuver her adversaries into a vulnerable position when she set her mind to it. Only a fool let his guard down around Isara.

"Yes," a deep voice said from the tablet's speaker.

Isara leaned back against the couch cushions, holding the tablet up in one hand. "I require your services," she replied. "There is a professor on Leyria who may cause my associates some difficulties."

"I'm not on Leyria right now."

"I can see that."

Irritation mixed with anxiety to form a claw that gripped Slade's chest. If the man wasn't on Leyria, it was unlikely that he would be able to dispatch the professor before Hunter got to him. Still… There were times when a wise man learned how to delegate, and this was one of them.

"How soon can you be there?"

"Two days."

Slade crossed his arms and leaned against the wall, hanging his head in frustration. "Is that the best you can do?" he asked. "I would remind you that Hunter may already *be* on Leyria."

Isara turned her head, allowing just a sliver of light to penetrate that hood, enough for him to see her frowning. "Col is my best operative," she said. "It isn't enough to kill the man; we must ensure that nothing leads back to us."

"We still haven't discussed payment," a voice came from the tablet. "I want the best weapons you can provide."

Chapter 7

The residential street that bordered the small patch of woodland behind his school was quiet on a Tuesday afternoon. As he walked, he saw a young girl playing on the front lawn of a red-brick house with large front windows. He caught sight of a kid who must have been nearing the end of middle school walking a dog, but that was it. Nothing out of the ordinary except for him.

Kevin walked along the sidewalk with hands shoved into his pockets, the hood of his sweatshirt pulled up to hide his face. *Don't make eye contact,* he thought as he passed the house with the little girl.

She was about seven years old and blonde as blonde could be, dressed in a pair of shorts and a blue t-shirt. "Hello," she said, waving as he passed. The fact that he refused to answer didn't seem to bother her.

Kevin grabbed the brim of his hood and pulled it down further, making sure to avoid looking at anyone. *They might have put your face on TV,* he noted. *You keep making slip-ups like that, and someone will recognize you.*

He flexed his fingers.

The device – or creature, or…whatever it was – that had attached itself to his palm was more than just a weapon; thirty-six hours of wearing the thing had been enough to make that clear to him. True, it could be used for destructive purposes, but it was so much more than that.

For one thing, he could sense the precipitation in the air, the electrostatic charge and the relative humidity. The device seemed to grant him a kind of intuitive knowledge of natural systems. Earlier this morning, he had touched a tree – simply touched it – and sensed its roots, its leaves, the sap flowing through it. Whatever this thing was, it had become an extension of his own body. He couldn't give it up now.

Not far ahead, the road curved slightly, and just past the bend, he found a strip mall with a laundromat and a convenience store. Several cars and one big blue van took up most of the parking spaces.

Kevin shut his eyes, breathing deeply. *Food*, he thought to himself. *You need to eat something before you faint from exhaustion. You can't keep surviving on just one meal a day.*

Keeping his hands hidden, he stepped onto the parking lot with his shoulders hunched up. Every trip to a public place left him feeling antsy. A black kid in a hoodie tended to put most people on edge, but if he let them see his face, he might find himself facing down a squad of cops.

Passing through the narrow space between two cars, he found a pair of young men standing beneath the strip mall's overhanging roof. Kevin froze in place. He knew these guys from school.

Danny Roberts was a tall, lanky boy in ripped jeans and an old black t-shirt. Pale as they come, he wore his dark hair combed forward emo-style and sported a light dusting of stubble on his hollow cheeks. "So she nags me about eating the cookies," he said. "I was like 'I didn't know they were for home-ec.'"

Next to him, Brian Robitaille pressed a fist to his mouth as he shook with laughter. "Dude," he said, shaking his head. "You ate her damn assignment." Shorter than Danny, he wore shorts and kept let his red hair fall to his shoulders.

Kevin stepped beneath the overhang.

If he could sneak into the store and get away without these kids noticing him, he might just be able to avoid some unwanted complications-

"Hey, wait!" Danny spoke up. "Harmon?"

Kevin froze.

"What the fuck?"

He spun around to find that Danny had come forward and now stood with his arms spread wide, snarling at him. "You go missing for three days, and you think you're gonna just pop by and score some smokes?"

"I'm fine," Kevin said, backing away from the other kids. "I was just…Look, I've got…I need to take care of a few things, that's all. I'll be fine."

"The whole damn school is looking for you."

"I'm sorry."

With a heavy sigh, Danny let his head hang. "Typical," he said. "You know my dad always says people like you are god-damn irresponsible."

"People like me?"

The other boy looked up with an expression that said he meant to do violence. "Yeah, you heard me," he barked. "Miss Sutherland's having a breakdown because you fucking took off."

Kevin felt heat in his own face. He reached up to grab the hood with both hands and slowly pulled it down. No sense in hiding now. "What I do and where I go is none of your god damn business."

Danny was hissing, tiny drops of spit flying from his lips. "Yeah, I bet it's not," he said, striding forward at a brisk pace, closing the distance in a few seconds. "Someone's gotta teach you some respect."

He threw a punch.

Kevin caught the guy's fist, and then – just like that – he had a flawless, intuitive understanding of the human nervous system. He could almost sense the electrical signals in Danny's body, trace every nerve ending with his thoughts. It wasn't hard to set them on fire. Every last one.

Squeezing his eyes shut, Danny threw his head back and screamed. He dropped to his knees, pawing at himself as if his clothes had suddenly burst into flame. *God help me. What have I done?*

Brian came at him.

Kevin raised a hand, and the air in front of his palm began to ripple, distorting their images as if they stood behind a curtain of falling water. Both boys stopped short. Kevin's reaction was instantaneous.

The shimmering curtain sped forward and hit the dumb-founded teens, knocking them flat on their asses. Somehow, he knew it was only a fraction of the device's power. If he had wanted, he could have killed them.

Click.

He turned to find a man in a denim jacket standing by the driver's side door of the big blue van, holding a revolver in one hand. "Now, that's enough, son," he said, pointing the gun at Kevin. "Drop whatever you've got there."

Kevin shut his eyes, sweat oozing from his pours. "I don't want to hurt you," he said, backing up until he was pressed to the window of the convenience store.

"Drop your weapon."

"Drop yours."

The man was flushed, his face scrunched up. "I'm not gonna tell you again," he said, gesturing with the gun. "Drop your weapon and get on your knees."

Kevin raised a hand, and the shimmering curtain reappeared. A barrier that would protect him from his enemies. Half a second later, the air was split by a vicious *CRACK! CRACK! CRACK!*

Bullets slammed into the rippling energy field, crumpled and dropped uselessly to the ground. Each mangled slug made a soft pinging noise that was distinct to his ears. Through the haze, Kevin saw the blurry image of one very frightened man.

He thrust a hand out.

The energy field sped forward with the momentum of a freight train, slamming into the man and sending him flying backward like a plastic bag in a gale-force wind. He went all the way to the edge of the parking lot before landing on his ass.

"Help!" someone shouted.

A quick scan of his surroundings revealed Brian Robitaille crawling on his belly with a cell phone pressed to his ear. "Send help! 1409 New Sycamore Drive!" He gasped a few times. "We've got a guy with a crazy weapon!"

Kevin turned to run.

Danny slammed into him from behind, wrapping both arms around Kevin's belly. "Come on, you mother fucker," he whispered in Kevin's ear. "You think you can just do that to me?"

The other boy's weight threw Kevin down on his belly, driving the air from his lungs when his body his the concrete. He struggled and squirmed, trying to force Danny off him. "Let go."

Kevin still had a free hand. He reached around behind himself, clamping his fingers around Danny's wrist. That was all it took: flesh to flesh contact with the device between them. He was able to map Danny's nervous system.

The human brain was a simple thing, really. A little oxytocin to make Danny bond with him, a little adrenaline to drown out the pain and leave the poor boy with an intense desire to do something. Stimulate the fight or flight response.

Danny stood.

When Kevin rolled onto his back, the kid who had wanted to knock him senseless just a few seconds earlier now stared down at him with perfect adulation. It was obvious that Danny was seething with rage, but he would never – not in a million years – direct it toward Kevin.

Danny stalked over to his trembling friend. "Put the phone down!" he shouted at Brian. "Put the fucking phone down before I bash your skull in!"

Danny squatted down and seized Brian's shirt. He then delivered a fierce punch to the other boy's face. Then another. Then *another*. The sight of it made Kevin nauseous. What had he done? It had been pure instinct: self-preservation fueled by knowledge he had gained with the device. He hadn't really been thinking about what he was doing. He never wanted *this!*

I have to get this thing off me.

Before he could even think, the harsh wail of sirens filled the air and two cop cars pulled into the lot, forming a makeshift barricade. There was no way out now. He could feel the urge to run and – if necessary – to fight for his life. *You can't let the damn thing control you,* he thought as he cowered against the window.

What was he going to do.

Anger flared up inside Anna, but she managed to keep it at a low simmer. Calling her had been something of an afterthought for the officers who had decided that the best way to handle a boy with an alien device was to corner him and point weapons at him. So far as she knew, the police had only been on scene for about five minutes before someone was wise enough to involve the Justice Keepers, but the status report she had been given suggested that they had the boy surrounded but were afraid to close in. Jack would call this a… something. Spanish Standoff?

Through the taxi cab's windshield, she saw a narrow suburban street with small houses on either side. Everything looked quiet and peaceful on a sunny afternoon. You would never have expected a life or death situation to break out.

The convenience store's parking lot was just a short ways off on her left, and she could already see two police cruisers blocking the entrance. Four uniformed men were using them as cover, aiming guns over the hood of each vehicle.

"You can stop here," she muttered. "Let me out by the curb and then get out of here."

The driver twisted in his seat to glare at her over his shoulder. "The fare is fourteen dollars," he said with a thick southern accent. "You ain't going nowhere until you pay for the service, little lady."

She handed him a bill.

His face twisted into something haggard, and she heard the soft sound of a hiss pass through his lips. "What the hell is this?" he asked, shaking the money at her. "God damn Canadian currency? Do I look like a bank?"

"Exchange it!"

She got out of the car with a sigh, reaching up with one hand to scrub a palm over her face. *Idiot man,* she thought, making her way toward the crime scene. *People's lives hang in the balance, and he quibbles over minutiae.*

One of the officers turned as she approached. He frowned, then looked her up and down. "You're the Justice Keeper?" he asked. "'Bout time you got here. The situation's getting out of control."

Craning her neck, Anna squinted at him. "Yeah, that's me," she said with a curt nod. "Next time, I'll try to be more punctual after you fail to call me before charging headlong into an unknown scenario."

"Listen-"

"What's the situation?"

As she approached the side of the police cruiser, she saw a young man standing in front of a window that looked in on the convenience store. He was tall and slim with a dark complexion, and even from this distance, she could tell that he felt cornered. "We asked him to let us tend the wounded," the cop said.

She noticed another pair of teenagers in front of the laundromat. One was lying flat on his back with a blood-stained face.

The other was on his knees a few feet away, hiding his face in his hands.

The officer who had decided to take on the role of her liaison stood behind her. "The kid wouldn't let us approach," he said. "We tried anyway, and he threw up some energy field. Bullets won't pierce it."

"You tried to shoot him?"

"He left us no choice."

Clenching her teeth, Anna shut her eyes tight. She tossed her head about in disgust. "Of course you did," she said. "From now on, you don't make a move without my say-so."

Kevin was still cowering in front of the window, staring into his palms as though he couldn't believe what he saw there. The kid was on edge, frightened. There was no telling how the Overseer device might have messed with his brain chemistry.

"Kevin?" she called out.

He looked up.

"I know you're frightened," Anna began. "It's okay; no one's going to hurt you. The device you're carrying is dangerous. We just want to help."

"You can't take it."

"Kevin, we-"

The kid thrust his palm out, pointing the strange Overseer device at her, and she had to admit that it was difficult to ignore the urge to draw her weapon. "It's mine!" he said. "I won't let you have it."

Anna sucked on her lower lip, then bowed her head to him. Thin strands of red hair dangled over her cheeks. "Sweetie, that device is going to kill you. It's already started to affect your mind."

"I know, but…" Kevin's words came out in a harsh squeak. "I don't know why, but…I have to hang on to it. I *feel* it in my head."

"I'm going to come closer now."

"No!"

In the blink of an eye, he had a hand pointed toward her, and she almost expected to see the rippling energy of a force-field. Luckily, he was still able to control himself. "No one with weapons gets anywhere near me."

Anna drew her pistol from the holster on her hip. She set it down on the hood of the police car. "No one's going to hurt you, Kevin," she assured him. "We're all going to put our weapons down, aren't we?"

The four men who stood on either side of her remained perfectly still, each aiming his weapon over the top of one of the vehicles. Not one was willing to follow her lead. Companion be praised this was a small town; a larger city would have had SWAT teams here by now.

Anna felt her cheeks burn with furious heat. She took a deep breath to calm herself. "Put your weapons down," she muttered under her breath. "The kid is only a danger if we threaten him."

The officer who had greeted her – a tall, well-muscled man who now stood on her immediate left – eyed her before speaking. "With all due respect, ma'am, we do that, and he might decide to flatten us."

Tossing her head back, Anna rolled her eyes at the clear blue sky. "Oh yes, because your bullets have been *so* effective thus far," she mocked. "Put your guns down; I'm not going to say it again."

One by one, the four officers lowered their weapons to point at the ground. Anna heard the odd muttered complaint, but they were wise enough to take direction when she forced the issue.

Kevin seemed to relax, lowering his hands. He was bent over, refusing to look up at her. "They need help," he said, gesturing to the other two boys. "I swear to god I didn't mean to hurt them."

Anna glanced over her shoulder.

The two men on her right holstered their weapons and made their way around the police car. In a few seconds, they were trotting across the parking lot, crouching down in front of the fallen boys.

Anna maneuvered through the narrow gap between both cars, and when Kevin did nothing to object, she started a slow march forward. With any luck, she would be able to defuse this situation before it got any worse.

Anna licked her lips, then lowered her eyes to the ground. "It's okay, Kevin," she said, moving forward with her hands in the air. "I won't hurt you. We're gonna take you up to Station Twelve and-"

She sensed someone on the store's roof.

The officer who had greeted her suddenly pointed his gun upward and fired with a *CRACK! CRACK! CRACK!* Just like that, the delicate cease fire that she had worked so hard to build fell apart.

Kevin raised a hand, and the air before him started to shimmer like ripples flowing across the surface of a pond. The two cops who were tending to the wounded boy looked up and reached for their weapons. "No!" Anna screamed. In her mind's eye, she saw the cop behind her aim for Kevin.

She threw herself down on her belly just before the gun went off with a thunderous roar. Bullets slammed into the force-field, but instead of bouncing off, they just hovered there. She had never witnessed anything like it.

Kevin gestured, and the force-field…pulsed, flinging each slug back in the direction it had come from. There were screams from behind her, the sound of shattered glass. Oh, Bleakness take her! This had been going so well!

Kevin ran around the side of the convenience store. Before she could even raise her voice, he was gone. *Damn it!* Rage flared within her. Couldn't those idiots keep their trigger fingers still for one fucking minute?

Anna got up.

She ran back to the police car, jumping to land on the roof. Crouched down upon the steel, she inspected her surroundings. One of the cops – the one who had greeted her – had taken a wound to the shoulder. A second officer was tending to him.

Ignoring the prickle of sweat on her brow, Anna shook her head. "Get him medical attention," she ordered. "Stay with him until the ambulance gets here, then follow me in the cruiser."

The other officer looked over his shoulder, frowning at her. "There's not much back there," he said, gesturing in the direction Kevin had fled. "Some woods and then the high school, but that's it."

"That's where he'll go," Anna muttered. "He'll know the area. Right now, his self-preservation instincts are nearly impossible to ignore. There have been cases like this one before. If we can keep him calm, he'll be all right, but spook him and the instinct to use the device kicks in."

The wounded cop was staring up at the sky with tears on his face. "The woman…" he said, tossing his head from side to side. "On the roof…I saw her…A woman in a ski-mask."

In the calamity, Anna had almost forgotten. She'd had the briefest glimpse of a tall figure standing on the roof just before the Bleakness took everything. Where that person had gone was a mystery to her, but it was hardly her primary concern. Someone had to get to Kevin before he did any more damage.

Anna slapped a hand over her face, groaning into her own palm. "So you're first instinct was to shoot at her? What part of 'don't frighten the boy' was so hard to understand?"

The man grunted.

"Never mind," she said, hopping off the cop car and turning away from them. "Get him help. I'll go after Kevin. Back me up as soon as you're able, but for the Companion's Blessed Love, learn to restrain yourselves."

Kevin would have a significant lead on her by now; she was going to have to rely on a little creativity if she wanted to close the distance. Anna took a second to survey her surroundings. There was a large blue van parked right in front of the convenience store. That would do nicely.

Anna ran toward it at full speed, then jumped and – with Keeper strength – easily crested the back end. She landed crouched on the top. Then she was charging headlong for the strip mall.

Anna leaped, somersaulting in midair. "Keeper girl!" She landed on the rooftop and resumed her frantic sprint. "Able to leap modestly-sized buildings with the aid of conveniently-positioned props!"

Behind the store, a small yard was surrounded by a chain-link fence that had been mangled. There was a great big hole in the mesh; Kevin had gone this way. A single elm tree stood tall and proud with branches that had sprouted green leaves.

Anna threw herself from the rooftop.

With a little help from Seth, she twisted gravity so that 'down' was now a horizontal line that would carry her across the yard. She flew with her arms outstretched, releasing the Bending as she neared the tree.

Catching a branch with both hands, Anna swung back and forth like a pendulum. *Have to maximize the arc,* she thought. The motion left a wonderful lurching sensation in her belly. She reached the peak of her swing and released the branch.

Tucking her knees into her chest, Anna back-flipped over the chain-link fence and landed poised on the other side. Dozens of trees rose up in front of her, packed so closely together they provided adequate shade from the sun.

She ran into the woodland.

In the distance, she could see a shadowy figure moving among the trees, following a twisting path as it snaked through the forest. "Kevin!" she shouted. He paused for half a moment. Then he was gone again.

Keepers were several times stronger than the average human being, which meant they could run like a demon when the need arose. She raced down the path at a speed that would leave most people gasping after thirty seconds.

On the far side of the woods, the trees gave way to a small field where she found yet *another* mangled fence. Beyond that, the red-bricked wall of James Polk high school stood with windows in all three stories.

She saw a door that had been ripped off its hinges, its frame mangled – Kevin was really racking up some impressive property damage – and beyond that, a wide hallway with yellow lockers in each wall stretched on to a distant stairwell.

Anna resumed her sprint.

Cool air slammed into her as soon as she passed through the door – the people were already using their air-conditioning system – and then she was running down the hallway. There was no sign of Kevin. He must have turned a corner or…

When she paused to catch her breath, she noticed something odd. The door to every classroom was shut except for the last one on her left. Her instincts said that something about that was a little too convenient, but if the kid was running on adrenaline, he likely wouldn't be thinking about concealing his trail.

She reached for the gun on her hip and found nothing.

Anna squeezed her eyes shut. "Of course," she said, starting down the hallway. "You left it on the hood of a police car! Jena catches word of this, and I might not be keeping that shiny new promotion."

She approached the door.

Inside, she saw nothing but an empty classroom with desks arranged in neat rows and a bulletin board on the back wall. There were pictures of this world's great literary figures – she recognized Shakespeare but none of the others – along with motivational posters proclaiming the same slogans that had annoyed the crap out of her as a teenager. Attitude was the key to success and all that. "Kevin?" Anna called out.

She crept into the room with a hand pressed to her stomach, turning her head to get a good look at every corner. Why she bothered was beyond her. As a Justice Keeper, she could sense her surroundings without having to use her eyes.

The desks were separated to form an aisle that ran through the middle of the room. Blinds over the windows filtered the sunlight into thin streams. Anna made her way to the back of the room, looking for a closet or a cupboard or any place where Kevin might be hiding. She found nothing. Something about all this felt odd…Why would a teacher leave this one door open when all the others had…

The revelation hit her like a smack to the face.

She had walked into a trap.

Chapter 8

A brief moment of fear faded into anger and then calm resolve. Anna focused. She stretched out with her senses and used her connection with Seth to watch every corner of the classroom. Sure enough, her instincts were confirmed within seconds.

Someone came through the door behind her.

Anna turned to find a tall woman in black pants and a matching t-shirt pacing through the space between the front row of desks and the blackboard. "You know…I had hoped to avoid this."

Just as the fallen cop had said, this woman was wearing a ski-mask with holes that revealed a hint of pale skin around the eyes. Her face was hidden, but that voice…Anna had never heard an accent like that, but somehow the voice was still familiar.

Crossing her arms, Anna stood in the middle of the aisle with her head held high. "Bad guys and ski masks," she said, eyebrows rising. "I'd suggest you try something a little more original, but honestly, your lack of creativity is probably the reason you guys keep losing."

The woman stopped short, letting out a soft sigh. "I don't want to kill you, my dear," she said, spinning around to face Anna. "Wasted life is always a tragedy, but you have made yourself a nuisance."

"Is that so?"

"I'll be taking the boy."

Anna clasped hands together behind her back, striding through the aisle between the desks with her head down. "So this is the script we'll be following?" she asked with a shrug. "You do a little posturing, I proclaim that scum like you will never win?"

"Your jokes do not amuse."

Tapping her lips with one finger, Anna narrowed her eyes. "I suppose they don't," she said. "So do you have a name? Because if we're gonna fight, I'll have to file a report, and those things have *so* many blanks to fill in."

The woman drew herself up, looming over Anna, and for just a brief moment, she inspired real fear. "I am called Isara," she said. "Not long ago, Slade offered you a place among us. I do the same in the hope that I will not have to kill you."

Isara… an odd name. It seemed almost Leyrian, but outdated. The kind of name that would have gone out of fashion maybe one hundred fifty years ago. "Well, you can just suck on the Bleakness itself," Anna growled. "Because there's no power in the universe that can make *that* possible."

Closing her eyes, the woman drew in a deep, calming breath. "That is as I feared," she muttered, pacing through the aisle to meet Anna halfway. "Such a shame. You would have been of great use to us."

Isara kicked high.

Leaning back, Anna reached up to catch the woman's foot with both hands. She gave a hard shove and threw her opponent off balance. Isara fell over backward, slapping her hands down on the floor.

She flipped upright, then jumped and kicked out. A steel-toed boot to the chest sent Anna stumbling backward. Pain flared up in her body as she watched the woman close in for the kill. Isara threw a mean right hook.

Anna crouched down, raising one hand to strike the woman's wrist and knock it aside. She used the other to deliver a palm-strike to the nose. Isara stumbled, very nearly losing her balance.

Anna moved in for a backhand strike.

The other woman caught her wrist in two hands, tugging on her arm and forcing her to double over. A swift kick to the belly drove the wind from Anna's lungs. The next thing she saw was a gloved hand strike her across the eyes, filling her vision with silver flecks that swirled about.

Two fists seized Anna's shirt, and then she was flying backward, propelled by Bent Gravity. She collided with the bulletin board at the back of the classroom, then landed on shaky legs.

As her vision cleared, she saw the masked woman stride forward with fists balled at her sides. Something in those dark eyes. In mere seconds, Isara had closed the distance.

She threw a punch.

Anna ducked, a gloved fist passing right over her head. She came up a few steps to the left, then flung her arm out to the side to strike the back of Isara's skull with her fist. The other woman went face-first into the wall.

Backing away with hands raised in a fighting stance, Anna felt blood leaking from her nose. "I don't suppose you want to tell me who you are?" she asked in a rasping voice. "Why you want to kill me?"

Isara rounded on her.

Lifting her chin, the woman studied her through the holes in that ski-mask. "You're on the wrong side, girl," she said. "It's been over two minutes and you're still standing. That is remarkably rare in an opponent."

"Yeah, well…You know me," Anna muttered. "I'm not the kind of girl who lets her partners go unsatisfied."

"You could join with us."

"To what end?"

The ski-mask's mouth hole allowed her to see a small smile on the other woman's face. "You will have to come see for yourself," Isara murmured. "I understand why Slade finds you so fascinating."

Keep the bitch talking, a small voice whispered in her mind. Combat was as much about the terrain as it was about the moves and counter-moves. If she could keep Isara focused on her words, the woman might fail to notice her slowly inching away from the back wall, making her way toward one of the desks.

"You know, I just don't get you," Anna mocked. "You guys in your secret societies, hatching dastardly plans for galactic domination. Okay, you want something called the Key. For what purpose? Do the Overseers just point in any random direction and you go? Are we really in full brain-trust land?"

Anna positioned herself behind a desk in the back row, watching as her opponent stood by the wall with arms folded. "We follow the will of God," Isara said. "It is enough that the Inzari speak and we obey."

Hissing softly, Anna shut her eyes tight. She brushed a strand of damp hair off her cheek. "Yeah, I'll bet you do…" she muttered. "In fact, I'll wager my favourite teddy bear that you guys sit around in your underwear paddling each other's bums just to see who's the most dedicated of all. Admit it; I've got you pegged."

"You should show respect."

"Try earning it."

Isara came at her.

Anna kicked the desk, applying a light Bending that sent it flying across the room. It collided with Isara, who raised her hands just in time to avoid getting knocked on her ass. Still, the woman was off balance.

Anna charged forward.

As the desk fell to the floor, she found herself staring down one very pissed off Isara. One very pissed off Isara who moved in for the kill like a shark that could smell blood in the water. Time to finish this bitch.

Anna punched her in the face. She spun at full force, one arm lashing out for a hard backhand strike. Her fist hit nothing but air.

When she came out of her spin, Isara popped up right in front of her. The next thing she saw was a fist colliding with her face. Blackness filled her vision, but she could still sense her opponent.

Isara tried to kick her stomach.

Anna doubled over, catching the woman's foot before it made contact. She growled and flung her opponent sideways, right into the back wall. The bitch let out a grunt as her shoulder hit the cinder-blocks.

Anna rounded on her.

She jumped for a high kick, but Isara danced out of the way at the very last second. When she landed, she was face to face with the wall. Then something grabbed the back of her collar and slammed her face-first into the bulletin board.

Anna jumped, pulling free of the woman's grip. She curled her legs up against her chest and back-flipped through the air. Pain made it hard to think, but her body moved on instinct. Pure instinct. She landed in the middle of the aisle between the desks.

Isara was in front of the wall, doubled over with a hand pressed to her chest. "By the depths of the Abyss, girl," she muttered under her breath. "It's been some time since anyone has caused me this much pain."

She leaped forward.

The woman landed hard on one desk, then lithely jumped to the next and the next, making her way to the front of the classroom. She hopped off and stood right in front of the blackboard. "There is no escape for you, girl."

Anna spun around.

Any attempt to go for the door would result in Isara descending on her like a wolf lunging for a rabbit, and the windows were probably off limits as well. The woman was too good for Anna to have any hope of defeating her – the best she could hope for was a stalemate – but that left her with few options. She had to find a way out of here before-

Two police officers stepped through the door and stopped short, freezing in place when they found themselves staring at a woman in a mask. In a heartbeat, both men drew their pistols.

"No! Don't!" Anna shouted.

Isara raised a hand, and the air before her rippled, light refracting until she was only a smear of dark colours. Gunshots filled the air, and bullets slowed to a crawl mere inches away from the woman's outstretched palm.

Each slug followed a looping path that turned it back on its master. They sped up, and both cops doubled over as bullets hit their armoured vests.

Isara turned and ran.

She charged right for the window, then jumped and crashed right through it with no remorse, pulling the blinds free in the process. A moment later, the woman landed outside and took off at a dead sprint.

Damn it! Anna felt the urge to chase her – there was no telling what the bitch might do next – but tending to the wounded cops was her first priority. Cops who – once again – had decided to lead with their pistols. There was probably a phallic reference in there somewhere, but she was too tired to be witty.

Anna went to them.

Clenching her teeth, she wiped sweat off her brow with the back of her hand. "Are you two all right?" she asked, surprised by the hoarseness of her voice. "Do I need to get you to a hospital?"

One cop was bent over with a hand pressed to his stomach, his face twisted into the kind of expression you might expect to find on a man who'd been kicked by a horse. "Vest took the brunt of it," he said. "Just a few bruises."

His companion nodded.

Anna breathed out a sigh of relief. So…after all that hard work, what did she have to show for it? Kevin had been spooked, and in all likelihood he would go even deeper into hiding now. Three cops had been injured along with two civilians. There was a woman with a symbiont loose in this town, and she would be looking for Kevin as well. Worst of all, Anna was going to have to explain all this in her next report. *I should have let Isara kill me,* she lamented. *It would have been easier.*

Chapter 9

The large quarter-dome shaped window on the Observation Deck looked out on an endless void with only a single point of light in the distance. From what Jack had read, that was a strange quirk of warp travel. He'd always imagined stars that streaked past as the ship flew, but apparently that wasn't how it worked.

The point of light broke apart into a million tiny stars, surrounding the ship on all sides, and then a planet seemed to expand from a single point, growing larger and larger until it almost filled the window.

Leyria.

It looked so very much like Earth, with vibrant blue oceans surrounding lush green continents. White clouds swirled playfully in the upper atmosphere, cutting off his view of the land below.

Off to his left, he saw a moon with a bright purple atmosphere. Summer perked up the instant his eyes fell upon it. The Nassai's emotions reminded him of what it felt like to go home for Christmas. Or rather, what it *should* have felt like to go home for Christmas. He cringed at the thought of the argument he had sat through last December.

Jack stood by the window with his hands on his hips, smiling down at his own feet. "So this is it," he muttered, taking a few steps forward. "You weren't lying; it really is a beautiful world."

Gabi was at his side in beige pants and a navy-blue t-shirt with a round neckline, her long black hair left to hang loose over her shoulders. "It's been almost two years," she murmured. "I've seen a dozen worlds in a dozen windows."

"But?"

"Nothing feels as good as coming home."

Jack touched his hand to the window pane and was surprised to find that it wasn't cold. Not that it should have surprised him; he knew perfectly well that the idea of space being frigid was a myth. Space was nothing. It had no temperature.

"Ladies and gentlemen," a voice came over the loud speaker. "This is your captain speaking. We've arrived in orbit of Leyria, and you will be allowed to disembark shortly. We ask that you gather your belongings and proceed to one of the two SlipGate chambers with appropriate customs documents."

"Come on," Gabi said. "We still have a ways to go."

Through the train's side window, Jack saw a clear blue sky with many skyscrapers glittering in the afternoon sunlight. A shuttle flew past overhead, descending toward some far off spot on the eastern horizon.

The train car was empty except for a few commuters who sat reading or listening to music. Enjoying their brief ride out to the suburbs. Leyrian cities were designed around public transit. In fact, if he looked out the window, he could sometimes catch glimpses of another monorail line in the distance, expanding out from the downtown core like a spoke on a wheel.

Jack leaned back in his seat with his arms crossed, turning his face up to the ceiling. "You're sure your mother won't mind me staying with you?" he asked. "I could just find a nice hotel."

Gabi sat across from him with hands on her knees, smiling into her own lap. "It should be fine," she replied with a shrug of her shoulders. "My mother has a guest room, and she likes company."

Pressing a fist to his mouth, Jack closed his eyes. He cleared his throat with some force. "Yeah well, where I come from, the random house guest is very seldom greeted with a great big smile."

Ben came shuffling through the aisle between seats, grabbing one of the metal bars that ran from floor to ceiling. "Oh it's good to be back home," he said. "Dude, you've got to come out with me tonight. I know this great little bar in Menara."

Jack grinned, a touch of heat in his cheeks. He scrubbed a hand through his thick brown hair. "That's all you ever do, man. You know, there's more to life than just hanging out in bars."

"Says the guy with no social life."

"Oh, I don't know about that," Gabi cut in.

She was leaning back in her chair with her head turned to stare out the window, a vacant expression on her face. As if this topic was of little interest to her. "His social life has been pretty active lately."

One perk of having a girlfriend? Someone was always there to defend your honour. At least in the presence of other guys. Then again, he still wasn't entirely sure if the term 'girlfriend' applied; Gabi wasn't clear on that point, but she seemed to be showing a little more enthusiasm. The plan for him to stay with her at her mother's house was something she had come up with just two days ago.

She lifted her chin and squinted when her eyes fell upon Ben. "Besides," she said with a quick bob of her head. "He's got a date tonight. No time for cheering you on while you hit on drunk Zero-G fans."

Ben sat down in the seat across the aisle, raising both hands as if he was facing a cop with a gun. "Hey, I'm a one-man guy," he replied. "And not all of us get the pleasure of multiple detours to smoochyville on our interstellar voyage."

"Smoochyville?" Jack asked.

"No good?"

"Your slanguage is a little off."

A date, he thought to himself. That was a new development. Either she had come up with the idea just a few seconds ago, or she had been planning to surprise him. Either one suited him just fine. Summer approved. Amazing how the Nassai had taken on the role of his older sister in matters related to his love life. The emotions he felt from her were enough to let him puzzle out her thoughts on the matter. *Well* someone *has to.*

"Tyree Station," a voice said over the loud speaker. "Approaching Tyree Station."

Gabi's mother lived in a small house just a few blocks from the monorail station, a dome-like structure with an arch-shaped overhang above the front entrance. There were round windows in the walls and something that looked like a skylight.

Large palm trees shielded the house from anyone who might come walking by on the street, and when you got past them, beds of flowers lined the perimeter of the front yard. It was truly a sight to see.

Jack puckered his lips and whistled. "Wow!" he said, shaking his head with some gusto. "I've seen a few pictures of Leyrian architecture, but they really don't do justice to the live show."

At his side, Gabi was smiling down at the ground, her cheeks strained by a touch of crimson. "I keep forgetting how new this is for you," she said. "Come on."

"Well then," Jack said, his eyebrows climbing upward. "You think Charles Strouse will want royalties? Because I'm *this* close to busting out my own rendition of 'I Think I'm Gonna Like it Here.'"

She glanced back at him.

"Never mind."

At the porch, Gabi stepped underneath the overhang and rang the bell. Jack still felt a little off about this whole thing. There was no doubt in his mind that Gabi's mother was a delightful woman, but no one liked surprise house guests. He thought about looking up the number of a good hotel, and then it hit him. How exactly did one *do* that on Leyria? Was there some kind of Leyrian Google? The computers back on Station Twelve received regular updates from the home world, but a live connection to the Link – what Leyrians called their Internet - simply wasn't possible given the stellar distances involved. Even Slip-Gates couldn't remain in active use *all the time.*

The door swung open, allowing a woman in tan pants and a bright blue t-shirt to step out. Sareena Valtez looked very much like her daughter but with black hair that was slowly graying and a few wrinkles. "You made it!" she said, throwing her arms around Gabi. "I've been excited all week!"

Gabi stepped out of the hug.

She turned partway, gesturing to Jack. "The young man I told you to expect." she said in smooth tones. So Gabi *had* made contact with her mother. "I'm sure you'll find him very…entertaining."

No pressure, Jack.

Sareena looked up at him with a great big smile, blinking as though unsure of what she saw. "Ah yes!" she exclaimed. "Your name sounded familiar when I read Gabrina's message. So…are you *the* Jack Hunter?"

"I'm a the?" Jack sputtered. "How did I become a the?"

"My dear boy, you are the first person from your world to bond a Nassai. Perhaps that doesn't mean much to your people, but Justice Keepers hold a place of honour here on Leyria!" He was famous? Oh boy, that didn't sit well with him. True, there had been accolades in the days after First Contact – he still cringed every time he recalled doing that damn interview with the CBC – but those had fizzled out when his natural tendency to turtle up and avoid social media had given people plenty of motivation to move on to the next passing fad. "Your name has already appeared in history textbooks," Sareena went on. "Tell me, what was it that compelled you to accept a symbiont?"

Jack scrunched up his face into a painful grimace. He tried to ignore the blush he couldn't fight off. "Not much of a story, really," he said. "The geeks on my world have always loved aliens. Captain Kirk slept with a green woman; Commander Shepard slept with a *blue* woman, but me? I got it on with bacteria!"

He expected a glare of disapproval.

Instead, Sareena threw her head back and roared with laughter. "My goodness!" she said, pressing a hand to her stomach. "Gabi, you didn't tell me he was so witty! Oh, I can tell the next few days are going to be very amusing."

Jack felt his lips curl, his cheeks burning noticeably. He closed his eyes and nodded to her. "Thank you for letting me stay here, and I promise to keep the snarky outbursts to a minimum."

"Nonsense! Come inside!"

A dining room table positioned right beneath the skylight supported a large bowl full of salad. Jack wasn't sure what really got him thinking: the similarity to a dish he might have tried on Earth or the fact that the entire meal was served by a human shaped robot who carried plates from the kitchen.

The bot – a five-foot tall creature with metal arms and legs – paused just in front of the table. It turned its camera lens to focus on Jack, then set a green plate down in front of him without a word.

He bit his lip as he studied the thing. "Um…Thank you?" he said, sliding his chair closer to the table. "Gabs, I'm a little confused by the customs here. Are we supposed to just ignore it?"

Gabi sat across from him with a fork in one hand, staring down at her empty plate. "Sweetie, it's a piece of technology," she murmured. "It doesn't mind serving plates any more than your dishwasher minds cleaning them."

Grinning at his girlfriend, Jack felt his eyebrows climb upward. "Well, just the same, I figure a little common courtesy goes a long way toward preventing a robot uprising."

On his left, Sareena lifted a glass of wine and paused just before taking a sip. "You aren't the only one to express such sentiments, Jack," she said. "When human-form bots were introduced, many people grew uncomfortable with the notion."

"I can see why."

The robot turned and left them.

In truth, he recognized it as something of a perceptual bias. If you were going to fight for robot rights, then you should be equally willing to stick up for those cylindrical things that cut the grass on board the starliner. Houses were designed for humans, and thus robots with arms and legs would have an easier time maneuvering through them. It was simple utilitarianism and nothing else.

A device didn't have a soul simply because it *looked* more like a human; sapience was a function of cognition, not appearance. In the early days of his Keeper training, he had read a bit of Leyrian history and learned that – almost two centuries ago – they had indeed created a real artificial intelligence. Fortunately, the people had been wise enough to treat it with respect.

But it was software, not hardware, a life-form that existed entirely in virtual space. As expected, its sapience had been an accident; the program had been created to oversee the resource management of an entire planet, and when it decided to forego those duties in favour of more fulfilling activities, the program had been kind enough to leave behind a replacement that could manage Leyria's systems without feeling... well, anything.

Jack used a pair of tongs to scoop salad out of the bowl and drop it onto his plate. The dish had kind of a south-west flavour with lettuce drizzled with some spicy dressing, sweet corn, black beans and diced chicken.

Jack stabbed a piece with his fork.

Lifting the meat up in front of his face, he squinted at it. "This isn't real chicken?" he asked.

"Genetically speaking, it's chicken," Sareena explained. "It's just that no animals had to die to make that piece. We clone animal tissue for food."

"There are still farms, of course," Gabi added. She sat back in her chair, smiling at him. "After centuries of domestication, most animals can't survive in the wild, but they aren't slaughtered for their meat."

Jack took a bite with more than a little apprehension – he had never eaten *cloned* meat before – but he very quickly let go of his concerns. It tasted like... Well, he wasn't willing to repeat a worn-out cliché, but he couldn't tell the difference between this and "the real thing." This was going to be an interesting trip; he just hoped they managed to get the professor back to Earth without incident.

And of course, even hoping for it jinxed him.

Chapter 10

A long hallway with carpeted floors was illuminated by purple moonlight that came in through windows on his left. At the far end, a large pair of double doors stood closed, soft light glinting off their metallic surfaces.

Ben stood in the middle of the corridor with his head down. *Don't chicken out now,* he thought, making his way forward. *You came this far.*

Potted plants with large green leaves that drooped stood on either side of the doors, and when he glanced over his shoulder, he saw the sides of other skyscrapers through the windows. It was a beautiful night without a cloud in the sky.

He stopped in front of the door.

Ben shut his eyes, then hung his head in frustration. *You have to know,* he thought to himself. *You get a head start on this, and you might be able to leave the system before-*

Before what?

Before he was arrested for treason? For delivering weapons to a hostile militia that was technically in an act of rebellion against the Leyrian government. Was he truly going to turn tail and run? Doing so would almost certainly mean an end to his relationship with Darrel. Not that he was planning on a lifelong commitment, but…

The doors slid open, revealing a large, open room with a single desk of polished Smartglass and some more potted plants in the corner. The soft moonlight was barely enough to let him see, but he had no desire to activate his ocular implant and no desire to turn on the lights.

This was a spare office in the new LIS building in downtown Saroga. Sometimes, field agents who were placed on colony worlds needed a work space when they returned to Leyria. This would do for now.

He went to the desk.

Brushing his fingertips along its surface, he brought up a square-shaped window that would allow for a user interface. "Computer," he said. "Sync with my multi-tool and access LIS investigation files."

The window on the desk's surface displayed a list of ongoing investigations with case file numbers for each one. He selected file 5127-CT, the investigation that had been launched three months ago when someone left an anonymous tip about missing weapons shipments on the Fringe. That someone had been Tyron, of course. When that bastard made a threat, he followed through.

A message window appeared informing him that he did not have authorization to view the contents of this file. Instantly, his stomach twisted itself in knots. Two weeks ago, he'd had full access. The fact that he could no longer view the contents of this file could only mean one thing.

He was a suspect.

"Companion have mercy," Ben muttered, shuffling over to the window. "It's already started, hasn't it?"

A set of stone steps built into a grassy hill were illuminated by small floodlights, and willow trees on the hilltop sighed softly with strings of lights laced through their branches and dangling alongside their leaves. Beds of flowers lined the hillside, blossoms sprouting in shades of red or violet. Gabi had said that these were the Nesaran Gardens: one of the most romantic spots on all of Leyria.

Jack stood on the path in a pair of gray pants and a green t-shirt with a V-neck, his hair a bit messier than usual. "Well, this is unexpected," he mumbled. "I know you said we had a date, but I was kind of expecting a coffee shop."

Gabi stepped up beside him in a white sundress with thin straps, her hair left loose to fall over her shoulders. She had put a purple flower in it, just above her right ear. "We only get three days here," she explained. "If I'm going to take you on a date, it should be one of the more memorable spots, no?"

"Good call."

He looked up to see the purple moon in the night sky shining bright and clear with a slight nimbus caused by a thin layer of cloud cover. Summer felt a burst of joy when his eyes fell on her home.

His lips curled into a small smile. "It's lovely here," he said. "Thanks for bringing me."

Gabi led him up the steps to a place where people stood with drinks in hand, taking in the sight of flowerbeds alongside the path with blossoms of yellow and orange and red. He spotted two men holding hands over a bed of tulips.

In the distance, a pavilion with a metallic roof that shimmered in the soft light was home to maybe twenty people who stood in pairs or little groups, making enough noise to fill the air with a buzz of conversation.

The whole place felt very… ritzy. Jack had to admit that when he imagined going on a date, this wasn't exactly what he had in mind. Still… it was nice. And he had never really had anyone go to such lengths on his behalf.

Underneath the pavilion, a circular bar with a counter that glowed with soft white light was covered in something that looked like vines. Canadian sensibilities made him wonder what would provoke someone into creating a structure like this – this pavilion offered absolutely no protection from the elements – but then he remembered that the Nesaran Gardens were located at a latitude where snow wouldn't be an issue.

Gabi took a bar stool and set her elbows on the counter, lacing her fingers tightly. "What would you like?" she asked with a glance in his direction. "Perhaps I should ask what Summer will let you have."

Jack smiled, hanging his head as he tried to fight off his embarrassment. "Gaining the power to bend space and time comes with a price," he muttered. "Got anything that's light on the alcohol?"

"*Light* on the alcohol?"

"She can handle a little bit."

Tapping her lips with a single finger, Gabi closed her eyes. "I've got it," she said. "Computer, I'd like one Stellar Cascade for my boyfriend and a glass of Zicaran white for me."

A hatch with edges so fine you wouldn't even notice unless you knew what to look for split apart, leaving a circular hole in the counter. Thirty seconds later, a platform with two drinks rose up. One was obviously a glass of wine.

The other.

Whatever Gabi had ordered for him came in a tall thin glass. It was blue and fizzy like soda. Jack wasn't quite sure what to make of it.

He lifted the glass to his lips and took a sip. The beverage was sweet and just a bit sour. And it tingled on his tongue just like soda. The real surprise came when some of it seemed to evaporate and fill his nostrils with a scent that matched the taste.

Clamping a hand over his mouth, Jack winced. "Oh my god!" he mumbled into his own palm. "Is it supposed to do that? Why do I get the impression this thing is a hit with college students?"

Gabi watched him over her shoulder, a sly smile on her face. "It's actually much more popular with teenagers," she said. "One of the few alcoholic beverages they can order. You'd have to drink ten before it really hit you."

"You let kids drink booze?"

"It isn't quite so cut and dry on our world," she explained. "We try to encourage responsibility by giving them the opportunity to experiment with milder drinks rather than simply denying them access to everything until they reach a certain age."

"How do you prevent them from just walking up here and ordering ten of these?"

"The bar's automated systems are programmed with biometrics. They assess the age of anyone who approaches the counter by measuring height, weight, body type and facial structure. A fifteen-year-old can order at most *one* Stellar Cascade. That number increases as they get older. New options also become available."

Jack took the stool next to her.

As dates went, this one was actually keeping him entertained. If nothing else, he was learning quite a bit about Leyrian culture. His girlfriend – it dawned on him that he was finally comfortable using that phrase – had a talent for planning a romantic evening. This was probably the most interesting date he'd ever been on, but…

But it wasn't frozen yogurt and sitting side by side on a bench next to the Ottawa River. He didn't have to wonder what that meant; he knew perfectly well what it meant, but the opportunities to go down that road had come and passed. Best to just put it out of his head right away. Still, a small selfish part of him wished that Anna could have been the one to tell him about Stellar Cascades.

A much larger part of him felt that he was being lax in his duties – they *had* come to Leyria on business, not pleasure – but their appointment with Professor Nareo was scheduled for tomorrow. They had to do *something* to pass the time.

Besides, it wasn't like things would go to hell if Jack Hunter took *one* night off.

Vetrid Col stood on a city street that curved slightly, a street lined with thick bushes and trees on either side. The bright lights left him feeling exposed. Leyrian cities used piezoelectric sensors so that the streetlights only came on when a car or a pedestrian passed through the area.

Col wore black: boots, pants and a light jacket with the hood down. His hollow-cheeked face of olive skin was shaved clean, and he kept his black hair cut short. Neat and tidy. Normally, he wouldn't be comfortable with his face exposed, but here, a man in a hood drew more attention than he would like. Besides, no one else was outside at this time of night.

He approached a gap in the trees lining the sidewalk, a gap that looked in on the front yard of a small house. Through it, he could see the small two-story structure with its dome-like roof. The thrill came over him now that he was close.

Col felt his mouth tighten. *Focus.* The thought came as a chastising rebuke that seemed to blend the voice of every teacher he'd ever had.

He crouched down at the edge of the property.

Slipping one hand into his pocket, he pulled out half a dozen small marbles with a glossy metallic surface. He left them in his palm for a moment before tapping each with his thumb to activate it.

He tossed them.

They landed on the path that cut through the front yard with a soft rattling sound, some rolling into the grass. Half a moment later, there was a soft hissing pop like wood crackling in a fire-pit.

The marbles had been a gift from Isara, each one programmed to deliver a sharp electromagnetic pulse that would short out any security systems. Most people used some combination of cameras and motion sensors to secure their homes. Getting inside would be difficult enough without accidentally setting off an alarm.

Col felt his lips peel back in a vicious smile. He let his head hang, sucking in a deep breath. *It's really nothing personal,* he thought at the owner of the house. *But Isara wants you dead, and I want to kill something.*

He started up the path through the yard, moving carefully, stealthily. The ability to walk without making too much noise – one of the simplest necessities of survival – was a skill too few people possessed nowadays. Too much coddling. When you built a society where no one had to struggle to find food, you inevitably bred weakness.

That wasn't why he killed.

He simply enjoyed the thrill of it: slipping past security measures, finding his target in a moment of vulnerability, removing any clues that might lead back to him. It was a challenge that pushed a man to his limits.

Around the side of the house, he found a rectangular window that looked in on the first floor. Inside, he saw nothing but darkness. There was no sign that the professor was home, but the man might have gone to bed.

Col unclipped a small disk from his belt.

He stuck it onto the window and watched as the blue LEDs blinked in quick, erratic patterns. The screen of his multi-tool lit up, and he checked the readout. This house was equipped with a standard security system: sensors would activate the alarm if he shattered the glass. Force-fields would keep him out, and the police would be here within minutes.

Fortunately, Col had made himself an asset to one of the most powerful women in Leyrian Space, and one of the perks of that association was access to military-grade tech. This little device could overpower most security systems.

Col stepped back.

A tap at the screen of his multi-tool caused the device to send out an EM pulse, and sparks flashed around the window pane as sensors and force-field generators exploded. Lights came on inside the house, and the alarm began to sound. *Bleakness!* His actions had triggered the security system.

He strode forward and seized the disk from the window, then drew a gun and fired several rounds into the glass. With the window shattered, he carefully climbed through into what appeared to be a rec room.

A gray couch faced the window on the other side of a coffee table, and there were a few shelves along the wall with various knickknacks on each one. To his left, a set of steps led up to a kitchen.

Pulling the hood of his sweater up over his head, Col frowned down at the floor. *I have to be quick about this,* he thought, striding toward the steps. *The police will be here in less than ten minutes.*

The kitchen was a spacious room with sleek, stainless steel cupboards and a glossy black refrigerator. Blinds on the window over the sink fluttered in the cool breeze; that one had been left open a crack.

He found another set of stairs that led up to the second floor where a hallway with carpeted floors stretched on for maybe ten paces. Each wall had exactly one door, and the professor had left them open a crack, revealing a linen closet at the end of the corridor and a small bathroom on his right.

Col opened the door on his left to find a bedroom that was kept neat and tidy with a few throw pillows on the bed. A wooden desk in the corner was bare except for a tablet that had been switched off.

There was no one here!

Col let his head hang and covered his face with a gloved hand. "All that for nothing!" he growled, spinning around. "The man picks tonight of all nights to be away from home!"

He ran back downstairs, into the rec room and out the window. He didn't make his way back to the street; instead, he sprinted through the backyard and charged down the gently-sloping hill behind the house.

Col winced, droplets of sweat rolling over his face. "Bleakness take me!" he said, tossing his head about in frustration. "This better be worth it, Isara. Because the price of my assistance just doubled."

At the base of the hill, he found a chain-link fence, and beyond it, an open field between this set of houses and those of the next street over. Far off in the distance, the skyscrapers of Calinar stabbed the night sky.

Lifting his fist, he tapped at the screen of his multi-tool. Nanobots emerged from the tiny metal disk, shaping themselves into a blade roughly twice the length of his hand. The software that allowed them to do so was illegal – you had to hack a multi-tool to give it the ability to fabricate weapons – but friendship with Isara had its perks.

He sliced through the fence with ease – the blade was sharp enough to allow it – and ducked through the opening.

Chapter 11

Like most others he had been in, the police station in Manchester, Tennessee had a bland feeling. Long hallways of white walls and wooden doors, officers shuffling about with their heads down. Harry felt right at home and also completely unwelcome. It was a strange sensation.

He wore a gray suit with a purple shirt as he strode through the corridor, sliding his sunglasses into place. "Excuse me," he said, stopping the twelfth officer he passed. "I'm looking for room 23-B."

The man looked up at him with lips pressed into a thin line, studying Harry as if he had just sprouted horns. "Second-last door on your right," he said, jerking his head in that direction. Cordial but forced. Harry supposed it was the best he could hope for.

He walked on.

As he passed through the door, he found a large room with an oval-shaped table, a room where half a dozen uniformed officers sat in the wan light that came in through the blinds on the windows. He could size up a cop's attitude simply by watching the man's posture, and this bunch... They were all grizzled men in their late thirties or early forties, and he was willing to bet that most were fed up with their jobs. That didn't bode well. A cop who was just counting the days until his pension had lost interest in justice as an abstract concept. If he'd ever had it. As expected, every last one of them was white.

The school principal was a pale man in a dark blue suit: a man who wore his hair parted to the side and kept his glasses pressed up against his face. Next to him, Harry saw a woman with long blonde hair. A guidance counselor unless he missed his guess.

And then there was Anna.

She leaned against the wall with her arms folded, dressed in gray pants and a black, short-sleeved blouse. Her bright red hair was tied back in a short little ponytail. Did she notice the dynamic here? A bunch of white people deciding the fate of a black kid.

The only person of colour in this room was obviously Kevin's father, and that man was about as relaxed as a deer who had just run straight into the middle of a wolf pack. He sat with hands folded over his stomach, trying not to look at anything.

The lead officer shot a glance in Harry's direction. "Who might you be?" he asked in that terse voice cops always developed. "This meeting is closed to the public."

Harry smiled, then bowed his head to the man. "I'm your liaison to the Keepers," he said, approaching the table. "You'll forgive me for saying so, but I think you boys could use a fresh perspective."

"He's legit," Anna said.

Harry took an empty chair without being asked, leaning back and taking in a deep breath. "Well, let's get started then," he said. "I've been briefed on the latest incident at the school."

The lead officer bit his lip, hanging his head as he looked over his papers. "We're thinking about calling in the FBI," he began. "This one is just too big for a small town police department."

Leaning against the wall with her arms crossed, Anna shook her head in disgust. "That's unnecessary," she replied in a breathy hiss. "You already have all the help you need, Lieutenant Biggs. I'm trained to handle these situations."

"With respect, Agent Lenai, you haven't exactly *handled* it thus far."

"Because your people don't follow orders."

For a moment, Harry considered intervening, but he'd known Anna long enough to know that when her righteous fury was hot, you had to let it burn itself out. Besides, the girl had a point. But for the itchy trigger fingers of a few idiots, this situation would have been resolved by now.

"The school board is concerned," Principal Jensen chimed in, even though no one had addressed him. "These incidents on school property put the lives of students at risk. I've been told to inform you that we expect a speedy resolution to this conflict."

Well, that settled it then!

One of the officers lifted a mug to his lips and slurped as he sipped his coffee. He turned his attention to the principal. "I say we bring in a TAC team. Next time we go up against this kid, we have snipers ready."

"Excuse me!" Trevor Harmon was on his feet in the blink of an eye, standing with his fists clenched. "You're talking about my *son.* If you think I'm going to stand by-"

"We're talking about a boy with the power to swat armed men like flies," the officer cut in. "This boy is a danger to anyone who crosses his path. Now, we must consider all possible options before we make a decision."

Anna strode forward with fists clenched at her sides, pausing next to the man who had spoken. "Let me make one thing perfectly clear," she said, fixing a death-glare on the back of his head. "This case is under Leyrian jurisdiction, which means Leyrian laws apply. You hurt that kid, and I will hunt you down like a dog.

"I'll see to it that you're charged with murder, and you will stand trial in a Leyrian court where, I can assure you, you will find no sympathy. Do we understand each other, Officer Hendricks?"

"Perfectly…Ma'am."

In all the years, he'd known her, Harry would never have described his friendship with Anna as anything more than cordial, but right then, he loved her like a daughter. Her stubborn insistence on following her own personal code no matter what anyone thought could be one of her most infuriating qualities, but when she took a stand on principle, it was a glorious thing to behold.

Principal Jensen pressed a fist to his mouth and cleared his throat. "Regardless," he said, swiveling nervously in his chair. "Young Kevin represents a threat to the safety of our community. The school board-"

"Which member of the school board?"

"Hmm?"

Anna glanced over her shoulder, thin strands of red hair falling over her face. "I'd like to know which member of the school board is pressing for action," she said, arching an eyebrow. "Is it Simmons?"

The principal went red, then lowered his eyes to stare into his lap. "It was a joint decision by all of them…" He slid his chair closer to the table. "You need to understand the value parents place on-"

"I understand perfectly well."

Lieutenant Biggs rounded on Harry. "You're supposed to be our go-between," he said, gesticulating. "Can you possibly convince her to settle down and see sense?"

"Could you be any more condes-"

"Anna," Harry broke in. "Give me a moment." The lieutenant let out a sigh of relief, and it was clear that he thought Harry was going to press for diplomacy. There was a time and place for diplomacy – sometimes it was necessary to smooth things over and get everyone back on track – but this wasn't it.

Pressing his lips together, Harry closed his eyes. He took a deep breath and then let it out slowly. "You want to know what

I think, Lieutenant?" he asked, standing up to give his words a little more gravitas.

"I think that the last ten years have seen a startling increase in the number of young black men shot dead by police officers. I think guns are a source of comfort to racist men who have no business wearing a badge, and now that one of these kids has demonstrated the ability to render your weapons useless, you're panicking. You want to escalate this, to reassert your control."

That left everyone speechless.

Anna walked around the table with her head down, forcing out a deep breath. "In case you've forgotten, you're on this case as a courtesy," she said. "And I've just decided that courtesy is no longer appropriate."

She whirled around to face them with her arms crossed, raising her chin to stare down her nose at the lot of them. "As of right now, you're off this investigation. All of you. If you see Kevin Harmon, you call me, but you are not to engage for any reason except to protect civilians."

Harry leaned back with fingers laced over his chest, frowning at the ceiling. "I guess you won't be needing a liaison," he said, eyebrows rising. "So, what's your next move, Agent Lenai?"

"I'm gonna find that kid," she said, "and get that damn thing off his hand."

Harry stared into his mug of coffee and watched his faint reflection ripple as he blew on the surface of the dark liquid. It was a little too warm for a hot beverage, but he really needed a caffeine fix.

This little coffee shop was empty except for a young man who stood behind the counter, cleaning the cake display with a cloth. Out the window, he saw cars rushing by on a busy city street.

Anna sat across from him with her elbow on the table, her chin resting in the palm of her hand. "What you said back there," she began. "About these cops being motivated by bigoted fears? Is that really what it's about?"

Harry closed his eyes. He let his head hang and chose his words with care. "It's a problem on this world. Cops tend to assume that people who look like me are dangerous."

Anna growled.

Lifting his chin, Harry narrowed his eyes. "This isn't something you were prepared for," he muttered, staring at the roof. "Anna, it's a reality that I have to live with every day."

She sat with arms crossed, bent forward so that he could only see the top of her head. "I knew race was a part of this," she hissed. "These cops had a bad attitude from the very start, but I never thought it would motivate them to kill."

"You were expecting some degree of integrity."

"Yes."

Harry brought the mug to his lips and slurped as he took a sip. He set it back down on the table. "Here's the sad reality, Anna. The egalitarian attitudes that your people take so much pride in were the result of centuries of struggle, and I'm willing to bet that if you scratch the surface, you'll find traces of those old prejudices in most people."

"You're probably right," Anna mumbled. "So now I have to finish this assignment alone."

"Not alone. You have me."

"Thanks."

"Not sure if this means anything to you," Harry said softly. "But I think Kevin's extremely lucky that you're the one working this case."

"If you say so."

"So, what do we do now?"

Anna looked up at the ceiling with her lips pursed, blinking as she considered the question. "The same thing we always do when an investigation hits a dead end. Go right back to square one."

He got up and shoved his hands into his pockets, standing before her with his head down. "Good luck with that," he said with a nod. "I think I'll go back to the police station and make sure they stay out of your hair."

"You really wanna put up with that hassle?"

"No," Harry admitted. "But I think it would do good for some of them to get used to taking orders from a black man. Might actually shake loose a few of their prejudices."

"Good luck."

"You too."

Amanda Simmons sat on a swing in a playground, clutching the chains with both hands. The girl was lovely in a white dress with lace on the sleeves, her hair left loose to fall over her shoulders.

Tracking her down had required some effort. With no other options, Anna went back to the school to interview anyone who might be able to give her some insight. Her instincts said that Amanda knew more than she let on. One of the students, a young man in the Christian Fellowship club, told her that Amanda sometimes went to the park near her home to read.

Anna stood in the grass in blue jeans and a matching t-shirt, the wind teasing her hair. *So sad,* she noted as she watched the girl. *Something's not right here, and I think I detect the father's scent.*

Amanda turned her head to smile at the young children who were squealing with delight as they ran through the playground. One of them, a young boy with short blonde hair, threw his hands up as he came down the slide.

Approaching cautiously, Anna let out a deep breath. "So I was hoping we could talk," she said as she neared the swings. "I didn't really have a chance to get to know you the other day."

Amanda looked up at her with big brown eyes that widened at the sight of her. "My dad doesn't want me to talk to you," she murmured. "He says you're part of the world. A temptation."

"What do *you* want?"

"I don't understand."

Anna forced her lips into a thin smile. She bowed her head and let out a soft sigh. "You're almost eighteen, Amanda. That's an adult in this country. You're going to have to start making decisions for yourself."

The girl shivered.

Anna took the swing next to her, gripping the chains as Amanda did. There had to be something she could say to get through. "You've heard about what happened the other day? When we tried to help Kevin?"

Amanda had tears on her cheeks. "I heard about it. Kevin's nice. He's funny. He doesn't deserve to have people shooting at him."

"Now, *there* we agree."

"You're going to help him?"

"I'm gonna try," Anna replied. "But if I'm going to help him, I'll need all the information I can get, and something tells me you haven't been totally honest."

For a very long moment, Amanda was still. Then she pushed herself on the swing and began a slow, gentle arc. "I just don't want anything to happen to Kevin," she said. "He's nice."

"You like him."

"What?"

Anna glanced over her shoulder with a stone-faced expression, the hot sun warming her skin. "Why didn't I see it sooner?" she whispered. "You've developed a little crush on Kevin, haven't you?"

The girl stopped herself by skidding her shoes in the sand. A shudder escaped her as she stood up. "He's just a nice boy!"

Amanda squeaked. "I…I don't like him that way, but I don't want anything bad to happen to him."

"Amanda, why are you lying to me?" Suddenly, she remembered her conversation with Harry. When she tried to think of reasons why Amanda might feel the need to hide her feelings for a "nice boy" like Kevin, only one thing came to mind.

But it didn't add up.

This girl displayed no outward signs of that kind of bigotry. It was possible that she hid it well, but Amanda seemed to be a gentle flower. Anna didn't think she was capable of harbouring negative thoughts about anyone.

The girl stood with her back turned, trembling as she struggled to express herself. "I'm sorry," she said. "I'm not allowed to feel that. When the time is right, my father will arrange a courtship."

Gritting her teeth, Anna stared down into her lap. The heat in her face was hard to ignore. "Right. Because your father's wishes are the ones that matter," she said. "It's your life, Amanda. You have every right to love whomever you want."

Amanda faced her with a shuddering breath. "He told me you'd say that." She rubbed her nose with the back of her hand. "The world tempts us to sin. I can't…"

"Why is it a sin?"

"Unsupervised dating can lead to sex."

Anna tossed her head back, rolling her eyes in exasperation. "Companion forbid it!" she said. "You might actually get to experience a little pleasure!"

She regretted the words as soon as they were out of her mouth. Mocking the girl would only make it harder to crack through that shell of indoctrination. Once again, she had spoken without thinking. "What do you think of me, Amanda?"

"What do you mean?"

Anna shrugged her shoulders, feeling self-conscious, then hung her head and let out a sigh. "As a person," she clarified.

"You don't know me that well, but tell me your first impressions."

Amanda stood there, hugging herself and rubbing her upper arms, shivering despite the warm afternoon. "You're a Justice Keeper," she mumbled. "You help people. I think that makes you a good person."

"Would you like to know how many people I've been intimate with?"

"I-I guess."

Anna held up five fingers.

The girl stared at her with eyes that seemed to pop out of their sockets. "That's…I wouldn't have expected that." She covered her mouth with one hand, breathing deeply. "That's…That's a lot. Aren't you worried that your husband will feel…cheated?"

"The first was a young man I dated casually after taking an assignment on Alios; his name was Elan, and he was very sweet. The second was a one-night stand. A man I met at a work function. The third was my friend Sinara. I didn't think I was capable of feeling desire for a woman until I met her. She was quite eager to be my girlfriend, but I didn't feel the same way. The fourth was a boyfriend I had for about three months last year. His name was Tierin. And the fifth is my current boyfriend. I can assure you he's not the least bit bothered by my past."

Anna stood up, pacing toward the girl. "I've been with five people," she said softly. "But I've saved more lives than I can count and stood against unspeakable evil. My worth as a human being is not determined by the number of people I've slept with."

Amanda shivered.

"And neither is yours." Anna laid a gentle hand on the girl's shoulder, trying to offer her support. "It's what we *do* that defines us, whether our actions help people or harm them. Date Kevin, don't date Kevin; it's really not my business. But if you know something, then you have a chance to help someone you obviously care about. So, the question is 'will you take it?'"

"He…" Amanda stammered. "He told me about a place he liked to visit."

"Show me."

Chapter 12

Five men sat around the table in the conference room on the second floor of the police station, bathed in warm afternoon sunlight. They all stared at him with wide eyes.

Harry stood before them with a tablet held up in front of his face. He lowered it to frown at the lot of them. "So let's go over this again," he began. "If one of your officers comes across Kevin Harmon…"

Lieutenant Biggs – a heavyset man with a sour expression on his face – leaned back in his chair with his arms crossed. "We keep our distance," he grumbled. "We call Agent Lenai, but we don't engage."

Harry closed his eyes, nodding to the man. "That's right," he said, approaching the table at a brisk pace. "Your people aren't equipped to deal with him, and it's important to defuse the situation."

The lieutenant swiveled in his chair to face his four subordinates. "So we're all clear on that then?" he asked with more than a little exasperation in his voice. "You don't go near the kid unless he starts harming civilians."

Biggs spun around to face Harry again. "Any other orders for us, sir?" he asked, bushy eyebrows rising. "Or can my men go back to doing their jobs like the simple folk they are?"

Harry felt his mouth grow tight, then shook his head with a growl. "Oh, I do have a few more things to say," he replied. "Specifically, I want to go over what your people should do if they're forced to engage Kevin."

"This oughtta be good," one of the others muttered.

"Something, Officer?"

A gaunt-cheeked man with a tiny scar over his left eyebrow looked up to fix his gaze on Harry. "Just wondering how you think we should handle it, sir," he said. "If we aren't to draw weapons, perhaps we should tickle him into submission?"

Several of the others laughed.

Harry had a hard time ignoring the anger in his chest. It had been like this for the last forty-five minutes, the officers paying attention with halfhearted interest when they weren't outright sneering at him. Well, he should have expected as much. There was no doubt in his mind that these men justified their behaviour with all sorts of excuses, but when you stripped it down to nuts and bolts, this was a case of white cops thinking that a black kid was dangerous and hating the fact that they had to take orders from a black man, orders that said "leave the kid alone."

Harry leaned forward, bracing his hands on the table's surface, and stared at the five laughing idiots. "This is funny to you?" he asked, raising an eyebrow. "Because, in case you haven't noticed, every time you escalate the situation, you put people's lives at risk."

The gaunt-cheeked man scowled. "All right," he muttered. "We understand your point. So how do you want us to handle a confrontation with the boy?"

"If it looks like civilians might be harmed, do whatever is necessary to remove them from the situation with *minimal* violence." The very fact that he had to speak such instructions out loud was a failure of epic proportions. "Kevin has shown willingness to work with us; so keep your weapons holstered – they won't do any good anyway – and approach him with caution. Assure him that he won't be harmed and that Justice Keepers have the technology to remove the device from his hand."

"Anything else?"

Harry stood up, frowning as he ran his gaze over all of them. "You're officers of the law!" he snapped. "Display a little professionalism for god's sake. If any one of you had been one of my subordinates, I'd have written you up."

"Yeah…" one muttered. "I'm sure you get all the hard cases up in Canadia."

Harry resisted the urge to respond to that. The comment was so mired in ignorance, there was nothing he could say anyway. All the hard cases? How about a Justice Keeper running around his city and getting into fights with maniacs who used energy weapons? How about a terrorist who used alien tech to kill and maim dozens of innocent people? How about god damn robots with no purpose other than to kill everything in sight?

"This briefing is over," he said. "Dismissed."

Tall trees rose up all around her with branches that stretched toward one another and leaves that caught the light of the sun in a sea of green. Down here, it was shady, but the mugginess was still fierce.

Anna stood with fists on her hips, peering into a small pit in the forest floor. "So, he would come here when he wanted to be alone?" she asked. "This was his sanctuary?"

There was nothing down there except dried up leaves and muck. A few twigs and candy wrappers littered the slope that led up to the other side of the pit. She did notice a nice big rock for sitting.

Pursing her lips, Anna turned her face up to the sky. She blinked several times. "This is where he would come whenever he felt like he was in trouble. That's what he told you when he brought you here?"

She turned.

"We were searching for a place to bury the time capsule," Amanda said. "We just sat a little while and talked. He said this was where he would go when he needed to clear his head."

"Well, it's a start."

Anna spun around, then hopped off the ledge. She landed crouched in the middle of the pit. "Candy wrappers," she muttered under her breath. "How much do you wanna bet Kevin's the one who left them here?"

"He doesn't seem like the kind of boy who would litter."

Mopping a hand over her face, Anna wiped sweat away. "Yeah, maybe not," she said. "But if he comes here to be alone, it stands to reason that not many people know about this place."

She extended her left arm to point a fist down at the ground. "Multi-tool active!" she ordered. "Full scan!"

The tool chirped in confirmation. There was a soft buzzing sound for a few brief moments, and then the results appeared on the display screen. Nothing noteworthy. Just some leaves and muck and…

Plastic?

She dug through the leaves like a dog trying to bury a bone, shoving them aside until she found a sandwich bag with a slip of paper inside. Now *that* must have been left here deliberately.

Someone had scrawled a phone number onto the slip of paper. The digits were written in faded black marker, but she could make them out. 931-555-7172. A jolt of excitement surged through her.

Anna tapped out the number on the screen of her multi-tool, then sent the call. A few seconds past while the phone rang, and then a deep voice answered her.

"Hello?"

"Kevin?"

There was silence for a moment, broken only by the sound of some heavy breathing on the phone, and then he spoke. "You're the Justice Keeper, aren't you? I had a feeling it would be you who found my quiet place."

Anna licked her lips, then let out a soft sigh. "It's me," she said with a nod. "Kevin, we want to help you. We can get that thing off you, but first I need to know where you are and if you're safe."

"I'm okay."

"Have you hurt anyone else?"

"No." That was a relief. The kid didn't strike her as violent, but she would be lying if she said she wasn't worried about what might happen if someone else tried to corner him. "I've been avoiding people for that reason. This thing…It's like a song in my head. I can control it, tune it out, but when I get frightened or angry…"

"Kevin, I assume you left this number here for someone to find."

"Yeah, I bought a burner yesterday," he explained. "I couldn't risk turning on my actual phone. They might try to track me that way. This way, if someone calls, I can be sure of who I'm talking to before I tell them anything. I left the number in my spot for you. I was hoping it would be you."

"So, you trust me?"

He hesitated. "Yes."

"Then I need to know where you are."

"You know the new housing development just east of I-24?" he asked. "I've been hiding out there in an unfinished house. I can turn on this thing's GPS if you want. You should be able to find me."

Finally! Some success! Her relief was so strong that it hit her like a splash of cold water. She'd been living with so much tension that she hadn't even noticed it until it was gone. "All right, Kevin, this is how it's gonna play out," she said. "I'm going to keep this low profile. No cops, no emergency response teams. Just me and a close friend that you can trust. His name is Harry. Once you have a chance to get to know us, we'll drive you to a landing site where a shuttle will take us up to Station Twelve. The doctors there can help you."

"Okay."

He hung up.

With the tension fading, Anna found herself feeling very tired. Too much stress for too long could leave you very drained. Hopefully, they would be able to bring Kevin to the station without any further incidents.

She climbed out of the pit to find Amanda standing there with her hands shaking, wearing a smile that would outshine the sun. "You found him!" the girl exclaimed. "So he's going to be all right?"

Anna smiled, then nodded to the young woman. "I found him," she said, exhaustion thickening her voice. "He should be fine so long as we can get him safely up to the station. Come on."

Their walk out of the woods was quick but uneventful. It took a few minutes to find the path that led to the back of the high school, and then it was just a short walk into the open sunlight. All the while, they discussed the importance of making choices. Hopefully Anna could impress upon this girl that her life was her own.

Once they were clear of the trees, the back of the high school loomed over them. Anna saw the chain-link fence that Kevin had ripped to shreds in his attempt to escape her and paused when she noticed her supervisor examining the hole.

Dressed in a pair of blue jeans and a pink t-shirt, Jena was down on one knee in the grass, scanning the mangled fence with her multi-tool. What would she be doing here? Why scan the fence? More to the point, if she'd wanted that done, why not simply ask Anna to do it?

Anna strode through the grass with her hands in her pockets, head bowed as she approached the other woman. "We found him," she said. "Kevin made contact with me just a few minutes ago."

Jena looked up at her with large dark eyes, almost as if she were surprised by the information. "You did?" she asked. "Well, that's wonderful. Where is the young man?"

Anna winced, shaking her head. "Doing what teenagers do best," she answered. "Hiding in one of the most unsafe locations imaginable. He's in an unfinished house just beyond the freeway."

"I take it you're on your way there?"

Anna crossed her arms, then turned her face up to the open sky. The wind teased her hair. "As soon as I can find Harry," she muttered. "The two of us can probably set Kevin at ease."

The fence was an absolute mess, its wiry mesh ripped and torn and singed in a few places. No doubt the principal was beside himself when he considered the cost of fixing it. "So what are you doing?" Anna inquired. "I mean… You can't think there might be a clue to Kevin's whereabouts here."

Jena frowned thoughtfully at the grass. "I was hoping I might be able to learn something about the device he carries," she said. "Compare the damage here to things we've seen from other Overseer weapons."

"Right."

"Who's the girl?"

When Anna turned, she saw Amanda standing just inside the treeline with a hand pressed to a tree. The girl kept her eyes glued to the ground beneath her feet. In all likelihood, she felt a little out of place, like a student overhearing a conversation between two teachers. "That would be Amanda Simmons," she answered. "The girl I told you about. Have you started the inquiry with Child Protective Services?"

"Inquiry?"

"Regarding Amanda," Anna snapped with more venom than she would have liked. "We talked about it the other day, remember? I'm concerned about the situation with her father."

"Oh, yes," Jena replied. "Thank you for reminding me. I'm sorry; I've been a little distracted with...with Jack's mission to Leyria. Do you think he's made contact with the professor yet?"

Now, *that* was an odd question. Jack had posted a mission status update last night, stating that his team had arrived on Leyria and that they intended to meet with Professor Nareo early the following morning. "I can't really say," she muttered. "What's the time difference between here and Kenthara Province?"

"Never mind." The silhouette of Jena stood up behind her, bracing one hand against the fence. "I'm worrying for no good reason. I like being able to contact my people on a moment's notice, and when I can't, it sets me on edge. You'd better go find Harry. I want this case settled as soon as possible."

Chapter 13

The first thing Jack noticed when consciousness seeped into his brain was the soft beeping of his multi-tool alerting him to the presence of an incoming call. He opened his eyes and saw Sareena's guest room in the early morning light.

His multi-tool was on the nightstand, still attached to the gauntlet he wore on his left wrist. The screen displayed the words "incoming call," and the metal disk attached to it buzzed to get his attention.

Jack squeezed his eyes shut, then forced them open again. "Multi-tool active." He sat up and scrubbed a hand over his face, threading fingers through his thick brown hair. "Answer call. Audio only."

"Agent Hunter?"

Jack pressed fists to his eye-sockets, rubbing the sleep away. "Yeah, that's me," he said in a rasp. "There some particular reason you decided to interrupt my date with the lovely Katniss Everdeen?"

"I'm sorry?"

"Never mind."

There was a brief moment of silence before the caller spoke again. By the soft light, he could tell that it was still early. The room was very spartan with only a dresser across from the foot of the bed as furniture. "Listen, Agent Hunter. This is Professor Aldin Nareo. We had an appointment this morning."

"Please tell me that you're not planning to cancel," Jack said. "I came a very long way to talk with you, Professor."

"It's not that. For the last three days, I've been attending a conference in M'Sia. I had just returned to my hotel room when I got a call from my local police department. Someone broke into my house last night, and from the look of it, they used some very advanced weaponry to bypass the security systems. The police believe that the intruder intended to kill me. An attempted murder less than twenty-four hours before our meeting. You will forgive me if I have a hard time believing these events are unconnected."

"Can't argue with that logic," Jack muttered. "Where are you now? Some place with *a lot* of security, right? Right?"

"I returned to my office for our meeting."

"Does anyone else know you're there?"

"I passed a few colleagues in the hallways."

Jack crossed his arms, leaning back against the wooden headboard. He looked up at the ceiling. "Okay," he said. "Stay where you are and keep a low profile. I can be there in just over an hour."

"You think I'm in danger?"

"With my luck? Yeah."

In less than five minutes, he was dressed and briefing his teammates in the dining room. Gabi stood on one side of the table in a pink housecoat, her long dark hair in need of a good brushing.

On the other side of the table, the half-dressed hologram of Ben hovered just a few feet off the floor. The other man was pinching his chin with his thumb and his forefinger. "So they actually tried to *kill* him?" he said. "Do you think Slade is behind this one?"

Jack felt his face twist into something haggard. "That would be my guess. Which means we've got to find him and get him someplace safe. 'Cause Slade isn't gonna give up after one try."

Gabi leaned her shoulder against the wall, standing with a hand gripping the fabric of her robe. The exhaustion on her face was unmistakable. "And we thought this would be a nice and easy assignment."

"Nothing's ever easy."

"No."

Closing his eyes, Jack breathed deeply through his nose. "All right," he said with a nod. "Ben, get down to the crime scene. Use your clearance; find out whatever the locals know about the break in."

"Will do."

"Gabi, I want you working low-pro real estate. We're going to need a safe place to take the professor once I retrieve him. I don't trust any of the Keeper offices – you never know where Slade might have agents – and I'd rather not bring him to a civilian's home if I can avoid it."

They stood there for a moment, both facing him with wide eyes, staring as if they'd never seen him before. The hologram of Ben wavered and then reappeared less than half a second later.

"What?" he asked.

Gabi smiled, gazing into his eyes. God have mercy, she was so damn beautiful! "Your new self-confidence is refreshing," she explained. "It's nice to watch you take charge of a mission."

"I'm sorry-"

"No." She forestalled him with a raised hand, coming toward him. "This is your mission, Jack. We follow your lead, remember?"

"All right then," he said. "Let's go."

The hallways of Lenasa University's archaeology department had a sleek, modern look to them. White tiles stretched through a corridor with green stripes on the pale walls. The door to every classroom was made of glass, and when you looked inside, you could see desks arranged in a kind of semi-circle around a central lectern.

Jack strode through the hallway in jeans and a brown jacket over his white t-shirt, keeping his head down. "Just my luck," he muttered under his breath. "Find a guy who can give me some answers, and now people are trying to kill him."

At the end of the hallway, he found a door on his right with Professor Aldin Nareo etched into the pane. The Smartglass was foggy, allowing for some privacy. You could choose to make it fully transparent if you were so inclined.

Jack knocked.

"Who's there?"

"Agent Hunter."

There was a soft buzzing noise, indicating that the door had been unlocked, and then Jack pushed it open to reveal a small office where the entire back wall was one big window that looked out on the campus. A slim, horseshoe-shaped desk – also made of Smartglass – and several wooden cupboards were the only pieces of furniture.

Nareo was a short man with olive skin and black hair that was turning gray at the temples. He sat at his desk with fingers laced over its glass surface, breathing deeply to stay calm. "Agent Hunter."

"We need to go."

The other man looked up at him with fierce brown eyes, and it was clear that they weren't going anywhere. "Not just yet," he said. "I want some answers before I agree to trust you with my life."

Chewing on his lip, Jack shut his eyes. "Okay," he said. "That's fair. But we haven't got a lot of time here, so how about I just skip to the part where I tell you everything."

"Fair enough?"

Jack took a chair across from him, setting his elbow on the armrest. He rested his chin on the knuckles of his fist. "I work with a team of Keepers on Earth. We're searching for a piece of Overseer technology called the Key."

"And you think I can help you find it," Nareo muttered. "You realize that any data on Overseer tech is sketchy at best."

"Any insight you provide is appreciated."

"What does this Key do?"

A grin blossomed on Jack's face, and he had to resist the urge to laugh. "I'm gonna go out on a limb and assume it opens something. But, you know, I *am* prone to flights of fancy."

Nareo pressed a hand to his mouth, coughing forcefully. "In other words, you don't know," he said with obvious frustration. "All right. Then why don't we move on to who's trying to kill me?"

"I can't be certain," Jack replied. "But if I were a gambling man, I'd bet everything I owned on Grecken Slade. That bastard wants the Key as much as we do."

Nareo studied him with lips pressed into a tight grimace. "Grecken Slade," he said softly. "The name sounds oddly familiar, but I can't recall why."

"He was the head of the Justice Keepers."

"So a *Keeper* wants me dead?"

"A *former* Keeper."

The professor leaned back in his chair, covering his face with both hands. A painful groan escaped him. "Regardless," he said. "It's a bit unnerving to find out that the people who are supposed to protect you are trying to kill you."

Jack doubled over with his arms folded, heaving out a sigh. "I hear you," he said, shaking his head. "You're wondering if you can trust me. If one Keeper can go bad, who's to say they aren't all corrupt?"

"Exactly."

Jack stood up slowly, towering over the other man with fists balled at his sides. He bowed his head respectfully. "Look, Professor, I don't think there's anything I can say to put you at ease. You're just going to have to make up your mind. Stay here and take your chances or come with me."

"And *why* should I trust you?"

"Well, I have a very honest face."

The other man wheezed with laughter, and Jack finally felt like he was beginning to make some progress. "All right," Nareo said. "You've persuaded me. If I survive this, I'll be happy to help you find your Key."

A few minutes later, they were out in the hallway, making their way quietly back to the elevator. There were no classes today – thank heaven for small miracles – but some of the faculty had come in to work on various projects. Best to avoid them. He would prefer it if no one knew the professor had left or where he had gone.

They turned a corner and started down a long hallway with glass doors that led into empty classrooms, most of which were open just a crack. The place was deserted except for a single man some fifty paces away.

He was a tall fellow in a long black coat that fell to his knees, a man with olive skin and short black hair. *Maybe we better turn around...* The man looked up and blinked when he saw Jack and Nareo.

He shrugged out of his coat, revealing thick, black armour underneath. In the blink of an eye, nanobots were crawling over his face, linking together to form a sleek black mask with a red visor.

Oh, my timing sucks! The assassin reached for the pistol on his belt, drawing it from its holster in one smooth motion. He powered up the weapon, and a high-pitched whine filled the air.

"Get down!"

Jack shoved Nareo sideways, sending the man sprawling through the open door of a classroom. The professor fell hard onto the white-tiled floor, stretched out in front of the first row of desks.

Black-Mask tried to adjust his aim.

Jack dove.

He somersaulted over the corridor floor, then came up on one knee, drawing his pistol from its holster. "Stun rounds!" he growled before aiming the weapon and pulling the trigger over and over.

The assassin stumbled as bullets slammed into his chest. His armour absorbed the electric charge, a jolt that would have knocked anyone else unconscious, but the constant fire prevented him from taking aim.

Jack stood up, clutching the pistol in both hands, and hissed as he paced through the corridor. "High impact!" he called out, and the gun responded. That would punch a hole in almost any body armour.

Black-Mask raised a hand up to shield himself, the gesture causing a wall of white static to appear before him. Jack's bullets hit the force-field and fell to the floor. Still, he kept on shooting. So long as that force-field was in place, his opponent couldn't return fire. He closed the distance in seconds.

The force-field flickered and then winked out.

Jack kicked the gun from the other man's hand. He spun and back-kicked, driving a foot into the assassin's chest. A sharp wheeze echoed through the hallway as Black-Mask stumbled backward.

He regained his balance quickly and studied Jack through that red visor. "Clever," he said, thrusting his arm out to point his fist at Jack. Two electrodes came flying from the man's gauntlet.

Leaning back, Jack caught the wires just before the sparking tips made contact with his face. *That* would have knocked him out. He gave a tug and ripped the taser right off the man's arm.

Jack swung the wire above his head like a propeller blade, picking up speed until the air whistled. The damaged taser unit lashed out and struck his opponent right between the eyes. If only that mask hadn't been there. Still, it was a distraction.

Jack leaped.

He snap-kicked, slamming a foot into the other man's face. The impact was enough to send Black-Mask falling backward, and within a few seconds, the assassin was sliding across the floor tiles.

He sat up and covered his face with a gloved hand. "I hate fighting Keepers," he said, grabbing something from his belt. Tension made a knot in Jack's chest as he readied himself for whatever was coming.

The other man threw something.

Two metal cylinders landed on the floor, and before Jack could so much as blink, there was a blinding flash of light and a terrible sound that left a ringing in his skull. It was hard to concentrate. He instinctively dropped his pistol to cover his ears, but it did nothing to ease his dizziness.

The assassin stood up, dusting himself off. He flung one arm out to the side, and something extended from the multi-tool he wore on his gauntlet. A blade of some kind. Likely very sharp.

Black-Mask strode forward.

Down on his knees, Jack had both hands over his ears. His teeth were clenched as he hissed and tried to ignore the pain in his skull. *Come on, Summer!* he thought at the Nassai. *We can do this.*

Black-Mask drew back his arm for a stab.

Jack fell backward, slapping both hands down on the floor. He brought one leg up to strike the other man's chin with his foot. That bought him a few seconds; the assassin stumbled about, trying to get his bearings.

Jack's pistol was on the floor.

He seized it and took aim, but the other man was quicker. Black-Mask tapped a button on his chest, triggering yet another force-field generator that shielded him with another screen of flickering static.

The man turned, backing through the open door of a classroom. Not the one Nareo had taken refuge in – in fact, this one was on the other side of the corridor – but it would provide him with some cover.

Jack was on his feet in an instant.

He winced and felt sweat running over his face. Mopping it away with one hand, he let out a breath. "Nothing's ever easy," he muttered, fighting off the last traces of dizziness. "Nothing at all."

Something floated out of the door that Black-Mask had gone through: a disk about the size of a man's palm with a single aperture on its edge. It whirled around to focus that small hole on Jack.

By instinct, Jack threw up a Bending that refracted the light into a smear of colour. Bullets jerked to a halt mere inches from his outstretched palm, then curved to the right and flew straight into the wall.

"Bloody hell!"

Jack threw himself sideways, into the room opposite the one that Black-Mask had gone into. He landed on the floor, then rolled like a log away from the door. *How many gadgets does that guy have?*

Jack got to his feet and backed up until his ass was pressed to the wall next to the door. He was doubled over, gasping for breath. "EMP!" he shouted and watched as the LEDs on his pistol turned white.

He flung his arm out to the side.

The drone floated through the door.

A single glowing bullet hit the edge of the disk, causing blue sparks to flash over its surface. The damn thing fell to the floor and sputtered a few times before it finally went still. At least it didn't explode the way Death Spheres did.

Jack stepped back into the hallway.

As expected, the armoured man was already halfway down the hallway, moving toward the room where Professor Nareo had taken refuge. The drone had been nothing but a distraction.

Jack lifted his pistol in both hands, cocking his head to the side. "High impact!" he said as he strode through the corridor. "And don't think for a second that I won't punch a hole in your chest."

The assassin froze.

He turned partway, glancing over his shoulder to study Jack through the lens of that red visor. "You're persistent," he said, one hand dropping to his belt where he might pull out yet another gadget.

Gritting his teeth, Jack let out a soft, menacing hiss. "We have that in common," he said, gesturing with his pistol. "Up against the wall. A high-impact round will pierce even your armour, and I'm betting your force-field generators are drained."

"You wouldn't kill me."

"What makes you so sure?"

The other man bowed his head, covering his masked face with a gloved hand. "I've learned a thing or two about Justice Keepers," he answered. "You're all so noble, so eager to preserve life at any cost."

A good con-artist knew how to keep you distracted while he pulled a little sleight of hand right under your nose, and this guy was no exception. Jack watched his hands as he spoke. The assassin was reaching for something on his belt. "No, I think that you will be quite willing to use any means-"

Jack lowered his aim.

He fired.

A spray of blood erupted from the man's leg, and then the assassin fell to his knees, squealing like a pig that had been stabbed with a hot poker. That was about as non-lethal as you could get with someone in armour that would deflect stun-rounds, but there was still a good chance the man would bleed out. "You're right," Jack said. "I would prefer to take you alive."

He lifted his forearm and rolled back the sleeve of his jacket to expose his multi-tool. A few taps at the screen allowed him to contact the local Keeper office. "This is Agent Jack Hunter at Lenasa University. There's been an incident."

Chapter 14

The line of maple trees that shielded Professor Nareo's house from the street had leaves that were turning yellow with the onset of fall. A small gap in the treeline led to the front yard.

Ben stood on the sidewalk with his head bowed, frowning down at himself. *Just once, I'd like an easy assignment,* he thought, starting forward. *Spend a few days on a starship, fetch the professor, bring him back...*

A group of men and women in gray uniforms with yellow stripes on their legs stood clustered on the front lawn, talking quietly with one another. One – a young woman with dark bronze skin – glanced over her shoulder and noticed him.

"This is a crime scene, sir," she said, spinning on her heels to face Ben. She strode through the grass as if she intended to mow him down. "I'm going to have to ask you to leave and check in with-"

Ben closed his eyes, sighing softly as he struggled to contain his exasperation. "I'm LIS," he said, lifting his forearm to tap at his multi-tool. A hologram shimmered between them, displaying his credentials.

The woman bowed her head, staring with consternation at the ground beneath her feet. "Another one," she said. "I didn't realize this professor merited that much attention. Was he developing weapons or something?"

"What do you mean 'another one?'"

"Your colleague is inside already."

Icy fingers closed around Ben's heart. It would never have occurred to him to think that someone else from the Service might want to investigate this crime scene. Now that he had exposed himself, it would draw too much attention to just leave, but his presence here would almost certainly raise a few eyebrows.

Worse yet, unless he was very much mistaken, the Service had finally begun to piece together his role in delivering weapons to Fringe Worlds five years ago. Not much of a role – all he had done was fail to confiscate a few shipments – but that still counted as aiding and abetting an arms dealer.

Ben started through the grass. "Thank you," he said, sparing a glance for the young police officer. "I'll meet with the other agent inside."

He scrubbed a hand over his face, wiping sweat off his brow with his palm. *Why, oh why, did I go to Palisa?* he wondered for the two millionth time. *Pissing off Tyron is always a bad idea..*

The front door was sheltered by a small roof that covered the front porch. It swung open before he got within ten feet of it, and a woman in black stepped out. She was tall and just a little plump, with dark skin and hair that she wore up in a bun.

Only three steps out the door, she froze when she saw Ben. "Who are you?" she asked, blinking at him.

Ben felt his cheeks burn. Closing his eyes, he nodded to her. "I'm Agent Tanaben Loranai with LIS," he explained. "I'm here to take a look at the crime scene and figure out exactly what we're dealing with."

The woman crossed her arms and frowned at him. "I wasn't told that anyone else had been assigned to this case," she said. "You want to present me with some credentials? Or shall I just call Director Sloan."

Lifting his forearm, he tapped a few commands into his multitool and generated a hologram of his LIS ID. The transparent rectangle of blue light hovered between them, and through it Ben could see the woman frowning.

He closed his eyes, bowing his head to her. "We're on the same team here," he said with a bit too much strain in his voice. "I was scheduled to meet with the professor this morning. I heard about the break in, and I just want some information."

The woman spun around, marching back to the door with a soft sigh. "I'd be happy to give you that information," she said, glancing over her shoulder. "Just as soon as I get authorization to do so."

"Mind if I ask your name?"

"Telena Blathe," she said. "Operative Telena Blathe."

Ben had never heard of her, but then the Service was a very large organization. There were tens of thousands of intelligence agents spread throughout Leyrian Space. It was ludicrous to think he would know all or even most of them. "I'm putting a call into Director Sloan's office," the woman said. "We'll get this sorted out."

She went back inside the house without another word, leaving him to chew on his anxieties. Ben waited. There was nothing else he could do. Coming here had been a bad idea – he saw that now – but there was no way he could have anticipated the presence of another agent.

Well, no. Even *that* was a little self-indulgent. A break-in like this was guaranteed to draw in Keepers and intelligence officers, but he'd been trying to keep up appearances. So far as he had known, they weren't directly tracking his movements, and telling Jack that he'd prefer to avoid visiting the crime scene would only lead to questions that he would rather not answer.

Ben watched the young police officers gathered together on the front lawn, huddled up so that he could only see the backs of their shirts. They were bored out of their skulls; he could tell. Someone from their department had to liaise with LIS, but these poor cops wouldn't get a crack at the crime scene until the higher ups were finished. That being the case, there was nothing for them to do but wait and gossip.

When the door swung open, the person who stepped out was not Telena Blathe but a shorter woman in green pants and a gray t-shirt. Raven-black hair framed a face of pale skin with cheekbones so sharp you might have cut yourself on them, and her eyes were a fierce emerald green. "Agent Loranai," she said.

"That's right."

She planted fists on her hips and stood there like a statue of Lenara, Goddess of Justice. "I'm Operative Calissa Narin," she said. "I've been instructed to bring you to the nearest Justice Keeper office."

"For what purpose?"

The woman gave him a stern-eyed glare and then stepped forward. "Agent, we can do this one of two ways," she said, stepping forward. "You can come with me now and spare yourself a great deal of embarrassment. Or I can formally arrest you, put you in handcuffs and drag you to the office myself."

Ben looked up to meet her gaze, struggling to keep his face smooth. "That's a nice tough girl act," he said, nodding slowly. "But it really doesn't change anything. You want me to come with you? You're gonna tell me why."

The woman sniffed. There was something about her… It took a moment for him to put it together, but Calissa Narin moved and spoke with too much authority for someone with such youthful features. She was a Justice Keeper.

Brilliant! Just what he needed! Not only did he have the Service monitoring him, but now the bloody Keepers were getting in on it.

Behind the other woman, Telena Blathe stepped into the front door and watched the whole scene with a wary expression. This wasn't going well at all. Clearly they'd received orders to apprehend him. If he forced a conflict with a Keeper, an intelligence agent and half a dozen cops…

Calissa studied him with nostrils flaring, contempt blazing in those hard green eyes. "I'm waiting, Agent," she said with enough volume to make the cops stop talking. "If you don't agree to come with me, I *will* arrest you."

"Sorry. I still-"

Calissa drew her gun from its holster, thrusting her arm out to point the barrel right in his face. Instinct kicked in before he could even think. Ben tapped a button on his belt, triggering a force-field generator.

A wall of flickering energy appeared before him just in time to intercept a slug that would have splattered his brains all over the yard. The smoking bullet fell to the ground. What in Bleakness was this? No Keeper would be so quick to use lethal force.

He tapped the button again.

The force-field jerked forward, but Calissa blurred into a streak of colour, moving a few steps to the left. Out of the way. Instead, the force-field zipped right past her and sent Telena Blathe flying back into the house.

The woman was right there!

Ben rounded on her.

He kicked the gun out of her hand, then moved in for a vicious palm strike. Calissa bent over backwards, moving with languid grace.

Her hand came up to seize his wrist, and the next thing Ben knew, there was a fist slamming into his nose. Everything went blurry for half a moment, tears welling up to fill his vision.

Two hands slammed into his chest, pushing him away with Keeper strength. Ben went flying backward, then landed hard on his ass in the middle of the front lawn. Pain made it difficult to breathe.

As his vision cleared, he saw the woman striding toward him, her face twisted into the kind of snarl you would only expect to find on a wounded animal. She intended to kill him with her bare hands!

Ben raised his right arm up in front of his face. "Multi-tool active!" he bellowed. "Execute Program Four." The screen on his gauntlet began to flash with brilliant white light in a strobing pattern.

Calissa stumbled for a moment.

It was all he needed.

Ben rolled to the side, then reached into his pocket to retrieve a disk about half the size of his palm. He threw it, and watched as adhesive on the back side allowed it to stick to the wall of the house.

Calissa was staggering backward with both hands raised up to shield her face. That strobe light would give anyone who looked directly at it quite a headache. "What are you waiting for?" she screamed at the cops. "Kill him!"

The uniformed officers just stood there, unsure of what to do. Some shared glances with one another, but no one moved to follow that order. They knew how it was supposed to work. Keepers went out of their way to *preserve* life; if Calissa was so eager to employ deadly force, she was probably on the wrong side of this conflict.

Ben thrust a fist toward her. "Target acquisition!"

His multi-tool spat a swarm of nanobots that converged upon Calissa and then dug into the fabric of her shirt. The woman stumbled backward in surprise, furiously trying to brush them away. "Execute Program Seven!" Ben ordered.

The disk that he had attached to the house suddenly came to life, unfolding like the petals of a blossoming flower to reveal a thin, tube-like protrusion underneath. That tube reoriented itself to point at Calissa.

It fired an orange particle beam.

Calissa blurred into a streak of colour, moving just a few steps closer to the house before solidifying again. The particle beam hit the ground where she had been standing, leaving a scorch mark in the grass.

His drone began to recharge its emitters. It would only fire at the nanobots he had released from his multi-tool. The police officers were safe so long as they didn't get too close to Calissa. This gave Ben a moment.

He got to his feet with some effort, drawing a pistol from his belt-holster. "Stun-rounds!" The LEDs on his weapon turned blue, indicating that it had switched to non-lethal ammunition.

He fired.

Calissa thrust a hand out toward him, and the air before her seemed to ripple just before a charged slug slowed to a stop in mid-flight. The bullet looped around in a tight arcing turn, then sped off across the front lawn.

It hit one of the cops square in the chest and caused the man to spasm before he fell to the ground in pain. *Damn it!* If Ben didn't put a stop to this soon, there would be a lot more than smuggled weapons weighing on his conscience.

His drone finished recharging.

It took aim once again.

Calissa jumped, flipping through the air and then uncurling to land just a few feet away. "You're a clever one," she said as the orange particle beam hit the ground where she had been just a few seconds earlier.

Ben hesitated before firing – he didn't want to give this bitch a chance to redirect his bullets toward the police officers – but that only provided her with an opportunity to turn her back on him and run toward the house.

She stooped low near the front entrance, snatching up her pistol before standing up straight again. In a heartbeat, she had the gun pointed up at the house. "EMP!"

A glowing bullet struck the drone that Ben had loosed, causing sparks to flash over its body. Half a moment later, the disk exploded in a bright flash that left a scorch mark on the wall of the house. The thing wasn't as powerful as a Death Sphere, but still very dangerous when destroyed.

Calissa turned on him, her face a mask of feral rage.

Ben watched as half a dozen people in gray uniforms ran past him, lifting pistols in both hands and pointing them at the Justice Keeper. "Freeze!" one of the women shouted. "Stay down or we'll put you down."

Licking his lips, Ben closed his eyes. "Even you can't evade that many bullets," he said, taking a cautious step forward. "My suggestion is to just stand down before we have to do something drastic."

The muzzle of a gun touched his back.

"The same goes for you."

He'd been unaware of the woman standing behind him – there were days when he would give up a lung for a Keeper's ability to watch all directions at the same time – but now she had him at point-blank range.

Ben hung his head, groaning in dismay. "I'm on your side here," he said, raising both hands defensively. "I was trying to keep you people alive! Bleakness take me, you must see that!"

"Doesn't matter," the cop said. "You're carrying all sorts of illegal goodies on your person. As far as I'm concerned, the two of you can have adjoining cells."

The windows in this twelfth-floor office looked out on a field of skyscrapers that pierced a blue sky with just a few thin clouds, sunlight streaming in to illuminate a desk of polished glass in the shape of a horseshoe. Two large gray couches faced each other on either side of a small wooden table.

Professor Nareo sat on one of those couches, hunched over with his face in his hands. The man looked exhausted, and what else would you expect? When your own home wasn't safe, it was hard to maintain a cheerful disposition.

Jack stood in the middle of the carpeted floor with a hand clamped onto the back of his neck, massaging away an ache.

"We'll get you someplace safe," he assured the other man. "Just give me a few minutes to smooth things over."

The door swung open.

A woman in a blue dress with short sleeves came striding through it, a woman with a dark complexion and long hair that she wore in a bun. "Jack Hunter," Larani Tal said with a touch of exasperation. "Why is it that when I heard about a potentially lethal altercation at a university, I was not the least bit surprised to learn you were involved."

Jack closed his eyes, breathing deeply. "I appreciate your frustration, ma'am," he said, trying to keep his composure. "But it was absolutely vital that we kept Professor Nareo safe from harm."

"Is that a fact?" Larani cast a glance over her shoulder, scowling when she saw the man sitting on her couch. "And outside of the fact that it's absolutely vital that we keep every single one of our citizens alive, what makes this man so special?"

"Slade wants him dead."

"Come again?"

Crossing his arms, Jack frowned down at the floor. "The professor's an expert on the Overseers." He turned his back on her, and paced over to the window. "We have cause to believe that Slade is trying to get his hands on Overseer tech."

In his mind's eye, he saw the blurry image of Larani standing near the couch with her chin clasped in one hand. "And how did you reach this conclusion, Agent Hunter?" she asked. "More importantly, why am I not aware of it?"

Jack watched his own faint reflection in the window pane, noting the visible tension in his face. "Do you remember the young telepath named Raynar?" he began. "He shared a glimpse of what he learned when he probed Slade's mind.

"We've kept the information out of our reports because we know Slade has people on the inside. The very fact that he was able to deduce my plan and send an assassin to kill the professor is proof of that."

Nareo stood up with a groan, pressing the heels of his hands to his eye-sockets. "Is it entirely rude for me to point out the fact that I want no part of this?" The man made his way over to Jack.

His posture was stiff, his face contorted to the point where even spatial awareness was enough for Jack to note his expression. "I'm just an academic. I don't know anything about infighting between the Keepers, and I don't want to."

Jack whirled around, pressing his back to the window pane. He doubled over with his arms crossed and let out a sigh. "I can appreciate how difficult this must be for you, but understand that we're talking about the lives of millions of people."

The other man lifted his chin to study him, a slight flush painting his cheeks with a rosy hue. "You're the one who got me into this," Nareo said. "Frankly, I wish you'd never reached out to me."

Larani sat down on the couch arm with hands clasped in her lap, sucking in a deep breath. "That's beside the point right now," she said. "Jack, I think you should start at the beginning. What is Slade looking for?"

"Something called the Key. We don't know what it is."

"And you?" Larani asked the professor. "Any guesses."

"Not one."

Closing his eyes, Jack took a calming breath and then let it out slowly. "Whatever this thing is," he began, "we can safely assume that Slade isn't planning to do anything good with it. That being the case, it's in our best interest to find it first."

When he looked up, Larani was still on the couch arm, but her expression was hard enough to crack walnuts. "Once again, I marvel at your failure to inform me," she said. "I suppose I should take that up with Director Morane."

"The more people who know," Jack said, "the more likely it is that Slade will figure out what we're up to." Come to think of it, he may have been a little too forthright in this conversation.

He trusted Larani to a point; she had always been willing to call Slade on his bullshit.

Nevertheless, they were in a full-on X-Files situation here. "Trust no one" was the new company policy. It wouldn't surprise him to learn that Slade had ordered one of his minions to show outward animosity toward him.

Still, it wasn't as if he had much choice in the matter. A showdown with an assassin bearing military-grade hardware was a major incident, not something he could just sweep under the rug. He had to tell Larani *something;* his only choice at this point was in how *much* he wanted to reveal.

Larani stood up with one hand on her hip as if she intended to lecture him. A scowl contorted her face. "I can understand the need for discretion, but I want to be informed of such matters in the future."

"Yes, ma'am."

"Now, let's get down to business." Lifting her forearm to tap furiously on the screen of her multi-tool, Larani activated the room's holographic projectors. The image of a man on a hospital bed rippled into existence over her desk.

The assassin.

"We've identified the man who attacked you as Vetrid Col," Larani explained. "He was a suspect in a high-profile murder case roughly four years ago, but we couldn't pin anything solid on him until now. At the moment, he's unconscious – he lost a lot of blood when you shot him – but once he wakes up, we'll get some answers."

Biting his lip, Jack looked up to study the image. He squinted. "So, that's the guy, eh?" He strode across the room, toward Larani. "We need to get the professor off world as soon as possible."

"Off world?" Nareo shouted.

"It'll be easier to protect you on Earth."

Nareo took a deep breath, then lowered his eyes to the floor. "All right," he said with obvious reluctance. "But just so that we're clear, I'm angry, and I resent the fact that you decided to involve me in your-"

A beep from Jack's multi-tool cut him off. When he checked the screen, he found Gabi staring back at him from what appeared to be a table in her mother's house. "Jack, we've got another problem," she said. "It's Ben."

Chapter 15

Through the passenger-side window, Anna watched as the car Harry had rented settled to a stop in front of an unfinished house that was little more than a two-story wooden box with holes where the windows should be. The front lawn was actually just a field of mud and dirt, and the driveway was made of gravel.

Anna closed her eyes, sinking into the passenger's seat. She pressed a palm to her forehead and massaged away a throbbing pain. "Okay, let's play this smart. No sudden, aggressive movements. Nothing that might scare the boy."

Harry sat with his hands on the steering wheel, staring straight ahead with a pensive expression. "You want me to come with you?" he asked. "The kid trusts you. He may not feel the same way about me."

"I think it's wise. He has to know you."

She got out of the car.

This dust-covered street lined with dozens of similar unfinished houses on either side was all but deserted despite the fact that the sun was still high. In the distance, she saw construction workers in orange vests digging the foundation of yet another home.

Anna shielded her eyes from the sun. "He can't stay here very long," she muttered under her breath. "Sooner or later, they're going to resume work on this house, and I'm guessing it'll be sooner."

Harry stood on the other side of the car with a hand resting on the roof, staring off into the distance. "Yeah," he agreed. "I'm surprised they haven't found him already. Most crews are pretty big on security. Liability and all that."

"He's probably moving from house to house."

They'd tracked Kevin using the GPS on his disposable phone. So far, it seemed that she and Harry were the only ones who knew what to look for, and if Anna had any say in the matter, she would keep it that way.

She strode up the driveway with a hand pressed to her belly, head hanging as she sucked in a deep breath. "Follow my lead," she said, approaching the front door. "And remember, stay calm."

Inside the house, she found the wooden framework of what would probably be a long front hallway and a great big hole in the floor that would eventually become a set of stairs. A rectangular opening in the back wall led into…a family room or a kitchen. She really couldn't say with the house in this condition. "Kevin?"

He stepped into the opening, dressed in the same dirty clothes he'd been wearing a few days ago. "Agent Lenai…" The expression on his face…The poor kid was frightened, unable to look at her.

Anna shut her eyes, taking a deep breath through her nose. "It's me," she said with a bob of her head. "You're safe now, Kevin. My friend and I just want to get that thing off your hand."

In her mind's eye, she saw the silhouette of Harry standing just outside the front door, his posture stiff. "We're going to bring you to Station Twelve," she went on. "The doctors there can help you."

Kevin let his head hang, fat tears running over his cheeks. "I'm so sorry," he said, rubbing them away with his fingertips. "I never meant for anyone to get hurt. This damn thing…It over-powers you."

"I know."

"I tried to control it-"

Anna winced, shaking her head in dismay. "It's not your fault," she said, leaning her shoulder against a wooden beam. "Lots of people have come into contact with Overseer tech, and the effect is always the same."

Harry stepped through the door, reached up to grab the arm of his sunglasses and remove them. "These devices weren't designed for humans, son," he explained. "No one can truly control them."

Kevin shuddered. "It's like…It's like a song in your head." He pressed fingers to his eyeballs. "You can ignore it if you try, but when you get scared…"

"We'll help you."

The boy nodded.

Anna crossed her arms with a quiet sigh, frowning down at the floor beneath her feet. "Do you trust us?" she asked. "Can you stay calm long enough for us to get you up to the station?"

"I think so."

"All right. Let's go."

Spinning around, she made her way back to the door. Bright sunlight hit her like a slap to the face, and it took a moment for her eyes to adjust. The afternoon was hot and muggy despite the fact that it was only the middle of April. She was beginning to grow weary of that. Hot weather could be wonderful when you wanted to relax on a beach, but right now she was aching for a crisp, cool afternoon. After months of winter, she wanted a little spring before launching straight into summer.

Behind her, Harry and Kevin walked side by side as they made their way down the driveway. The boy was tense, his posture stiff and rigid, and he seemed to flinch at every unexplained sound. Anna couldn't blame him. Five days on the run, terrified that the very people who should have helped him might try to shoot him, and then there was that damn Overseer device that kept pumping up his adrenaline. It was enough to make anyone feel on edge.

Anna made her way around the back of the car, opening a door on the driver's side for Kevin. "It's gonna be all right," she said, glancing in his direction. "You just wait. In a few hours, you'll be free of that thing."

Kevin stood with one hand resting on the car's trunk, his face twisted into a painful grimace. "I know," he whispered hoarsely. "I've got it under control. Let's just get all of this over with, okay?"

"Okay."

A spike of alarm shot through Anna, one that was not her own. Sometimes Seth sensed things before she did.

Anna spun around in time to see someone hop over the peak of the house across the street and land perched on the shingled roof. A tall woman in black pants and a matching t-shirt, she wore a ski-mask to hide her face.

She stood up straight with thumbs hooked into the waistband of her pants, staring down at them. "I'm sorry to interrupt!" Isara shouted. "But I'm afraid that the boy will be coming with me now."

Harry was halfway around the car's front end when he froze in place and shivered at the sound of her voice. He drew aside his jacket, reaching for his pistol. "Anna, get the kid out of here!"

She reached for Kevin, but he was faster.

The boy whirled around, thrusting one hand toward the house across the street, and a wall of rippling energy appeared before him, colours blurred into a hazy whirlpool. The forcefield jerked forward.

It sped across the street in half a second, struck the wooden face of the unfinished house and shattered it into hundreds of tiny fragments. A part of the roof collapsed.

Isara leaped, somersaulting through the air and then uncurling to drop slowly to the ground. Contact with Seth allowed Anna to sense the other woman's effort to warp space-time and weaken gravity's pull.

Isara stood up straight, dusting herself off with a click of her tongue. "Bit quick on the draw there, isn't he?" she asked, striding through the muck that would one day be the house's front lawn. "Still, I have to thank you for leading me to him. I couldn't have done it without you."

There were shouts in the distance.

The construction workers were too far away for her to sense with spatial awareness, but a quick glance over her shoulder revealed that they were scurrying about like bees from a hive that had been disturbed. Clearly some of them had witnessed Kevin's poorly-timed display of destructive power, and now they were reacting. Chances were good that some of them had already called 911. The cops would be here soon.

"You're not taking him," Anna spat.

Isara shrugged. "I don't really need *him*," she said. "Just the device. Give it to me now, Kevin, and this can all be over."

Kevin shut his eyes, tears streaming over his face. "I can't," he whispered, shaking his head. "It won't come off."

"A pity."

Anna stood in the street with a hand on her holstered pistol, setting her jaw as she stared down the other woman. "You really think I'm gonna let you take him?" she asked. "Might be time to review your history lessons. Last time we fought-"

"You barely survived and had to rely on some of your police friends to chase me off." The woman clamped a hand over the mouth-hole of her ski-mask, trembling as she giggled. "I bet a dozen officers are already on their way here. I wonder how they'll react when they see Kevin."

The boy flinched.

Anna glanced over her shoulder, snarling at him. "Get behind cover!" she growled, jerking her head toward the car. "And whatever you do, stay put! You run away now, and I can't protect you."

He backed up around the trunk, crouching low on the passenger side. The frenzied light in his eyes...He was spooked. Right now, every instinct would be screaming at him to either run or lash out with the device again. The fact that Kevin had done neither was a testament to his strength of character.

Isara strode forward with all the confidence of a queen descending the palace steps. "I'm not really interested in you, Kevin," she said. "I'd rather you come with me of your own free will, but if necessary, I'll kill you."

"Kill me?"

"Mmhmm."

Isara drew herself up to full height, lifting her chin to stare at them through the eye-holes of that ski-mask. "The device won't remain attached to a corpse," she explained. "If you can't release it to me, I'll take it by the most efficient means possible."

Harry stood near the front end of the car with a pistol held in both hands, pointing the weapon at Isara. "Stay put, Kevin," he shouted. "Anna and I will protect you. She can't overpower both of us."

"Keep telling yourself that, Detective."

Anna stepped forward with fists raised in a fighting stance, shaking her head with enough force to send strands of hair flying. "You're not getting anywhere near that kid."

Tilting her head to one side, Isara smiled at her through the mask. "Is that so?" she asked, batting her eyes. "Kevin, did you know that there are many different ways to kill a man with your bare hands."

The boy wheezed.

"I prefer choking," Isara went on. She was trying to psych him out, trying to make him run. For a moment, Anna wondered why her opponent would do such a thing – after all, if Kevin ran, finding him again would be much more difficult – but then the answer came to her. In chess, frustrating your opponent's gambits was every bit as important as successfully executing your own.

Isara had to know that the chances of walking away from this with the device in her possession were slim. So if she couldn't accomplish her primary objective, she'd settle for keeping the device out of Anna's hands. Worst of all, Anna couldn't do a damn thing but stall and hope the cops would scare Isara off. If she started a fight now, Kevin would run. "This isn't going to-."

"Of course," the woman cut in, pacing a wide circle around Anna to put herself on a line of sight with the boy. "You could just wait for the police to arrive. I think they would rather just shoot you."

"I think you'll be their first priority," Harry said.

Isara clasped her hands together behind her back, pacing a line through the middle of the road. "Perhaps," she said with a halfhearted shrug. "But I think some of them want payback after Kevin put several of their colleagues in the hospital."

She covered her mouth with three fingers, closed her eyes and giggled once again. "Of course, I could be wrong," she added. "Who knows? These men might be willing to rise above their less than charitable inclinations. They *have* displayed enormous amounts of tolerance and restraint. I suppose I should be worried that they might take one look at me and decide that I'm the real danger here. But then again...I'm white."

"Stay put, Kevin!" Anna barked.

"Yes! Stay put!" Isara shouted. "Let the Justice Keeper lead you to the slaughter like the innocent lamb that you are."

Kevin turned and bolted, sprinting through the muck like a man with rabid dogs on his tail. He leaped through the front door of the house he'd been using as a hiding place. And then he was gone!

Anna winced so hard she trembled. "*That* was a mistake!" she hissed. "One that you're gonna pay for with a whole lot of pain!"

Anna ran forward.

The other woman jumped, flipping over her head and then uncurling to land in the space between Anna and the parked car. Isara turned with fluid grace, stretching a hand out toward Harry.

The former detective raised his gun in both hands, snarling as he took aim. "Harry, no!" Anna shouted. "Don't do it!"

A Bending appeared before Isara, colours stretched into a blurry smear, and panic seized Anna's heart. If Harry tried to shoot her, the bullets would reflect back at him, and then there would be one more-

Harry raised his pistol to point at something above Isara's head, then fired with a *CRACK! CRACK! CRACK!* Bullets passed right over her, flying uselessly into the clear blue sky. Why would he-

He was keeping the bitch busy!

Anna took the opportunity, closing the distance between herself and the other woman while Harry emptied half a clip. Isara would hear the roaring gunfire, but it would take a moment for her to comprehend Harry's plan.

The woman let her Bending vanish, rounding on Anna.

Anna kicked her in the belly. She spun and hook-kicked, one foot whirling around to clip Isara across the cheek. The other woman stumbled about in confusion.

Anna came round to face her.

She jumped and kicked-out, driving a foot into Isara's chest. Driven backward by the impact, the masked woman wheezed as she was slammed into the side of the car. She let out a groan and doubled over.

Drawing a pistol from her belt holster, Anna pointed it at her opponent. "High impact!" she barked and watched as the LEDs turned red.

Isara became a blur just before Anna pulled the trigger, moving aside in the blink of an eye. A dent about the size of a man's chest appeared in the car's driver's-side door and smoke rose from the point of impact.

Isara charged forward like a freight train. The woman leaped and used a touch of Bent Gravity to propel herself in a long arc that took her right over Anna's head. *Do not let her get the drop on you.*

Anna turned in time to see the masked woman jump and snap-kick. An old gray sneaker came right at her face, and then she was stumbling, dropping the pistol. In her mind's eye, a foggy silhouette came at her.

Isara threw a punch.

Anna ducked and let the woman's fist pass over her head. She grabbed Isara's shirt with two hands. Bent gravity did the rest. Her skin tingled as she called upon Seth for a burst of power.

Isara went straight up, then arced and fell flat on her back on the car's hood, landing with a harsh *CLANG.* The woman groaned and rolled onto her belly, pressing her body up against the windshield.

CRACK! CRACK!

Harry strode forward with the pistol in his hands, his face a mask of pure rage and hatred. "Stay where you are!" he shouted, stopping about ten paces back from the car. "You can't fight off both of us."

Isara wiped her mouth with the back of her hand, then turned her head and spat a gob of saliva onto the road. "You really believe that, don't you, Detective?" she mocked. "Would you like to know how long I've carried a symbiont?"

"Oh good!" Harry said. "I haven't made enough small talk today."

"Hey!" Anna shouted. "I get the one-liners!"

Before anyone could say another word, the harsh wail of a siren cut through the air. Two police cruisers turned onto this street from an intersection several blocks away and began speeding toward them.

Isara leaped from the car, passing over Anna's head with a touch of Bent Gravity. She landed in the middle of the street with her arms spread wide. "I'm afraid we'll have to finish our little threesome another time."

The woman jumped, and suddenly, she was yanked upward toward the roof of the house across the street. She landed gently on the black shingles, then vanished behind the building.

Anna pressed a palm to her nose, massaging her eyelids with the tips of her fingers. "She's not going after Kevin." The words came out as a shrill squeak. "We've got to find him before anyone else corners him."

Harry stared at her with lips pressed into a thin line. "Shouldn't we wait for the others?" he asked, gesturing to the approaching cop cars. "We should at least give them a status update."

"I don't trust them."

"Anna…"

She bit her lip and tried to ignore the aches and pains in her body. "You tell them what they need to know," she said. "I'm the only one here who has any chance of locating Kevin."

"How you gonna do that?"

Anna smiled. "Parkour."

Closing her eyes, she took a deep breath and focused her thoughts. Seth's presence was there in her mind, a warm comforting sense of kinship. Once the Nassai understood her plan, he reacted with approval.

Anna jumped and back-flipped through the air, Bending gravity with the aid of her symbiont. She was yanked upward by an invisible tether and then deposited on the roof of the house Kevin had used as a hiding place.

She turned and ran up the slanted rooftop, pausing at the very peak. From here, she could see the entire neighbourhood. The next street over was lined with more unfinished houses, as was the one after that.

Only one thing to do.

Anna leaped.

Her skin tingled as she called upon Seth for another jolt of Bent Gravity, and then she was flying over the backyard to the next house. She landed on the roof with a grunt, then took off in a mad dash.

When she reached the peak, she took a moment to observe her surroundings. Yet another police cruiser was driving up the street below. Bleakness! How many officers did they send?

She spotted Kevin on the sidewalk across the street. The kid was down on his knees with fingers laced over the back of his head, and even at this distance, she could tell that he was gasping for breath.

The cruiser settled to a stop several houses away from him and then flashed its lights with a brief squeak of the siren. Both officers exited at the same time, each one drawing a gun from his holster.

"No!" Anna screamed.

Kevin heard her voice and looked over his shoulder. When he noticed the two cops, he thrust a hand out and protected himself behind a force-field of rippling energy. *Damn it all!* If those two idiots started shooting…

So far Kevin had avoided doing anything aggressive. The force-field would protect him, but maintaining it for more than a minute or two would leave him exhausted. The cops could wait him out.

Anna jumped from the rooftop.

One more surge of Bent Gravity – and this time the tingling in her skin became a thousand fiery pinpricks – was enough to send her flying toward the officers. Both men looked up when they noticed her.

Anna landed in the middle of the road, doubling over on impact. She wiped sweat off her brow with the knuckles of one fist. "Stand down, both of you. I'm taking Kevin to Station Twelve for treatment."

The two cops stood side by side in front of their cruiser, each man holding his gun in two hands, each wearing the intently focused expression you often saw on people at the shooting range. "I said stand down!" she bellowed.

The one on her left came forward, squinting as he took aim. "Lieutenant Biggs has authorized the use of lethal force," he said, marching past Anna. "If that kid puts up any resistance, we shoot to kill."

"I'm countermanding those orders!" she insisted.

The officer glanced over his shoulder with his lips peeled back. "Your authority doesn't count for much around here, Agent Lenai." He returned his attention to Kevin, but thankfully, he did not shoot. "That boy is a menace. If we don't bring him in, he'll tear this whole damn city apart."

"You're frightening him!"

"What the hell is wrong with you, girl?" That came from the second cop, the one who still stood in front of the cruiser. He directed a thin-lipped frown toward Anna. "We tried using the kid gloves, remember? Every single time we do, the boy just slips away. Your methods don't work."

Anna hissed air through her teeth, tiny drops of spit flying from her mouth. "I'm ordering you to stand down," she said. "You disobey, and I'll have you both on report."

A glance over her shoulder revealed the blurry image of Kevin hiding behind his force-field. The first cop took a few steps forward. "Kid's getting tired," he said. "When he loses concentration, we take him."

"No!"

"Don't get your panties in a bunch, Agent Lenai," he said with obvious disdain in his voice. "We'll *try* to take him alive for you."

This was getting her nowhere. Any moment now, Kevin would lose the ability to maintain his force-field, and then…Well, it would play out one of three ways. Either the poor kid would end up shot, or he'd lash out with the device in some unexpected fashion, or he'd just wind up on the run again. She had to do something. "Hey!"

The second cop spun to face her, lowering his weapon.

Anna jumped, turning belly-up in midair. She kicked out to slam both feet into the man's face, the impact driving him backward until he was sprawled out on the hood of the cruiser.

Anna back-flipped through the air, then dropped to land in a crouch with the other cop behind her. In her mind's eye, she saw him whirl around and point his pistol in her direction, aiming for the spot where her chest would be if she were standing.

He fired without looking.

Bullets whizzed right over her.

She slapped her hands down on the pavement and brought one foot up to strike the underside of his wrist with her heel, knocking the gun away. The cop let out a yelp as he stumbled backward.

Anna stood.

She spun around to find him standing there, empty-handed with a look of pure rage in his eyes. His features were twisted into something feral, his brow shining with the sheen of sweat.

Anna squinted at him, holding the man's gaze for a long moment. "Still think guns are the ultimate weapon?" she asked. "Still feel secure in your ability to dominate any situation with violence?"

The man growled, his face twisting with unbridled fury. He pulled the night-stick from his belt and strode forward, lifting the weapon high above his head.

He swung for her.

Anna leaned to the side, the baton whistling through the air next to her shoulder. She slipped past him on the right, then

166

kicked out behind herself to strike the back of his leg. The cop fell to his knees.

Her elbow slammed into the back of his skull, knocking him senseless, and then he was down on all fours, groaning. In her mind's eye, she saw the other man on the hood of the cruiser getting to his feet.

Anna spun around.

She seized the man she had just incapacitated by the shoulders and lifted him until he was standing. Then she gave a quick shove and sent him stumbling head-first toward his partner.

They collided like a pair of drunken college boys staggering out of a bar, then fell to the ground in a tangle of limbs. Grunts and moans were the only things that either man could use to communicate.

Violence. It was a terrible thing – damaging to the soul, in her opinion – but there were times when the use of force was necessary. Whether or not it was justified was a whole other philosophical quandary. The necessary thing was not always the right thing. Now she just had to-

Despair came over her when she turned around to find that Kevin was nowhere to be seen. The boy had run off again, using the distraction Anna had provided to escape. *Bleakness take it all!*

After all that work, all that struggle – not to mention the pain of taxing herself and her Nassai – she had lost him *again!* For a moment, she just wanted to sit down on the sidewalk and cry. *Maybe later*, a small voice whispered. She could deal with the fallout of all this stress later. Right now, she had to find the kid before someone else attacked him.

Kevin ran through the space between two houses, then doubled over with his hands on his knees in the dirt that would one day be someone's back yard. None of the lots had been fenced off yet, and he could move freely between them.

The streets were off limits to him for the time being. If he went out there, he would be cornered by another pair of ambitious cops, and then he would either have to let loose with the device or…Or…He wasn't sure what.

The strange piece of alien technology sang in his head, whispering promises of the power he could wield, urging him to stay away from anyone who might try to take it from him. It was *his!* He couldn't let them-

No!

This thing was a danger, and it was killing him. The terror he felt whenever anyone spoke of removing it, the urge to lash out: these were not his impulses. They were only the product of an alien mind trying to influence his thoughts. He was Kevin Harmon. He had a life of his own, and he wasn't going to let some *thing* take that away from him.

I have to go back to Agent Lenai.

That was the rational thing to do. He just had to keep calm and make his way back to her. She would take him to the space station, and he would finally be free of this thing. *Amanda,* he thought. If he made it through this in one piece, he was definitely asking her out, and damn whatever her stupid father thought. That would be his motivation. He had to make it through this. For her.

Harry drove along the dusty street lined with unfinished houses, doing everything in his power to ignore the crushing sense of helplessness and the rage that threatened to flare up whenever he let himself think on it for more than a few seconds. The driver's-side door was mangled, but the car still worked.

All his life, he had been a man who believed in working within the bounds of the law, a paladin as Jack would say. He had waited for those officers, hoping that he could relate to them, one cop to another. They had barely acknowledged his presence.

So, now he was stuck, feeling useless and driving around a neighbourhood filled with half-finished homes, hoping that by some stroke of luck he could spot young Kevin before someone else did. The rational part of his brain said that he should just go back to his hotel room. Anna was a competent officer, and she could cover more ground than he could even with a car. What could Harry do? He was no Keeper. Just a middle-aged ex-cop with some good intentions and-

It was sheer dumb luck that made him glance through the passenger-side window as he was passing in front of two houses. Through the narrow gap between them, he saw a young man standing in the dirt.

Harry slammed on the brakes.

It took him all of ten seconds to park the car, and then he was running through that gap, panting as he got closer. Kevin seemed not to notice him. The kid just stood there, staring off into space.

"Hey!" Harry called out.

That got the boy's attention. Turning partway, Kevin glanced over his shoulder and froze when he saw Harry. "It's you," he said. "Thank god. Can you help me get back to Agent Lenai?"

Harry closed his eyes, nodding to the young man. "I can," he said hoarsely. "But we're going to have to be careful. This neighbourhood is crawling with police who seem to think you're a threat to the whole town."

"Yeah, I know," Kevin said. "Two of them came at me just a few minutes ago, but Agent Lenai fought them off. I…I ran."

"That was smart."

"Smart?"

Licking his lips as he tried to calm his anxiety, Harry looked up to meet the boy's gaze. "If it's that or fight, run every time," he said. "Violence is only going to result in even more people thinking you're a threat to public safety."

"I don't mean to be."

"I know."

Kevin kicked a clump of dirt with the toe of his shoe, sending it flying a good ten feet before it fell to the ground. "I controlled it, this time," he panted. "It takes so much willpower, but I used the energy field to protect myself. I didn't attack them."

Harry clapped the lad on his shoulder and watched as the tension drained right out of him. That the boy was able to exert that much control…Resisting the influence of an Overseer device was not impossible, but it was incredibly difficult.

"You have to understand the song," Kevin explained. "When this thing first bonded with me, I couldn't distinguish my own thoughts from the ideas it slipped into my mind. I wanted to protect myself. The device wanted me to do whatever was necessary to prevent anyone from taking it from me. But it wasn't what *I* wanted. So long as I remember that, I can control it."

"Are you saying you want to keep it?"

Kevin shook his head violently, turning his back on Harry. He laced fingers over the top of his head. "You don't know what it's like," he said. "It's there all the time, singing in your mind. It's easier when I'm not under stress, but you never get a moment's rest. You have to constantly remind yourself that it doesn't control you."

"Okay. Let's get-"

Footsteps behind him.

Harry turned to find two uniformed officers moving through the gap between houses, approaching cautiously with weapons drawn. Each man wore a hard expression, the thousand-yard stare of someone who knew that he was going to have to do something very unpleasant. "Step aside, Mr. Carlson," one said.

"I can't do that."

The cop lifted his gun and frowned at Harry over the length of his extended arm. "You think I won't shoot you," he said, arching a thick, bushy eyebrow. "I'd rather not have to, but we're bringing the boy down to lock-up."

Harry felt his face burn, tears leaking from his eyes to roll over his cheeks. "Oh, I have no doubt that you'll shoot me," he replied. "But violence is only going to make this situation worse. You've seen what happens when you resort to bullets over brains."

Kevin was tense, and he clung to Harry's jacket with both hands, trembling. The boy was whispering something. If Harry strained, he could just pick it up. "You do not want to hurt them. You do not want to hurt them. You do not…"

"Please," Harry implored them.

The second cop ignored him and focused on Kevin. "We don't want to hurt the kid," he said. "But he has caused an insane amount of property damage and put several people in the hospital."

"It wasn't his fault."

"That's for a court to determine."

Harry showed his teeth with a vicious growl, then shook his head forcefully enough to make himself dizzy. "Let us take him to the space station," he said. "We can remove the device and sort out the legalities later."

"I'm not authorized to do that," the first cop insisted. "You try to stop us, and you're aiding and abetting a wanted felon. Step aside, Mr. Carlson. If you force my hand, I *will* have to shoot you."

Harry refused to budge, choosing instead to shield Kevin with his own body. Damn it, but one way or another, this kid was leaving here alive. "I get it," Harry said. "You're scared. You've seen the kind of destructive power Kevin can unleash, and you've decided that enough is enough. No one should be allowed to terrorize an entire community. You'd be surprised how well I can relate to that.

"I come from a city that was terrorized by a single individual not once, but *twice.* Murderers running around with alien technology, blowing holes in the sides of buildings, leaving people afraid. You think I haven't seen this? You think I don't under-stand the urge to end the threat by any means necessary?

"But if you stop and think for five seconds, you'll realize there's a huge difference between a man who inflicts terror be-cause he *likes* seeing people suffer and a kid who got in over his head. Kevin never meant to hurt anyone.

"So, I want you to look within yourselves and ask yourselves one question. When you look at this kid, do you see a scared young man or an animal on the verge of losing control? You might take note of the fact that he's not attacking you right now.

"Think long and hard on that question, Officers, because the answer will determine a lot more than whether or not you're the kind of men who let prejudice influence their decisions. It will determine the state of your souls; it will determine whether or not you walk out of here with a murder on your conscience."

His heart was pounding, but Harry did everything in his power to keep his voice even. He took one step forward with his hands raised in the air. "I'm a human being," he said. "Kevin's a human being. And your failure to recognize that fact doesn't make it any less true.

"So go ahead then," Harry urged. "Put a bullet in my chest. Take the life of a fellow human being. Squeeze those triggers, and be all you can be. Or…if you'd prefer, you can put away your weapons, and we can solve this problem without anyone else getting hurt."

The cop stood there with his eyes shut. "I'm sorry," he whis-pered. "My orders-"

"Fuck your orders!" Harry shouted. "You've got a mind of your own. Use it." In all his years, he would never have expected *those* words to come out of his mouth.

The cop lowered his weapon, and half a moment later, his partner did the same. A sigh of relief exploded from Harry as he watched them holster their guns and turn their backs. "Call

Agent Lenai," the first cop said. "Bring the kid up to the space station. I'll tell the other guys you're already gone."

They left without another word.

Kevin took one step forward and threw his arms around Harry, squeezing him like a long lost father. "It's over?"

"It's over," Harry whispered. "You're safe now."

Kevin shivered.

Harry returned the hug, patting him on the back. "It's okay, Kevin," he said softly. "I won't let anyone hurt you. I promise."

The End of Part 1.

Interlude

"So, you failed."

The hologram of Isara stood before him: a translucent woman in a black dress with the hood of her cloak pulled up to hide her face. Her expression was unreadable, but there was no doubt in Slade's mind that she wanted to claw his eyes out.

He stood in the small bedroom of his apartment with his arms crossed, frowning at his errant servant. "You failed to recover the Inzari device," he said, his eyebrows rising. "Your assassin failed to kill the professor."

Isara stood there with her head bowed, the image flickering several times before it solidified once again. "A minor setback," she insisted. "If necessary, I will travel to the Justice Keeper station and-"

Slade winced, hissing as he shook his head. "You would expose yourself before we are ready for it," he said softly. "No, the device will have to remain with Lenai for now. It was not crucial to our plans."

Isara took that in stride.

He turned away from the ghostly woman, sighing as he paced across the hardwood floor. "We will simply have to accelerate our timetable," he went on. "I find it unlikely that Lenai and her friends will glean anything useful from the device, but that girl has surprised me in the past."

Clamping a hand over his mouth, Slade narrowed his eyes. "We've scanned every inch of this planet's surface," he muttered into his own palm. "Nothing…Nothing to give us even the slightest clue."

"I can't hear you."

He whirled around to find the hologram staring at him from the depths of her hood. No doubt Isara was growing impatient. He couldn't blame her. Pennfield had spent over a decade searching for the Key before Lenai and Hunter frustrated his plans. A decade with nothing to show for it but useless data.

Four years ago, when Leyria had first made contact with this backward little world, Slade had held out some hope that the ability to use ships to scan the planet from orbit would result in progress, but that had ended in nothing but more failure. Even the Inzari did not know the Key's location. The ones who had hidden it had done their jobs well.

Slade leaned against the wall with his arms folded, tilting his head back to scowl at the ceiling. "There may yet be an opportunity to turn this to our advantage," he muttered. "It's time we started playing to our strengths."

"What does that mean?"

"You never really did possess a thorough understanding of the game." Slade took a few cautious steps toward the hologram. "Never act directly when you can force your opponent to act on your behalf."

She looked up at him, and for a brief moment, enough light penetrated the hood for him to see a flash of irritation on her beautiful face. "We are influence peddlers, Isara," Slade went on. "We were fools to act outside that arena."

"So how shall we use influence peddling to our advantage?"

Slade chuckled. "I'm going to destroy Anna Lenai."

The fence in his backyard would need replacing in another year or two. After two decades of harsh Canadian winters, the wooden planks were showing signs of wear and tear. Some were chipped and cracked.

Arthur Hunter paced through the damp grass with his hands shoved into the pockets of his brown leather coat. A tall man with a dark beard that was slowly graying and thick brown hair, he stopped in front of the fence.

He dropped to a crouch, then rubbed his forehead with the back of his hand. *Next, summer,* he said to himself. *It'll last until then.*

Strange that he would focus on this tiny detail, as if fixing the battered old fence could somehow correct everything else that had gone wrong. He tried not to think too much on that. Nothing would be accomplished by dwelling on the things he couldn't change. Crystal was gone. It was what it was.

He stood up, dusting his hands, then whirled around to face the house once again. *It's for the best anyway,* he repeated for the thousandth time. *If she's that eager to leave, we'll both be happier this way.*

The back of the house loomed up before him with yellow aluminum siding on the wall and green shutters framing the large window that looked into the kitchen. Keeping this old place in order was the only thing that took his mind off the frustration. Retired cops didn't have much else to occupy their time.

He made his way around the side of the house, pushing the squeaky gate open with a grunt. A rain-slick driveway stretched through the grass all the way to the curb of this quiet suburban street, but he was surprised to find a car parked there.

Not his car.

This was a sleek, black Volvo that practically glistened despite the lack of sunlight, and the man who leaned against the hood with hands folded over his stomach had the air of someone who could throw money around just for fun.

He was a tall, slender fellow in black pants and a matching trenchcoat, a handsome man just shy of middle age with dark hair that he kept neatly combed and thin glasses on his face. "Mr. Hunter," he said in a dry, emotionless voice.

Arthur closed his eyes, bowing his head to the man. "That's right," he said, starting down the driveway. "I wasn't expecting any visitors. Is there something that I can do for you, Mr…"

"Pennfield," the man said. "Wesley Pennfield."

The name tickled Arthur's memory.

His visitor grinned the kind of toothy grin you'd expect to find on a cat that had just cornered a field mouse. "I've been looking forward to meeting you," Pennfield added. "I wanted to tell you how impressed I am with your son."

It all snapped into place. Memories of conversations that took place several years ago suddenly lit up his mind like fireworks. This was the man Jack had captured shortly after receiving his symbiont.

Arthur kept his eyes fixed on the ground. "What do you want?" he spat. "Maybe you haven't noticed, but my kid isn't here. He doesn't come around all that often."

The other man stood up straight, smoothing his coat with a gloved hand. He strode forward with his eyes closed. "Yes, well…I'd like to change that. In fact, I would like you to deliver a message to Jack for me."

Arthur turned and ran.

Hair stood on the back of his neck when he felt something pass over him, and then the other man was landing before him with his back turned.

Pennfield spun around to face him with a cold, menacing smile. "I am not the kind of man who takes no for an answer," he said. "Really, Arthur, did you honestly think that you could evade me?"

Arthur winced, a flush setting his cheeks on fire. "Worth a shot," he whispered. "You want me to deliver a message to Jack? Why? Too cowardly to tell him yourself?"

"It's not the kind of message you tell."

Pennfield drew aside his coat to reveal a holstered gun on his hip. In a heartbeat, he had the weapon drawn and pointing at Arthur. "I've given serious thought as to whether or not I should kill you. Do you believe in fate, Arthur?"

Oh, Christ Almighty, was Pennfield really the kind of murderer who felt the need to philosophize before he finished off his victims? Arthur thought that was the kind of thing that only happened in the movies. No wonder Jack considered this man to be his nemesis. They both overthought everything. "What the fuck does it matter?"

"I've never believed in fate," Pennfield said, ignoring the question. "I've always felt that people who do are simply making excuses for their failures. A man takes his destiny in his own hands, or he descends into mediocrity."

"Look, if you're going to shoot me-"

Pennfield shook his head in disgust, a rasping breath passing through his lips. "Arthur, Arthur, Arthur," he said with obvious exasperation. "This will be a defining moment for both of us. Treat it with the reverence it deserves."

"No, I don't believe in fate."

"As I suspected."

Pennfield lifted the gun up in front of his face, squinting as he studied it. "I once considered myself to be a man who focused on the bigger picture," he said. "A man who was not concerned with petty vendettas."

Craning his neck, Arthur stared up at the sky. "What changed?" he asked, deep wrinkles lining his brow. "I'm guessing it's got something to do with parents who never loved you or some such new-age bullshit."

"Your son took something from me."

"Then he did something right at least once in his life."

A menacing smile stretched across Pennfield's face, one that made Arthur think of the Joker on those old Batman comics.

"Your son humbled me, Arthur. Humiliated me in the eyes of my masters."

The other man thrust his arm out to aim the gun down at Arthur's leg. A thunderclap filled the air, and then pain ripped through Arthur's body. Before he could even think, he was tumbling backward.

His body hit wet gravel, but he barely even felt it. The agony in his shin drowned out every other sensation. Somehow, he was dimly aware of the endless pounding of his own heart. He'd been shot before, of course – you didn't spend twenty years on the force without encountering gunfire – but each time, he had been wearing Kevlar. This...This was something entirely different.

A hazy image stood over him, and it took him a moment to recognize Pennfield in his black trenchcoat. The man was speaking. What was he saying? "...never about you, Arthur. I want your son. I want his little bitch as well, and I want you to live so that you can tell them who did this to you."

Arthur groaned.

Pennfield returned the gun to its holster, then started down the driveway with his back turned. "They will come for me, of course," he said, almost as if he was musing to himself. "I look forward to it. No one takes from Wesley Pennfield."

The man turned, reaching into his pocket to pull out a disposable phone. He tossed it to the ground where it skittered before landing just a few feet away from Arthur. "Call the authorities if you wish," Pennfield said. "Tell them who did this. I have nothing to hide. I welcome the scrutiny."

He turned and walked back to his car, laughing all the while.

Part 2

Chapter 16

She watched Kevin.

The kid was lying on a bed in the Med-Lab, his eyes closed and his head nestled against the pillow. His breathing was slow and steady. After everything he'd been through in the last few days, he must have been exhausted.

In the end, it was Harry who brought him in. Harry, a man with no symbiont and no special weapons, had stood his ground against two men who had promised to kill him if he didn't back down. It was a feat of bravery that left Anna awestruck. Would she have been able to do the same under such circumstances?

Kevin stirred, sitting up straight with a groan. He touched a hand to the side of his head. "Where am I?" The words came out as a whimper. "Agent Lenai? Did anyone else get hurt? It's all so foggy…"

Anna sat at his bedside with hands on her knees, smiling into her lap. "You're in the Med-Lab on Station Twelve," she said. "Nobody else got hurt. Not by you, anyway."

"What do you mean?"

"I had to knock out a pair of cops."

Kevin stiffened, breathing deeply through his nose. The soft grunt that followed was barely audible. "I remember," he said. "They were gonna shoot me. I'm sorry. I shouldn't have ran away like that."

Anna sat forward with her elbows on her thighs, resting her chin on laced fingers. "It's all right," she murmured, noting the exhaustion in her own voice. "We were able to remove the device. How do you feel?"

The kid lifted his hands up in front of his face, examining them as if he thought it odd to find nothing but his own skin there. "Like I was run over by a car," he said. "After being mauled by a bear. But the song in my head is gone."

"Good."

Anna stood up, doubling over when a wave of fatigue hit her. She rubbed her eyes with the tips of her fingers. "You're going to need a few days rest before you can go back to school, and we'd like to keep an eye on you."

He stared at her with his lips compressed, tension clearly visible in his expression. "I'm in trouble, aren't I?" Kevin asked. "Everyone must be pissed about the damage I've caused."

"Not if I have anything to say about it," she answered. "It wasn't your fault, and I'm gonna make sure everyone in that town knows it."

"Thanks."

"We got you this far, Kevin," she added. "Trust us to get you the rest of the way." She turned to go, shuffling toward the door, but the sound of his voice made her pause.

"What happened to the device?" he asked.

"We took it to a science lab," she said. "Some of our best engineers are looking it over." That was about all the conversation she could manage; so she bid him farewell and made her way out to the corridor. Her skin was still tingling after pushing Seth so hard; she needed a rest.

The first thing she was going to do when she got back to her apartment was sink into a nice, hot bubble bath, complete with scented candles. After that, she was going to curl up in her bed and sleep for twelve hours. *Maybe there should be food,* she noted. Of course, that would require *effort.* Anna loved cooking.

She had always prided herself on being the kind of girl who prepared her own meals – it gave one the chance to experiment – but right now, she really wanted to employ one of those serving bots.

Her multi-tool beeped.

Checking the screen, she found Jena staring at her from behind a desk. "Anna, get up here," the woman said. "We've got a problem. It's about Jack."

Harry pushed open the front door to his house to find Melissa standing over the stove in their narrow kitchen, cooking something that looked like a quesadilla in a frying pan. The girl had a sour expression, and she seemed consumed with her task.

Harry shut the door behind himself, leaning against it. He touched three fingers to his forehead. "You're back," he muttered. "Did you have a nice time with your mother?"

Melissa looked over her shoulder, her face hardening when she saw him. "Yeah," she said softly. "I did. And I'm sorry if things got a little tense between us. It's just really important to me that I follow this-"

"I understand."

She froze.

Harry stepped into the open doorway that separated the foyer from the kitchen, leaning his shoulder against the frame. A deep breath exploded from his lungs, and he suddenly became aware of fatigue in his muscles. "I saved a kid's life today," he went on. "At least I think I did."

The whole time, his daughter watched him with a guarded expression, wariness shining in those dark eyes of hers. "I was in Tennessee," Harry explained. "A bunch of cops were about to shoot this poor boy. I wasn't going to let that happen; so, I put myself in front of them, knowing they might shoot me."

Guilt crept into his heart, and he had to struggle to resist the urge to shrink away from his daughter's gaze. What exactly had he been thinking? He had a responsibility to these kids; he couldn't just throw himself into dangerous situations without thinking. He was a father!

That didn't change the fact that he'd do it again if he were forced into that situation. A man had two choices when he found himself face to face with injustice. He could either shrink away, or he could take a stand. Harry chose the latter. Every time.

Melissa's smile was infectious, but she covered it with two fingers. "And that's my dad," she said. "Always putting himself on the line for other people. Seems like you had a good day."

Closing his eyes, Harry turned his face up to the ceiling. He paused for a second to collect his thoughts. "You really want to be a Justice Keeper?" he said. "You really want to dedicate your life to that?"

"I know it's dangerous."

Harry strode into the kitchen with his arms crossed, hanging his head as he tried to ignore the anxiety in his chest. "Dangerous isn't really the point, is it?" he mumbled. "I've had a bit of an epiphany."

Melissa stood over the stove with her back turned, seemingly transfixed by the contents of her frying pan. "What kind of epiphany?" she asked in a voice so quiet he might have thought he'd imagined it.

"I was willing to die for what I believed in today," he whispered. "I've got all these responsibilities, and yet I was willing to do it anyway."

He leaned against the cupboards opposite Melissa, clamping both hands onto the counter. "If I'm willing to do that myself," he began. "I can hardly tell you you're wrong to make the same choice."

His daughter dumped her quesadilla onto a plate, then set the pan back down on the burner. The silence that followed seemed to last ages, though, on some level, Harry knew it was only a few moments. Why should he feel like he had to prove himself to his child? He was the adult in this situation, for god's sake.

When Melissa turned around, she was grinning at him, nodding as if she were a teacher and he her errant student. "I'm glad we got that sorted out," she said. "I know you worry about me, Dad, but it's what I want."

"Even if it cuts your life in half?"

"Yes."

"And denies you the chance to have a family?"

Melissa closed her eyes, breathing deeply through her nose. "Not every woman is interested in having children," she said. "And there are plenty of ways to have a family. I've thought long and hard about adopting a child."

When…When exactly had *that* happened? Jesus, you thought your kids told you everything – all the important stuff anyway – but the things they held back could leave you with a serious case of the chills. He naturally assumed that, as a teenager, Melissa would be focused on boys and homework and possibly her efforts to choose a career. But children? She was contemplating whether or not she might want to adopt one day? Had he entertained such thoughts at that age? He couldn't remember; it had been so long ago.

Harry pressed a hand to the top of his head, running fingers through his hair. "Well then…" he muttered, leaning back against the counter. "I guess you've got it figured out. If this is what you want, of course I'll support you."

His daughter stepped forward and slipped her arms around him, resting her head against his chest. "Thank you," she said, giving him a squeeze. "I'm glad you're with me. Because I don't think I could do it without you."

"Well, if you want to be a Keeper, now's a good time to start."

"What do you mean?"

"I think…" Harry began. "I think I might know someone who could use your help."

Thin rays of sunlight streamed through a window of frosted glass that looked out on a small yard of green grass. In the distance, the blurry image of a high gray wall made the view less than spectacular.

His cell was more than large enough for him to stretch his legs, complete with a bed that stood in the light of the window and potted plants in the corner. A set of comfortable chairs faced a screen of Smartglass hung on the wall.

Ben sat at a table with his elbow on its surface, his cheek leaned against the palm of his hand. *Thirty-six hours,* he thought to himself. *If anybody was going to come for me, they'd have done it by now.*

He'd been charged with carrying illegal weapons – no small offense on Leyria – but he was more than certain that would not be the charge that stuck. No, they were going to pin him to the wall for what he had done five years ago.

The door behind him slid open.

A glance over his shoulder revealed a man in a long gray coat that dropped to mid- thigh, a handsome fellow with thin glasses on his pale face and hair that was just a little too dark for his complexion. "Tanaben Loranai?"

Ben shut his eyes, then covered his nose with one hand. "Yeah, that's me," he said, turning away from the other man. "I take it you're here to tell me just how bad things are starting to look?"

The other man strode forward to stand at Ben's side, bathed in the light that came in through the window. "Garin Covern," he said. "I'm your attorney, and not to put too fine a point on it, but things are bad."

"How bad?"

Mr. Covern heaved out a sigh, then turned on his heel to face Ben with hands pressed to his thighs. He refused to look up. "Well, they inspected your multi-tool and found a lot of illegal mods."

"What'll that get me?"

"Four months of rehabilitation therapy and a discharge from LIS."

Ben stretched out in his chair with hands folded behind his head, smiling up at the ceiling. "Guess I should start rehearsing before I meet the therapists," he said. "Tell me how this sounds. 'It all started when I realized my mother never loved me.'"

Covern's mouth twisted, and then he turned his head to stare at the wall. "This is hardly the time for jokes, Agent Loranai," he grumbled. "At the moment, you're under suspicion for your involvement with an arms dealer named Tyron Senaro. Now, with a little coaxing, I might be able to make them drop-"

"I did it."

"Excuse me?"

Ben stared into his own lap, a flush setting his face on fire. "I did it," he said, his eyebrows climbing upward. "Five years ago, I caught Tyron red-handed with smuggled weapons, and I let him continue his operation."

Covern licked his lips, then hung his head as he let out a sigh of frustration. "Well, it's good that you've been forthright with me," he began. "But I would suggest that you avoid addressing those-"

"No."

In a heartbeat, Ben was on his feet and pacing across the small room with fingers clenching and unclenching. A painful ache in his chest made it difficult to speak, but he managed. "I'm confessing...to all of it."

His attorney just stood there with a dumbstruck expression. "Are you sure that's what you want?" the man said softly. "If you do, you could be looking at several years of rehabilitative therapy, and an end to your career."

"I'm sure," Ben said. "I did what I did to help people who were suffering. But it doesn't matter how good your reasons are, when you do something wrong, you have to pay the price for it. It's time I stopped running from that."

Chapter 17

This time, there was no cruise ship to carry them through the long empty lightyears of Dead Space. No arboretums full of lush plants or grand windows that looked out upon breathtaking stellar vistas. No night club where they could soothe their boredom with a good drink and some tolerable music.

Jack didn't want any of Slade's agents getting close to the professor. A cruise ship was open to just about anyone with a valid passport, and not every assassin would be as obvious in his methods as their dear friend Vetrid Col. A poisoned drink would kill just as quickly as a bullet to the head.

This time, Jack had booked passage back to Earth on a military ship. That didn't make him feel any safer – Slade had agents everywhere – but it did limit the number of potential threats to a crew of roughly one hundred fifty. Much more manageable.

Of course, the scenery redefined the word "drab" for him.

Gray carpets stretched through a corridor with gray walls and bright lights in the ceiling. Doors at even intervals – each a slightly darker shade of gray – were shut tight and secure. Nothing to see here. But he had it on good authority the place was modeled on that level in the deepest pits of Hell where Satan sent souls who needed a time out.

Jack wore a pair of blue jeans and a t-shirt the exact shade of turquoise you saw in tropical waters. It was a conscious act of rebellion. If he was going to be surrounded by drabness, then damn it, he'd find a way to insert a little colour.

He stopped at the professor's quarters and rang the chime.

The door slid open to reveal a small room with a glass table in the corner and a cot propped up against the far wall. Half a second later, Professor Nareo stepped into view, wearing a scowl that could set ice on fire. "There you are," he spat. "I've been trapped in this, this *coffin* since last night. I resent this entire trip."

Closing his eyes, Jack took a deep breath and then let it out. "Nice to see you too, Doc," he said with a curt nod. "And really, it's not that bad! By tomorrow night, we'll be back on Station Twelve where you can spend your days staring at an entirely *different* set of drab gray walls."

He entered the room.

Jack strode to the far wall with his arms hanging stiffly, then paused and let out a sigh. "I know it's been hard," he said without turning. "But you really are making a good choice. Both for yourself and for Leyria."

In his mind's eye, the other man stood with arms crossed just in front of the door that was now sliding shut. "Yes, so I've been told," Nareo muttered. "I've gone through my notes, but I find nothing that might correspond to this Key."

"That doesn't surprise me."

"No?"

Jack crumpled his face into a painful expression, then shook his head with enough force to make himself dizzy. "Everything you know about the Overseers comes from the records they left behind."

He turned

Aldin Nareo stood with one shoulder pressed to the wall, watching him with a guarded expression. "Those records were *meant* to be found," Jack went on. "This Key almost certainly isn't."

"Then why bring me along?"

Biting his lower lip, Jack let his head hang. "For kicks?" he offered, deep creases forming in his brow. "You study the remnants of an alien civilization; I'm a rogue agent who doesn't play by the rules. Throw in some Nazis, and we've got a thirty-three million dollar opening weekend."

The other man shut his eyes, resting the back of his head against the wall. "You're a strange man, Agent Hunter," he muttered. "Has anyone ever told you that?"

"It's the first sentence in my online dating profile."

"I see."

"Listen, Doc," Jack began. "You want to know why you're here? Because we need a fresh set of eyes to look at the data."

"You're hoping that a lifetime spent studying the Overseers will grant me some insight," Nareo muttered. "I'll see something you missed."

"Got it in one."

With a sigh, the man shuffled past Jack to stand over his small bed. A brief moment passed before he spoke again. "I suppose we won't know if it will work until we try," he said. "And helping you is better than dying."

"That's the spirit!"

Jack left the other man to muse on his own thoughts. He had other matters to attend to anyway, and being cooped up on this ship was going to drive him stir-crazy faster than a Transformers movie marathon. This ship… The damn thing was built for efficiency, not for comfort. Which was a good thing in some ways. Still…

No arboretum, no night club…No Ben either. The man's arrest had left Jack feeling baffled, and his superiors had been unwilling to say more than two words about it. What could Ben have possibly done to get himself in that kind of trouble? Over the years, Jack had deduced that his friend had made a few questionable mods to his multi-tool, but still. That sort of thing should have been a slap on the wrist in his opinion.

For the last two days, he and Gabi had taken turns trying to soothe the professor's anxieties, keeping the man company to prevent him from bouncing off the walls. Jack could tell that his girlfriend was getting fed up with it.

The mess hall was a large room with square-shaped tables spread out in a grid-like pattern, most of which were occupied by men and women in the sleek black uniforms of the Space Corps. He found Gabi sitting in the corner.

She wore black pants and a maroon shirt with a round neck, and for some reason, she had put her hair up in a ponytail. The expression on her face as she studied the tablet in her hand made him think that he was about to hear some bad news.

Jack sat down across from her.

Covering his eyes with both hands, he let out a groan. "Tell me you have something good to report," he muttered, surprised at the strain in his voice. "Did you learn anything about Ben's situation?"

She studied him with an expression as smooth as ice. "I'm afraid not," she said. "I check my e-mail every time we drop out of warp for a communications update, but so far, no one has told me anything."

"Not even a scrap?"

Gabi shook her head in dismay. "Usually, I can find out what I need to know with a little needling." She slid her chair closer to the table and spoke at a lower volume. "But this time…LIS doesn't make it a policy to hide things from its agents. The fact that I don't know…"

She didn't have to finish that sentence. Something was very wrong here; either Ben had committed a *major* offense, or… Or what? Could Slade be in on this somehow? Jack put a stop to that line of reasoning.

If he saw Slade's fingertips on everything that didn't go his way, he'd turn into the same kind of conspiracy buff who had insisted that Barack Obama wasn't an American citizen. There was only one shooter; 9-11 was an *outside* job, and Grecken Slade did not have agents in every single branch of the Leyrian government.

"How are you holding up?" he asked.

"I'm surviving."

Jack grinned, then lowered his eyes to stare into his lap. "I've been thinking," he said with a casual shrug of his shoulders. "When we get back to Earth and this crisis is over, maybe we can go on a date."

His girlfriend wore a smile that could have melted snow, and she laughed softly. "That sounds nice," she said, taking both of his hands in hers. She gave a squeeze, and for a moment, he felt a little better.

It didn't last.

The bubble jerked to a halt, and through its shimmering surface, Jack saw a box-like room of gray walls. The control console was right in front of him, but the image was too blurry for him to make out the person pushing buttons.

The bubble popped.

Jack stood with Gabi on his left and Professor Nareo on his right in the middle of the Gate Room on Station Twelve. A soft humming from behind him slowly faded as the SlipGate powered down.

Anna stood behind the control console, scowling down at its surface as she locked the Gate to prevent anyone else from coming aboard. That look…He'd seen it many times over the last few years. Something was wrong.

At his side, Nareo closed his eyes and let out a huff. "I suppose that we should get settled in," he said, taking a few steps forward. "I assume that you've arranged quarters for me while I'm here."

"We ha-"

Anna strode across the room with her arms swinging, her face a mask of anguish. "I need to speak to Jack," she said, stopping right in front of him. "Gabi, why don't you help the professor settle in?"

Gabi wore a tight frown, but aside from that, her face betrayed not the tiniest hint of emotions. Spies…Always with the perfect composure. "Of course," she said, nodding to Anna. "Follow me, Professor."

She flowed across the room with an elegant grace, pausing at the door that led to the hallway. A moment later, Nareo joined her, carrying a suitcase full of clothing in one hand. The man was muttering to himself. More complaints, unless Jack missed his guess.

When they were gone, Anna slammed into him at full force, wrapping him up in the fiercest hug he'd experienced since…the last time she hugged him. There was no doubt in his mind now; something was wrong. It was almost like she was trying to protect him.

"Anna?" he whispered.

She looked up at him with those big blue eyes. "It's your father," she squeaked. "Pennfield…He's back, Jack. He went to your house and shot your father in the leg."

"Jesus Christ!"

"Your dad's alive," she assured him.

Baring his teeth, Jack winced and felt his face burn. He shook his head with a hiss. "As if we don't have enough problems! Now Agent Smith's third-string understudy thinks he's gonna take another crack at us?"

Anna nuzzled his chest, sniffling. By instinct, he rested a hand on the top of her head and gently stroked her hair. "What are you gonna do?" she asked.

"I'm gonna check on my father," Jack said. "And then I'm gonna find Pennfield and make him sorry he ever dragged his skinny ass out of hiding."

He should have been devastated. Why wasn't he devastated? Those were the only thoughts that kept running through Jack's mind as he made his way through a hospital corridor with light blue walls and doors that looked into rooms where sunlight came in through the windows.

A nurse in blue scrubs wheeled an empty gurney through the corridor, and behind him two more walked side by side, scanning the contents of some poor patient's chart. Hospitals were busy at all hours of the day.

Jack strode through the corridor in gray cargo pants and a bright green t-shirt, heaving out a frustrated sigh. *It's always something,* he thought to himself. *Would you look at me? He's got me quoting Rick Springfield.*

A door on his right looked into a room where the bed was propped up at an angle, bathed in warm afternoon sunlight. His father sat with a remote in one hand, frowning at the TV screen.

Jack stepped into the room.

Arthur turned his head to study him with a thin-lipped grimace, his blue eyes as hard as diamonds. "You made it," he said in a gruff voice. "I was wondering when you'd show up."

Jack crossed his arms, then looked down at himself. "Already we start in with the disapproval," he said, moving closer to the bed. "Hello, Dad. What's that you say? Oh, you're all right, and I shouldn't worry? Well thank God for that!"

"I've had worse."

"Really doubt that."

The other man kept his eyes glued to the TV screen and did his best to maintain that trademark Hunter composure Jack had never learned. "Just a shot in the leg," he said. "It didn't hit any major arteries. People have shot at me before."

"Yeah, but they never hit you." Jack replied in the gentlest tone he could manage. "They never put you in the hospital. It's okay if you're a little freaked out."

"I'm wondering what you're gonna do about this man."

Dropping into a chair with his hands gripping the armrests, Jack hunched over and let out a soft sigh. "Well, the guy's tolerable but not nearly handsome enough to tempt me," he replied. "A gentle rebuke by post should suffice."

"Jack…"

A flush burned through Jack's face, one that he quickly hid behind the palm of his hand. "I'm gonna track him down, Dad," he muttered. "I'm gonna put him in a pair of handcuffs and lock him in the deepest, darkest cell I can find."

When he looked up, his father was watching him over one shoulder, wearing an expression that he couldn't read. "Good," Arthur said with a curt nod. "The sooner that man is off the streets, the better."

"Can we talk about you now?"

"I already told you about me."

Jack figured he would leave it at that. One thing he had learned after twenty years of living with his father: sometimes the best thing they could share was silence. Arthur didn't want to talk, and he didn't want to force the issue.

He'd come straight here after meeting Anna in the Gate Room, and throughout the whole cab ride to the hospital, he had been unable to get his mind off Wesley Pennfield. Why had the man come back now, after four years? Where had he been? And if he was working with Slade, as Jack suspected, then why draw attention to himself by attacking Jack's father?

Slade was an evil son of a bitch, but he wasn't petty. If Pennfield was out pursuing vendettas, he was likely doing so against orders. Unless, of course, they weren't actually working together. Or maybe Pennfield was in charge? Jack wasn't exactly sure how the dynamics of their little cabal worked.

"You have that look."

A glance to the side revealed Arthur lying against the mattress and directing a scowl up at the ceiling. "That look you get when you're putting the pieces of a puzzle together," he went on. "Something you want to share?"

Jack closed his eyes, taking a deep breath before he spoke. "I don't know," he said. "I've got a few vague ideas, but I haven't had a chance to sit down and go over it... The plate."

"What plate?"

Jack sat forward, setting his elbows on his thighs and resting his chin on the heels of his hands. "Pennfield's license plate," he mumbled. "Did you get a good look at it before he drove away?"

Arthur's face contorted as if the question brought him as much pain as the shot to his leg. "I caught the digits," he said. "Had a friend down at the station run it for me. The plate's not registered to anyone."

"A fake?"

"Looks like."

"Well, that's just grand." It seemed as though Dear Old Wesley had come prepared. There were a few things Jack could do to find the man; he could monitor security camera footage from the SlipGate terminals, check sensor logs to see if any shuttles had touched down near Winnipeg. But if Pennfield had taken off in a car, things would be much, much harder. Worst of all, he could feel his father watching him.

This would be one of those moments where if Jack Hunter failed to produce results, it would be even more proof that he was a horrible son. And that made him angry. Damn it, why was everything in this universe on his shoulders?

He waited silently, reviewing the crime scene report on his multi-tool while his dad watched TV. When his mother arrived, Jack quietly excused himself. The sooner he got to work on this case, the more likely he was to find Pennfield.

And taking out his frustrations on that bastard's face was exactly what he needed.

Chapter 18

Their small booth on the second-floor balcony of a trendy bar in Vancouver was lit by a Tiffany lamp that cast colourful light on the brick wall and wooden tabletop. Up here, the music was quiet enough to allow for pleasant conversation.

Jena sat on one bench with hands on her knees, frowning at a menu. "You're sure about this?" she said, arching a thin eyebrow. "Because I like a little protein in my diet."

Across from her, young Anna had her back pressed against the seat cushion, her eyes shut tight. "Yeah, I know," the girl said. "I didn't realize it when I first came here, but these people actually *kill* animals for their meat."

"So you're a vegetarian until you go back home?"

"Essentially."

Jena crossed her arms, then turned her head to direct a tight frown at the wall. "You gotta be careful, kid," she murmured. "These people do a lot of things wrong, but we're not exactly saints either."

Their conversation was interrupted by the arrival of a waitress in a white shirt and black vest who carried a tray of drinks. She set one down in front of Anna – a simple glass of wine – and for Jena, it was whiskey.

The waitress straightened and paused for a moment to show them a bright smile that could melt butter. "Anything else?"

she asked in a voice with just a little too much sugar. Earthers had strange expectations of the people they made servants, and…Damn it! Now *she* was doing it too. She could lecture Anna all day and all night about not judging other cultures, but she was just as guilty.

Planting her elbow on the table, Jena leaned her cheek against the knuckles of her fist. "Just drinks for now," she said softly. "And you don't have to worry about us. If we want anything, we'll come down to the bar."

"Thank you."

The waitress turned to go.

Anna lifted her glass as if in a toast, but her expression was quizzical. "*You're* sure about this?" she asked, her brow furrowing. "Because Seth will be very cranky if I make him feel sick."

Jena smiled down at the table with a burst of laughter. "You named your Nassai," she said, shaking her head. "Over four hundred years of humans bonding symbionts, and you're the first one who has to give yours a personality."

"Actually, Jack-"

"Oh yes! I forgot about Summer."

Folding her hands on the table's surface, Jena leaned in close to share a warm smile with the other woman. "The trick with alcohol is to find the sweet spot," she said. "Drink just to the point where you're a *little* tipsy, and your Nassai will become very mellow and share those emotions with you."

"And caffeine?"

"You have to be careful with caffeine," Jena explained. "Most people who bond a symbiont have already developed a tolerance – so they don't notice it as much – but too much will make…Seth…very uneasy and you'll be fighting off anxiety for the rest of the day. Not pleasant."

Anna took a sip, then paused for a moment to stare into her glass. "I forgot that I like wine," she said. "I haven't had all that much of it since I was sixteen."

"Well, be careful."

"Oh?"

Jena chuckled, shaking her head. "When normal people get drunk, they end up in bed with an idiot," she began. "If *you* get too drunk, you'll be unable to stand up for several very painful hours."

"I never heard that!"

"That's because Keepers have developed such a religion around not imbibing that most of them have forgotten why it can be a problem. Your brain has learned to rely on the spatial awareness provided by your symbiont. Get the poor thing *too* intoxicated, and you'll feel as if the room is upside down and spinning."

Sharing your body with another living being: in a way, it was more intimate than anything you could experience with even the most passionate lover. Shared emotions, shared experiences. You were never truly alone after you Bonded a Nassai. However, it meant giving up certain freedoms. It wasn't just *your* body anymore.

Leaning back in the booth with her arms folded, Jena looked up at the ceiling. "So," she murmured. "Care to indulge my insatiable curiosity and tell me every last detail about your personal life?"

Anna was smiling, her cheeks flushed to a deep red. "I didn't think you cared about other people's personal lives," she said, brushing a lock of hair off her forehead. "You're kind of remote up in that office."

"I've never had a little sister," Jena said. "Humor me."

"Well, I've been seeing this guy for a few months," Anna began. "He's nice…He's very sweet."

"And?"

"And what?"

"Well, it just seems a little sparse of detail," Jena replied. "Which, more often than not, means there's something on your mind."

Grinning sheepishly, Anna shut her eyes and shook her head. "He's curious about my work," she said. "It makes for some interesting conversations whenever I get an e-mail that I can't discuss with him. And you? How are things with Harry?"

Jena pressed her lips into a thin line, ignoring the heat in her cheeks. "I'm not sure," she answered honestly. "He's very serious. I think he might be picturing me as the new stepmom to his kids."

"Is that a problem?"

A frown tugged at the corners of Jena's mouth, one that she tried without success to hide. "I don't do permanent," she said. "I've always been a bit of a lone wolf. Sooner or later, something calls me off into the great dark yonder."

She was cut off by the sound of her multi-tool beeping.

Swiping her finger across the screen, Jena watched as the round face of Glin Karon appeared. "Is Agent Lenai with you?" he asked in that stern voice of his. "I need to speak with both of you immediately."

"What's wrong?"

"I think perhaps you had better come up to Station Three."

The only thing Anna could see was the back of Jena's white shirt when the other woman froze in the open doorway to Glin Karon's office. "All right, what's this about?" Jena demanded of her fellow director.

Anna folded hands over her stomach, hanging her head as a wave of anxiety went through her. *It can't be good,* a tiny voice whispered in her mind. *You only get called to the principal's office when you're about to get detention.*

Jena strode in.

Anna followed.

Glin's office was a large open room with shelves lined with potted plants that grew under the light of bright fluorescent bulbs. The large rectangular windows that should have peered out into space were shaded with dark curtains.

Director Karon stood in front of his desk with a tablet in his hand, turned so that Anna saw him in profile. A man of average height with what Jack would call "Asian features," he frowned into the screen.

A quick glance over his shoulder allowed him to direct that scowl at Jena instead. "We've received a rather disturbing complaint about one of your agents," he explained. "It seems Agent Lenai assaulted two officers of the Manchester Police Department."

"I knew it!" Anna snapped. "They were going to kill that poor kid. I tried several times to reason with them, but-"

Jena cut her off with a wave.

The other woman stepped forward to stand between Anna and the man who now stood in judgment over her. "I've read Anna's report," she said in a voice so cold it could extinguish the sun. "You're aware of what the Earth-Leyria Accords say. Justice Keepers have authority over local law enforcement.

"Anna ordered them to stand down; they refused. Both men displayed intent to use deadly force against a civilian. She was within her rights to respond accordingly."

Glin closed his eyes with a deep breath, then grunted in frustration. The look on his face told Anna that it wasn't nearly so simple. "The Manchester police are claiming that you used excessive force against them."

"Of course they are!" Anna snapped.

"They want the matter investigated."

Anna crossed her arms, striding forward with her eyes downcast. "So what are you going to do?" she asked in a gruff voice. "I've never had to use force against an officer of the law before. How does this play out?"

Glin watched her with a tight frown, his eyes flicking from side to side. "It's highly unlikely that they will be able to try you in an Earth court," he said. "But a tribunal of six directors will review the situation."

"And if they find me guilty?"

"You could be suspended."

"Make sure I'm on that tribunal," Jena said in a low, menacing voice. "I won't have-"

A look from Glin was all it took to silence her. The man arched one eyebrow, and just like that, he had the floor again. "I'm sure that you can understand why that would be considered a conflict of interest."

He lifted his chin to stare down his nose, and suddenly Anna felt like a little girl who had made a mess in the kitchen. "It's easy to insist that other people are using force excessively," he said. "Much harder when you must justify your own use of it."

Anna flinched.

"Perhaps," Glin went on, "it would be best if I relieved you of duty for now. I've called Larani and suggested that she come as soon as possible. She's been flying back and forth to Leyria ever since she took up Slade's duties. In the meantime, take a break. Spend a few days hiking. This planet has some beautiful nature trai-"

Anna didn't even bother listening. Before he could finish his sentence, she whirled around and walked right out of the office. Anger threatened to push bile right to the tip of her tongue, and if she stayed one moment longer, all that primal fury would lash out at the first available target. Most likely Glin.

Wasn't that just what she needed? Snarling at a superior officer on top of knocking out a pair of cops? That would do wonders for her credibility. Nevertheless, the rational voice that told her to keep her cool was swallowed in a sea of indignation.

Two men had planned to murder a boy for no other reason than to sate fear born out of prejudice, and she had stopped them. Now she was to be punished for that choice? Not if she could do anything about it! It was vile. It was immoral. It was...overwhelming.

The law existed to protect citizens from harm, but in her short time on this planet, she had discovered that Earthers learned how to twist it to their advantage. It was a sad byproduct of their culture; they saw everything as a game in which they tried to gain a competitive edge, and now...Now, they were going to ruin her career because she chose to save a boy's life.

Anna covered her face with both hands, trembling as tears leaked from her eyes. *Keep it together, Lenai,* she told herself through a fit of sniffles. *You're going to survive this. Jena won't let them undermine you.*

The words sounded hollow to her.

The Science Lab doors slid apart to reveal a room with black floor tiles and light gray walls. Long, rectangular tables supported all sorts of equipment: scanners, powerful microscopes and some things Jena couldn't identify.

At the very back of the room, a man sat with his back turned, facing a container that looked very much like a fish tank that had been drained of water. Inside, a thin sheet of membranous skin was stretched out and suspended from metal clamps.

Looking at it made her shiver.

Jena strode into the room with her fists balled at her sides, dressed in black pants and a white t-shirt. "I hate looking at that thing," she muttered, shaking her head. "Any luck figuring out how it works?"

The man swiveled in his chair.

Professor Nareo was short and compact with a handsome face for an older man and gray hair that was thinning. "Some," he said, getting out of the chair. "This isn't the first Overseer device we've encountered."

"And?"

Nareo hung his head to look down at himself. "They all work the same way," he said with a shrug. "They're designed to bond with another organism and to receive input through the central nervous system. So if you can mimic that…"

"That thing nearly destroyed some poor kid's life." Jena said. "It seems to me it almost takes over your central nervous system."

"It wasn't designed for humans."

"You sure about that?" she asked, moving past the man. "Maybe this is exactly what the Overseers want."

That Bleakness-taken sheet of skin was just hanging there inside the containment unit, stretched out with veins pulsing despite the fact that it wasn't attached to anything. Just looking at it seemed to have an effect on her.

Jena knew what it was; she knew it was dangerous, and yet for some reason that she couldn't quite articulate, she wanted it. It whispered in her mind, urging her to come closer, to take it and-

Jena turned away.

Nareo was facing her with his arms crossed, frowning as if she had said something very stupid. "You think this is what the Overseers wanted?" he asked. "To leave us with a piece of technology that would destabilize its user?"

"It wouldn't surprise me."

"That's an interesting theory."

How did she go about explaining *this* one? To her knowledge, no one else had ever seen what she had seen. The events on that ship, the monstrosities the Overseers created to do their bidding: all of that was coming sooner or later. It reminded her of a book she had read as a child: *The High Winds* by Bili Tarson.

Just beyond the edges of civilization, the Infernals were gathering their forces, and no one was the wiser. She could tell people, of course, if she wanted to be published in this month's issue of "Crazy People Ranting."

No one would believe her.

By some blessed miracle, the small team she had put together since coming here had taken her seriously, but even they required a little coaxing. Worse yet, if she spoke openly about what was happening, she would only be making herself a target. "It's just something that makes sense to me," she said. "I've never been able to believe that a race of beings who make it their business to take primitive people from their home world and dump them all over the galaxy has benign intentions."

Nareo grunted.

Scratching her chin with three fingers, Jena squinted at the man. "So, can this thing be used for anything other than violence and destruction?" she asked. "Is there any point to keeping it around, or should I find the nearest airlock."

"If I'm right," Nareo said in the pedantic tones you could only get from a professor – not that she had ever been to university - "this thing likely has data that would give us a better understanding of the Overseers."

"Data?"

"Oh yes! These things have memories.

Covering her mouth with the tips of two fingers, Jena felt her eyes widen. "Well," she said under her breath. "Isn't that just peachy? Any guesses as to what you might find in that thing?"

"I'm afraid not," Nareo replied. "The only people to have successfully extracted information from one of these things have done so while bonded with it. But as I said, my colleagues have been working on a neural interface that-"

Knock knock knock!

Jena spun around to find that the two metal doors that led out to the hallway were still shut tight, but someone was pounding on them. Desperately knocking as if a wolf stood just outside and this was the only sanctuary they could find. The computer would only let authorized personnel into the lab.

"Open!" Jena commanded.

The doors slid apart to reveal young Raynar – the telepath – standing in the hallway in a pair of black pants and a gray shirt. The boy had grown out his blonde hair and now wore it parted in the middle. He had also put on a few pounds. It was a welcome sight. After three months, he no longer looked like a refugee fleeing a war zone. "What have you got in here?" he demanded.

Jena licked her lips, then looked down at the floor. "Raynar," she said, starting toward the boy. "This is a restricted area. Only station personnel have access to the lab. If you need to talk-"

He looked up at her with hard gray eyes that reflected the lights in the ceiling. "I've been down on the surface for three days," he said. "Dr. Kalaro thought I should get some fresh air. I Slipped up just an hour ago."

"Raynar-"

"And the instant I set foot on this station, I felt something pulling me to this room," he went on. "It was irresistible. I didn't even know where I was going. I just wandered the hallways and felt the tension fade as I got closer."

Hearing that left Jena with an icy lump in her stomach. Nareo, on the other hand, seemed to find the whole thing fascinating. He shuffled over to the boy with a hand over his mouth. "Interesting," he said. "Overseer devices draw people to them – that is likely why Kevin chose that exact spot to plant his time capsule – but the range should be limited to this room and possibly the hallway. For the boy to feel it all the way from the SlipGate chamber…"

"He's a telepath."

"Ah!" Nareo exclaimed. He now stood in front of Raynar, blocking her view of the boy. "Well, that explains it then! We've never considered what effect these devices might have on the mind of a telepath."

"Um…" Raynar mumbled.

Jena closed her eyes, a sigh escaping her. "Can you live with it, Raynar?" she asked. "Can you learn to tune it out? If not, we'll find you quarters on one of the other stations."

The boy leaned sideways to peek at her around Nareo, By the stunned expression he wore, she could tell he was still trying to process everything. "I think a better question might be 'is there anything I can do to help?'"

Nareo turned in the blink of an eye, facing her with a broad grin on his face. "The boy's insights would be invaluable," he added. "So far, we've been mimicking the electrical signals from the human nervous system and relying on trial and error to see what makes the device respond, but a telepath might-"

Jena shut him up with a sharp wave of her hand.

"First we find out if the device poses any danger to him," she insisted. "*Then* we determine if putting a telepath and an Overseer device in the same room puts the station at risk. And then – only then – do we even *consider* what you're asking. Am I clear?"

"Crystal clear."

"Excellent."

Anxiety, guilt and anger came together to form a knot of pain in Anna's chest, and she had to struggle to maintain her composure. She managed it with some effort, making her way home from the SlipGate terminal.

When she pushed open the door to her apartment, she found Bradley standing right in front of the big living room window. He was almost a silhouette to her eyes, a shadowy figure with his back turned.

"I forgot that we were going to have dinner," she said, shutting the door behind herself.

Bradley turned.

He faced her with relaxed posture: a gorgeous man with unkempt hair and a sweet, boyish smile. "That's all right," he said, striding across the living room. "That just means it'll be a surprise."

Anna felt a smile blossom, her cheeks suddenly burning. "You're way too good to me," she said. "But I'm probably not very good company right now. I had an absolutely miserable afternoon."

"What happened?"

"It's…" The words were there on the tip of her tongue, but she just couldn't bring herself to speak them out loud. The shame was still too fresh. Worse yet, on some level, she knew that she had done nothing wrong, but she felt ashamed anyway. How, by the Holy Companion's name, was *that* possible?

You beat the crap out of two people, she noted. *Is there any reason you wouldn't feel like garbage?* Anna had never been very comfortable with the idea of doing violence to another human being, but she had come to recognize the necessity. Still, there was a part of her that felt she had finally gotten her just punishment for all the men and women she had knocked around.

Anna shuffled forward.

A moment later, Bradley was slipping his arms around her, and she leaned her cheek against his chest. "I'll tell you later," she murmured. "Right now, I want to forget about it for a little while."

"Okay," he said. "Do you want me to start din-"

Anna stood up on her toes. Seizing his face in both hands, she pulled him close and kissed him full on the mouth. Right then, she didn't want to talk. She didn't want to *think.* The only thing she wanted was warmth and affection and love.

An hour or so later, she was lying with her cheek pressed to his bare chest, a thin sheet pulled up over her shoulder. "That was nice," she whispered, nuzzling him. "If you like, you can start dinner now."

Bradley was grinning up at her, lost in his own little world. "Maybe I will, in a few minutes." He gently stroked her hair with his fingertips. "Why don't you tell me what has you so upset?"

"Do I have to?"

"No, but…"

Propping herself up on one elbow, Anna rested her chin in the palm of her hand. Her red hair was in a state of disarray with thin strands falling over her face. "I've been suspended from duty," she said. "I beat up a pair of cops to prevent them from shooting that poor kid."

Bradley squeezed his eyes shut, grunting softly to himself. "Well, it's not that bad," he managed after a few moments. "They'll probably give you a slap on the wrist. In the meantime, think of it as an impromptu vacation."

There were many things he might have said to ease her frustrations, but *that* wasn't one of them. Bleakness take her, did he think this was some kind of joke? She didn't want a vacation.

Anna rolled onto her side, turning away from him and pulling the covers up over herself. "We should probably get dressed," she muttered. "It's getting late, and I've got a few things I still have to do."

"Everything all right?"

"Yeah," she said, deliberately softening her tone, ignoring the tears that threatened to well up. The very last thing she needed on top of everything else was a fight with her boyfriend. He was trying! It wasn't fair to expect him to read her mind and say the right thing in every possible situation. Relationships didn't work like that in real life. She was angry with her superiors, and taking it out on Bradley would be inexcusable.

When she turned back to him, he was lying on his side, facing her with a concerned expression on his face. "I know it's gotta be awful," he said. "But you're the most capable person I've ever met. You'll sort it out."

Anna leaned in close, touching her nose to the side of his neck, then pressing kisses to the soft skin. "I am one very lucky woman," she whispered to him. "You always make me feel better."

Well, most of the time, he did.

His arms slipped around her, trailing fingertips over her bare back. "I just wish that I could do more," Bradley murmured. "I wish you'd tell me about whatever big project you're working on. I might be able to offer ideas."

That brought a surge of irritation that she quickly smothered. She didn't need any suggestions on how to do her job. Still…this was his way of showing her that he cared. Anna gave him a smooch on the forehead. "I can't," she said. "I know you want to help, but I've been ordered not to divulge any information."

There were days when she wanted to tell them about their hunt for the Key, but in addition to Jena's insistence that she avoid discussing it with anyone outside their little council, she wasn't entirely sure how Bradley would react to it. The Overseers had left a powerful device somewhere on this planet, and if Slade got his hands on it, he would use it to do…something bad.

Being shot at, punched and exposed to life-threatening danger on a regular basis had a way of steeling your nerves.

Bradley, on the other hand, had none of that experience. When you got right down to it, he was just a guy who wanted to go into work every day and create apps for smart phones. How would he react to the knowledge that his planet might blow up? Would he tell people? Start a panic?

Her musings were cut off by a soft beeping sound. When she rolled over, she saw her multi-tool sitting on the nightstand, its screen lit up with the words "Incoming Call." She snatched it up by reflex.

"Answer call," Anna said. "Audio only. Hello?"

"How you doing, girl?" Jena's voice came through the speaker.

Anna shut her eyes tight. "I'll be fine," she said. "My boyfriend advises me that I should look on this as an unscheduled vacation."

"That's the spirit," Jena replied. "Look, I know you must be pretty shook up. I was thinking I would stop by and we could talk. Say in half an hour?"

"Sure. That'd be fine."

Chapter 19

The screen of his tablet displayed black-and-white security camera footage of the Winnipeg SlipGate terminal, and it was pretty much what you would expect. A bunch of people stood in line, shuffling slowly forward as they passed through scanners. No sign of Pennfield.

Not that he would have had much luck catching the man with the naked eye – not when the facial recognition software that analyzed the footage had been unable to do the job – but sometimes he had to try.

Chewing on his lower lip, Jack shut his eyes tight. "This is getting me nowhere," he said. "Put the tablet down, Jack. If you don't see him after several hours, it's time to let go of your fun new obsession."

He threw himself back against the plush couch cushions, turning his face up to the ceiling. "What do you think, Summer?" he asked the Nassai. "See anything I might have missed? Like a tall skinny guy with glasses and an obvious stick up his ass?"

Unlike him, Summer would remember every second of that footage – every single frame – with perfect, vivid clarity. He would put his mind into a relaxed state so that she could communicate more directly, but before he even took the first step, his symbiont's emotions told him that the answer was a resounding no.

Jack sighed.

The living room of his apartment was lit by late afternoon sunlight, sunlight that fell on the couch, his wooden coffee table, and the big blue easy chair across from it.

After nearly four years, he had grown used to the place. He could have moved out when Anna left for Alios – he had no need for the extra bedroom once she was gone – but he stayed because this place reminded him of her. Did he still feel that way? After nearly four years, he supposed he didn't really need the reminder, but it was his home now.

A knock at the door brought him out of his reverie.

"It's open."

The front door swung inward to admit a tall, slender woman in black pants and a white t-shirt. Jena wore her auburn hair cut short and parted in the middle. "So this is the place, huh?"

Grinning into his lap, Jack shook his head. "Not quite what you'd been expecting?" he asked, eyebrows rising. "Hey, wait a minute. How the hell did you get up here without me buzzing you?"

His boss stood with arms folded in the entrance to his living room, staring down at herself. "I was visiting Anna," she said, taking a step forward. "After the day she's had, I'd wager the girl was ready to punch a hole in the wall."

"What happened?"

Jena filled him in on everything: Anna's search for the boy who had bonded with the Overseer device, her altercations with a strange masked woman who carried a Nassai of her own – as if they needed *another* maniac with Keeper powers on the loose – and the police with their unfortunate refusal to exercise restraint. Now Anna was suspended pending the results of a formal inquiry.

Jack almost groaned. He knew exactly how his best friend would react under such circumstances. There was no doubt in his mind that if he had been in Anna's place, he would have done exactly as she did. He would have protected the boy and accepted the consequences of that decision. The difference between them, however, was that Jack was *used* to being a pariah. He had come to accept it, even to like it.

Anna, on the other hand, believed in the Keepers. They weren't so different when you got right down to it – like him, she'd follow her conscience, throw public perception to the wind and accept the consequences – but she desperately wanted to believe that she and the people she worked for were on the same side. She wanted their approval even if she was willing to throw it away in the service of what she thought was right.

Jack winced, doubling over to press a fist to his forehead. "She's blaming herself for it, isn't she?" he muttered. "No, not even that. She's trying to act like she's letting it roll off her back, but it's killing her."

"You know her well."

"Sometimes better than she knows herself."

"Well, talk to her when you get a spare moment," Jena said. "In the meantime, I'd like to have a chat with you about our dear friend Wesley Pennfield."

"I'm trying to track him."

"You do realize that we have agents up on Station Twelve trying to do the same thing." Her tone suggested that this would be one of those conversations where she took on the role of mentor and he the role of errant pupil. "Why aren't you working with them?"

Jack frowned into his own lap, shaking his head. "Well, you know me," he said. "I could go up there and make nice with the other agents, but that would ruin this lone wolf image I've been working so hard to cultivate."

"I see."

With a heavy sigh, Jena dropped into the easy chair on the other side of the coffee table and crossed one leg over the other.

Her expression was stern. "So you're *not* going to run off and attack Pennfield all by yourself."

Closing his eyes, Jack took a deep, soothing breath. "Is that what you're worried about?" he asked, leaning back against the couch cushions. "You think I'm gonna go on some vengeance crusade?"

"The thought crossed my mind."

"I suppose a simple 'no' isn't good enough."

Leaning forward, Jena sat with her hands on her knees. Her face was so contorted you might have thought she had been punched in the belly. "Look, Jack, if you need a few days off to look after your dad – or even just to sort out your own feelings – that's fine. If you wanna work, work with us."

He paused for a moment, considering what his boss had just said. The truth was, he wasn't feeling up to social interaction – not after finding out that his father had been shot by an enemy who should have stayed gone and forgotten – but he was also feeling more than a little restless. He had to *do* something, to find some clue that would lead them to Pennfield, but he had no intention of running off to beat the man senseless with his own bare hands.

Still, six months as Harry's girlfriend would have exposed Jena to more than her fair share of action movies. She had to know the tropes by now, and her concern was not unreasonable. "Okay," he said. "I'll come up to the station tomorrow."

"Okay." She offered a warm smile, one that made him feel a little less tense. "In the meantime, why don't you go do something fun?"

"Yeah, I guess I should."

Melissa was surprised by just how warm Tennessee could be when temperatures in Ottawa had only just risen above freezing a few weeks ago. The hot sun was bright in the clear blue sky, beaming down on a small park in the middle of a field of green grass.

About a hundred feet away, a jungle gym of brightly coloured metal bars was just overflowing with little kids who ran about, shouting with glee as they chased each other. Beyond that, small houses stood on the other side of the street that bordered the field.

Melissa wore beige pants and a red tanktop with thin straps, allowing the warm sun to caress her bare shoulders. Her dark hair was pulled back with a clip, and the strap of her purse was heavy against her skin. "So, are you recovering from your experience?"

At her side, Kevin Harmon – a young man in shorts and a dark blue t-shirt – stood with a sullen expression, staring off into the distance. "That isn't the hard part," he said. "The hard part will be going back to school."

Pressing her lips into a thin line, Melissa stared down at the grass under her feet. "Yeah," she said. "I hear you. But I think you'll be okay."

Yesterday, her father had taken her up to Station Twelve to meet this young man who was recovering in the Med-Lab. After spending one very long night there herself, she could understand how staring at the walls would eventually drive anyone insane. Kevin was nice, very pleasant.

She couldn't begin to guess what he was going through, having been exposed to that strange piece of alien technology that had overpowered his mind and body, that had forced him to do things he would never have wanted. It made her heart break.

"Come on," Melissa said. "Show me around. Manchester seems like a nice place to live."

They made their way through the field toward the jungle gym, giving the kids a wide birth. One boy chased his sister with a water gun and sprayed the back of her shirt until his babysitter shouted for him to stop. How long had it been since Melissa had done stuff like that? The answer came to her in a flash.

Last Summer.

Claire was still at an age where she found annoying her older sister to be the best fun she'd ever had. Last year, a few of the neighbourhood kids had pelted her with water balloons on her way home from the community centre. Still, there was something sweet and innocent in all-

She noticed that Kevin had stopped and now stood perfectly still, staring at a girl in a green dress with short sleeves, a girl who wore her dark hair in ringlets that spilled over her shoulders.

A frown put creases in Kevin's brow. For a moment, it looked as though he wanted to say something, but he quickly got a hold of himself, shook his head and started onward without another word.

The girl was another matter.

She looked up, blinking at him. "Kevin?" she asked, starting toward him at a quick pace. "You're all right? Oh, thank goodness! They told me the Justice Keepers found you, but I didn't know…"

"Amanda, I'm so sorry." Kevin's words were hoarse, strained. "I never meant to frighten you, but that alien thing has a way of screwing with your-"

The girl slammed into him, slipping her arms around his neck. "I'm just glad you're all right," she murmured. After a moment, Kevin found the nerve to return the hug.

Well, this was interesting. Admittedly, Melissa had only known this boy for a mere twenty-four hours, but he had never mentioned anything about a crush. It was clear that these two liked each other.

Melissa stood with her arms crossed, smiling down at herself. "So are you going to introduce me?" she asked, moseying closer to the pair. "Also, you seem to be unaware of the rule that says when someone keeps you company in the hospital, you are required to pass the time by sharing all the juicy gossip."

Amanda glanced over her shoulder with a tight expression, her eyes fluttering as if she had never seen a girl in a tank top before. "Oh…" she murmured, backing away from Kevin. "I didn't realize…"

Closing her eyes, Melissa shook her head. "No, you don't understand," she said through a fit of laughter. "My father works with the Justice Keepers. He thought Kevin could use a little company."

The young man was blushing, his eyes downcast so that he wouldn't have to look at Amanda. "This is Melissa," he muttered under his breath. "I only just met her yesterday. She's a good friend."

Of all things, Amanda hugged herself and shivered. What could…The girl seemed flustered by the implications that she might have feelings for Kevin. But why…Melissa remembered the story her father had told. She prayed to God Almighty that racism wasn't the cause of that reaction.

"Amanda!"

The sound of a gruff voice shouting her name caused the girl to jump and cover her mouth with both hands. When Melissa turned around, she began to understand Amanda's jumpiness. *This can't be good.*

A man in a gray suit and white shirt with the collar left open came striding through the grass. He was handsome enough for an older guy: tall with a stern face and short gray hair. "What are you doing, talking to that boy?"

Amanda shut her eyes, then covered her face with her hand. "I was just worried about him," she mumbled halfheartedly. "He went through a horrible experience. The Christian thing to do would be to show concern."

The man's lips pulled back, revealing clenched teeth, and his face turned several shades of crimson. "Stay away from my daughter," he said, fixing his gaze on Kevin. "You've done enough damage to this town."

Kevin sucked on his lower lip and kept his eyes focused on the ground. "I was just apologizing," he said, backing away. "The alien device is gone now. Your daughter is in no danger."

"She's in plenty of danger if you're around."

That was when Melissa began to understand. It wasn't Amanda's racism that made the girl afraid to admit her feelings for Kevin. No, that bigotry came from the girl's father. But what to do about it?

Three months spent training with the Keepers had given her plenty of role models to look up to. Anna would launch into a fiery tirade, exposing the man's vile attitudes the way one might peel off a bandage to reveal a festering wound. Jack would employ a well-timed comeback, deflating the man's ego with razor wit. Jena would probably find some way to entrap him, but Melissa…

What was her approach to these situations?

She watched as Amanda wilted, head hanging as she backed away from her father. "He's a good person," she murmured with so little volume it was barely audible. "It was not his fault."

And then it hit her.

Melissa wasn't fiery; she wasn't impulsive. The few times she had listened to her gut instincts, she had regretted it. No, deep down, Melissa was a thinker, and when she analyzed the situation, she realized that her first priority was ensuring the wellbeing of the people under her care. Kevin and Amanda.

Carefully, she reached into her purse and swiped her thumb across the screen of her cell phone. Tapping a little green icon with a microphone activated the voice recorder. If this got serious, she wanted to be able to corroborate her story.

She wasn't afraid to start an open confrontation – there were times when you had to draw a line in the sand – but if circumstances forced her down that road, she wanted to be sure she had all the information first. Let an idiot talk long enough, and he almost always gave you something to exploit.

"Amanda, you're here to babysit," Simmons insisted. "Look after the kids. And as for you, boy, I strongly suggest that you leave this park *now.*"

Well, *that* didn't take long.

"It's a public park," Melissa said. "He has every right to be here."

Red-cheeked and fuming, Simmons glared at her. "And who might you be?" he asked, creases forming in his forehead. "This might be a public park, but the police are just itching for a reason to put that kid in handcuffs."

"So you're saying the police carry out vendettas."

"I said nothing of the-"

Melissa closed her eyes, bowing her head to the man. The heat in her face was hard to ignore. "I wonder what kind of media attention that would draw," she went on. "Public servants accused of prioritizing petty grudges over the law."

The man recoiled as if she had suddenly become a hissing snake, his nostrils flaring with every breath. Clearly he hadn't been prepared for any kind of civilized debate. "I am *not* here to argue with a-"

Melissa cut him off by opening her purse and revealing the phone nestled safely atop her things, quietly recording this entire conversation. Mr. Simmons took a step back, his eyes widening when he saw it. "Care to have your views exposed on social media?" Melissa asked. "I know plenty of people who would *love* to retweet it."

The man growled, spinning around and stalking away through the grass. He paused a few paces from them. "Amanda," he said without turning. "You're to finish babysitting, and the instant you're done, you're to return home immediately."

Once he was gone, Melissa let out a deep breath. The few seconds of joy she felt at her "victory" quickly turned to pain when she realized that Amanda would bear the brunt of this man's anger. This was why it was always best to think before you acted; however, a Keeper couldn't just let injustice go unanswered.

When she looked to her two new friends, she realized that her fears were valid. Kevin and Amanda both looked crestfallen, and Melissa had a painful realization that she had a privilege they lacked. When this was over, she could go home to her comfortable house and loving family; Kevin and Amanda would have to live with the consequences of what happened here for years to come. There had to be *something* she could do.

"I have got an idea," Melissa said.

"What's that?" Amanda murmured.

"I'm gonna teach you two everything I've learned in the last little while."

There was a small coffee shop not far from Jack's apartment building: a cute little place with blue tiles on the floor and lamps that hung over the counter, casting light on a display case full of cakes. At this time of evening, the place was busy with over a dozen people scattered throughout the room at small tables.

He found Anna sitting on a stool with her back to the door, hunched over and likely staring into a cup of tea. She liked peppermint tea when she was feeling stressed out and tired, and today would be one of those days.

Jack closed his eyes, breathing deeply through his nose. *Time to be a good friend,* he thought, nodding to himself. *Which means keeping your observations about Justice Keeper politics to yourself.*

He shuffled across the room.

Setting his elbows on the counter, Jack laced his fingers and rested his chin on top of them. "So," he said. "Is this a good time to talk about my unfinished graphic novel?"

Anna smiled, a faint curling of her lips. "I think you came to the wrong place," she said, rubbing. "This counter is reserved for people who want to engage in silent moping."

Jack hopped onto the stool next to her.

He sat with hands on the countertop, staring into his own lap. "Oh, really? So you mean this isn't the place where aspiring artists go to meet gorgeous young women who will see the creative genius lurking beneath their brooding exterior?"

Anna covered her face with one hand, rubbing her nose with her palm. "No, you're misreading the tropes," she said. "You see, the brooding artist is supposed to fall for the quirky girl with an unshakable sense of wonder at everything around her. All you'll find here is one pissed off cop who's been suspended from active duty."

"Tell me what happened."

"Don't you know?"

Jack turned his face up to the ceiling, blinking slowly as he chose his words with care. "I do," he said. "But I think I'd like to hear you tell the story anyway. Sometimes it helps to say these things out loud."

A heavy sigh exploded from her, and she leaned over with her arms folded on the counter. "The whole time I was there," Anna began, "it was a constant battle just to make those idiots listen to me.

"They get spooked, and the only thing they can think to do is shoot whatever it is that frightened them. It didn't even occur to me that Kevin's skin would be a factor in this. Not until Harry showed up. And it's just… You should have seen them, Jack. It's like they were *looking* for an excuse to use deadly force."

She went on, relaying the details of the event, her attempts to bring Kevin safely up to Station Twelve, the constant interference by a masked woman with a symbiont – Jack still shivered every time he considered the prospect of another Pennfield on the loose – and the local cops who offered no help at all. All the while, he just listened, occasionally resting a comforting hand on her back. It was what she needed from him.

"And you wanna know the worst part?" Anna leaned over the counter and buried her face in her folded arms. "By the time it came down to it, I think a part of me *wanted* to hurt them.

"To teach them a harsh lesson, to make them realize what happens when you rely on violence to solve your problems. So, there's my secret, Jack. In the end, I'm no better than any of those men. I'm just as bad, and that's why I deserve whatever I get."

Jack couldn't help himself.

He grinned into his own lap, a slight warmth in his cheeks. "You think I'm gonna judge you?" he asked, shaking his head. "We all feel the urge to do violence – that's only human – but I don't know *anyone* who does a better job of showing restraint.

"Your reverence for life is nothing short of miraculous. Anna, you are the bravest, kindest, most resourceful person that I have ever met. I've never told you this before, but you're my hero."

When she looked up, her face was flushed. "You don't really mean that."

"If necessary, I *will* start singing 'Wind Beneath My Wings.'"

"You dork."

"Just for that, I'm gonna throw in 'From a Distance.'"

A brief moment of silence was broken when she suddenly took his hand and gave it a gentle squeeze. "How do you do it?" Anna whispered. "How do you make everything better with just a few words?"

She was watching with a smile on her face, a light in those big blue eyes. Dear god, she was so beautiful! Right then, he wanted nothing more than to slip his arm around her, press his lips to hers and-

Jesus Christ, what was he thinking? Anna was his best friend, and she had a partner, and she would *never* forgive him if he ever broke that trust. On top of that, *he* was seeing someone else! No, no, no, this had to stop. He was not going to let these feelings of his ruin a wonderful friendship. For some reason, he felt an echo of his own disappointment. *Summer* disapproved of his refusal to indulge those emotions? She of all people should have understood why honouring his commitments mattered. Jack would have to talk it over with her later.

Gently, he pulled his hand away.

Anna looked crestfallen, her bright smile fading to a frown that she smothered so quickly you might have thought you'd imagined it. "Thank you," she said softly. "You're really good at figuring out exactly what I need to hear."

"Did you talk about it with Brad?"

"I don't know *how* to talk about it with Bradley," she answered. "He keeps asking about things I can't tell him."

"Like what?"

For a moment, Anna was silent, glancing around in all directions as if she thought someone might attack her. When she was satisfied that they were alone, she leaned in close and said, "Like what we talk about at our weekly meetings. It's not like I can tell him about the Key or what might happen if Slade finds it."

Ah. Jack had to admit, he had never considered that angle. Dating Gabi meant that he could share just about anything that happened to him throughout his day – she was in on all the big secrets – but for Anna… Well, it must be like walking a tightrope. Keep too much back, and your partner would start to feel shut out. Share something classified, and you risked your career.

So it all came down to the person then. Was Brad the type of guy who could handle that kind of information? Jack didn't know him well, but he seemed pretty solid. "Mind a piece of advice?"

"Not at all."

"Tell him," he said with a curt nod. "Tell him everything. I know it's against the rules, but…your soul mate is the person you trust with anything."

"I guess you're right."

"Besides," Jack went on. "If you can't hold on to this guy, I might just have to pick him up. He sounds dreamy!"

Anna giggled, covering her mouth with one hand as she trembled on her stool. "I didn't know you were interested in men."

"I can learn!"

She touched his shoulder. "Thank you."

"Anytime."

They sat together for a few minutes, enjoying a comfortable silence before they got up and made their way back to their building. Anna had a big day tomorrow, and Jack, Jack had to find the murderer who had wounded his father, captured his symbiont and killed a whole bunch of CSIS officers right in front of his eyes. *The glorious life of a Keeper,* he thought. *I should have gone into Nascar. It's way safer.*

Chapter 20

They used a small conference room for Anna's tribunal hearing, a box-like room with gray walls and a long table where three senior officers sat side by side. Glin Karon was on the left. Today, he wore a black coat with silver trim on the cuff of each sleeve and silver flowers on the lapels.

Next to him, Tiassa Navram sat prim and proper in a sleeveless blouse. Anna had never met her before, but the woman was absolutely stunning with long blonde hair and blue eyes that belonged on a hawk.

The third was a woman named Kaydie Cadanzar. Tall and slender, she had a stern face with an olive complexion and dark hair that fell to the small of her back. The few rumors that Anna had heard about her suggested that she was the kind of supervisor who expected strict adherence to policy.

Anna sat at a smaller table across from them, bent over with her elbows on its surface and her forehead pressed to laced fingers. *Don't lose your temper,* she chastised herself for the fourteenth time.

Next to her, Harry sat with hands in his lap, dressed in a gray suit with a red tie that stood in contrast to his lily-white shirt. The look of concern on his face said that he wanted to be here even less than she did.

Jena was on his other side, slouched down with arms folded and staring up at the ceiling. Her contempt for all of this was obvious. Anna didn't blame her. It was good to know that *someone* believed in her!

This was an internal matter – a review of Anna's decisions to see if disciplinary action was necessary – and since no criminal charges had been filed, Anna had no right to an attorney right now. Still, she felt a little sick to her stomach, and Seth was so tense she could feel it despite his efforts to hide those emotions. Nassai believed in commonality. Individuality was something of a foreign concept to them. As such, if Anna's actions were deemed incorrect, then in Seth's eyes, they might *become* incorrect, and thus he would be complicit for his part in them.

Still, the symbiont had been with her long enough to know that sometimes humans did not agree on the rightness or wrongness of any given event. And that sometimes the individual was correct even when the crowd insisted otherwise.

"I believe we can get started," Tiassa said.

Another table on Anna's right was occupied by three officers of the Manchester Police Department, and each man wore a dress uniform complete with a cap and jacket over his shirt and tie.

Lieutenant Biggs stood up with a grunt, maneuvering around the side of his table to approach the three senior Keepers. "We've taken footage from the squad car's dashboard camera. That should be all that we need."

Glin Karon looked up with a dark scowl, staring so hard at the other man you might have thought he intended to start a fistfight right here in the conference room. "Computer, play video file Karon-2315, holographic output."

White light streamed up along the wall to her left, slowly resolving into the image of a car's windshield. Through the glass, Anna saw a street lined with unfinished houses, but her view was blocked by the backside of a cop who stood just in front of the car.

His large body partially hid the other cop who had moved a few paces away from the car and now stood with his back turned, pointing a gun at Kevin.

Something slammed into the cop nearest the camera, and when he fell back against the hood of the cruiser, Anna caught a brief glimpse of herself falling to land crouched on the black pavement.

The other cop turned, pointing his gun.

Anna saw her own foot come up to strike his wrist and knock the weapon out of his hand. Half a moment later, she was standing and facing the man.

The cop swung a nightstick at her.

On the screen, Anna slipped past him, kicked the back of his leg and knocked him down to his knees. The camera didn't have quite the right angle to catch her elbowing the back of his head, but she remembered that moment. In the heat of battle, she had felt rage and – to her shame – a touch of satisfaction. Now…Now, all she felt was disgusted with herself.

The cop who had landed atop the cruiser was getting to his feet, standing up on shaky legs. His partner came stumbling forward, and the two collided gracelessly, each man dropping to the pavement.

The hologram vanished.

"May I ask a question?" Harry said before anyone could speak.

Tiassa nodded to him.

Harry stood up, smoothing wrinkles from his shirt, then faced the three judges with a hard expression. The same expression you might find on a man who expected to be dodging gunfire any moment now. "Agent Lenai has already stipulated to all of this," he said. "She has already admitted her actions and fully documented the injuries that she inflicted on Officers Crowley and Simpson. What is the point in making us watch this?"

"The point?" Biggs said, turning to Harry. A nasty snarl twisted his features into something vicious. "The point is to give you a visceral understanding of the brutality she displayed."

"Trying to pull on our heartstrings then." Jena slid her chair closer to the table, shaking her head in contempt. "Too bad we can't have a visceral understanding of the brutality your officers displayed when they decided to employ lethal force against a helpless kid."

"I don't appreciate your tone."

"And I don't appreciate seeing one of the best officers I've ever worked with being dragged through the mud on a bullshit complaint."

Harry closed his eyes, breathing deeply. No doubt he was wishing that Jena might show a little more restraint. "The fact remains that Agent Lenai ordered your people to stand down," he said. "By refusing to do so, they've put themselves in violation of the Earth-Leyria Accord which stipulates that Justice Keepers have authority over all local law enforcement agencies."

"I'm aware of the-"

"Furthermore," Harry continued, striding around the table to stand toe to toe with the other man, "there is grounds to claim that your people intended to use excessive force against Kevin Harmon, which means that Agent Lenai was justified in ending the threat to an innocent life."

Pressing her lips together, Anna stared into her lap. Damn it, Harry, you just walked right into his trap! she thought. *He's only going to take your logic and twist it around.*

It was a tenuous argument because it left Biggs free to claim that Anna had used excessive force in her attempt to prevent the use of excessive force. Round and round the carousel went.

Lieutenant Biggs crossed his arms and stepped back, regarding Harry with a self-satisfied smile. "Did she have to put two of my men in the hospital?" he asked. "From what I've read, your girl has a habit of going a little too far."

"What are you talking about?"

The lieutenant scowled, shaking his head in disgust. "I'm talking about over half a dozen security guards who worked at Penworth Enterprises," he said. "On her first visit to our world, Agent Lenai did some serious damage-"

Jena stood up with a growl, her frosty glare threatening to peel strips off the man's hide. "That's enough!" she said. "The fact remains, your people were out of line. Anna did what she had to do."

Of course, that line of reasoning made Anna sound remarkably similar to the men who claimed that, in pointing a gun at Kevin, they were only doing what they had to do. Which might have been the lieutenant's whole purpose.

"Perhaps," Tiassa cut in. "A short recess is in order."

A domed ceiling of glass with metal grating spread out like a spiderweb allowed sunlight to fill a courtroom where wood-paneled walls were carved with delicate flowers. Three glass tables stood side by side – the outer two placed slightly askew so as to form a semicircle – and each was occupied by an arbiter in dark blue robes.

There were three – criminal trials always involved three arbiters – but Ben didn't know any of them. Not that he was familiar with many people in the justice system, but when you worked in intelligence, you generally made connections.

The woman on the left had short black hair and a dark complexion; the man in the middle was an older fellow with graying hair and rosy cheeks. And finally, the man on the right had blonde hair and a thick goatee that seemed at odds with his tanned skin.

Ben stood at the entrance to the courtroom with hands clasped behind his back, his head bowed respectfully. That was part of the formality. Any moment now, he would be called forward to hear the charges against him.

At his side, Garin Covern waited with stiff posture. The man wore black pants and a red coat that fell to mid-thigh, a coat that drew the eye with the gold trim along the hem and the cuffs of each sleeve.

"Tanaben Loranai," the head arbiter called out. "Approach."

Closing his eyes, Ben took a deep breath to calm his nerves. *You can do this,* he thought, nodding to himself. *You always said that you would accept the consequences of your actions. Time to make good on that.*

He started down an aisle that ran through rows of wooden bench seats that were – for the most part – unoccupied. He spotted a few of the cops that he'd spoken to outside Professor Nareo's house, but other than them, the three arbiters, two lawyers and himself, the courtroom was empty.

The prosecuting attorney was an older woman in a blue coat with silver trim. Until this moment, he had only interacted with her once, on the day when he agreed to a plea bargain. Three months of psychiatric rehabilitation and a formal discharge from the LIS. On top of that, he would be unable to travel off-world until he completed his sentence. All in all, it could be a lot worse.

Ben approached a table on the left side of the aisle, waiting patiently for permission to sit. Seconds later, his attorney joined him. In the hush that followed, Ben could swear that he heard his own heart beating.

The middle arbiter looked up to frown at him. "This is Case XJ-734C," he began. "Arraignment of one Tanaben Loranai in the matter of weapons smuggling and possession of illegal military-grade weapons technology."

"Ms. Kyson," the female arbiter said. "Are you ready to proceed?"

Across the aisle, the prosecuting attorney stood up tall, straight-backed and proud as an eagle soaring the open skies. "I am, Arbiter," she said in a crisp, clear voice.

The third arbiter – the younger man with the blonde goatee – studied Ben intently. "Mr. Covern," he said in a voice that echoed through the entire courtroom. "Is your client ready to proceed?"

"He is, Arbiter."

The middle arbiter stood and stared into the distance, his eyes fixed on nothing in particular. "Tanaben Loranai," he said in a voice that echoed through the entire room. "To the charge of possession of illegal, military-grade weapons tech, how do you plead?"

"Guilty."

"To the charge of weapons smuggling, how do you plead?"

Ben shut his eyes tight, hanging his head in shame. He felt warmth in his cheeks. "Guilty, Arbiter." The words came out hoarsely, but he managed to hang on to some small scrap of dignity.

With a heavy sigh, the arbiter dropped back into his chair and folded his hands on the table. "The terms stipulated in the plea agreement state that the defendant will be immediately discharged from-"

"A moment, Arbiter."

The voice that echoed through the courtroom spoke with such authority it brought a hush to everyone present. Out of the corner of his eye, Ben saw the prosecuting attorney fidgeting uncomfortably.

Turning around made him flinch in surprise. A tall, slender woman in gray pants and a black short-sleeved blouse came striding through the aisle between the bench seats. One look at her, and you could tell she meant business.

Her face was nothing short of lovely, with dark skin and almond-shaped eyes, and her hair was pulled back in a ponytail. It took Ben a moment to recognize her. Larani Tal. The new head of the Justice Keepers.

The middle arbiter looked up with a frown, squinting at her. "This is most irregular, Director Tal," he said with obvious discomfort. "Interrupting an arraignment before we can pass sentence is-"

"Unfortunately necessary."

Larani Tal paused at the end of the aisle with her arms folded, craning her neck to fix her gaze on the man. "I wish to offer the defendant a way to repay his debt to society, as it were." Now what did *that* mean? Ben didn't have time to contemplate it because she just kept right on talking. "I have need of his services."

"Mr. Loranai has been discharged from the LIS."

"Then he can operate as a civilian consultant," she said coolly. "One of my Keepers attacked this man, and I need to know why. Attempts to interrogate Calissa Narin have been less than successful."

A lump of anxiety fell into the pit of Ben's stomach. After nearly a week spent focusing on his impending trial, he had almost forgotten about Calissa Narin; after all, the woman was *supposed* to be safely tucked away in a cell. He had no desire to interact with a rogue Keeper, but... A part of him felt compelled to try.

Besides, while his sentence was in effect, he would be unable to leave Leyria. He had promised Darrel that he would get back to Earth as soon as possible – that he would only be gone a few weeks – but it was clear now that he would not be able to keep that promise. The thought of leaving his partner alone with the abusive people that he called family was devastating. He'd been forbidden from calling anyone but his lawyer while he was held in custody. Hopefully Jack had explained the situation to Darrel.

If there was something Ben could do to shorten his sentence...

The prosecuting attorney stood with her hands folded over her stomach, her eyes fixed on the arbiter. "A gesture of good faith would go a long way toward helping Mr. Loranai to complete his rehabilitative therapy."

"Well, Mr. Loranai?" the arbiter inquired.

"I'll do it," Ben said, nodding to the other man. "Just promise me that I don't have to be within arm's reach of that monster. Once was enough."

"I think," Larani said. "That can be arranged."

A long, rectangular window in the wall looked into a cell with a bed and a small table, a bookshelf and several paintings on the wall. The woman who stood inside with her back turned was as still as a statue.

Calissa Narin wore a simple pair of beige pants and a white tank top, her long, dark hair spilling over her shoulders to the small of her back. She seemed to be focused on one of the paintings.

Ben stood in the small observation room, trying his damnedest to ignore the anxiety he felt. This woman had very nearly ripped him to pieces, and now here he was, putting himself in her crosshairs once again. His rational mind said that there was nothing she could do to him from inside that cell but Keepers inspired a kind of awe in the general populace. They were heroic figures, larger than life, and when one of them went bad, that sense of awe became horror.

Was Calissa the woman who attacked him on Palissa? He snorted at that. If he'd had any talent for poetry, he would have sculpted that sentence into a beautiful rhyming couplet. Amusement died quickly, however. The hooded woman who had tried to kill him in Tyron's bar had also been a fallen Keeper. What were the odds that he would come up against two? Still he remembered the hooded woman's voice. It didn't match.

Larani Tal was on his right, standing stiffly with her arms folded, and staring into the cell. "That glass won't crack even if you hit it with high-impact rounds," she said. "It's as safe as can be."

Ben frowned.

Inside the cell, Calissa turned and gave a start when she saw them watching her through the window. A moment later, she was smiling.

Larani activated the speaker.

"Ah good," Calissa said, bowing her head as she flowed toward the window with the grace of a Sinthala dancer. "Back for more questions, I see. What is it you'd like to know this time?"

"Where did you get your symbiont?"

A sly little grin blossomed on Calissa's face, but she kept her eyes fixed on the floor. "I thought I'd already told you that," she said. "I was given a symbiont after graduating from-"

Thrusting her chin out, Larani squinted at the other woman. "Enough," she said, stepping forward to position herself right in front of the window. "No Nassai would ever allow you to use your abilities for such violence."

The grin on Calissa's face widened, and when she looked up, it was like watching contemplate whether it wanted to pounce. "Perhaps you don't know the Nassai as well as you think," she offered. "Breslan, Slade...Now me. Plenty of rogue symbionts, it seems."

She turned her attention to Ben, and those green eyes blazed with a feral hunger. "And you...the man who refused to die." It took a great deal of resolve to prevent himself from wilting under that stare. "No matter. Your time will come."

"Yeah, let's talk about that," Ben replied.

He clenched his fists and moved closer to the window, forcing himself to maintain eye contact. "Your boss wants me dead," he said, arching one eyebrow. "How did I get on his radar?"

"What makes you think I have a boss?"

Chuckling softly, Ben shook his head. "Nice try, darling," he shot back, surprised by his own bravado. "People like you don't get to be where they are without a lot of help from the inside."

Calissa tapped her lips with one finger, her eyes widening as she studied him. "You could be right about that," she murmured, her voice barely audible through the speaker. "Except I was just an ordinary Keeper who decided to kill you."

"Your symbiont," Larani insisted

"Where do you think I got it?"

Ben was fairly certain that he knew the answer, but he wasn't comfortable saying it out loud. Anna had discovered Earth while she was chasing a criminal who had stolen a symbiont. Everything he'd read on the incident suggested that Wesley Pennfield intended to experiment on the creature.

Nassai could deny their hosts access to the space-bending powers that made Justice Keepers so formidable in battle. If a Keeper went too far, his Nassai might simply decide to stop cooperating, but Calissa suffered from no such restriction. That being the case, it wasn't much of a stretch to think that the purpose of Wesley Pennfield's experiments was to remove the Nassai's ability to resist.

That wasn't what scared him.

Cal Breslan had been a Justice Keeper for close to twenty years, and though the man's service record indicated a less than friendly disposition, the man had done his job adequately. So did Breslan have a corrupted symbiont from the very beginning? Or had something changed?

Ben felt his mouth tighten, then rubbed his forehead with the back of his hand. "All right," he said. "Let's try this again. I don't think you realize just how much trouble you're in. A rogue Keeper?"

Calissa lifted her chin to stare down her nose at him. It was almost a sneer. "Yes," she said. "I can imagine that such a thing would almost be enough to cause a panic. Why, it would cast doubt on everything the Keepers stand for."

"They're gonna bury you in a hole."

"Indeed."

Shutting his eyes, Ben took a deep breath through his nose. "Right," he said with a curt nod. "You're still putting on a brave face because you still think it's only a matter of time before you walk out of here."

The scowl that Calissa quickly smothered beneath an expressionless mask told him that he'd hit a nerve. "It was Slade, wasn't it?" Ben went on. "You're one of his, and you think he's coming for you."

Quick as a flash of lightning, Calissa spun around and marched across the cell. Ben recognized the tactic. Keep her back turned so that they would have a harder time reading her body language. "You know nothing, little man," she said. "But feel free to remain safely wrapped in your arrogance."

Pursing his lips, Ben looked up at the ceiling. He felt creases form in his brow. "I don't know," he began. "Seems to me I know a little more than you'd like. Must be rough when someone sees right through you."

She turned.

Clamping a hand over his mouth, Ben squeezed his eyes shut. He shook with soft laughter. "That's it, isn't it? It's been what? A week and a half since they dragged you in here? You must be wondering what's keeping Slade."

The caged woman hissed like a cat, striding toward him as if she intended to punch her way through the glass and kill him right there. "Think you've found a soft spot, hmm? You can't imagine what's in store."

"Oh no!" he mocked. "Slade has an evil plan!"

From the corner of his eye, he saw Larani glance over her shoulder and show him a thin smile. It seemed he'd gained a measure of her respect. His success should have come as no surprise to her. Intelligence was what he *did.* "Whatever Slade's planning," he said, "it's probably...What's a good synonym for pathetic?"

"Wait and see."

Ben stood before her with arms crossed, hanging his head with a sigh. "Perhaps I will," he said. "You can wait with me. After all, it's not like you'll be going anywhere anytime soon."

"He *will* come for me."

"Well, that's something."

Calissa's mouth opened, but she forced it shut again when she realized that she had revealed too much. A grimace betrayed her shame. "Grecken Slade is a great man." So, she was committed now. Perhaps she figured that since she had already slipped up, no more harm could come of it. "You wish to know why I tried to kill you? It is enough that he asked, and I obeyed."

Before Ben could say one word, Larani stepped forward. "So you just come right out and admit it, then?" she said. "You're not even going to *try* to hide your allegiance."

"You fool," Calissa said softly. "Slade held your position for almost ten years. Do you know what a clever man can accomplish in that time."

The thought sent chills down Ben's spine.

"Ten years is a very long time," Calissa went on. "Slowly, piece by piece, bit by bit, Slade maneuvered his people into key positions. We are *everywhere*, Larani, eating away at your organization from the inside.

Calissa lifted a hand, and the air before her rippled, light refracting until she was a smear of colour. Then, just like that, she was solid once again. "This symbiont I carry?" she said. "It's not the one you gave me eight years ago."

She turned so that Ben saw her in profile, then paced a line right in front of the window. "This symbiont obeys *my* commands! Yet another gift from Slade. Power without being subject to the whims of a Nassai."

Ben swallowed.

For some reason that he couldn't fathom, this woman was confirming all of their worst fears. It made no sense. Any knowledge she gave them would only make it that much easier for them to-

Abruptly, Calissa rounded on them and flashed a smile so cold it was enough to make a grown man sweat. "You're wondering why I would tell you all this," she said. "Why let you in on the big secret, hmm?"

She leaned in close until her nose was almost touching the window. "It's because there is *nothing* you can do to stop it. And the suspicion as you wonder which of your people are secretly working for us will tear you apart."

Those words seemed to hang in the air for a moment.

"Sleep well, Larani," Calissa said softly. "Sleep well."

Chapter 21

Blinds on the window split the sunlight into thin bands that fell upon a hospital bed, but otherwise the room was dim. The same sounds you always heard in a place like this filled the air: a strange, non-localized whirring, people's footsteps in the hallway, muffled voices and the occasional beep.

Arthur Hunter sat in a wheelchair with hands resting on his knees, frowning into his own lap. Today, he wore blue jeans and a gray sweater with the hood pulled back. "What is taking so long?" he muttered.

Jack let out an exasperated sigh.

His mother stood at the window with her back turned, peeking through the blinds at the scenery outside. "They're just working on your discharge papers. We'll be on our way soon."

Arthur was unsatisfied, and he showed it by casting a glare in his son's direction. "Never mind that," he grumbled. "I want to know what *you* are doing to locate the man who did this to me."

Jack stood by the wall with his arms hanging limp, his eyes fixed on the floor tiles. "We tracked Pennfield's car to a parking lot downtown," he explained. "We don't know where he went from there.

"Pennfield was presumed dead three years ago, his accounts frozen and his assets seized. So any funds he's using are coming from unknown accounts. Sadly, we won't be able to trace him that way."

"Marvelous."

At that less than charitable comment, Crystal turned and fixed a steely gaze on her ex-husband. She said nothing, however, and quickly went back to the window. Jack didn't blame her. Fighting with Arthur when he was feeling surly never got you anything but a whole lot of grief.

For the hundredth time since this morning, he wondered whether coming here had been a good idea. He could have insisted that the search for Pennfield was too important – and his father would almost certainly approve – but somehow, Jack felt as if it was *his* fault that his dad was currently sitting in a wheelchair.

"So you've got nothing?" Arthur murmured.

Jack winced so hard it hurt, then banged the back of his head against the wall. "I'd like to remind you that this is the man who ran an interstellar smuggling ring for *years,*" he snapped. "Pennfield is *extremely* dangerous."

"All the more reason to put him in a cell."

Crystal glanced over her shoulder with a tight frown, her face flushed to a soft pink. "That's enough, Arthur!" she snapped. "They're working as fast as they can. *You* can just focus on getting better."

"I think I'll go grab a coffee," Jack said. "Do either of you want anything? Tea? Water? Maybe something to eat?"

"No thank you," Crystal said softly.

Arthur echoed her sentiment.

Once he was alone, Jack breathed out a soft sigh of relief. His father had a way of putting him on edge, and the man was particularly bad lately. Not that Jack could blame him. Getting shot in the leg would leave anyone feeling angry with the world. He needed to find Pennfield and end this quickly.

Of course, even with the resources of the Justice Keepers at his disposal, that task was proving to be exceptionally difficult. So far as anyone could tell, the man had just up and disappeared. Forensic specialists had covered every inch of that parking lot without uncovering a spec of evidence. Just an empty car. What he really needed was Anna. The two of them were almost unstoppable when they worked together, but she had problems of her own right now.

He rounded a corner into a hallway where bright lights shone down on the polished floor tiles and the plain white walls were each marked with a single blue stripe at chest height. Doors to his right looked into hospital rooms, some allowing the sounds of TV shows to spill out.

In the distance, he spotted a nurse in green scrubs making her way toward the end of the corridor, but other than that, there was no one around. Not that he minded. Right then, he really didn't want to deal with people.

Jack started up the corridor with his hands clasped behind himself, head hanging in shame. "What are *you* doing to locate the man who did this to me?" he said, imitating his father. "As if you'd do much better."

Someone came around the corner behind him. He saw it through his connection to Summer: the blurry image of a man in a suit who stood imperiously with one fist on his hip. "The lengths I have to go to just to get your attention."

That voice!

Jack spun around.

Wesley Pennfield stood tall and proud in the middle of the corridor, grinning like a cat who had decided that he could play with a mouse before finishing the job. "Honestly, Jack, it's really quite a nuisance."

With his mouth hanging open, Jack shook his head. "You have *got* to be kidding me," he said, striding toward the other man.

"All the effort I go through just to find you, and you dump yourself in my lap?"

Wesley came forward at an even pace, smiling down at himself. "You really must forgive me," he said, shaking his head. "I don't have the months it would take to wait for you to find me on your own."

"Is that right?"

"Come now, Jack, surely you know how this works," he went on. "I kill you. Lenai comes after me. Then I kill *her* and regain my power."

Crossing his arms over his chest, Jack lifted his chin to hold the other man's gaze. "Got a whole lot of confidence there, Sparky," he said. "But I seem to remember kicking your ass the last time we met."

A sly grin split Pennfield's face in two, and his soft chuckle was more menacing than the angry roar of a mob enforcer with a gun. "You got lucky four years ago, boy," he said. "Luck won't save you this time."

"No, it won't," Jack admitted. "But I've been working out."

A moment of tense silence passed with agonizing slowness, a cold, nerve-racking moment where Pennfield closed the distance between them. Jack was suddenly aware of the pounding in his own chest, but it wasn't the thought of losing that made sweat prickle on his brow. Pennfield had come from *behind* him, from the direction where his parents were. What exactly did the man mean when he spoke of the lengths he would go just to get Jack's attention?

Wesley leaned in close with a triumphant giggle, light glinting off the lenses of his glasses. "Would you care to test your-"

Jack punched him square in the nose.

The other man fell over backwards, catching himself with both hands and twisting to land on his side. He hooked one foot around the back of Jack's leg and pulled. *Oh, no! No! No!*

Toppling over backwards, Jack slammed his hands down on the floor. He rose into a handstand, then flipped upright just in time to see his opponent pop up right in front of him, moving forward with menacing grace.

Wesley jumped and kicked out.

A blow to the stomach drove the wind from Jack's lungs, but it was Bent Gravity that did the real damage. Jack went flying backward through the corridor, yanked away by unseen forces.

He landed a moment later with a hand pressed to his chest, bent over and breathing hard. Being hit by a Bending always left him feeling disoriented. He shook the cobwebs from his head.

Pennfield strode through the corridor with a grim expression, his cheeks flushed to a deep red. It was rare for him to show such emotion; usually the man was ice. *Maybe that's the hole in his armour,* Jack thought as his opponent drew near.

Wesley threw a punch.

Crouching down, Jack brought one hand up to strike the man's wrist and deflect the blow. He used the other to drive a fierce punch into Wesley's chest, one that would break ribs in anyone not carrying a symbiont. The other man stumbled.

Jack spun to deliver a backhand blow, his fist whirling around to clip Wesley on the chin. Knocked senseless by the impact, the evil bastard went stumbling sideways until his shoulder hit the wall.

In a heartbeat, Jack was running past him. Somewhere in his mind, a small voice was whispering that he needed to finish this now, but panic drowned out every last scrap of rational thought. What had Pennfield done to his parents? He had to know, had to see! With a little help from Summer, he was able to keep an eye on his opponent.

Wesley was doubled over with arms folded, shaking from the pain of his injuries. He tossed his head about. "This isn't over, boy," he said, standing up straight. "Not even *close* to over."

He drew a pistol from his belt.

Jack whirled around to find the other man facing him with one hand thrust out to point a gun at him. "You really think I would be unprepared?" Pennfield asked, cocking his head to one side.

On instinct, Jack brought his hands up and called on Summer's aid. The air before him began to ripple, and through it, he saw a hallway that wobbled like Jell-O that had been struck by a spoon.

CRACK!

A bullet appeared right in front of him, then turned, following the curve of bent space-time to the wall on his right. It struck the plaster with enough force to send chips flying.

Though it brought him pain – little pinpricks like the vicious stings of a thousand angry hornets – Jack changed the shape of his Bending. He formed a bubble, immersing himself in a sphere of accelerated time.

Through its rippling surface, he saw a blurred image of the hallway. Pennfield stood there with the pistol in one hand. Jack dropped to a crouch, getting himself out of the line of fire. He needed time to think, to plan. *You don't have time.*

His skin was already burning, a warning that Summer was being taxed to her limits, and his temples were starting to throb. The instant he dropped this bubble, Wesley would start shooting. He couldn't dodge forever. *Have to get the gun away.*

But how?

Jack pulled his wallet from his blue jeans pocket, holding it tightly in his right hand. This would be a long shot, but it was all he had. With a nod of thanks for Summer, he let the bubble collapse.

CRACK!

A bullet whizzed over his head. Jack threw himself forward. He somersaulted over the linoleum tiles, then came up on one knee, tossing the wallet. It tumbled end over end through the air.

Wesley adjusted his aim just in time for the wallet to hit his gun and knock it right out of his grip. The pistol went flying from his hand, leaving a very pissed off Pennfield snarling in the hallway.

Jack ran forward.

He jumped and snap-kicked, aiming for Wesley's face. The other man leaned back and caught his ankle before he made contact. The next thing he knew, he was flying up until his head hit the ceiling. Painfully.

He landed in time to see the fuzzy image of a man in a gray suit standing before him. Wesley swiped at his head.

Ducking low, Jack felt the blow pass right over him. He slammed both fists into the other man's chest, staggering him. A high-pitched wheeze filled the air as Pennfield tried to regain his balance.

Jack jumped.

He spun in midair, kicking out behind himself to drive a foot into the other man's face. Those expensive glasses were mangled on impact. Wesley cried out, covering his eyes with one hand as he stumbled away.

"You've gotten better at this, boy," he said, doubling over in obvious pain. Only then did Jack notice the blood leaking through the cracks between his fingers. Some of those lens shards must have found their way into Wesley's eyes. Time to end this. The world would be a better place without Pennfield in it.

Jack started forward.

Wesley turned and ran into the nearest room, cradling his face the whole time. *No you don't!* There was no way this bastard was getting away this time. With a symbiont of his own, the man would still be able to see.

Jack slipped through the door just in time to see his opponent charge headlong for the sixth-story window. Wesley leaped and crashed through the glass without a moment's hesitation. Well *that* was a bonehead move! A Keeper might be able to slow his descent enough to avoid doing any serious damage to his body – *might*; it was quite a drop – but it would leave his symbiont exhausted.

Contact with Summer allowed him to perceive what he could only describe as a warping sensation. Normally, when somebody employed Bent Gravity, he was too busy trying to stay alive to focus on the impressions coming from his Nassai.

He reached the window in time to see Pennfield running across the hospital parking lot, making is way toward a black limousine that was parked near the street. Jesus Christ! How was the man still on his feet?

Pennfield opened the limo's door and scrambled into the back seat. A moment later, the vehicle lurched into motion, making its way toward the exit.

Footsteps behind him.

In his mind's eye, Jack saw security guards fill the doorway. "Sir, are you all right?" one asked in a gruff voice. "We heard gunshots! Was anyone injured? Do you know who discharged the weapon?"

Jack closed his eyes, breathing deeply to calm himself. "Yes, I do," he answered. "Post guards at every entrance to the hospital. I've got some bad news for you."

"He was here!"

Arthur wheeled his chair across the length of the hospital room, cursing as he tried to work out his frustration. "The man who shot me was here? He walked right into this hospital without incident?"

Jack sat on the bed, doubled up with his elbows on his knees, his face in his hands. "That's the gist of it, yeah," he groaned. "I scared him off for now, but he's not done tormenting us."

If not for his ability to perceive the world around him through spatial awareness, he would have jumped when his mother came up behind him to lay a hand on his shoulder. Adrenaline was still pumping through his system. Now wasn't exactly a good time to get inside his personal space.

Arthur stared into the distance, shaking his head. "You're not going after him?" he asked, glancing at Jack. "There's a murderer running around this city, and you're not even going to try to apprehend him?"

Closing his eyes, Jack touched his fingertips to his forehead and massaged away a headache. "I've already alerted the other Keepers," he said. "I just pushed Summer pretty hard, which means if I go after him, there's a good chance I'll pass out."

Arthur grunted.

Tossing his head back, Jack squinted at the ceiling. "Let's hear it, Dad," he said, getting to his feet. "The standard 'Be a man' speech. Come on. Tell me to go risk my life on some stupid vendetta."

To his surprise, Arthur only shot a glance in his direction and frowned. "I wouldn't suggest that you put your life at risk," he muttered. "Forgive me, Jack, but I don't exactly know how all this Keeper stuff works."

Arthur wheeled his chair around with more deftness than you would expect from a man who had lived his whole life on two legs. "I thought that you people healed quickly," he said. "I didn't know you had limits."

"Well, we do."

Crystal's hand on the back of his head, gently stroking his hair, was almost enough to take the edge off his emotions. Almost. "Half a dozen Keepers can bring Wesley in just fine," Jack went on. "It doesn't really matter *who* does it so long as someone does. But I'll be going to join them as soon as I can."

"Right," Arthur said. "So, what now?"

"Now, we make sure you're somewhere Pennfield can't get to you."

Chapter 22

The limo moved forward, but Wesley was barely aware of the motion, barely aware of anything except the pain and the fatigue. Hunter had taxed him to his limits. Clearly he had underestimated the boy.

He sat doubled over with his face in his hands, the seat belt digging into his belly. He didn't care. "Damn it!" Wesley whispered. "So close! I was so close!"

He should have killed the boy's family – that had been his intended goal – but sheer dumb luck had allowed him to catch sight of young Hunter moving through the hallways, and he didn't really care about two middle-aged nobodies. With Hunter right in front of him, he had been unable to pass up an opportunity to end this.

Against his better judgment, Wesley prodded the eye that had been cut when Hunter shattered his glasses. The wound was gone. The Drethen he carried had been able to heal it, but in so doing, it had taxed itself even further. Unlike a Nassai, his symbiont was little more than a seething mass of emotion, responsive only to his commands, but that meant *he* had to be responsible for how hard he pushed the creature. A Nassai could refuse to craft a Bending if it was too exhausted. Drethen would push themselves until they died of fatigue, taking their hosts with them.

The wail of a siren assaulted him.

He turned, glancing out the back window.

His vision was blurry, but he didn't need crisp lines to recognize the flashing blue and red lights coming up behind him. Police cruisers. In truth, he had expected as much. Hunter had called for backup.

"How far are we from the warehouse?" Wesley called out to the driver. "Can we escape before these wretched little plebs surround us?"

"Five minutes, sir," Gilbert replied.

Too long.

Wesley shut his eyes. Their sting reminded him of his humiliation. "Then I will deal with them myself," he said softly. "Keep focused on the road."

Wesley reached up and tapped a button that caused the sun roof to slide open. Cool air came streaming in, ripping the warmth from his body, and he had a brief glimpse of clouds drifting across the darkening sky. With a grunt, he retrieved a pistol from the small compartment. It was always good to keep a few extra weapons around when you went out seeking vengeance.

He undid his seat belt.

Once again, he called upon his Drethen, and the sting in his skin that had faded to a mild prickle flared up again with renewed vigor. He crafted a Bending that would reverse gravity's pull on his body.

He shot upward through the gap, then tucked his knees into his chest and flipped to land crouched on the roof of the limousine. His head swiveled as he tried to get a sense of where he was.

They were on a busy street with skyscrapers on either side, heading eastward under a sky that was quickly fading to a deep twilight blue. Ahead of him, cars were moving at a good pace, but one of the stoplights in the distance turned yellow as he glanced around.

He looked back over his shoulder.

Framed against the light of the setting sun, two police cruisers drove side by side, taking up both lanes of this road. A third was following from behind, and there were no other cars for at least half a block. No one wanted to get anywhere near this.

Wesley twisted on the roof.

Though his vision was blurred, he used the innate spatial awareness that came from Bonding a symbiont to guide his aim. It wasn't hard to get a sense of where each car was in relation to himself and then to estimate where each driver would be inside each car. Aim for the cruiser on his left.

He fired.

A hole appeared in the windshield, and the driver inside jerked backward as a bullet pierced his skull. Instantly, the car went out of control, veering off to his left and crashing through the front window of a convenience store. The sound it made on impact was both painful and deliciously satisfying.

The second cop car was speeding up.

Wesley shot its front tire.

With a dreadful screech, the car turned sideways, creating a barricade that blocked both lanes. The third cruiser coming up behind it was unable to stop in time. It smashed right into the side of the immobilized cop car, knocking the thing over.

Wesley smiled a gleeful little smile, then shook his head in dismay. "Pitiful," he said to himself. "You fools really think you can best a man who has been touched by the Old Ones? By divinity itself?"

The limo was slowing.

The cars in front of him had been smart enough to clear a lane, but it still required a bit of careful maneuvering. Wesley slipped back through the sun roof and took his seat once again. No sense exposing himself to danger.

A pleased smile blossomed, and before he knew it, he was covering his mouth and trembling with soft laughter. "Irony," he muttered into his own palm. "Victory is always best when seasoned with it."

Six months ago, he had sent that fool Leo to Earth to sow chaos and distrust. Now, with a few quick twitches of his index finger, he had completed the work started by that wretch.

More sirens.

Wesley shut his eyes and let out a soft sigh. "Drive carefully," he said. "Make sure that we're spotted pulling into the warehouse. I want Hunter to know where to find me."

A line of yellow police tape formed a barrier across the paved surface of a parking lot, and beyond it, a garage door in the side of an old gray building was open, revealing a warehouse where uniformed cops stood talking in little clusters. The sting in his skin had faded to a soft tingle – Summer had recovered – but he still felt as if he had run ten miles without rest or water.

Jack squeezed his eyes shut, trembling with impotent rage. "Never ends, does it?" he muttered, ducking under the police tape. "No matter where we go, someone's always trying to kill us."

He went to the door.

One of the officers spun to face him: a gruff man with a barrel chest and thick gray stubble on his jawline. "This is a crime scene, son," he said in that terse voice cops liked so much. "You can't be here."

Jack closed his eyes, bowing his head to the man. "I'm Agent Jack Hunter with the Justice Keepers," he said. "Now, if you'll excuse me, some of my people are in there, and I'd like to see what they found."

Before the cop could say anything, he brought up his multitool and activated the hologram that displayed his badge. The transparent image of a four-pointed star on a circle of blue floated between them.

The cop turned his head so that he wouldn't have to make eye contact. "Right," he said, clearly embarrassed by the oversight. "Go on in. Your forensics team is scurrying around like someone just kicked up their ant hill."

When he got inside, Jack saw that it was no exaggeration. The room was essentially a great big cube with nothing in it except maybe twenty-five people who flitted about like bees gathering honey. There were cops hanging out by the door, but everyone else had come down here from Station Twelve.

He spotted Ali Layson standing with her back turned, dressed in a sleek gray skirt and a black blouse with a lacy fringe on the neckline. As usual, she was all business, her blonde hair pulled back in a ponytail.

Jack crossed his arms as he strode across the room, sighing softly. "Hey," he said, coming up behind her. "Find anything that might tell us where that son of a bitch scampered off to?"

She stiffened, then took control of herself and turned to face him. Ali was a lovely woman with fair skin and big glasses that gave her something of a sexy librarian vibe. And he felt positively wretched that his mind would go to such a place at a time like this. "Well, there is something."

"Something?"

Ali winced, then covered her face with one hand, massaging away what appeared to be a very nasty headache. "You're not gonna believe it until you see it," she muttered. "I have several of my people scanning it right now."

Only then did Jack realize that not everyone in this room was affiliated with the Justice Keepers. Some wore badges that revealed them to be agents of CSIS. So, this had become a joint operation, had it?

A familiar image solidified in his mind's eye: a tall woman who came up behind him as if she intended to bulldoze anyone standing in her way. Though her form was blurry, Jack knew exactly who he was dealing with.

He spun around.

Aamani Patel looked as sharp as ever in a black pantsuit. A tall woman who wore her black hair pulled back in a clip, she looked him up and down, then gave a quick sniff of disdain.

Thrusting his chin out, Jack narrowed his eyes. "What are you doing here?" he asked. "The last I heard, you weren't exactly fond of working with people like me."

Aamani smiled, then bowed her head, chuckling softly. "Good to see you too," she said. "And I'm here because our government is losing faith in the idea that people like you can do anything to keep this country safe."

"Is that a fact."

"One you can take to your superiors."

"I don't have time for this, Aamani," he said. "You want to work with us? Fine. Share what you know, and we'll do the same."

The woman just stood there with a blank expression, blinking as if she had never seen a man before. "I thought you of all people would be sympathetic," she murmured. "Most Keepers are from other worlds – they're used to this danger – but you! You know first hand what it's like to get swept up in the wake of forces that could squash you like a bug and not even notice."

"Which is why you should let us do our jobs."

"Oh? And what has that gotten us?" Aamani clasped her hands together in front of herself, then cleared her throat as if she were about to give a speech. "Two people dead and five injured thanks to Wesley Pennfield's little downtown rampage."

Jack felt his mouth tighten, then pressed the heel of his hand to his forehead. "Yeah, you will get no argument from me there," he said. "But again, do *you* have the resources to stop him?"

"We're developing-"

"I didn't think so."

He turned his back on her and found himself confronted by a group of three men who were crouched side by side, scanning…something they had spread out on the floor. It looked like a thin sheet of flesh with veins that pulsed, and it seemed to drink in the light from the nearby lamps.

In fact, it looked just like the device that had attached itself to Kevin Harmon, only this thing was big enough that you could use it as a blanket if you were feeling chilly. An Overseer device? And if size was any indication of power, then this thing was much more dangerous that whatever Anna had taken off Kevin.

Just looking at it made Jack's stomach turn, and he could sense Summer's growing apprehension as clear as sunlight on a warm spring day. This must have been what Ali was trying to tell him.

The tiny blonde woman had been content to remain silent during his confrontation with Aamani, but she stepped forward and grimaced when she saw the thing. "Yes," she said as if she could read his thoughts. "Your suspicions are correct. That is an Overseer device, and we have no clue what it does."

Biting his lower lip, Jack let his head hang. "I bet I can guess," he said. "Pennfield's limo is outside, but he's nowhere to be found. Smart money says this thing transported him somewhere."

"And you think you can find him?" Aamani asked.

"Given enough time, I know we can."

The woman stepped forward until she was standing right beside him, her face as smooth as porcelain while she studied the device. "You may not *have* enough time. He will strike again."

"I'm aware of that."

"Then you-"

Jack rounded on her with arms folded, drawing himself up to his full height. "Then I what?" he asked, stepping forward. "My question from before remains. Do you have the resources to contain a man like Pennfield?"

"We are developing new technologies-"

"Uh huh? Like what?"

A flush put some colour in Aamani's cheeks. "Cells reinforced with force-field generators," she said. "Weapons based on Leyrian technology with multiple settings."

"Oh, well, that's just wonderful," Jack snapped. At this point, he wasn't even trying to moderate his tone. The anger was just bubbling to the surface, and he couldn't spare the mental energy necessary to keep it bottled up. "So what are you gonna do when he crafts a Bending that reflects those bullets right back at your people? When he activates a Death Sphere that rips your officers to shreds?

"Fuck, Aamani, you of all people should understand why we need the Leyrians. I was *there.* I saw what happened in that parking garage; I watched those battle drones cut down your officers one by one while your best efforts barely even scratched their paint. Anna is the *only* reason that you and I are still standing right now, and rather than accept that simple reality, you've decided to pick up a copy of 'Xenophobia for Dummies.'"

He was seething – and Summer as well – but he didn't care. Once upon a time, he had felt a great deal of respect for this woman. Once upon a time, he would have been too afraid, too convinced of his own inadequacy, to bother telling her what he really believed. No more. No, he was in this game now, and that meant he'd better start playing to win.

The words just kept spilling out of him.

"What are you gonna do when the Antaurans show up with ships?" Jack went on. "When they offer the nations of this world two choices: allow them to strip our planet of every last resource or watch helplessly as they obliterate us from orbit?

"Hell, it doesn't even have to be an official military. Some guy in a dinky little fifty-year-old shuttle could hold this planet hostage by floating in orbit and threatening to drop a few plasma bombs on just *one* of our major cities. The Leyrians prevent that. They may not be perfect – and sometimes I want to kick my superiors halfway across Dead Space – but they are the reason our culture continues to exist."

Aamani was watching him with big brown eyes, and for a moment, he almost felt as though she were seeing him for the first time. No. this was not the Jack she had been expecting. Not the uncertain boy who covered his self-loathing with jokes about maple-glazed Timbits. Sometimes he still hated himself, but he knew what he was doing now.

"I will… think on that," Aamani said.

"Good," Jack grumbled. "Ali, would you please call in a Hazmat team? Let's get this thing up to the station."

Samuel Elwood – that was his alias for the time being, and he had better get used to thinking of himself in that way – watched as two women in Hazmat gear carried the Overseer device out of the warehouse. Those suits were bulky with big thick visors, and you could hear the soft rasp of their breathing. No one wanted to risk letting exposed skin come into contact with Overseer technology.

He stood in the corner with his arms folded, staring down at the floor beneath his feet. *What scheme is this,* he wondered in the privacy of his own mind. It was an effort to keep his thoughts quiet. *What are you planning, Slade?*

Aamani Patel came striding over to him. Her posture made it clear that she was tired. "As usual, the Keepers will be taking their prize," she muttered. "I wonder what we could have learned from it."

Samuel looked up to meet her gaze, blinking several times. "Not much, ma'am," he said, shaking his head. "Our best scientists can barely puzzle out how Leyrian technology works. That stuff is a whole other ballpark."

He was pleased with himself. Adding a touch of Earth slang gave him even more credibility. The badge he wore on his jacket pocket, declaring his affiliation with CSIS, would not do very much good if he couldn't act like one of the locals. Now to drive home his point…

Samuel opened his mind to the sensations all around him, allowing the thoughts of others to seep into his consciousness. Aamani's were strongest. She was right in front of him and focused on him. Images flickered in his mind: memories of Agent Hunter and some little blonde woman. But he was not interested in her thoughts, only her emotions.

He sensed Aamani's frustration, her feelings of being shut out, unable to take part in the search for Pennfield, unable to *do* anything to bolster the security of her country when she had dedicated her very life to that purpose. Once upon a time, she had been relevant, an important figure in government's hierarchy. Hers was a voice that carried weight.

Then the Leyrians came and took all that away from her. Years of slowly climbing the ranks, of proving that she was not just *as* capable as any man but *more* capable. Years of refusing to back down until she finally achieved her goals, only to be made obsolete by a group of space cops with better technology. She hated it.

Samuel stoked those emotions. Just a tweak – too much, and he would be noticed – but it would do the trick. "Agent Hunter was right, ma'am," he said. "The Leyrians are better equipped to study that thing." A gentle caress of her mind, flaring the distrust that she naturally felt. It would leave her confused and disoriented, his words pushing her in one direction, his thoughts in another.

And there it was!

He felt it well up inside her like an eruption from a volcano. Resentment. Disgust at the notion that technological superiority would give someone the right to set policy. He could hear the question burning in her mind. "Why should the Leyrians get their way just because they have better tools?"

Aamani grimaced, touching three fingers to the side of her forehead. "You're right," she said, backing away from him. "Though I don't have to like it. I suppose we'll have to work with Hunter if we want any answers."

Leaning against the wall with his arms crossed, Samuel shut his eyes. He drew in a deep breath. "It seems that way, ma'am," he said. "But you can trust him. You've worked with Agent Hunter before, right?"

"Yes…"

"Good."

The woman forced out a sigh, bracing one arm against the wall to her left. "I think it's time we left this place," she muttered under her breath. "Do you need a ride back to the SlipGate terminal?"

He shook his head. "No, I think I'm gonna get some food," Samuel said, feigning exhaustion to the best of his ability. "I'll catch a cab back when I'm done. See you in the office tomorrow then?"

"Okay."

It was some time before everyone was gone – the Leyrians wanted to go over the whole place with a scanner – so he made his cover that much more believable by actually going for food. The things these primitives ate! After several years on this planet, he had grown used to hamburgers and french fries, but what he wouldn't give for a nice lean cut of fish with some garlic seasoning.

When he returned to the warehouse, the place was empty, the police tape removed and the lights turned out. The only illumination came through the open garage door, and that wasn't much. He wasn't nervous; he would have sensed another mind long before he was in any danger.

Samuel retrieved a multi-tool from his pocket, a metal disk with buttons on top. He didn't bother wearing the gauntlet with its touchscreen interface. That would have raised too many questions.

Tapping one button caused a rectangle of soft blue light to appear before him, the hologram displaying icons would allow him to access the tool's functions. He waved his finger through one and the image rippled to be replaced by the tool's communication's application. After that, it was a fairly simple process to place a call.

The hologram of Grecken Slade stood before him: tall and proud in a pair of gray pants and a black coat with gold trim. The man wore his long dark hair hanging loose and kept his expression neutral. "Report."

Bathed in the light of the hologram, Samuel shut his eyes and bowed his head. "It seems Pennfield has left a piece of Inzari technology for Hunter to find," he said. "I have no doubt it is some form of bait."

Folding his arms with a grunt, Slade craned his neck to stare at something above Samuel's head. "Yes, I would agree," he muttered. "So it seems our errant servant is still spinning his own web."

"It appears so."

With a sigh, Slade covered his face with one hand and gently massaged his eyelids. "Idiot man," he said into his own palm. "His insistence on carrying out this vendetta has forced us to accelerate our timetable."

Samuel frowned down at the floor, his brows drawn together. "Would you like me to remove him from the game?" he asked, ignoring the chill that ran down his spine. "It can be done, but I will need assistance."

"No," Slade answered quickly. "Don't bother. Pennfield is nothing but a distraction at this point, and if he keeps Hunter occupied..."

"What if he manages to kill the young Keeper?"

Slade shrugged as if it were no concern of his. "One way or another, Jack Hunter must be dealt with," he explained. "He is a resourceful young man – so I would prefer to bring him around to our way of thinking – but if that proves to be impossible, his death will do just as well. Leave Pennfield in play for the moment."

Cocking his head to one side, Slade frowned at him with puckered lips. "And how is Aamani?" he asked, raising a thin eyebrow. "I trust that her conversion is progressing according to schedule."

"It is."

"Good. I'd hate to have to replace you."

"That will not be necessary," Samuel muttered. "Aamani Patel is naturally suspicious of anyone that she deems to be an outsider. A few gentle nudges are all she needs."

"You're certain?"

Samuel looked up to squint at the other man. "Quite certain," he replied with a nod. "Telepathy is a subtle art, Lord Slade. Push someone too hard, and they will detect your touch and counter it. You were wise to choose her. She was already close enough to being exactly what we need her to be."

"Very well, then," Slade said. "You are dismissed."

The hologram rippled out of existence.

Chapter 23

"You're too tense," Melissa said.

The sun was beating down from a clear blue sky, casting rays of silver light upon a field of green grass not far from the park where Amanda Simmons did her babysitting. The girl was off today, which made it a good time for training.

Melissa stood in the grass with hands folded behind herself, dressed in a pair of white shorts and a black tank top. "You need to loosen up a little," she said, striding toward Amanda. "Let muscle memory guide you."

The other girl wore a similar outfit and stood with her fists raised in an attempt at a boxer's stance, up in front of her face so that it would be hard to see. "We've been at this for almost a week now."

Melissa scowled, nodding her agreement. "We have," she said, approaching the other girl. "But I've been training for over three months, and I'm only *starting* to hit the point where I feel competent."

Amanda looked up at her with lips pressed into a thin line, her face betraying her confusion. Or maybe it was skepticism. "If you say so," she mumbled. "It's just… This Tae Kwon Do stuff isn't me."

Well, that was a good thing since Melissa was actually teaching her a Leyrian self-defense style called Dejara. Jena had claimed that it was best for someone who preferred to let her opponent strike first and then capitalize on whatever opening presented itself. Still, Melissa could understand the girl's lack of confidence.

Not too far away, Kevin sat in the grass with his knees drawn up against his chest, smiling as he watched the whole thing. "You can do it, Amanda!" he called out. It was obvious he liked her as much as she liked him.

"Kevin, get up here."

He stood.

This was their third training session, and by now, the young man had learned his role. One thing that spoke well of him: he didn't seem to mind Melissa repeatedly tossing him on his ass as part of a demonstration.

Melissa turned her back on him, standing with fists balled at her sides, head bowed. "It's fairly simple," she said. "It doesn't matter how big he is. The only thing that counts is how smart *you* are."

Kevin seized her in a bear hug.

Melissa squeezed her eyes shut, then slammed the back of her head into his nose. Not hard enough to do damage, but even that small impact would stun him. She flung her arms upward, pulling free.

Kevin gasped.

Crouching down, Melissa drove one elbow into his stomach, just barely making contact. She had no desire to hurt the guy. "He's twice my size," she said. "But I can still get free if I know what I'm doing."

Amanda hugged herself, turning so that Melissa couldn't see her expression. "And I'm sure that will help against school bullies," she said, pacing a line in the grass. "But what am I supposed to do when…"

When her father was the bully?

Turning around, Melissa found Kevin standing a few feet away with a solemn expression. "Sorry," she murmured, suddenly very embarrassed. "I hope that didn't hurt."

"Nothing major."

He let his arm drop, then fixed a bright smile on Amanda. "It's not about being the best brawler on campus," he said, striding toward her. "It's about looking within yourself and seeing that you're amazing."

Amanda was blushing, her cheeks stained red as she bowed her head to him. "I'm not that special," she mumbled, shifting her weight from one foot to the other. "I'm not like you, Melissa. I'm not strong."

"I disagree."

The other girl shuddered, crossing her arms and doubling over like a delicate flower bent by a fierce wind. "It's been like this my whole life," she muttered. "My father says I need to accept my-"

"What your father says is irrelevant." Some people might have felt anger hearing Amanda talk about herself in that way – and Melissa had to admit, that on an academic level, this kind of thing *did* piss her off – but what she really felt when she looked at this poor girl was grief. That someone could do something like this to their own child...

What would her life have been like if her father had sliced away at her self-worth with one barbed comment after another, if her father had insisted that she was worth less than all the boys around her. Perhaps she hadn't really appreciated just how good she had it, comparatively speaking. Harry could be overprotective, but he *believed* in her. How many girls – or boys, for that matter – could say the same?

Amanda looked flustered.

Closing her eyes, Melissa let her head hang and tried to ignore the sticky sweat on her face. "Maybe it's time for a break," she said softly. "Why don't you guys go and grab something to drink; I'll catch up with you."

Kevin turned slightly, looking over his shoulder with a wary expression. "You're not going to come with us?" he asked, raising an eyebrow.

"No, I should check in with my dad."

As a minor, she had a difficult time traveling by SlipGate without at least one of her parents present. A volunteer ID issued by the Justice Keepers along with written consent by her father had allowed her to come down here and spend some time with Amanda and Kevin. Harry seemed to approve of her desire to help them both, but one of his conditions was that she text him at least once an hour.

Watching the two of them walk side by side, Melissa had to fight the urge to squee. It was clear they really cared for each other. She was sure that Kevin was ready to admit it – everything he did made his affection clear – but Amanda? The girl would need some time. Not to acknowledge her feelings but to give herself permission to explore them.

Hopefully, a little time alone with Kevin would see to that. *Bit by bit,* Melissa thought to herself. *You took the girl apart, old man. But give me enough time, and I will put her back together.*

The things I do for the people I love. Right then, Jena should have been prepping for the next session of Anna's hearing. So far, the process had been agonizing with the Manchester cops insisting that one of her agents was essentially a brute who knocked skulls together to get her way. She *should* have been prepping for the next session, but here she was, granting one of Anna's requests.

The small house had blue aluminum siding and a big front window that looked into a living room with burgundy walls. A wooden porch was lit by a single light that cast a yellow glow.

Dressed in black pants and a red t-shirt with a square neck, Jena climbed the steps with her head down. "I must be nuts," she muttered. "The girl's gone and made me as naive as she is."

She banged on the door.

A moment later, it swung inward to reveal a tall woman in a pair of faded jeans and a gray t-shirt: a gorgeous lady with a round face and long blonde hair that fell over her shoulders. "Yes?"

Jena squeezed her eyes shut, taking in a deep breath. "Clara Randall?" she asked, backing away from the door. "My name is Jena Morane. I'm with the Justice Keepers."

The woman's eyes widened, and she took a step back as if hoping to find shelter in the safety of her own home. "Is there something that I can do for you?" she spluttered. "I didn't have anything to do with the trouble a couple weeks back."

"I'm aware of that, ma'am."

"Then why are you here?"

Leaning against the wooden porch railing with her arms folded, Jena felt her mouth twist into a frown. "I'm here to talk about your niece," she replied. "Amanda Simmons is your late sister's daughter, correct?"

Clara Randall braced one arm against the door frame and watched Jena with such intensity you might have thought that Jena meant to kill the woman. "Now, why would you be coming to talk about her?"

Jena looked up, blinking at the other woman. "One of my agents interviewed your niece during the search for Kevin Harmon," she explained. "The girl's behaviour made us think that maybe-"

"My brother-in-law pecks away at her self-esteem until she's nothing but an empty shell of a human being." A flush painted Clara's face, but she stepped out onto the porch with cold control. "I'm well aware of the problem, but there's very little I can do."

"You can testify against him."

"What good would that do?"

A grimace tugged at the corners of Jena's mouth, and she wiped sweat off her brow with the back of her hand. "I've spoken with Child Protective Services," she said, pushing past her anxiety. This wasn't exactly her area of expertise. Apprehending criminals who tried to shoot her? No problem. But this... "They admit there's cause for concern, but they can't take any action without some kind of evidence."

Clara strode across the porch, passing Jena and gripping the wooden railing with both hands. "Vic would never hit Amanda," she said, staring out at the houses across the street. "But he *will* attack her confidence."

The woman glanced over her shoulder with a vicious scowl, fine lines visible at the corners of her eyes. "He's one of those traditionalists," she went on. "He believes that a woman's role is one of obedience."

Instantly, Jena understood why Anna had been in a lather over this. The girl was always two inches from punching someone whenever she was forced to deal with this planet's outdated gender politics. It didn't produce the same kind of hot rage in Jena. No, her anger was of a colder sort, the kind that made her want to take down assholes like Vic Simmons with one calculated move.

But what should that move be?

"You can't let her stay in that environment," she said insisted. "It could ruin the rest of her life."

"You think I don't know that?"

"Then do something."

"Like what?"

Jena spun around to lean over the railing. Right now, it felt as if the stress she had been battling for days had become a boulder strapped to her back. "You could give Amanda an alternative."

Clara stiffened. "You don't get it. I go up against Vic, and he turns the whole damn town against me."

"But-"

"No," the woman insisted. "It's not happening, okay? I'd like you to leave now."

"The situation is clear."

Lieutenant Biggs stood with his back turned, facing the table where Glin Karon, Tiassa Navram and Kaydie Cadanzar sat side by side. What Anna would have given to see the smug expression on his face. Then again, that would almost certainly lead to her punching him and thereby proving his point.

The officer kept his back straight, his shoulders square, and faced them with the kind of quiet dignity you might expect from a diplomat. "Agent Lenai tossed my men around like rag-dolls. If you want to prove goodwill between our two peoples, you can't let transgressions like this go unpunished."

With her mouth hanging open, Anna looked up to blink at him. *Oh, you have* got *to be kidding me!* she thought, sliding her chair closer to the table. *He wants them to offer me up as a sacrificial lamb to prove their goodwill?*

At her side, Harry sat stroking his chin and watching the whole thing with concern on his face. "Agent Lenai acted to protect the life of an innocent," he said. "That is her first and most important duty."

Biggs turned.

His smug, self-satisfied grin was just repulsive, and to make matters worse, he tipped his cap to Anna. "One might say my that officers have the same duty," he replied. "And yet you felt justified in attacking them."

Anna wrinkled her nose in disgust, then shook her head. "I can't win this," she said, getting out of her chair. "Make whatever snide insinuations you like; it doesn't change the fact that your men were planning to commit murder."

Biggs moved aside, granting her a view of her three would-be "judges." Glin Karon sat with his hands folded on the table, patiently watching her with a neutral expression. It seemed that he was the one most likely to support her.

Tiassa slouched in her chair with arms folded, and by this point, it was clear that she was fed up with this whole thing. Most of her comments over the last few days had betrayed her sensibilities. The woman saw Lieutenant Biggs as nothing but a swaggering, self-righteous fool, but she wasn't supportive of Anna either. She seemed to blame Anna for the fact that this mess had landed in her lap, so to speak.

And then there was Kaydie Cadanzar. That one was watching them like a hawk. Of the three, she was the hardest to read.

Anna approached the trio with her hands clasped behind her back, her head bowed respectfully. "This whole thing has become a circus," she said. "Make whatever judgment you want, and let's get on with our lives."

In her mind's eye, she saw Harry doubled over in his chair, "face-palming" as Jack would say. The man wanted her to be a little more tactful. At the moment, tact was simply beyond her.

"Very well," Glin said.

He stood up with fists clenched at his sides, running his gaze over everyone else. "We have deliberated this in private," he began. "Our conclusion is that Agent Lenai's intention to protect Kevin Harmon is in line with the mandate of the Justice Keepers. It is our duty to oppose corruption even in those who serve the law."

Anna felt a swell of pride.

That emotion vanished when Glin let out a sigh of dismay. "However," he went on, leaning forward with his hands braced on the table. "The fact remains that violence is and should always be a last resort."

Tiassa looked up at the ceiling, sniffing to show her disdain. "Agent Lenai's actions have damaged relations between our people and the citizens of Earth." Her mouth twisted with obvious disapproval. "It is our assessment that she could have defused the situation without resorting to such extreme measures."

"Therefore," Glin concluded, "she will be suspended from active duty for a period of three Earth weeks, and a formal reprimand will appear in her record."

The words hit like a punch to the chest.

Anna closed her eyes, pinching the bridge of her nose with thumb and forefinger. She sighed into her own palm. "All right then. Now that the jackals have been placated, can we end this farce?"

"This hearing is ended," Glin said.

On her way out the door, Harry reached for her, and she let him offer a few comforting words. This wasn't his fault, after all, but a part of her wanted to scream at him. People always wanted to comfort you, even when they should just leave well enough alone. If she rebuked his kindness, he would be offended, but it seemed grossly unfair to her that she should have to take care of his feelings on top of everything else.

Ten minutes later, she was wandering the hallways of Station Twelve, lost in her own musings. The station wasn't off limits to her – civilians came up here all the time for one reason or another – only the restricted areas. No shuttle access, no access to any of the weapons' lockers.

What was she supposed to do now? Slink back home and tell her boyfriend the sad news? Would he ever look at her the same way again? It ripped her apart inside, knowing that she had been shamed in this way.

At least Seth was still on her side. She could feel the symbiont's love for her and his support as well. Of course, Seth's perceptions were coloured by her own, but that didn't make it any less comforting.

Anna sighed.

A few years ago, it never would have occurred to her that she might ever have a reprimand on her record, but there it was. She was beginning to understand Jack's point of view. All this time, she had believed that Earth cynicism had distorted how he saw his fellow Keepers, but maybe he was right.

Maybe the senior directors *were* more interested in politics than they were in doing their damn jobs! It was a scary thought. Shouldn't a Nassai reject anyone who was prone to that kind of thinking?

She went home with a dull ache in her chest.

Chapter 24

Jack watched the SlipGate power up, watched the sinuous grooves that ran from the base of that metal triangle all the way to its pointed tip light up with a fierce white glow. There was a soft, whirring sound, and then a bubble appeared, expanding from a single point to something large enough to hold a dozen people.

Inside, a blurry figure stood with her head down. The light that passed through the surface of the bubble was refracted, making it difficult to determine who was inside, and Jack couldn't rely on spatial awareness either. His Keeper senses detected nothing but a big spherical gap in the fabric of reality.

The bubble was a pocket of folded space-time that had been translated from one point to another through SlipSpace. Matter could not pass through the barrier; that was why travelers did not have to fear that the oxygen that traveled with them might disperse.

The bubble popped.

Aamani Patel stood before him in a blue pantsuit, her eyes downcast as though she found something fascinating in the floor tiles. "I must admit, you've left me intrigued, Hunter," she said. "Why did you call me here?"

Jack smiled, a flush burning his cheeks. "Well," he began. "You seem to think that you can't trust me, Aamani. By the time we've finished, I hope you'll feel differently."

"What did you have in mind?"

He powered down the gate.

Jack stepped out from behind the console, approaching her with his hands shoved into his pockets. "I figure you could fall backwards, and I'll catch you," he said with a shrug. "Sixty-six percent of the time, it goes off without a hitch."

She snorted.

"Come on," Jack said. "You wanted a look at the ugly, veiny slab of flesh that Wes left on the floor. Well, I'm inclined to indulge you."

A thin sheet of skin slightly larger than Jack's palm was suspended from hooks on a metal bar, the veins pulsing as if the thing was still alive. Which it was. Exactly how that was possible remained a mystery. Professor Nareo seemed to think that the lack of direct sunlight had caused the object to slow its metabolic rate by several orders of magnitude.

The man stood a few feet from the table with his shoulders slumped, frowning intently at the device. "It's been like this for days," he began. "We've made some small progress in scanning some of its memory, but…"

Clasping his chin in one hand, Jack squinted at the thing. "Do you think it might react with the device Wesley left in the warehouse?" he asked. "Is it wise to keep them both in the same room?"

The professor sighed, his head drooping as if he could barely fight off his own exhaustion. "I've been over this with Director Morane," he muttered. "So far, we have seen no sign that they will interact."

Jack turned.

Aamani Patel stood side by side with Raynar, and both had adopted the exact same posture: hands pressed to their sides, heads held high with smooth expressions. Jack had noticed that the young man did that sometimes, subconsciously mirroring other people. From what he had read, it was an instinct found in most humans, the urge to mimic each other's body language. It stood to reason that instinct would be even more pronounced in a telepath.

Aamani closed her eyes, sighing softly as she strode forward. "This is the weapon that Lenai recovered from the young man in Tennessee?" Every syllable betrayed a keen fascination with the object. "Could its power be harnessed for any useful purpose?"

Puckering his lips, Jack shut his eyes and blew out a breath. "Not from what we've seen," he answered. "The device triggers a fight or flight response in anyone who tries to use it."

Nareo's only response was a quick nod. "It increases production of dopamine, acetylcholine and adrenaline." He scraped a gnarled knuckle across his forehead. "The result leaves one unstable."

Aamani studied the thing with her lips pressed together, her face as smooth as crisp, clean ice. "Still…" she mumbled absently. "With proper study, we might be able to adapt it for human use."

"My people have tried," Nareo chimed in.

"Aamani."

Cautiously, she turned to him.

Jack lifted his chin and held her gaze for one very long moment. "That's not our goal," he said with as much delicacy as he could manage. "We're hoping that this thing might shed *some* light on what Slade is planning."

At the mention of Slade's name, Aamani went bone white. Now *there* was an odd flash of emotion. Jack figured he couldn't blame the woman; by this point, the story of what Slade had done on Station One – shutting down the whole system, including life support, while he made his escape – had reached just about every major news outlet.

The man had become public enemy number one on Earth, and yet, somehow, no law enforcement agency had been able to find him since he went to ground four months ago. That in and of itself was a bad sign; it meant Slade had connections, influence that he could exploit.

It took him a moment to notice Raynar, but the young man was as intensely focused on Aamani as he was. Had Raynar sensed something? Some fleeting thought that might put Aamani's reaction in context? Jack decided that he would resist the temptation to ask. People had a right to their privacy. "So what do we know?"

Raynar perked up at the question, shaking his head as if to clear away the thoughts that had distracted him. "Attempting to devise a technological interface is slow going at best," he answered. "But I have managed to…read the thing's memory."

Jack blinked.

The boy licked his lips, then bowed his head as if the topic had become a source of embarrassment. "It's hard to explain in words," he went on. "But I can show you if you're willing. Share the experience with you."

"Let's do it," Jack said.

"I would like to see as well," Aamani added.

Less than a minute later, Jack was standing in the middle of the room with hands folded over his stomach, waiting patiently for Raynar to do…whatever it was he planned on doing. Aamani was at his side with posture fit for a soldier, staring warily at the young man as he approached.

Raynar closed his eyes, breathing deeply. "This may be somewhat disorienting," he said, touching one index finger to Jack's forehead and the other to Aamani's. "But it will pass quickly."

Jack was yanked forward – or so it seemed – and suddenly the world around him was drowned out in a void of infinite blackness. Images floated in the distance, swirls of colour that he couldn't identify, but they quickly solidified.

Two bright eyes glowing like a pair of suns, bearing down on him and threatening to pull him in. On some level, he understood what they were. This was an Overseer, his maker, his designer, and it had instructions for him.

His function was to be versatile, to serve in many ways: as a sensory organ to study the world around him, as a tool to reshape flesh toward his master's desires, as a weapon to protect his master from harm. His mind was filled with knowledge: dates, locations, events. He couldn't make sense of any of it. It was as though he were looking at records in another language, possessing a vague intuition as to what kinds of information they held but unable to access the specifics.

So much raw data!

Too much for one mind to handle. He tried to sift through it, but it became nothing but sound and fury, totally incoherent. Something about that made him want to panic, and he pulled away, trying to rid his mind of those images.

Raynar severed the link.

Jack shut his eyes, ignoring the throbbing pain that threatened to knock him over. "I'm gonna have a headache for a week," he muttered. "But I think we finally have a sense of what this thing is."

Aamani was next to him with one hand pressed to her temple, wincing as if she felt terrible pain. "How did you stand it?" she asked in a hoarse voice. "Being overwhelmed by it. It's like I was swimming in a sea of noise."

"Yeah…"

Turning to face her with his arms crossed, Jack frowned down at himself. "But you sensed it, right?" he mumbled, shivering despite his attempts to prevent it. "Your function is to be versatile."

"I did."

Not ten paces away, Nareo was tapping his lips with one finger. "You're saying it has some significance?" he asked. "Beyond the fact that this is a multipurpose device?"

"I'm saying it has a basic operating system," Jack said. "A rudimentary simulated intelligence that will allow it to interface and respond to its owner's wishes. I'm saying this thing is the Overseer equivalent of a multi-tool."

His declaration left everyone a little flabbergasted, though it really shouldn't have been *that* much of a surprise. They had already known that the device was capable of a wide variety of tasks. Perhaps it was just the fact that the Overseers – inscrutable, god-like aliens who were the living embodiment of Clarke's Third Law – might use tools on a day-to-day basis.

Now, on to the bigger mystery.

In the corner of the room, the sheet of skin that they had recovered from Wesley Pennfield's warehouse was stretched out on the floor, soaking up the light from the bulbs in the ceiling. Another shiver went through him when he looked at it. Organic technology. Would wonders never cease?

He shuffled over.

As he drew near to it, Summer grew tense, so tense that he could feel the sudden spike of alarm as if it were his own emotion. That was rare. Usually a Nassai's emotions felt like a faint, distant echo of what he might feel.

Closing his eyes, Jack tilted his head back. *Are you okay?* he thought at the Nassai. *I know you don't like being around things that remind you of your creators, but you didn't react that way to the other device.*

Of course, she couldn't answer him with words. Nassai could only share feelings, not complex thoughts. Not while he was fully conscious, anyway. But the emotion his symbiont shared was…terror mixed with wonder. Something was wrong. "I need to talk to Summer for a moment," he told the others. "Just ignore me."

Jack sat down on the floor, drawing his legs up against his chest, and he worked to calm his mind, to banish all superfluous thought and slip into a peaceful, relaxed state. Teetering on the edge of sleep and wakefulness. With practice, a Keeper could learn to commune with his symbiont in a matter of moments.

The world slipped away, and he found himself standing in the middle of a forest of tall maple trees. Their branches reached for one another, nearly touching in some places, and provided shade against the hot afternoon sun.

Summer glided toward him in a strapless white dress with a skirt that flared and cute little shoes. Over the years, she had developed a taste for Earth fashions. Or maybe those were his own preferences reflected back at him.

Her golden hair was left to hang loose in waves that fell to the small of her back, framing a lovely face that was somehow a composite of every woman he'd ever looked up to – both real and fictional.

"You look lovely, as always," Jack said. "What's up?"

Her face was a blank mask, but she did blink several times as she came close. "One of my kind is trapped inside the larger device," she said. "I couldn't sense it until we got close, but I'm sure of it."

"A Nassai?"

"Yes."

"Inside the device?"

"Yes."

"Didn't you once tell me that the Overseers created the Nassai to be the means by which their ships would travel faster than light?"

Summer shut her eyes and nodded to him. "We were created for that purpose," she explained. "But the Progenitors abandoned us on the moon that orbits Leyria."

"Some of you anyway."

"What do you mean?"

"Well, the Overseers were zipping through space at speeds much faster than light." He turned away from her, making his way down a muddy path that cut through the trees. "Their ships must have employed *some* kind of propulsion. Perhaps they didn't leave all of you on Laras. Perhaps you were…excess inventory."

He felt awful describing one of his dearest friends in those terms, but if Summer was offended, she gave no sign of it. Instead, she came up behind him, resting one hand on his shoulder. "What should we do?" Jack asked.

When he turned, she was watching him with her lips pursed, her large brown eyes slowly expanding. "I would like to try something," she said. "If we get close enough, I may be able to reach out to the Nassai inside the device."

"Will it understand you?"

"Unknown." Touching two fingers to her forehead, she scrunched up her face as if she were fighting off a painful headache. "Thousands of your years have passed since the Progenitors left us on Laras. Our patterns of thought have evolved in that time, growing even more complex when we met your kind and discovered concepts such as love, justice and self-determination."

"Right."

"The Nassai inside that device may be feral," she went on. "It may not be capable of truly complex thought."

"Well, it's worth a shot," Jack said.

The forest faded away in a blur as he felt himself being pulled back into his body. Awareness of his limbs, his breathing and of the presence of Aamani, Nareo and Raynar seeped back into his mind. The three of them were standing side by side behind him, all watching him as if they expected him to grow horns. For him, it had felt like minutes, but he knew that in the physical world, less than thirty seconds had passed since he'd entered the trance.

Jack stood up on shaky legs, doubling up with his hands on his knees. "There's a Nassai inside the larger device," he said, shaking his head. "Summer can feel it, and she wants to try contacting it."

"What?" Aamani said.

In his mind's eye, Jack saw the blurry image of Nareo stride forward until the man was almost within arm's reach. "That's impossible," he said. "Director Morane has been in half a dozen times since we brought that thing up, and she's felt nothing."

"Did she ever get within five feet of it?"

Nareo paused, his mouth agape as he stared at the back of Jack's head. "No," he said. "She's been very cautious about going anywhere near either device. She said we should all do the same."

Jack whirled around to face the other man, head hanging as he let out a deep breath. "Well, there's your answer then," he muttered. "Summer wasn't able to feel anything until I was almost close enough to touch it."

Raynar looked up with a frown, his brow furrowing as he made eye contact. "But I've gotten within five feet of it," he said. "I even touched it with my bare hand, and I can tell you that I sensed nothing."

"You're not a Nassai, kid."

"Be that as it may," the young telepath countered, "I would have felt the presence of another sentient mind. All I felt from that big thing over there was the same…I don't even know what to call it. These devices, they have a rudimentary consciousness, but it has no desire except to serve."

"Well, there's really only one solution then," Jack said. "Let's have Summer take a peek and see what she comes up with."

He made his way toward the slab of skin. His intention was to get down on his knees and touch it ever so gently with one finger – Nassai needed physical contact to speak to other Nassai in other bodies – but as soon as he got close enough, the sheet of flesh began to writhe.

A bulge formed in its surface, growing larger and larger until it split into an upside-down V that rose up toward the ceiling. It happened so quickly! Jack was so mystified by the speed with which this thing changed shape that it barely registered when the device became a seven-foot tall triangle of flesh.

Wait. A triangle?

Jack understood at the last second.

He spun around, intending to get away, but it was too late. A bubble formed around him, cutting him off even as Aamani rushed over to help. He saw her only as a blurry figure who came toward him with one hand outstretched. *No! No! No! No!* Panic welled up. He had to get out, but how-

The bubble sped forward, pulling him into SlipSpace.

Chapter 25

The bubble jerked to a halt in a small room lit by two lamps on wooden tables on either side of a door that led into a hallway. Through the shimmering curtain of folded space-time, Jack saw two black lumps standing in that corridor. Men, he assumed. And dressed in full tactical gear. Matter couldn't pass in or out of a SlipGate bubble once it had formed – Jack was essentially in his own mini-universe, at the moment – but he had at most ten seconds before everything went to hell.

Jack closed his eyes, letting his head hang. *Just my luck,* he thought, covering his face with one hand. *I have to give you this much, Pennfield. When it comes to evil plans, you go above and beyond.*

The bubble popped.

He immediately threw up another, forged of a Bending that he made with Summer's assistance. The air before him rippled and pulsed, and it seemed as if he viewed his two attackers through a wall of falling water.

In that split second between when the SlipGate had deposited him back into normal space and when he had thrown up his Time Bubble, the two uniformed men had pulled the triggers on their assault rifles. And now bullets erupted from the barrels of each, slowly spiraling toward him. When they crossed the barrier into his time-frame, they would rip through his body like a dog tearing up an old rag. With a groan, Jack crouched down to get out of the line of fire.

His bubble vanished.

He somersaulted across the polished floor tiles while thunder filled his ears and bullets zipped through the space above him to hit the metal SlipGate with harsh pinging sounds. Jack came up on one knee between the two men.

He flung his arms out to the sides, catching the back of each man's leg. Like a pair of dominoes, they both tumbled backwards to land face-up in the middle of the hallway, the one on his left still firing bullets up at the ceiling.

Jack turned to the one on his right.

He slammed a fist down into the man's throat, crushing the trachea with a sickening *squish.* The guard's eyes widened behind his visor, and he let out a squeal when he realized that he could no longer breathe. His hands clawed at his throat.

The one on his left was moving.

Jack fell onto his backside, lying flat on the floor. The remaining guard managed to roll and point his gun at an oblique angle, loosing a steady stream of bullets at the wall on the other side of the corridor.

Jack brought one leg up, striking the underside of the rifle, and ripping it right out of the man's hand to land several paces down the corridor. The silence that followed was so unexpected it almost made him jump.

The guard sat up.

Jack did the same.

For a moment that seemed to stretch into endless eternities, he stared through a clear visor at the face of a man who was probably only a few years older than himself. A face locked into slack-jawed terror.

Clenching his teeth with a hiss, Jack squeezed his eyes shut. "Go," he whispered, pointing down the corridor. "Don't reach for your sidearm; you'll be dead before you get it out of the holster. Just go."

The young man did as he was told.

He stood up on shaky legs, then spun around and bolted down the corridor to what appeared to be an open foyer at the far end. Gasping and sobbing, he ducked around the corner and never looked back.

That was probably a mistake. Right now, the guy was frightened out of his wits, but when he regrouped with his buddies – and there was simply no way to tell how many of them were crawling around this place – he would probably regain his courage. Being part of a group had that effect.

The practical part of Jack's mind said that all he had done was guarantee that he would have to finish the job whenever the man decided to take another shot at him. His conscience didn't give a damn. He had taken his first life today, and he wasn't intending to let that particular scorecard fill up with tick-marks.

He stood.

Shutting his eyes, Jack felt tears on his face. *You had to do it,* he thought. *They threw you into this with no weapons, no body armour. Nothing but your wits and a Nassai.*

He knew the protocol. In a situation like that, you took down your opponent by any means necessary. Non-lethal force was always preferable if you could manage it, but his instructors had been clear on this point. Sometimes the enemy left you no alternatives.

A man appeared at the end of the corridor, standing tall and proud in a gray suit with a navy blue tie. Wesley Pennfield was looking a lot better, his eyes healed and his mangled glasses replaced by a stunning new pair of designer frames. "A pleasure to see you, Jack," he said with a nod. "Once again, you continue to impress."

Jack felt his face burn. "You son of a bitch," he said, marching down the corridor. "What? Were you too scared to face me yourself? Easier to send a pair of hired goons. Is that it?"

A wicked grin split the other man's face, and he lifted his chin to stare imperiously through the lenses of his glasses. "I'm sorry. Was I supposed to fight fair?" The mocking tone set Jack's blood on fire. "I see you have become the typical Justice Keeper. Nothing short of brilliant when it comes to ripping through enemies while your blood is hot. But true strategy eludes you."

Jack dove.

He somersaulted through the corridor, catching the fallen assault rifle on his way, then came up on one knee. Half a second later, he was standing, pointing the weapon at his opponent.

Wesley just stood there with one hand outstretched, a quizzical expression on his face. "Really?" he asked, arching one eyebrow above the rim of his glasses. "You know I'll just reflect them back at you."

Grinning like a kid with stolen cookies, Jack shut his eyes. He shook his head ever so slowly. "You really think I'm planning to *kill* you with this? No, moron, this is to tire you out before the real fun begins."

"Strategy?"

"Capital S."

Wesley glided backward with a swan's grace, retreating until he stood in the middle of the foyer. He bent his knees and leaped, shooting upward with a surge of Bent Gravity. "Come find me then." His voice echoed from above.

Jack ran forward.

At the end of the hallway, he found an open space with a large front door to his left, frosted glass on the windows admitting the fierce light of early afternoon. To his right, a curving staircase with a marble railing led up to a landing that overlooked the foyer. Wesley stood there with his hands behind his back.

The man leaned forward, smiling down at Jack. "I must say," he began with a shrug of his shoulders. "Bringing you here was quite the effort. Honestly, I thought I'd do away with you in the hospital. This trap was for Lenai."

"Well, she gets invited to all the good parties."

"Yes, but you get to meet all the best people."

It was only then that Jack noticed someone coming up behind Wesley, a tall, bare-chested figure with abs that would leave any teenage girl dazed and drooling. This guy had smooth copper skin without a spec of hair on his bald head.

He leaped over the railing with no effort.

Descending to the floor below, he landed in the middle of the foyer, then dropped to a crouch. There was no warping sensation, no sign that he had employed Bent Gravity. So when the newcomer stood up on legs that seemed unharmed by the impact, Jack had to stifle a wave of dread.

The man turned to face the corridor, and Jack got a good look at his face. He might have been handsome if not for the nasty scar where his left eyebrow should have been. In fact, the guy *had* no eyebrows, but that was not what made Jack pause.

No, it was the eyes themselves.

They were inhuman: cornea, iris and pupil replaced with a silver sheen that almost reflected the world back at whomever had the courage to gaze into them. Something about that tugged at Jack's memory – something Jena had said once – but he couldn't quite recall... *The ship!* a small voice whispered. *She fought these things on a ship near the Belos colony.*

Wesley stood over the railing with arms folded, a shit-eating grin on his face. "It's called a *ziarogat*," he said. "Even those who resist the Old Ones can be put to good use. We made them specifically for you, Jack."

"For me?"

"For you and all the other Keepers." Wesley turned, pacing a line at the edge of the landing, trailing his fingers along the railing. "It won't attack until I give the order. Total obedience. The pinnacle of military prowess."

The man – Jack refused to think of him as an *it* – just stood there, waiting patiently. Whatever Pennfield had done to him had stripped away all free will. A name! It was too easy to see this person as nothing but a mindless drone, but a name was a reminder of his humanity. But what to call him? Jack doubted he would remember anything from his old life, and there was nothing that really stood out…Except that nasty scar. Scar would have to do for now.

"Good bye, Jack," Pennfield said from above. "It's been nice sparring with you. I admit, you provided a pleasant surprise. But play time's over. Now we have to focus on more important things. *Ziarogat*, terminate."

Scar lifted his arm, revealing a metal gauntlet strapped to his wrist.

At the last second, Jack fell backward, catching himself with one hand while three slugs sped past above him. He used the other hand to lift the assault rifle and fire. Keeper strength let him hold it steady.

Bullets chewed through Scar's stomach, but instead of blood, some strange silvery liquid burst from the wounds. The man stumbled, but if the gunfire did any serious harm to him, he didn't show it.

With some help from Summer, Jack put up another Time Bubble, speeding himself up by a factor of hundreds. It seemed as if the world beyond that shimmering curtain had come to a complete stop, though Scar adjusted his aim slowly, inch by laborious inch. He had no gun. That gauntlet on his wrist would spit bullets in a three-round burst.

Jack used the extra seconds to stand and take one step to the right, putting himself out of the line of fire. Already, the tingling in his skin was becoming a painful, stinging sensation. He let the bubble drop.

Bullets flew past him.

Jack raced into the foyer, veering to the right to put himself underneath the landing. He whirled around to find Scar facing him, lifting his forum to take another shot. Jack let loose with the assault rifle.

A wall of flickering energy appeared in front of Scar, intercepting the bullets before they made contact and sending them falling to the floor. So, these things had to protect themselves. They couldn't take an endless amount of punishment. Jack ran out of ammo.

The force-field vanished.

Jack threw the rifle with all his strength.

It flew through the air at blinding speed, the stock colliding with Scar's face before he could take aim, knocking him senseless. He went stumbling away as he tried to regain his balance.

Jack ran forward.

He jumped and kicked out, driving a foot into the other man's chest. The impact sent his opponent sprawling backward, all the way to the front door. A forceful collision shattered the window, and Scar doubled over, giving Jack the few precious seconds that he needed to get close.

The *ziarogat* lifted his weapon.

Crouching down, Jack seized the man's wrist and pointed it upward just before a stream of three bullets erupted from the nozzle on that gauntlet. As if by some automated program, a rectangular cartridge slid out of the gauntlet. An empty clip.

Jack took the opportunity to punch his opponent in the face, raining blows down upon the other man. It did little good. The *ziarogat* was unfazed. Scar's knee came up, slamming into Jack's belly.

Jack went staggering backward, doubled over with one hand pressed to his chest. Breath exploded from his lungs like a raging fire. And Scar came at him with no visible sign of emotion.

The *ziarogat* spun for a hook-kick.

Jack stayed low, allowing the blow to pass right over him. He waited for the other man to come around.

Jack punched him in the chest with one fist then the other. He drew back his arm and delivered a mean right hook to Scar's cheek, a hit that landed with a gut-wrenching *crunch.* Did these things even feel pain?

Using the momentum to his advantage, Scar backed away until he was standing in front of the door again. The man raised a hand, and just like that, there was a force-field flickering in front of him. It sped forward.

Oh no… The wall of electrostatic energy slammed into Jack before he could move aside, sending a jolt that set every nerve in his body on fire. His muscles were spasming, his head spinning.

He flew backward like a leaf kicked up by the force of a tornado, thrown across the foyer all the way to the space underneath the landing. He hit the wall at full force, then dropped to the floor.

Tears blurred his vision, but he was able to catch a brief glimpse of Scar retrieving another rectangular cartridge from his belt and sliding it into the slot on his gauntlet. *Oh shit… It just never ends.*

Scar took aim.

Lying flat on his back, Jack reached out to Summer and threw up yet another Time Bubble, the world distorting, light refracting as if the whole room had been submerged in water. He used it for only a second, just long enough to roll out of the way, and then he let the bubble collapse.

Bullets hit the floor behind him.

Up above, Wesley cackled.

Anna rushed down the stairs from the monorail platform, huffing and puffing with every step. Of course, it wasn't exertion that left her winded. The call she'd received from Jena just a few minutes earlier – a frantic declaration in which the other woman revealed that the alien device they had recovered from Pennfield's warehouse was a SlipGate that had transported Jack to some unknown destination – left her out of breath. Suspension or no suspension, she wasn't going to do nothing while her friend was in danger.

At the foot of the stairs, Jena stood in the hallway with her hands shaking, watching Anna with brows drawn together. "You made it," she said. "Good. He's been gone nearly ten minutes. I don't need to tell you what that means."

"You just left that thing out in the open?" Anna spat. "No safeguards or precautions of any kind?"

Jena raised her chin, then sniffed to show her disdain. "I *left* that thing in Professor Nareo's care," she said, whirling around and starting up the hallway. "I figured he would know the potential hazards. We had nearly a dozen hazmat specialists carrying it up here from Earth. It never once reacted to any of them."

Which meant that either Jack had done something to trigger the Gate, or it was keyed to respond to him and him alone. A wave of nausea came over her when she put the pieces together. Pennfield was looking for revenge on Jack – and on her as well, it seemed – and he had left behind a piece of Overseer technology that forensic analysts would be unable to resist.

No doubt the strange organic SlipGate was how Pennfield had escaped from the warehouse while the police were closing in. She could see the basic elements of his plan. They'd take the SlipGate up to the station and study it. Jack would insist on being part of that investigation. Sooner or later, he would get close enough to activate the Gate…

They rounded a corner and started up another hallway.

Anna walked with her arms folded, staring down at herself. "We played right into his hand," she said, shaking her head. "This was exactly what Pennfield wanted, and we gave it to him."

Jena glanced over her shoulder with a frown, her expression cold enough to freeze a hardened criminal's blood. "Recriminations will get us nowhere," she snapped. "Right now, I need you to tell me everything you know about Pennfield."

"There's not much."

"I don't care. Think."

Halfway up the corridor, they came to a door on the left, a door that slid open as soon as Jena got near it. Inside, the Science Lab was a flurry of activity with Professor Nareo pacing back and forth and muttering to himself.

Raynar was squatting in front of the SlipGate, which had reverted to its previous form as a puddle of flesh. "Nothing," he said, shaking his head. "I've scanned it over and over. I can't get a sense of where it sent him."

"Get away from that!" Jena shouted.

The boy stiffened.

On the other side of the room, Aamani Patel was leaning against the wall with her eyes closed, taking deep calming breaths. What was she doing here? "A plan," she said as if speaking to herself. "There has to be a way to locate him."

"His multi-tool," Anna said, spinning on her heel to face her supervising officer. "We can use its GPS."

Squeezing her eyes shut, Jena buried her face in the palm of her hand. "We already tried that," she explained. "We've scanned the whole planet three times now and found no sign of him. Wherever he is, he's being jammed."

"Damn it!"

Pressing a hand to her stomach, Anna paced across the room. "All right," she said, stopping in front of the wall. "Think... Use your brain. Where would Pennfield take him?"

The problem was, she didn't have the slightest clue. Four years had passed since she had tangled with Wesley Pennfield, and in that time, she had barely given him a second thought. Bleakness take her, she hadn't even thought that much on him on her first visit to this planet. In was Jack who had guided her in her attempts to rescue Summer, Jack who had deduced where Pennfield might be keeping a symbiont.

She knew nothing about the man, about his assets, his contacts. Jack could be just about anywhere on the planet below. Companion have mercy, he could even be on the moon. If the Gate had linked to another of its kind on a starship, then Jack could be well on his way to another solar system.

In her mind's eye, she saw Jena pacing across the room, crouching down next to Raynar and resting a hand on his shoulder. "Kid," she said with more gentleness than Anna would have expected. "Stay away from this thing."

"But I need to scan-"

"We don't know what activates it," Jena cut in. "You might trigger something, and then I'll be looking for you too."

With a soft sigh, Raynar stood and tugged on his shirt to smooth it. He turned his back on the Gate and walked across the room. Well, that was for the best. The last thing they needed was *another* missing person.

Jena stood over the Gate with fists on her hips, shaking her head in disgust. "Not a damn thing," she growled. "I thought maybe it would react to the presence of a symbiont, but the damn thing just sits there."

The presence of a symbiont...

So, Jena was hoping that the Gate would send her wherever Jack had gone – that it would work for any Justice Keeper – but that was obviously a failed hypothesis. No, this trap had been designed for one person, one *specific* person. Pennfield had a grudge, and he wanted some alone time with Jack.

Damn it all to the Bleakness! It was a good idea. The Gate was likely programmed to send any traveler to one specific destination. If they could just find a way to activate it, they could get to Jack without needing to know where he was.

Anna spun on her heel.

She strode across the room with fists balled at her sides, head hanging in shame. "I should have been there for him," she muttered to herself. "We took on Pennfield together. The man hates both of us. I should have been working side by side with Jack, but instead, I was dealing with some *bullshit* disciplinary hearing!"

Anna froze.

Of course! That was it! Elation quickly turned to nerve-racking anxiety when she got near the Gate and felt Seth react to it. Her Nassai was nervous but also curious. Well, it only made sense that the Overseers would employ one of his kind in any technology that would bend the fabric of space-time.

Jena was crouched down in front of the puddle of veiny flesh, watching it like a hawk. So long as she stayed there, the Gate would remain dormant. Pennfield wouldn't want any unexpected company. Worse yet, Jena could sense anyone coming up behind her. This was going to be tricky.

Anna paused for half a second, just long enough to ask herself if she wanted to go through with this. If she did, it would be a direct violation of the terms of her suspension, and that could mean all sorts of nasty consequences. Possibly even the end of her career. That was exceedingly unlikely, of course – Keepers were rare enough that the directors rarely let one go no matter how badly he or she had screwed up – but it *had* happened in the past. They couldn't take her symbiont, but they *could* take her badge. That in and of itself wasn't so bad, but if Jena had the slightest inkling about what Anna was planning, she would be livid to say the least.

So…Decision time. Did she want to risk alienating her supervisor and pissing off the senior directors? Anna was proud to realize that she didn't even have to think about it. Her best friend was down there, and she was *not* going to leave him. "Jen," she said, approaching the other woman from behind.

"Hmm?"

Anna squatted down next to her supervisor, breathing out a sigh of frustration. "I just want you to know that I'm sorry." She gently laid a hand on the other woman's shoulder. "If there were any other way…"

Before the meaning of her words could sink in, Anna called upon Seth and crafted a Bending that twisted gravity. Jena was yanked backwards, pulled to the other side of the room.

That was all it took.

The puddle of flesh contorted, rising to become a triangle that stretched almost to the ceiling. Anna stood with it, watching the bubble form around her body. Her suspicion had been correct. Pennfield hated her almost as much as he hated Jack, maybe even more. The Gate had been programmed to respond to either one of them.

She turned around in time to see three blurry people rushing toward her, but it was too late. They were cut off, unable to do a damn thing to help her. And that was just fine with Anna; if she was going to die today, she didn't plan on taking anyone else with her.

She smiled as the bubble lurched forward.

Now the fun starts.

Chapter 26

Jack somersaulted across the floor tiles, scooping up a handful of fallen slugs that were still warm to the touch. He came up on one knee, then flung them at his opponent, applying a light Bending to each.

Bullets zipped across the room, slamming into Scar with enough force to kick up silver fluid from his wounds. The *ziaro-gat* stumbled, bracing himself against the ruined front door. That was what Jack needed.

He got to his feet, and exhaustion nearly knocked him right back down again. Doubling over with a hand pressed to his chest, Jack scrambled into the hallway and nearly fell flat on his face.

His vision dimmed until the SlipGate that loomed some twenty paces away faded to black only to come back in full colour. His head was swimming, and more than anything else, he wanted to lie down.

It was Summer, he realized. All that Bending had pushed her to her limits, and now she was having a hard time regulating his body's natural functions. A Keeper was the most dangerous thing this side of the Galactic Core. Until he overtaxed his Nassai, that was. After that, he was as helpless as a baby.

Scar was coming for him.

Jack braced a hand against the corridor wall, doubling over and wheezing in pain. "Keep going, Hunter," he whispered to himself, limping forward. "You're still alive, and you're going to stay that way."

Another assault rifle on the floor next to the guard who had suffocated after Jack crushed his throat. That would do. He stooped low, picking it up. Christ, why was it so damn heavy? What happened to his strength?

He turned around.

Scar stepped into the opening that led out to the foyer, his wounds leaking silver blood over that handsome muscular torso. The man's face was still a blank mask, as if he were oblivious to the damage his body had sustained. He tried to aim.

Jack didn't give him the opportunity. Lifting the assault rifle in fumbling hands, he pulled the trigger and watched as the muzzle flashed and spat a bunch of bullets. It didn't matter that his aim was terrible. Enough would hit.

Scar staggered as bullets pierced his flesh, raising one hand to shield himself. No force-field appeared to protect him. Perhaps the man had exhausted his power supply. It was good to know that Jack had pushed *him* to his limits as well.

The *ziarogat* stumbled.

With a snarl, Jack fled into the room with the SlipGate, pressing his shoulder to the wall next to the door. Every muscle in his body ached, and his skin was on fire. The dizziness made him want to pass out.

Jack squeezed his eyes shut, sucking air into his lungs. "Come on," he said, shaking his head. "You can do better than this! Are you just gonna leave Anna to take on Slade all by herself?"

Footsteps in the hallway.

It took some willpower, but Jack ventured a glance around the corner, popping out just long enough to catch a glimpse of the other man shuffling toward him on a wounded leg. Scar's wounds were knitting themselves, the holes in his chest slowly closing. Still, it seemed as though the *ziarogat* had been weakened.

Jack ducked back into cover.

He closed his eyes, tilting his head back. Breathing slowly, he tried to calm himself. *Focus… The guy is wounded. You just have to surprise him when he tries to come in here, and then…*

And then what? He had some hope that he might be able to take down Scar, but that still left Pennfield. And while Jack was exhausted, pushed to the point of nearly passing out, Wesley was fresh as a daisy. The shuffling sounds grew louder.

Scar poked his head through the door.

Jack slammed the rifle into his face, knocking him back into the hallway. The man lost his balance, toppling over sideways until his shoulder hit the corridor wall. He tried to stand, but that wounded leg made him falter.

Now! Finish it!

Jack opened fire.

Gunshots echoed from below, but Wesley remained calm, waiting on the landing for the grisly affair to play out. From what little he had seen – and that wasn't much; only a fool poked his head into the open when bullets were flying in all directions – it was clear that Hunter was overtaxed. The boy had retreated into the corridor, leaving Wesley's dutiful servant to chase after him.

Wesley suppressed a grin – he had been far too free with his emotions lately – and found his calm centre. The icy mountaintop at the core of his being. A lesser man would have been tempted to go down there. A lesser man would have reasoned that two against one ensured a better chance of victory, but that was the product of a mind with no talent for strategy. Why risk his own life when his proxy could do the job just as well? A stray bullet was as deadly to him as it was to anyone else, and the ability to Bend space-time would not save him from a moment of distraction. Wesley was not afraid to get his hands dirty – the Old Ones had no use for cowards – but he had not survived five centuries of conflict by giving in to his passions.

The *ziarogat* was expendable; better to let it suffer the brunt of Hunter's fury. One way or another, things would play out in Wesley's favour. Either the *ziarogat* would end Hunter – in which case, it might be salvaged to be used again another day – or Hunter would emerge victorious. Even if that happened, the boy would be so weakened by the experience that he would make easy prey.

Best to wait.

A wise man was always patient.

Scar stumbled when a hole appeared in his skull, and silver blood spattered against the wall behind him. The *ziarogat* shuffled about for half a moment, then slowly sank to the floor, leaving a trail of blood on the plaster.

Closing his eyes, Jack let his head hang. He mopped a hand over his face. "That's it," he whispered. "Sorry, friend, but you weren't leaving me with a lot of options."

He wondered whether this should count as another tick-mark on his scorecard. *Had* he killed Scar? Or had the man inside that monster died a long time ago? No way for him to be certain, and he decided that he was *not* going to torture himself over it. Jack Hunter had enough on his plate already.

He turned back to the Gate.

Dealing with Pennfield would have to wait; he was in no condition to fight. The smartest move would be to get out of here as soon as possible, and that meant taking the Bubble Express back to Station Twelve. Or anywhere else.

A few quick taps at his multi-tool nixed that plan in short order. The Gate wouldn't respond to his commands. Brilliant! Wesley had decided to make him the guest of honour at a very special party, and there was no leaving until the festivities were over.

The front door.

He started up the hallway.

Jack winced, his head aching from the exertion. "Pennfield's gonna rip you to pieces," he whispered to himself. "But hey! At least you'll get a few good taunts in."

A whirring sound behind him made him turn around just in time to see the grooves on the SlipGate's metal surface light up with a furious glow. *Oh no!* A bubble expanded from out of nothing, and he could just make out a figure inside.

It popped, revealing Anna in a pair of black dress pants and a red, short-sleeved blouse, her head hanging. "Jack," she said, looking up at him. "Oh thank the Companion you're safe."

She rushed forward.

Her eyes widened when she noticed the assault rifle he carried, and then she turned her head to inspect the damage to the walls. "Quite the party," she muttered. "And...What in Bleakness is *that?*"

She was looking at the smear of silver blood that Scar had left when he dropped to the floor. "It's a long story," Jack answered, noticing the way his voice grated for the first time. "Pennfield's here, and he's trying to kill me."

Anna looked up at him with big blue eyes, blinking as though his words took a second to sink in. "You've overtaxed yourself." It wasn't a question. "Stay here. I'll deal with our dear friend Wesley."

"I can help."

Crossing her arms with a sigh, Anna gave him the kind of scowl he was used to seeing on his mother. "Really?" she asked, raising an eyebrow. "You're going to help, are you?"

"Yeah..."

"No. In your current condition, you're more likely to get me killed." Just like that, she was striding past him, making her way toward the foyer. "Stay."

"All right."

She turned back to him, then came over and hugged him for all she was worth. "It's okay," she whispered, guiding him to the wall where he could rest. "I won't let him hurt you. I will never let *anyone* hurt you."

He believed her. There was no doubt in his mind that she meant every single word of it, and the warmth it brought to his heart was so bright it eclipsed the aches and pains throughout his body. For a few seconds anyway. "Do you want this?" Jack asked, lifting the rifle for her inspection.

Anna frowned, then lowered her eyes to the floor. "No," she said softly. "I won't leave you defenseless. You never know who might come through the SlipGate or from somewhere else in this house."

He was going to argue, but he knew better than to try. When Anna made up her mind that she was going to be noble, your only option was to get out of her way. It was one of the things he loved about her. "Good luck," he said.

"Stay safe."

The foyer in this rather large house would have been gorgeous even to someone with her Leyrian sensibilities if not for the bullet holes in the floor tiles and the front door that was a shattered wreck of its former glory. The cream-coloured walls were scarred in several places.

To her right, curving stairs rose up to a landing that was lit primarily by daylight that came in from the front door. Pennfield was up there somewhere. Anna's blood was boiling – *no one* hurt the people she loved – but you would never know it to look at her. She was a painter, a chef, an artist in all things, and battle was no different. It had taken several years of bringing in violent criminals for her to come to a simple understanding: she was *good* at this.

Craning her neck, Anna pursed her lips as she stared up at the landing. *I've fought in weirder places,* she thought, her eyebrows rising. *Besides, it will be all sorts of fun to wreck Wesley's nice things.*

She started up the stairs.

At the top, she found a carpeted area where a leather couch was propped up against the railing that overlooked the foyer and a hallway branched off in two directions. Of all things, there were masks hung up on the wall. African tribal masks unless she missed her guess. And swords.

One was long and elegant with an ornate crossguard and a blade that was edged on both sides. A rapier? Was that what it was called? The other was of Japanese design, with a single edge and a blade that curved ever so slightly. She had forgotten the name for this weapon, but on closer inspection, she noticed a smaller version of it hung on the wall.

Wesley emerged from the hallway, smoothing the jacket of his fine, gray suit and frowning at her. "My, my," he said, striding into the open space. "I wasn't expecting you, but I suppose we had to meet sooner or later."

Anna thrust her chin out, squinting at the man. "Not happy to see me, Wes?" she asked in a singsong voice. "That's funny because I've been meaning to say hello. I never did thank you for shooting me."

Wesley showed her an ugly rictus smile, his face turning a deep, violent red. "I'll do more than shoot you this time, girl." He turned slightly, grabbing the rapier's hilt and gently lifting it off its mounting. "This time I intend to gut you."

"Really? We're gonna sword fight?"

Pennfield lifted the weapon up in front of his face, perfectly in line with his nose. "It's a sport I've kept up with," he said, flowing toward her. "I was once acclaimed as a master swordsman; did you know that?"

Anna dove, slapping her palms down on the carpet and rising into a handstand. She quickly flipped upright near the back wall, grabbing the Japanese sword before Wesley could get too close.

The cockiness she'd felt down below quickly evaporated. Pennfield had strength and reflexes to match her own, and he was actually *trained* in this form of combat. Anna had never bothered to learn fencing; why would she? What use would a Justice Keeper have for bladed melee weapons. *Why didn't I take the assault rifle?*

She turned.

Wesley was standing at the mouth of the hallway with his sword raised in a guarded stance, watching her as if he expected her to spit fire. "Well then," he murmured. "This might actually be fun."

Quickly, she ran through everything she knew about sword fighting. *Don't block a strike with the edge of your blade. It creates nicks. Always use the flat side.* And…that was it. Bleakness take her.

The grin on her opponent's face told her that this had been one of his contingencies. Pennfield was a man who liked to have an advantage. He seldom went for the kill unless he knew he would find an easy victory. In a straight up fistfight, they would at least be evenly matched, and there was a good chance that Anna would take him down. After all, she *did* this on a regular basis. Pennfield avoided a fight whenever possible.

He flowed toward her with impeccable grace: a lion on the hunt. The only thing Anna could think to do was lift her weapon in both hands and hope that the ferocious pounding of her heart wouldn't be a distraction.

Wesley swung at her neck.

Anna brought her weapon up. Blade met blade with a harsh, clear ring, and she turned his sword aside. She spun and back-kicked, driving a foot into Wesley's stomach. The impact sent him stumbling backward.

Anna rounded on him.

She jumped and brought her blade down like a headsman's ax, a swift vertical arc that made the air whistle. Wesley lifted his sword horizontally, catching her attack at the very last second, dazing her while she landed.

He kicked her in the chest, knocking her off balance. Winded by the sudden jolt, Anna wheezed and doubled over in pain. She needed a few seconds to recover, but that gleaming blade was already coming at her. So, she did the only thing she could.

With Seth's help, she threw up a bubble that accelerated the flow of time around her and left the world outside a frozen still-life where every heartbeat lasted minutes from her perspective. The blurry image of Wesley stood with one leg lifted, his blade inching its way toward the surface of her bubble.

Anna hopped back.

She let the bubble vanish and watched the tip of Wesley's blade pass within inches of her shirt, almost close enough to cut fabric. The man was over-extended, his middle left unguarded.

Anna stabbed at his belly.

The tip of her blade drew blood, but Wesley flowed backwards with a serpentine grace, enhanced reflexes allowing him to keep pace with her thrust. In the end, it was only a flesh wound.

Stoking the rage within her, Anna advanced on him. Their swords met in a flurry of cuts, each strike and parry producing a soft ringing sound that echoed through the house. Wesley performed some kind of twirling motion, ripping the sword right out of her hands and sending it tumbling over his head to land behind him.

Falling over backward, Anna slapped her hands down on carpet and brought one leg up to kick him in the chest. A wheeze exploded from his lungs as Wesley stumbled backward, giving her the few seconds she needed.

She snapped herself upright.

Anna dove past him, somersaulting across the floor. She came up on her knees, then quickly recovered her fallen weapon and lifted it over her head, the blade parallel to her spine.

Just in time to stop a cut that would have sliced through the back of her neck. With a throaty growl, Anna flung her blade upward in a vertical arc and tore the rapier out of Wesley's hands.

She got up and spun around in time to see Wesley dancing backward across the landing, positioning himself under his sword as it fell and catching it with smooth grace. A sly smile spread on his face.

Anna charged at him.

The next thing she saw was a gleaming length of metal coming for her eyes. She ducked and felt the blade pass over her head. Then she swung at his legs.

That should have incapacitated him, but Wesley jumped with inhuman height, and her swing went underneath him. He landed right in front of her, then brought the pommel of his sword down on her head.

Silver flecks filled her vision, and she moved backward as quickly as her legs could carry her, putting some distance between herself and her opponent. Spatial awareness let her sense Wesley's approach.

Anna was moving backward through the corridor, toward the bedrooms, and she was quite dizzy. Vertigo brought with it an urge to empty her stomach right there on the expensive gray carpet. *You have to stay alert,* a small voice whispered. *Give him even the tiniest opening, and he'll slaughter you.*

Her opponent chuckled softly as he followed her into the hallway. "Not bad, girl," he said with a shrug of his shoulders. "Better than I would have expected, though your success comes by the fact that you refuse to play by the rules."

The rules?

Her vision cleared, blurring colours resolving into the image of Wesley coming at her with the rapier held at his side, its blade pointed down at the carpet. What rules was she supposed to be following? Pennfield considered himself a swordsman. He had been doing this for some time…which meant that his thinking was structured by the years of practice. No traditional swordsman would have access to a Nassai's abilities. You would never see Time Bubbles and acrobatics in a true fencing match.

At last, she understood. Pennfield wanted her to stand her ground and swing her arm about like a *civilized* opponent, countering every cut with a skillful parry and then a riposte. Well, fuck that! It was Pennfield's biggest weakness, she realized. He was a man who had grown used to seeing the world in a very specific light. He knew his place and the place of everyone beneath him. Four years ago, she and Jack had upended his world, and that more than anything else produced the visceral hatred he held for both of them.

"You will never destroy me, girl," Wesley said, twirling the sword with nimble fingers. A full turn one way and then another in the opposite direction. "Even now, I can see it in your eyes. You want to be the good little Keeper. You want to bring me to justice so that I can stand before my accusers and accept the punishment deemed appropriate by your sad little society."

Wesley paused, bracing his free hand against the wall, hanging his head with a soft sigh. "You'll never kill me, Anna," he said. "You're too gentle and pure. Too enamoured with the foolish customs of your benighted little world."

His laughter stoked her rage, producing a furious flame in her chest that threatened to rip right through her. "You Leyrians think yourselves the pinnacle of civilization," he went on. "You are nothing! Dust before the storm of the Old Ones!"

The grin returned to Wesley's face: a vicious, predatory smile that promised agonies beyond imagining once he got his hands on her. "You know what will happen if you try to imprison me?"

he asked. "The Old Ones will free me as they did last time. Then I will find you and kill you. I'll kill Hunter as well. And your family, and *his* family. Unlike the pawns I've sent against you, I have eternities to act. I have the patience to ensure that my gambits strip away that which is most precious to you.

"I am not Leo, raging against the confines of his cell, struggling in impotent fury to exact his vengeance. I am calm, cool and collected. My name is Wesley Pennfield, and no one takes from me! Slade was wrong about you, girl. Everything you know and love will die because you lack the stomach to do what is necessary!"

Anna screamed, charging at him.

Seconds later, she realized that had been a mistake. The whole speech had been designed to leave her blind with rage, to exploit an emotional weakness that would allow Pennfield to slip past her defenses.

Wesley was a whirlwind, slicing and cutting, forcing her to rely on every precious millisecond her enhanced reflexes could give her. A storm of metal flashed through the hallway, blade ringing against blade, and each riposte came closer and closer to opening Anna's veins. She couldn't keep this up. *He's forcing you to play his game*, she realized. *Don't let him. Don't play by his rules.*

Anna jumped and kicked out, planting a foot in the man's chest. She pushed off and back-flipped through the air, uncurling to land poised in the middle of the hallway. That little stunt left Wesley off balance.

He was doubled over, wheezing.

Anna rushed forward, trying to stab him through the chest, but his blade came up and casually flicked hers aside. Her sword went into the wall; so she let it go rather than wasting seconds trying to pull it free.

Using her momentum, Anna spun for a hook-kick, her foot whirling around to strike Wesley across the cheek. The man went stumbling sideways, slamming his shoulder into the wall and groaning on impact.

Anna dropped to a crouch.

She punched him in the gut with one fist then the other, then laced her fingers and brought them up to strike the underside of Pennfield's chin. Her opponent threw his head back with a painful shriek.

Growling under her breath, Anna dug her sword out of the wall. She thrust it forward, sliding the blade home through Wesley's chest with enough force to pierce his rib-cage, all the way through his heart.

Pennfield's eyes widened behind his glasses.

He doubled over, revealing a length of red blade sticking out of his back, then sank to his knees. "It's not possible," he croaked, "You… You… You… don't have the stomach to do what is… " His words cut off with one final, pitiful gasp.

Anna stood over him with arms folded, frowning down at his corpse. "I think you'll find," she began, "that you don't know the first damn thing about me, Wesley Pennfield. Give the Bleakness my regards."

Chapter 27

On the second floor, they found a door that led out to a balcony with a wide stone railing that overlooked a sandy beach. The crystal blue waters of a vast ocean – Anna wasn't sure which one, but it was clear they were someplace tropical – lapped at the shoreline with a soft, sighing sound.

Jack was sitting with his back pressed against the railing, legs stretched out before him as he tried to recover his strength. "Lovely vacation spot," he said, lifting a bottle of water that he'd pilfered from Wesley's fridge. "Just perfect for romantic moonlit strolls, sun-bathing and, oh yeah, murder!"

Anna closed her eyes, hanging her head. "We'll be all right," she said, sitting on the railing across from him. "After all, we've been through a lot worse than this. Remember those damn battle drones?"

Jack smiled, his face flushed and glistening with sweat. "Yeah, that was pretty bad," he said, rubbing at his eyes. "But it's got nothing on the horrors of a Hunter family Christmas dinner."

"Ugh! Don't remind me!"

"So, what now?"

Anna got up and paced across the balcony with her arms folded, pausing to stare out at the horizon. "I've been trying to find whatever Pennfield used to jam our multi-tools," she said. "No luck."

The beach stretched on as far as she could see, and to the best of her knowledge, this was the only house within half a kilometer. No one would have heard the gunfire; there was little chance of the local police showing up. On the plus side, the fridge and pantry were both full of food, and there were cars in the garage.

Anna knelt down before him with hands folded over her belly, staring into her lap. "When you feel better, we'll go for a drive," she said. "I figure once we get far enough from this house, we can call Jena."

Jack replied with a small smile, and then his head sank until his chin touched his chest. "Always positive, An," he muttered, lifting the water bottle as if in a toast. "That's what I love about you."

"How are you feeling?"

"My skin's not on fire anymore."

Closing her eyes, Anna turned her face up to the warm sunlight. "Good," she said with a curt nod. "That means you're recovering. If you're not in pain, then you're not in any danger."

A grin blossomed that she could not smother, and she hid it behind her fingertips. "Listen to me," she murmured. "Still talking to you like this is all new to you. I think you proved yourself in there."

Jack looked up at her with eyes that were narrowed to slits, pausing for a moment before he spoke. "You're kidding, right?" he asked in a strained voice. "Just look at me! I don't see *you* on the verge of passing out."

"I didn't have to rely on Bendings to keep me alive," she countered. "If we had switched opponents, I'd be where you are now." Or worse, she realized. Some of the best Keepers she knew would have been overwhelmed by that monstrosity Jack fought. After checking the house to ensure there were no further surprises, she'd gone back down to the hallway to scan that thing with her multi-tool.

Its blood was some kind of technorganic compound, filled with microscopic semi-organic nanobots that could repair damaged tissue. Its brain was half flesh, half circuitry, and whatever they had done it had increased both strength and durability.

As usual, Jack failed to give himself enough credit. The very fact that he was still breathing after fighting that thing was an accomplishment in and of itself. "We'll need to get a forensics team down here."

When she looked up, Jack was watching her with those gorgeous blue eyes of his. Somehow, he could always see past her defenses. "How are you doing?" he asked. "After Pennfield, I mean… Do you feel… "

Anna sucked on her lower lip, a lock of red hair falling over her face. She brushed it away with one hand. "That's the crazy thing," she said softly. "I'm strangely okay with what happened."

Why *was* she so calm?

Shouldn't there be an ache in her chest that no amount of comforting words could soothe? Was she in shock? The only thing she felt right then was physical exhaustion, and, Companion have mercy, was she actually *proud* of what she'd done?

After a moment of reflection, she realized that it wasn't exactly pride, per se, but rather a certainty that she had done the right thing. Pennfield would have overwhelmed her if she didn't put him down permanently, and then he would have gone for Jack. Even if they somehow managed to dump him back into a cell, he had demonstrated the ability to escape before. His final words had signed his death warrant.

Pennfield was right; he *wasn't* Leo. This trap was well thought-out, meticulously planned and absolutely deadly. Even with most of his assets seized, his resources severely diminished, the man was still a threat. Anna refused to accept any line of reasoning that insisted someone was too dangerous to be left alive – once you start down that road, it becomes far too easy to justify murder – but if an enemy threw himself against you with no remorse, insisted that it was you or him with no possibility of compromise, if he made it clear that it wasn't just *your* life he intended to take but those of hundreds of innocents as well… "I feel unreasonably good about it."

"Good," Jack replied. "I'm glad. Because, Anna, you are the most moral person I know, and you did the right thing."

Anna shut her eyes tight, a single tear rolling over her cheek. "Here I am blathering on about myself," she whispered, "when you had to take a life as well. I'm so sorry, Jack. But it wasn't your fault."

He looked up, and for a moment, there was something dangerous in his eyes; then his expression softened. "You killed a monster," Jack said. "I killed a man. Karmically speaking, your soul is better off than mine."

Anna crawled over to him.

The next thing she knew, her cheek was pressed to his shoulder, her eyes shut tight as she let her guard down. Every muscle in her body relaxed. Jack's hand cupped the back of her head, holding her close.

And that was when she let herself really contemplate it. For a while there, she had held out some hope that she would go through her whole career without ever having to take a life. A shame, but she didn't hate herself for it. That was something. And Jack still thought she was wonderful.

She would always protect him, but it surprised her to realize how safe she felt in his arms, how comforting it was to know that he would always protect *her* as well. As equals, fighting side by side. She let herself melt into the embrace…

…For a few blessed moments.

Then reality reasserted itself, and she pulled away from him. This, this was a little more intimacy than two friends ought to have, and she had commitments to keep, promises she had made to another. It was time to stop indulging childish fantasies.

Anna looked up, strands of hair falling over her face. She blinked several times. "Come on," she said, her voice barely audible. "I think it's time that we got out of here, don't you?"

A metal railing overlooked the concourse on Station Twelve, a bustling area where dozens of people walked across the black floor tiles, some stopping in at the restaurants or fabrication stations on either wall, others making their way to the set of stairs that led up to the monorail platform. Automated restaurants, automated fabrication stations that required no money: the Leyrians offered a new way of life. She had to admit that scared her more than she would like.

Gripping the railing in both hands, Aamani leaned over to peer down at the people below. She still wore her blue pantsuit, but she was tired and the long black hair that she usually wore pulled back in a clip was slightly mussed.

What exactly was she doing here? Her instincts told her that coming here had been a mistake – the Leyrians couldn't be trusted – but everything Jack had said back in that warehouse made perfect sense. Her rational brain told her that the young man had been spot on on every point, and when confronted with logic vs emotion, Aamani Patel took pride in choosing logic every time. But she rarely had such difficulty reconciling the two. So why was this time different? Perhaps she should return to-

"Excuse me."

Aamani stiffened.

Hunching up her shoulders with a soft hiss, she trembled as a shiver went through her body. "My apologies," she said, turning around. "Usually, I'm not so easily startled. It's been a stressful day."

The young boy from the Science Lab – Raynar? – stood before her in a pair of beige khaki pants and a blue button-up shirt that he left untucked. His short blonde hair was parted in the middle, falling to the nape of his neck.

Raynar closed his eyes and bowed his head, breathing deeply through his nose. "I'm sorry to disturb you," he said, approaching cautiously. "But we need to speak before you return to the surface."

Aamani leaned against the railing with her arms crossed, watching him for a very long moment. "All right," she said. "You've got my attention. So, what would you like to discuss with me?"

The boy sighed, refusing to look up at her. He gripped a handful of his own hair. "When I touched your mind to show you the data from the Overseer device...I sensed something."

Aamani felt her mouth tighten despite her best efforts. "If you've read my thoughts without permission..."

"No, not that!"

"Then what?"

The boy had large gray eyes, and he blinked slowly as he studied her. "I cannot be certain without a deep scan," he said, stepping forward. "But your emotions have been influenced by a telepath."

"What?"

"Someone is manipulating you, ma'am."

She felt cold inside, as if she'd been stabbed through the heart with an icicle. How? What little she knew of the galaxy beyond this solar system said that telepaths were only found in Antauran Space. A genetic quirk of some kind in their evolution. She had never imagined that one might be here.

But of course, that was their greatest weapon, wasn't it? The vision unfolded before her with chilling clarity. Conquering Earth by military might would be impossible so long as the Leyrians remained in this system, but a full-scale military strike was often the last resort of a good tactician. How much easier would it be to simply "nudge" events in the right direction, and if you had access to agents who could perform mind control...

Aamani scowled, shaking her head in disgust. "Perform the scan," she said, stepping up to the boy. "Do whatever you need to do, and do it quickly, before I change my mind. If you are correct…"

Raynar touched her forehead.

It was not nearly as painful as she would have expected, merely a sense of another presence. As if she had been alone all her life only to discover for the first time at the age of forty-three that someone else existed in her universe. She understood Raynar in a way that she had understood few other people. It was…

…Over. As quickly as he had come into her thoughts, he vanished from them, and the profound understanding went with him. As if she had forgotten most of what she'd learned in those few seconds.

Blushing hard, the young man squeezed his eyes shut. He turned his head so that she could only see him in profile. "It's true," he said softly. "You've been influenced by a telepath. Many times."

"How can you tell?"

"It's not something that is easily expressed in words," he said. "Human emotions are smooth; they blend together naturally. When someone tweaks them, influences them against their natural inclination, they become jagged. The stronger the tweak, the more noticeable the change.

"What they did to you was subtle: just a few nudges here and there, but…" Raynar turned, gesturing with his hands to show two paths diverging from a single point. "When an object is in space, and you nudge it just a centimetre, thirty thousand years from now, it ends up lightyears away from where it would have been if you'd left it alone. A small nudge, and the choice you might have made one time out of a hundred suddenly becomes the most probable outcome."

"And this was done to me?" Aamani whispered. "When? How? Most importantly, *who* did this to me?"

"There's no way to know."

Raynar strode past her, folding his arms on the railing and leaning over it to watch the people below. "Telepaths develop a…a style, I guess you could say." He seemed to be having trouble with the language. Perhaps English lacked the words to express what he was feeling. "Whoever did this to you, I've never seen their work before."

The anxiety that had tied her stomach in knots intensified. It could be anyone, and that meant guarding against it was going to be exceedingly difficult. Aamani sighed. She needed allies…and that meant she would have to do something she would rather avoid.

But first…

"I'll pay you well for an hour of your time, Raynar," she said. "I want you to teach me how to guard against it."

Dressed in black slacks and a gray sweater with a round neck, Jena strode across the room like a meteor on course for some miserable little planet, making her way toward a table where three senior Justice Keeper sat by side, watching her. The same three who had pronounced judgment on Anna just yesterday. Jena had a few choice words of her own for the girl, but in the end, she understood. What else could Anna do? You didn't leave a loved one to suffer at the hands of a psychopath. Now, if only those two could finally admit what they really felt for each other.

Glin Karon wore a sad expression as he looked up to meet her eyes. Next to him, Tiassa Navram was leaning over the table, scanning through something on her tablet. And then there was Kaydie Cadanzar. Cold, implacable Kaydie Cadanzar. Getting a read on her was next to impossible.

Jena refused to slow down.

Harry and Anna walked side by side behind her, flanked by Jack and Melissa, with Raynar and Gabi bringing up the rear. They had dragged in every last one of her people, even the ones who didn't actually work for her. That left her feeling anxious, but Jena had a few good tricks up her sleeve.

Tiassa stood up, her statuesque face framed by long blonde hair that fell over her shoulders. "Now then," she said, running her gaze over the lot of them. "We can finally get started. The question of your competence has been raised more than once, Director Morane. Your people seem to have a knack for causing trouble."

Kaydie sat with her hands folded in her lap, frowning down at the table's surface. "What's more," she added. "After being removed from active duty, one of your officers decided that she would ignore her suspension and pursue a dangerous criminal."

Jena forced a small smile, hanging her head in frustration. "That's all you got?" she asked, her eyebrows climbing. "Lenai acted to save the life of one of her fellow officers, and you're upset because, on paper, she didn't have authority to do so?"

"This is no laughing matter," Glin cut in.

"This latest incident shows a trend of insubordination." Leaning forward with her hands braced on the table, Tiassa stared her down. "The very first officer you recruited was suspended from duty at the time."

"By order of a traitor."

The other woman carried on as if Jena hadn't spoken, shaking her head in disgust the whole time. "Half of your so-called team consists of people who don't even carry a symbiont. You openly consort with enemies of the state." Raynar stiffened at that. "And you've even brought a *child* into your council."

In her mind's eye, Jena watched the silhouette of Melissa flinch and back away as if she'd been slapped. The poor girl. Not the best way to start her relationship with her future bosses. "A child who will one day be an incredible Justice Keeper," Jena insisted. "And if you have a problem with me building bridges, then I humbly suggest that you don't know how to do your jobs."

A flush set Jena's cheeks on fire, but she ignored it, hissing softly with every breath. "We need to establish trust with the people of Earth," she went on. "That means working side by side with them."

Jena turned slightly, gesturing to the people behind her. "You don't like working with Antaurans?" It was hard to keep the venom from her voice. She didn't even try. "I don't like war. So maybe if people like you were a little more willing to compromise, we wouldn't have to keep fighting each other."

The only one who seemed affected by that was Glin, and he showed it only by staring vacantly down at the table. Kaydie was as unreadable as ever; she just sat there, taking it all in. But Tiassa...

The woman crossed arms in front of her chest, stood up straight and spoke like a queen pronouncing judgment. "Be that as it may," she began, "Your team has become an unstable element in this organization, and we believe that-"

Lifting her forearm, Jena tapped away at the screen of her multi-tool. It was time to play her hand and hope for the best. A pair of holograms appeared before her – black text on a white background – one oriented so that she could read it, the other facing the three senior directors.

"Director Morane's team operates under my authority," Jena began. "And it is my intention that they should continue their efforts unhindered. Though unconventional, their methods have proven effective on many occasions. Agent Lenai is to complete her three-week suspension and return to duty without further punishment. You may be assured that Director Morane and her team have my complete confidence.

"Signed: Larani Tal, Chief Director of the Justice Keepers on the second day of Azaran, 752 NA."

Jena let her arm drop, the holograms vanishing to reveal three stunned faces staring at her like cats peering through a basement window. Everyone was speechless. They had not expected that little trick. Well, she deserved a little awestruck confusion after all that. Securing Larani's support had been easy enough once she got a hold of the woman. One advantage to her team's somewhat tarnished reputation was the fact that no one would suspect them of being part of Slade's little cabal.

Larani had told her what she'd learned from the woman who had tried to kill Ben. Moles in the Justice Keepers, traitors eating away at their organization from the inside. People with symbionts that no longer demanded any kind of accountability. In a climate like that, it was hard to trust anyone. Larani opposed Slade; Jena opposed Slade. That made them allies for the moment.

Tiassa drew herself up to full height, standing behind the table with arms folded, her face a mask of bitter resentment. "Larani Tal can't protect you forever," she threatened. "Sooner or later, you're going to have to account for yourself."

Grinning ferociously, Jena looked up at the ceiling. "That may be so," she said, nodding to the other woman. "But for the moment, I think we've wasted enough time on this hearing, don't you?"

She turned to go.

Her people followed her direction, Anna and Harry spinning around and following Jack, Melissa and Gabi to the door. One more battle over. One more check mark in her column of victories. The sad reality about fighting the good fight was one that very few people stated out loud: sooner or later, you lost. Sooner or later, the people who greased the gears that kept the engines of corruption turning would bring institutional power against you. On that day, you would go down.

All you could really do is last as long as you can.

Raindrops slid down the window pane in what was now Ben's living room, the gray light of an overcast afternoon leaving a gloomy feeling that almost made him want to turn on the lights. Almost. His new dwellings were simple; this tiny house in the residential zone of Denabria had been assigned to him just one week ago. The courts had decided that he wasn't a dangerous criminal, and so he was allowed a private residence so long as he stayed within city limits during his rehabilitation.

Through the rain-streaked window, he saw the green grass of his lawn and a line of trees that marked the edge of the property. One of the small, rectangular robots was busy trimming the grass despite the lousy weather.

Ben sat on a sofa, bent over with arms pressed to his stomach. A grimace twisted his features. *Stuck here for three months,* he lamented. *Unable to call anyone off-world. Darrel probably thinks I abandoned him.*

Gloominess suited him just now.

Ben stood and shuffled over to the window, pausing there for a very long while. *It could be worse,* he reminded himself for the hundredth time. *Weapons' smugglers usually get a stiffer punishment.*

A knock at the door.

"Come in!"

To his left, the front door swung open, allowing a half-soaked Larani Tal to step inside and close her umbrella. If Ben had been the sort of man who preferred women, he would certainly have preferred Larani. She was tall and reed-slender with dark chocolate-brown skin and long black hair that she wore in a ponytail. It was a mess at the moment, but that only added to her beauty.

Larani closed her eyes, exhaling slowly. "You'll forgive me for intruding on your quiet reflection," she said, approaching the open doorway where the foyer met the living room. "I thought we should talk."

Ben spun to face her.

He felt his mouth tighten, then bowed his head to her. "I'm taking it you've had no luck with Calissa." Mentioning the woman left a sick feeling in his stomach. "She's still making threats and grand boasts."

"To say the least." Larani glanced from side to side, looking for a place to hang her coat, and when she found none, she simply shrugged out of it and folded it over one arm. "I've received news from Earth. Wesley Pennfield is dead."

Covering his lips with three fingers, Ben squinted up at the floor. "I feel like I should know that name," he mumbled to himself. "He was involved in the case that led Anna to Earth, right?"

Larani stood before him with her arms folded, her eyes downcast as if this subject had become a source of personal shame. "From what we can tell, Pennfield was running a smuggling ring that trafficked in symbionts. Which brings me to my next point."

"Calissa's ominous predictions."

"Yes. I don't suppose I could trouble you for a cup of tea."

Ben was more than happy to oblige her – after all, it wasn't every day that you got a visit from the Head of the Justice Keepers – and besides, the mail bots had just delivered his groceries, and he had more than enough to spare.

About ten minutes later, Larani was sitting in the big comfy chair with both hands cradling the cup that she balanced in her lap, steam wafting up toward her face. "I have your friends looking into the symbiont they recovered from Pennfield," she said softly. "Trying to determine how he was able to circumvent the checks a Nassai would usually insist upon."

Standing in front of the window with his arms crossed, Ben frowned down at the floor. "Have they come up with anything useful?" he murmured. "Maybe even some way we might *test* each Keeper for the presence of an evil Nassai?"

"Nothing yet."

"Well, damn it."

Larani looked up at him with a solemn expression, daylight reflected in her large dark eyes. "The fact is, Tanaben," she began. "There is simply no way to know precisely how many of my agents have been compromised."

Ben squeezed his eyes shut, trembling as he drew in a long breath. "Right," he said with a curt nod. "So now you're desperate, and you can't even order one of your people to investigate because you don't know if he's one of Slade's moles."

"Trust is a valuable commodity."

"So what makes you trust me?"

In response, Larani sat back in the chair and lifted her cup in two hands. She took a long, slow sip. "I trust you because Jack trusts you," she said simply. "And that man has an impeccable moral compass.

"So, until further notice, you're working for me. Unofficially at first, but I'm going to pull every string I can to somehow get you reinstated with the LIS. Once you complete your 'rehabilitation,' I'm sending you back to Earth because I need *every last resource* I have pointed directly at Grecken Slade. You may not be a Justice Keeper, but I can count on one hand the number of people I trust right now. So, I'm stuck with you."

"You certainly know how to fill a man with confidence," Ben muttered. Of course, if he had half the brains he claimed to have, he would shut up and take the offer. It was a chance to get back to Darrel. Just thinking of his partner facing down that awful family of his without any support from Ben was a knife in his chest.

"In the meantime," Larani went on, "you are going to become the very *definition* of a reformed convict. You will attend every therapy session, deduce precisely what your councilor wants to hear and say exactly that with such conviction that jaded cynics would *weep* at the sincerity in your voice. You will abide by the terms of your parole, remaining inside the city limits at all times unless authorized to do otherwise. And finally, you will express a fervent support of Leyrian foreign policy that borders on jingoism. Do you have a problem with any of this, Mr. Loranai?"

"No, ma'am."

"Then I can count on you?" she asked with a raised eyebrow.

"Yeah," Ben said. "You can count on me."

Chapter 28

The sun was high in the clear blue sky, shining down on a street lined with small, one-story houses. Just two lanes of black asphalt and no sidewalk. Deep ditches on either side would allow quite the nasty fall to anyone who wasn't careful.

Melissa walked with a hand pressed to her stomach, head hanging as she let out a deep breath. "We could really kick up trouble with this one," she said, glancing over her shoulder. "Amanda's father isn't going to like it."

At her side, Jena strolled casually up the street in a pair of denim shorts and a blue tank top. She wore a blank expression, her face unreadable, but the wind played with her short auburn hair. "One thing you learn in this business, kid," she murmured. "You can't be afraid to piss off assholes who abuse their power."

Melissa smiled down at the road, unable to suppress a chuckle. "Very true," she said. "But even if this works, Amanda still has to live with the man for at least three more months, so…"

Not far ahead, another street intersected with this one, and Melissa could see that at least some of the houses there were a little bigger, the cars in each driveway a little more expensive. The text she'd received from Amanda said that the girl was babysitting at one of the houses on that street, making this an ideal time to catch her without worrying about her father's interference.

After turning the corner, she realized that the homes here were much larger and newer. In a small town like Manchester, there wasn't much of a divide between poor neighbourhoods and richer ones.

By a twist of luck, she spotted Amanda coming up the street in a blue dress with short sleeves. The girl shuffled along with her arms folded, her eyes fixed on the ground right in front of her.

"Hey!" Melissa called out.

Amanda looked up, blinking. "Hi!" she exclaimed, picking up the pace to join them on the corner. "Michael's father got back early; so he sent me home. Paid me a full night's fee, though."

"Sometimes luck goes your way."

Jena stepped forward, thrusting out her hand in greeting. The bright smile on her face would have made even the most insecure person feel at ease. Melissa wished she could do that. "Hello, Amanda. I'm Jena Morane."

"Nice to meet you."

They shook hands, but the look of skepticism on Amanda's face made it clear that she already suspected that Melissa had an ulterior motive for bringing someone new into her life. Well, that was mostly accurate. But they could exchange a few pleasantries first. There were certain social niceties you just didn't ignore. "How've you been?" she asked. "Are you practising the forms I showed you?"

Amanda smiled down at herself, a lock of hair falling over her cheek. "I try," she mumbled. "But it's hard to find a chance to do it when my father's not looking. I'm not as… free-spirited as you."

Blushing hard, Melissa closed her eyes and took a deep breath through her nose. "That's actually why we're here," she said softly. "There's an opportunity we wanted to discuss with you."

"An opportunity?"

Melissa retrieved a small tablet from her purse, powering it up to reveal a document on the screen. "A cultural exchange program," she said, handing the device to Amanda. "You'd be invited to attend a Leyrian university."

Amanda took the tablet and began skimming through its contents, her eyes slowly widening as she absorbed the details. "This is amazing!" she squeaked. "By why would they want to take me?"

"I pulled a few strings," Jena explained, "called in a few favours, had them take a look at your transcripts. They say you're a talented young woman who could benefit from a broader experience. This would be an opportunity for you to study science, philosophy, literature. Whatever you choose. Best of all, your material needs would be seen to. You could live on Leyria for as long as you please, free of charge."

"I…I don't know what to say."

Jena smiled, bowing her head to the girl. "Say yes," she replied with a quick shrug of her shoulders. "You wouldn't be legally eligible until after you've reached the age of majority, which I believe is eighteen here."

"But what about…"

Melissa thrust her chin out, studying the girl for a very long moment. "Kevin?" she asked, raising one dark eyebrow. "It's funny you should ask. We just stopped by his place and made him a similar offer. His father was ecstatic."

The girl looked stunned.

"I won't lie to you, Amanda," Jena broke in. "Once you turn eighteen, your father can't stop you from joining this program, but that doesn't mean he won't try. If you do this, it will almost certainly strain your relationship with him, but…It will also give you a chance to live your life on your own terms."

For a moment, Amanda looked apprehensive, but stone-faced resolve quickly replaced any anxiety she might have felt. "May I keep the tablet?" she asked.

Anna was stretched out on her belly across the couch in her living room, her legs curled so that her feet were almost touching her butt. She looked up with strands of red hair falling over her face. "Sweetie, could you grab my tea?"

The kitchen in her little apartment had brown wooden cupboards and an island with a white countertop. Her boyfriend stood there with his eyes downcast, staring into a mug that sent steam flowing up toward the ceiling. Something had been bothering him all day, but every time she asked, he just said it was nothing.

Bradley took the cup and strode into the living room, bending over to set it down on the coffee table. "There you go," he said. "Peppermint tea with milk and a teaspoon of sugar."

Planting her elbow on the couch cushion, Anna rested her chin in the palm of her hand. "Okay," she said, her eyebrows rising. "Do you think you might be able to tell me why you're so unhappy?"

His face crumpled like one of those soda cans in the fist of an angry ten-year-old. "It's nothing," he muttered, dropping into the chair on the other side of the room. "I've just had a long week."

Anna frowned, then scrubbed a hand over her face, brushing bangs back from her forehead. "If you insist," she murmured. "But don't say I didn't try to be a good girlfriend."

He grunted.

"What?"

Bradley scowled, turning his head to stare down at the floor beside his chair. "You are a wonderful girlfriend." The words sounded so forced it actually left a knot of anxiety in her chest.

Anna sat up straight.

Drawing her legs up against her chest, she hugged them and watched her partner for a very tense few seconds. "All right, now I'm insisting," she said. "If you're going to be sullen – and clearly I'm the cause – let's talk about it."

"It's not-"

"Enough." Her chest was so tight with fear that she was surprised her shirt wasn't drenched with sweat. She hated fighting, hated rocking the boat in any relationship, but there were times when you just *had* to get things out in the open. "What did I do? Let's just confront this now."

He sank down in the chair with his arms folded, then threw his head back to look at the ceiling. "It's not what you did," he replied gently. "It's what you *didn't* do. What you *never* do."

"And what do I never do?"

"You never let me in."

Anna was on her feet in two seconds, standing before him with both hands gripping the hem of her shirt, her head hanging in frustration. "I did not realize you felt that way," she said. "I try to be as open as I can with you."

"You never tell me anything!"

Anna felt tears on her cheeks, heat burning in her skin. "I tell you *everything!*" she shouted, striding toward him with the fury of a hurricane. "When I feel stressed, I tell you! When one of my cases goes sideways, I tell you!"

Bradley stood up, towering over her, but if that was supposed to leave her feeling intimidated, she had to admit she was unimpressed. The pain on his face, however... *that* took the wind from her lungs. "And do you want to know what you tell me about most? Jack fucking Hunter. Everything he does, everything he says."

"Because he's my partner?"

"Really? I thought *I* was your partner."

Crossing her arms with a soft sigh, Anna frowned down at herself. "That's not what I mean," she whispered. "He's the person that I interact with every day, and it's not fair of you to twist my words."

In response, Bradley turned so that she saw him in profile and went to the window. He remained there for a little while, hands gripping the wooden windowsill as he stared out at the city. "And you don't see a problem here?"

"Why would I?"

A small part of her – a tiny voice that she had been ignoring for several days now – whispered that Bradley had noticed something that she was trying very hard not to notice. That moment of tenderness between her and Jack. Some part of her wondered if maybe they had gone just a little too far. She had wanted to believe it was nothing but a figment of her imagination, a product of her own insecurity. But if Bradley saw it too…

The anxiety that had been nothing but a hot knife in her chest mere moments ago suddenly became a black hole threatening to crush her from the inside. She couldn't lose Jack. She *couldn't* lose Jack! But at the same time, she had responsibilities. When friendship crossed the line and threatened your relationship, what else could you do?

The tears were flowing freely now. Companion have mercy, why did this always happen whenever she got into it with one of her partners? She could handle gunfire with stone-faced serenity, but confront her with the unsavory reality that she had hurt someone she loved, and Leana Delnara Lenai became a quivering mess. "I'm sorry." The words came out hoarsely. "Maybe I need to take some time away from Jack."

"I don't want you to take time away from Jack," Bradley muttered. He tensed up, shivering as he spoke. "I want you to decide for yourself whom you spend time with, but that said, I need to feel like I'm the person you come to first."

Anna closed her eyes, then pinched the bridge of her nose. "I know," she said into her own palm. "This is all my fault…Sweetie, there's no one in this world that I love as much as I love you."

He turned around, leaning against the windowsill with his head hanging. "Yeah," he said with a shrug of his shoulders. "I know. I just…I get that you can't tell me everything you do, but I feel so out of the loop."

"Maybe it's time we changed that."

"What do you mean?"

She opened her mouth to speak, then immediately swallowed her own words and replaced them with something that wouldn't pour oil on the fire. "A friend told me that your soulmate is the person you share everything with." Best to avoid telling him that advice had come from Jack. "We're searching for something called the Key; we have no idea what it does, but if Slade gets his hands on it, things could go very wrong. Jena was hoping that that thing I recovered in Tennessee might give us some clues to what…"

Isara flowed through a hallway of scarred walls, her cloak flapping behind her with every step. The sheer destruction. Bullet holes everywhere, smears of dried blood with a distinctive silver sheen. At the end of the corridor, a small room stood empty. No doubt the Keepers had taken Pennfield's SlipGate.

Isara crouched down.

Clothed in a navy blue dress that left her arms bare and matching gloves on each hand, she tugged the hood up a little further. One never knew when it might be pertinent to hide one's face.

A sliver of light penetrated the hood, enough that she would be recognized if there had been anyone here to see her, but she allowed herself to smile anyway. "Fool," she said, shaking her head. "Insubordinate, disobedient fool."

She tapped a spot of dried blood on the floor tiles, then rubbed her thumb and her index finger together. The substance flaked away, but she had no doubt that there were microscopic nanobots on the surface of her glove.

She produced a metal disk from a pouch on her belt – a multi-tool – and she pushed a button on its surface to bring up the main menu. A few gestures with one hand allowed her to place a call to Slade, and then she set the tool down on the floor.

The man's hologram appeared before her, standing tall and proud in a black silk robe, his head turned to stare at something off to his left. "Report," he growled in tones that indicated he was in no mood for pleasantries.

"Pennfield is dead," she said, rising gracefully, drawing herself up so that he could see her at full height. Subtle things about one's image would create the right impression: clothing, posture, the way in which one moved. She used them all to her advantage. "The Keepers have been here, and I have no doubt they took his body. Which means they have his symbiont as well."

A frown twisted Slade's mouth, and he sighed before bowing his head to her. "We had anticipated this eventuality," he said. "A shame. I had hoped that Pennfield would do away with Jack Hunter."

"You always overestimated his competence."

"And *you* overestimate my patience."

Isara crossed her arms, frowning down at the large sapphire that dangled from her necklace. "Do you wish me to recover the symbiont?" she asked, raising one shoulder in a halfhearted shrug. "It can be done."

"No." Slade clasped hands together behind his back, assuming the posture of a man who intended to give a speech. "Even *you* would not survive the attempt. Not on a station full of Justice Keepers."

"But if they are allowed to uncover its secrets…"

"An inevitability at this point."

Tapping her lips with one gloved finger, Isara shut her eyes. "There is one more thing to report," she began. "Pennfield chose to use a *ziarogat* against Hunter."

"He did *what?*"

Soft, musical laughter filled the hallway while Isara contemplated the delicious irony of Slade's failure. Master manipulator indeed. "Did you expect Wesley to exercise *prudence* in the pursuit of his vendetta?" What a rare joy it was to see Slade off balance. "Our long term goals were of no consequence to him, not when he was in the grip of his foolish need to assert his own dominance."

Slade was stroking his chin with the fingertips of one hand, his eyes narrowed to slits as he considered this new eventuality. "And the Keepers have the *ziarogat* as well?" he asked. "You can be certain of this?"

"Quite certain."

"Then it seems we must accelerate our timetable," Slade murmured. "Report back to me at once, Isara. It's time we concluded our business on this miserable little planet."

The hologram rippled and faded away.

Chapter 29

The small containment unit looked very much like a fish tank, but instead of water, it held swirling clouds of pink gas that flashed as if a lightning storm were brewing inside. Angry lightning. Perhaps it was just his imagination, but something in those brief pulses of light felt hostile.

Jack was bent over with his hands on his knees, peering into the containment unit. "So that's Pennfield's symbiont," he muttered. "Have we been able to communicate with it?"

Behind him, Nareo sat at the table with his elbow on its surface, his chin resting on the knuckles of his fist. He was fixated on the smaller Overseer device that still hung from metal hooks. "Several Nassai specialists have been in and out of here over the last few days," he said absently. "They're not sure what to make of it."

Jack stood up straight, crossing his arms with a heavy sigh. A frown tugged at the corners of his mouth. "I'm not sure either," he said, turning away from the containment unit. "Summer felt hatred and malice from that thing."

"Is that odd for a Nassai?"

"Very."

Glancing over his shoulder, Nareo wore the kind of skeptical expression you would expect from a scientist. "Perhaps it's simply a matter of lived experience," he suggested. "Being Bonded to a man like Pennfield would have been torture for that thing."

Jack closed his eyes, sighing softly. "It's possible," he said, nodding once. "But it wouldn't account for Wesley's abilities to craft Bendings. Host and symbiont must work together to Bend space-time, and no Nassai ever would."

Summer echoed his sentiments with a burst of pride.

Swiveling in his chair, Nareo faced him with hands on his thighs, head hanging as though the topic were a source of great frustration to him. "Well, then I will tell you what little they told me," he said. "Nassai exhibit patterns in the electrical activity they display. Patterns that indicate sapience."

"And this thing?"

"Doctors Kavinar and Venshal tried to communicate with the symbiont in the same way those pioneering scientists communicated with the first Nassai they recovered from Laras. They tried to induce electrical activity in the gas and see if the symbiont would mimic the patterns. The first Nassai we brought back from Laras did precisely that. This thing doesn't, almost as if…"

"As if it has no will of its own," Jack finished. He covered his face with one hand, massaging his eyelids with the tips of his fingers. "So is that it? That's the only attempt we've made at communication?"

"What else would you suggest?"

Tossing his head back, Jack felt his eyebrows climb upward. "Well, it all depends on how creative you want to get," he said. "One should never underestimate the ability to find common ground through the power of interpretive dance."

The lab doors split apart, revealing Jena and Raynar standing side by side in the hallway. As usual, Jena took the lead, striding into the room like a whirlwind on course for a dilapidated farm. "Lab techs have been in a fury all day," she declared. "You guys just keep bringing in more stuff for them to poke at."

"The *ziarogat*?"

Jena scowled, shaking her head. "They don't even know *what* to make of that…thing," she said, stopping in the middle of the room. "But they're sure of one thing: that man has Overseer technology in his body."

"Is it the same thing you fought on that ship?"

"Definitely."

Clamping a hand over his mouth, Jack shut his eyes tight. "Well, that's just grand," he muttered into his own palm. "If they've been mass producing these things for over a year, there's no telling how many are out there."

"Yeah, I had the same thought," Jena said. "I was hoping that whatever those things were, it was just some kind of random experiment."

"But if they're building an army…"

No one wanted to finish that thought, but Jack was suddenly aware of Nareo and Raynar. His words had sucked the life right out of the room. *Ziarogati.* Jack could still hear Pennfield's voice in the back of his mind. *The pinnacle of military prowess.* That thing was quite *literally* a killing machine. To call it merciless was wholly inaccurate. It had no motivation of its own, no impulse other than serving the ends of its master. There had been no malice in its attempt to kill Jack, just cold machine-like precision.

An army of these things, each one a match for the very best Justice Keepers, each one outfitted with weapons that responded to a single thought. How much damage could they do? There were fewer than three thousand Keepers operating in Leyrian Space: less than three thousand people responsible for the lives of billions. How could they stop an entire army of *ziarogati*?

Raynar stood in the middle of the room with three fingers pressed to his lips, his eyes fixed on the Overseer device. What exactly was the kid doing? *Just leave him to it,* Jack told himself. *You have larger concerns.*

"It's not often that irony kicks me in the ass," Jena muttered, pacing a line with her hands shoved into her pockets. "All those times when I lectured Anna about being able to make the hard choices, and now I wish that she had kept Pennfield alive so that we could question him."

"He wouldn't have told us anything."

"Probably not."

Jack sat down in a chair, breath exploding from his lungs. "The man clearly had friends in high places," he muttered. "Pennfield escaped from one of our cells before; if we took him alive, he'd probably-"

"Gods be good!"

Jack looked up.

Raynar's eyes were so wide they might have fallen out of his head, his skin so pale you might have thought he'd seen a ghost. "I know where it is," he whispered. "Jack, I know where it is! I know where it is!"

"Where *what* is?"

The boy gave his head a shake, then touched his fingertips to his temples and let out a groan. "The Key," he said. "The thing that Slade's been looking for. That Overseer device has *records*, Jack! Records of where they left their technology. Computer, give me a holographic display of Earth."

In the middle of the room, a transparent globe nearly six feet in height rippled into existence. Raynar made a motion with his hand as if he intended to spin the thing, and the motion sensors interpreted his gesture by having the globe turn its axis.

He brought Africa around to face him, then spread his hands apart to zoom in. Closer and closer. Eventually, the globe vanished to be replaced with a flat image of the land from above. Jack had to walk to the other side of the room to see it from Raynar's perspective. Lush green fields dotted with trees.

Raynar took a step back, then pointed. "There," he said. "Those coordinates. That's where you'll find your Key."

"Western Kenya," Jack said. "Less than a dozen kilometers from the place where they unearthed that first SlipGate." But surely, if there was anything of value, *someone* would have found it by now.

He turned to Jena.

She stood with fists balled at her sides, staring at the hologram with an open mouth. "All right," she said, nodding slowly. "New orders. *Nobody* hears a word about this until Jack and I have a chance to check it out."

"So we're going?"

"Get your ass up to the shuttle bay, kid," she replied. "We're about to take a little trip."

Through the shuttle's cockpit window, Jack saw green fields that stretched to the horizon under a blue sky that was slowly darkening with the onset of evening. Jena set them down gently with a jolt so mild he barely felt it.

He could only see the back of her seat, but he didn't have to observe her posture to know that she was tense. The soft sigh she let out while she powered down the shuttle's systems was evidence enough of that.

Stroking his chin with the tips of his fingers, Jack narrowed his eyes. "You realize this could be a wild goose chase," he murmured. "We're not exactly on the border of a major city, but there have been archaeology teams in this region."

Jena swiveled around.

She stood up with a grunt, crossing her arms and shutting her eyes tight. "I know," she said, nodding to him. "But we've been looking for this thing for months, and I will take any lead I can get."

Jack turned around, marching to the back of the cockpit, hesitating there while the doors to the cabin slid open. "So what's your play?" he asked. "Do we go in armed, or is this a 'we come in peace' thing?"

"I'm not sure," Jena replied. "But my instincts say be careful. Light pistols only. If there *is* anything down here, I'd rather not spook it."

That seemed like as good a plan as anything. At the back of the cabin, there was a compartment that opened with a biometric palm scan followed by his latest access code. Inside, he found several pistols holstered side by side. Jack took one for himself and then offered one to his boss.

They exited the shuttle cautiously despite the fact that they were probably the only human beings within ten kilometers of this spot. The sun was sinking toward the western horizon, painting the sky orange and yellow and finally a deep dark blue with tiny stars twinkling up above.

"Let's go," Jena said.

Northward, they walked through nearly two hundred meters of open grassland with nothing but the odd tree or boulder, the ground sloping gently upward toward a rock wall with grass on top. It was hot and sticky even without the sun beating down. This close to the equator, it was always hot.

They said nothing, of course – Jena could be pretty damn taciturn when there was something on her mind – but Jack had plenty to occupy his thoughts. He kept imagining what he'd find. Some kind of Overseer device? A ship? Was it underground? If not, then why had no one ever found it?

Jena stopped in front of him some ten feet away from the rock wall, planting fists on her hips. "Well, this is the place," she said, turning her head to survey the surrounding area. "Whole lot of nothing."

Biting his underlip, Jack lowered his eyes to the ground. "You think Raynar was wrong?" he asked, his eyebrows slowly climbing. "The kid seemed pretty sure we'd find *something* out here."

He stepped forward.

As expected, there was nothing here except a wall of rock with grass sprouting from the top. The sounds of cicadas began to fill the air; this would make for a lovely campsite, but-

He saw it.

A hole in the rock just wide enough for one person to walk through, leading down into what seemed to be a cave. That had to be where the Key was. Unless maybe Raynar had misread what he saw in the device…

Jack slipped both hands into his pockets, bowing his head until he looked like some kid standing in the corner at this first high school dance. "Well, then," he muttered. "Who votes we look inside the creepy, ominous cave?"

Jena turned her head to watch him with a flat expression, her eyes full of challenge. "You think that's a good idea?" she asked. "In all likelihood, the only thing you'll find in there is a broken ankle."

"We came this far."

He turned on his heel, trailing his fingers over the rock wall until he reached the mouth of the cave. Something inside him felt tense; he was dimly aware of the beating of his own heart. When he peered into the hole, only darkness stared back at him.

Thrusting his left fist out, Jack said, "Multi-tool active. Flashlight." A bright cone of radiance penetrated the cave, illuminating dark gray walls and an uneven floor that sloped slowly downward. Not that he would need light to see – Summer could handle that – but it was best to rely on *all* his senses.

Jack stooped low.

He shuffled through the opening with a grunt, then stood up straight and blinked to give himself time to adjust. "Aliens just have no standards anymore," he said, descending the rough incline. "If they're gonna leave their stuff in the middle of nowhere, you would think they'd at least put up some defenses. An energy shield or a-"

His light fell on something.

A cylindrical device about as tall as his knee sat in the middle of the floor with red LEDs blinking on its surface. But this wasn't Overseer technology; Jack had seen devices like this before. It was a portable, holographic generator.

An image rippled into existence before him: a large, blue rectangle with the Leyrian phrase "placing call" blinking at him in huge letters. He was dimly aware of Jena coming up behind and cursing when she saw it.

The hologram vanished to be replaced with the transparent image of a tall man in black pants and a white shirt with the collar left open, a man with smooth skin, tilted eyes and long dark hair. "Jack!" Grecken Slade exclaimed. "I was hoping that it would be you. I really must congratulate you on defeating Wesley."

Craning his neck to stare at the hologram, Jack narrowed his eyes. "Slade!" he said, stepping closer to the ghostly image. "Does this mean you found the Key? Not enough to just take your prize, eh? You have to gloat as well?"

Slade crossed his arms with a sigh, smiling down at himself. "Oh heavens, no!" he said through a lighthearted chuckle. "If only it were that simple. Honestly, Jack, did you really think we wouldn't try checking Inzari devices for the Key's location?"

"You've already been here?"

"Many times."

Jack closed his eyes, breathing deeply to calm himself. "Which means the place is empty," he said. "How is *that* possible? Why would the Overseers put false information in their own devices?"

Spreading his arms wide, Slade bowed low as if putting on a performance. "Isn't it obvious?" he asked. "One would think that your clever mind would have put the pieces together. The Key *was* here, but they've moved it."

"How?"

Jena stepped forward to stand beside him with hands folded over her thighs, her face as hard as rock. "Moved it," she asked, raising one eyebrow. "I thought the Key was a place. How do you move a place?"

"Station Twelve is a place," Slade answered. "Fire its thrusters to adjust its orbit, and you will have successfully moved it."

Pinching his chin with thumb and forefinger, Jack squinted at the other man. "Wait, this makes no sense," he said. "You work for the Overseers, don't you? Why don't your bosses just *tell* you where the Key is?"

"That's why I want you on my side, Jack," Slade murmured. He turned to Jena with a sour expression. "You, on the other hand, can die at your earliest convenience. I have no use for you.

"A small reward for your cleverness. The Inzari created the Key for us, intending for us to claim it when we were ready to wield its power. But a small number of them – a faction that believed it was wrong to direct humanity's evolution to their ends – hid the Key and masked it so that even Inzari technology could not detect it.

"Only humans can solve the puzzle, and we have spent *decades* searching for the Key. Everything you think to try, every new idea you come up with, we've done it first. But I thought I'd leave this little greeting for you in the event you should stumble upon this place. You see, now I know you're looking for the Key too."

Mopping a hand over his face, Jack raked fingers through his sweat-slick hair. "Isn't that just grand?" he grumbled. "I guess you're gonna tell me that the cave is empty. You'll have to forgive me if I don't take your word for it."

A wicked grin appeared on Slade's face, and he replied with cruel, self-satisfied laughter. "I wouldn't say that it's *empty,*" he said. "Explore the cave if you wish, Jack. But you won't like what you find."

The hologram vanished.

At his side, Jena stood with her lips pursed, gazing into the darkness. "No time like the present," she said, starting forward. "Come on, kid. Let's go find something we know we won't like."

"You want to go on?"

She turned partway around, glancing over her shoulder to study him for a very long moment. "If there's something down here, I want to know what it is," she said. "Besides, where's your sense of adventure?"

They journeyed deeper into the cave, to a point where the ground leveled off and he could hear a soft dripping sound in the distance. His flashlight allowed him to see a small area right in front of him, but spatial awareness did the rest. He could sense the uneven ceiling, the pits and dips in the floor.

A small ledge rose up before them to the height of Jack's waist. Being a gentleman, he climbed up first, then turned and offered a hand to his companion. She murmured her thanks and then pressed onward, her own flashlight swiveling this way and that.

A few minutes later, he sensed it.

A circle of spikes rising out of the ground, each curving inward like teeth from a perfectly round mouth. At first, he thought they were stalagmites, but that wasn't likely. They were far too smooth, far too uniform. Someone had *constructed* these things.

Jack dropped to one knee on the cold, damp ground, thrusting one fist out to shine a light on the structure. "Okay…That's unnerving," he muttered. "You ever get hit hard with a sudden burst of genre savvy?"

"What are you talking-"

The walls lit up with a soft blue glow, a radiance that permeated the entire chamber from floor to ceiling. It should have been frightening – and he could sense tension from Summer – but for some reason, Jack found himself feeling strangely calm. Hey, if he was gonna die in some Eldritch abomination's stomach, at least his story would have a cool ending. Find the silver lining in everything.

Something that looked very much like black smoke rose up from inside the circle of spikes, coalescing into a cloud that hovered just a few feet below the ceiling. Two yellow eyes appeared, blazing with the heat of a thousand suns.

Amateur parlour tricks.

Jack tapped away at his multi-tool, bringing up the scanning feature. As expected, this creature was nothing but a hologram. A very sophisticated hologram, but sculpted light nonetheless.

The yellow eyes flared, and the cloud seemed to loom over him, tendrils of smoke reaching out like tentacles. "They come again!" a deep voice boomed. "Seeking answers, seeking meaning. Seeking us."

Pressing his lips into a thin line, Jack blinked at the thing. "I'm guessing you're an Overseer," he said. "Well, if you don't mind, maybe you could give us a little insight as to-"

The cloud trembled, yellow light flashing within as if it intended to spit lightning bolts at him. Hell, maybe it did. There was no telling what these things were capable of. "Overseer," it said. "A new term for that which you can never comprehend."

"Oh, I get it," Jack mocked. "This is the 'I'm old and inscrutable' speech. Hang on while I fish out my book full of cosmic horror clichés. I do believe your next line should include something about us being the dust at your feet."

"I saw what you did on that ship!" Jena barked. "The people that you turned into monsters. You're building an army!"

"What need would we have for an army?"

"You plan to wipe us out!"

The cloud pulsed, yellow lightning flashing within. The rumbling he heard sounded so very much like mocking laughter. "What purpose would be served by your extinction?" it asked in mocking tones. "Limited creatures. You struggle for understanding, but the true nature of the universe yet eludes you."

Jack got to his feet.

He crossed his arms with a quiet sigh, frowning down at himself. "Okay," he said, pacing toward the apparition. "You've got my attention. If you don't want to kill us, then what *do* you want with us?"

The cloud expanded, wisps of smoke curling up toward the ceiling, and the yellow eyes were suddenly fixed upon him. Twin infernos that threatened to scorch him to ash with a single glance. "Your species considers itself the pinnacle of evolution," the cloud thundered. "You sculpt metal to serve your will and think yourselves gods. We sculpt flesh to serve our will. You are flesh; you will serve our will."

Terror seized Jack's heart in icy fingers. Was this thing saying what he thought it was saying? Was humanity just one more piece of organic technology to be used by these Overseers? That couldn't be possible! It was a lie; it had to be! Jack wasn't just a cog in some great machine. He had a *soul,* god damn it!

Or did he…

The Nassai had been created by the Overseers to allow organic ships to reach faster than light travel. An entire species created and then abandoned because it had outlived its usefulness. If the Overseers could do that to Summer's people, then why not to humans? Was anything he had been taught in school correct?

"I don't accept that," he said, shaking his head. "Not for one god damn minute! Humans aren't so easily controlled. We will fight you."

"In resisting, you serve us still."

"How?"

The cloud pulsed, yellow light flickering within. It reached out with one smokey tendril, and there was a pressure on his mind.

A white flash drowned out everything, and suddenly he was standing in his sister's living room, just inside the front door, the containment unit that carried Summer resting on the table beside him.

A uniformed cop with an ugly face stood with a pistol clutched in both hands, its barrel pointed right at Jack's chest. Hutchinson. He remembered this moment. "Defiance is your purpose," the voice echoed. "Your function."

Another flash, and then he was standing in Slade's office, watching as the former head of the Justice Keepers approached a window that looked out upon a field of stars. The man stood with his back turned, hands clasped behind himself. Jack knew this moment as well; this was the day he had been suspended for defying Breslan's orders and capturing Nicolae Petrov. "Defiance is your central imperative. It is coded into the very essence of your being. In following that imperative, you serve us."

A flash returned him to the cave.

Jack squeezed his eyes shut. "That's not true," he said, his voice thick with hatred. "Break out whatever mind screw you want, but you do not *own* me!"

"Ownership. A human concept."

Something touched his arm.

A glance over his shoulder revealed Jena standing there with a thin smile on her face. "Come on," she said, jerking her head toward the cave's entrance. "Let's go. There's nothing for us here besides a bunch of empty posturing."

"Your arrogance blinds you," the voice boomed.

"Funny," Jena replied. "I was about to say the same thing."

Despite his anger, Jack allowed himself to be led away from the strange hologram, back to the mouth of the cave. The walls dimmed as they went, and they had to rely on their flashlights once again. "Serve your function, Justice Keeper," a deep voice echoed from behind them. "The next phase will soon begin."

Chapter 30

No more dead babies.

Thin rays of sunlight came through the skylight in the ceiling, illuminating a large lobby with gray carpets and a curved wooden desk along the wall opposite the door. Half a dozen people – most of them women – knelt in front of the bench seats in the middle of the room with fingers laced over their heads.

Christopher tossed the receptionist to the floor.

A tall woman in a black skirt and matching blouse, she landed on all fours, her dark hair fanning over her back. "Please," she whimpered, her body shaking with every gasp. "You don't have to do this."

Christopher stood over her in blue jeans and a gray t-shirt, the gun in his right hand pointed at the back of her head. He was a tall man with pale skin, stubble on his jawline and dark hair that he wore neatly combed.

Christopher flinched, turning his face away from her. "You kill babies," he growled, kicking her in the short ribs. "Use their bodies for your twisted experiments, and yet you are afraid to die?"

One of the women near the door rose.

In a heartbeat, Christopher had the gun pointed at her, and she froze in a crouch, raising both hands into the air. "Stay on your fucking knees, whore!" he spat. "That's where you belong. All of you. Murdering children to avoid responsibility for-"

His phone rang.

That damn police sergeant wanted to talk again. As if he would entertain anything the other man had to say. If there were any justice in this world, those officers out there would be on *his* side, but America had thrown justice to the wind over fifty years ago. *Someone* had to take a stand. *Someone* had to speak for God.

He answered the phone, lifting the receiver to his ear. "How you doing in there, Chris?" Sergeant Matthews's voice came through the speaker. "I'm hoping you've had a few moments to calm down."

"Calm down?" Christopher said. "You want me to calm down? You've got twenty men surrounding this building, and you want me to calm down?"

"No one wants to hurt you, Chris," Matthews assured him. "We want to help you get better, but in order to do that, you're going to have to give us a show of good faith. How 'bout releasing two of the hostages?"

"Fuck you!"

"Chris, you're gonna have to play ball here."

By instinct, he moved to the back of the lobby, near the wooden door that led to the examination room. The front windows were all frosted glass, the better to let these sinners escape the eyes of judgment, but he didn't want their sharpshooters getting any bright ideas. "How far you've fallen," he whispered into the phone. "These people butcher children, and you *defend* them?"

"I understand what you're feeling, Chris, but-"

"There was a time when this country stood for something!" He rolled up his sleeve to reveal a tattoo of Old Glory on his upper arm. Seven red stripes, six white stripes and fifty stars: once upon a time, it was a symbol, a beacon to the rest of the world.

But now, America was nothing but a hollow shell of its former self, a nation that had turned its back on God and suffered for it.

"Chris…"

Shutting his eyes tight, Christopher gave his head a shake. "I'm not giving you any of the hostages," he said. "You pull your people back, give me some breathing room, and maybe we'll talk."

"Chris, I need you to-"

The line went dead all of a sudden, and before Christopher could even wonder what had caused the disruption, gunfire erupted, filling the air with a vicious roar. Hostages shrieked and dropped to the floor in terror, but none of those shots hit the window. Not one stray bullet found its way into the clinic. Whatever the cops were shooting at, it certainly wasn't him.

The shots stopped, leaving a silence that felt like going deaf, but he could just make out the sounds of voices outside. "Jesus Christ!" someone shouted. "How in God's name did they do that? Did we hit one?"

One what?

A moment later, the skylight shattered, raining shards of glass down on frightened people, and once again, the lobby was an echo chamber of screams and pleas to the God who had long since forsaken these sinners. "Shut up!" Chris bellowed, gesturing with his pistol. "Shut your fucking mouths!"

A man dropped through the opening, landing on one knee in the middle of the floor. Tall and lithe, he wore black pants and a red coat. He was Asian, with delicate features and long dark hair. "Greetings," he said, rising.

Three others followed him through the skylight. A woman in beige pants and a white t-shirt landed just behind the newcomer, swiveling around to point pistols at the cowering hostages. Her face was hidden behind a ski-mask.

Next came a black man who wore simple gray clothing. His face was handsome with a square jaw, and his dark hair was kept short in a crew cut. The smile he directed at everyone in the room made Christopher think of a cat that had just cornered its lunch.

Finally, another woman dropped from the roof into the lobby, this one short and slim with olive skin and brown hair that fell over her shoulders in curls. She looked like she could kill with a glance.

Christopher stared at them with a gaping mouth, blinking slowly. "Who are you?" he said, raising his gun to defend himself. "Who...Why would you? What do you want with me?"

The Asian man turned with his hands raised defensively, a sly, satisfied smile on his face. "Please...You have nothing to fear from us," he replied, starting toward Christopher at a measured pace. "Your faith and dedication have been rewarded."

"Rewarded?"

"Why have you come here, my son?"

Red-cheeked, Christopher squeezed his eyes shut and let his head hang. "These people are murderers," he muttered. "Somebody has to take a stand for justice!"

"They have transgressed?"

"They kill babies!"

The Asian man's smile deepened, and he bowed his head almost respectfully. "Do you know who I am, my child?" he asked in a voice as smooth as silk. "I am a servant of the Divine. My name is Grecken Slade."

Something about that name tickled Christopher's memory, but he couldn't say what. He'd heard it before, but he didn't know where. Not that it mattered. If this man intended to stand in his way, he would simply pull the trigger. "That's close enough!" Christopher shouted, gesturing with his pistol.

Slade stopped in his tracks.

The man turned his head to direct a frown over his shoulder. "You are a man of true dedication," he said, nodding with satisfaction. "It takes an enormous amount of courage to stand up for your convictions."

"What are you doing here?"

"Allow me to introduce my companions," Slade said, gesturing at the black man. "This is Arin. He has only recently joined us."

Before Christopher could speak, Slade was facing the masked woman. "Isara," he said, striding forward and clapping her on the shoulder. "By far my most skilled warrior. She has been at my side for over a hundred years."

Some of the hostages perked up at that, exchanging startled glances with one another. The receptionist was so shocked by what she heard that she actually got up on her knees so she could get a good look at the woman. Christopher couldn't say that he blamed her. Over a hundred years? Was the mask hiding an ugly, withered face?

Twirling on his heel, Slade approached his third companion with his head down. This one had the appearance of a lioness, and whenever she looked at Christopher, he couldn't help but feel like she was thinking about ripping him to pieces. "Valeth," Slade said, gently touching the woman's arm. "Our newest recruit."

"Why are you telling me this?" Christopher wondered aloud.

"Because we would have you join us."

"Join you?"

Taking a position in the middle of the room, Slade spread his arms wide and bowed his head. "Your commitment to the Divine is commendable," he said. "Now join with me, and I will show you the face of God."

Christopher shut his eyes, tilting his head back until he felt warm sunlight on his skin. He took a deep breath and then let it out. "I know the face of God already. He who died for our sins."

"Yes, that is one of his faces." The other man flowed across the room, caressing a strange circular device that he wore on his belt. "Consider this a baptism into a new life, my son. You oppose sin. Your purity will be rewarded."

"You can't be serious."

The small smile on Slade's face could have frozen the most violent volcano. "You have prayed to the Lord for a sign," he said. "And the Lord has provided. Will you now reject the honour that has been given to you?"

Christopher swallowed, then glanced about from side to side. "What do I have to do?" he asked, his brow furrowing. "How do I…How do I accept the place the Lord has set aside for me?"

"Kneel before me, my son."

Christopher did as he was ordered, dropping to his knees and letting his head hang. A shiver ran down his spine, and he had to resist the urge to tremble. He would meet his Lord with the dignity expected of a man.

Slade held the circular device before him, and he saw that it was some strange kind of container with a blinking green LED. What could possibly be in there? "Accept this," Slade intoned. "Be one with the Lord, and you shall be transformed into a new and better incarnation. Place your hand on the device."

Christopher did so.

Slade pressed two buttons with his thumbs, and then Christopher felt something warm and moist against his palm. There was a brief tingling sensation, but it lasted only seconds before raw energy coursed through every cell in his body. Pure, undiluted power. The essence of God himself.

His skin was glowing with brilliant white light, his hand luminous as he flexed his fingers. The ecstasy! The sweet, glorious fury of it. He felt… something. Some other force that was blending with him. And it was enraged. He could feel it in his mind, in his very soul; this was God's divine wrath, and it had been given to him to wield. Sinners would pay for their crimes in droves. He would break them all with his bare hands.

Christopher toppled over, catching himself by slamming hands down on the carpet. "What was that?" he asked. "What, what did you do to me?"

When he looked up, Slade was smiling down at him, chuckling softly to himself. "I made you one with the Divine," he said. "Your old life is forgotten. The man you were is no more. You must choose a new name."

"A new name?"

One of the hostages stirred, hoping to use this distraction to her advantage, but Isara kicked the woman hard across the chin, breaking her jaw on contact. "Stay down! All of you!" she ordered, gesturing with the pistols in her hand.

The men and women who cowered under their seats began to whimper, a sound that filled Christopher with delicious glee. He relished their suffering. It was as if his desire to inflict pain on these miserable excuses for human garbage had been amplified. "When we join with the Divine," Slade began. "We each take a new name. You must now do so. Let go of your old life, and commit to a greater purpose."

What name should he choose? One of the apostles perhaps? Or a great figure from American history? A real man who stood for righteousness? No, none of that would do. He needed something simple, something that suited him.

Out of the corner of his eye, he noticed the tattoo on his arm, and the answer came in a blinding flash of inspiration. "Flagg," he said. "My name is Flagg."

The woman called Valeth turned her head, frowning at Slade with her brows drawn together. "We can't stay here forever," she said. "Sooner or later, those officers outside will try to reestablish control of the situation."

"Then perhaps we should send them a message."

"What kind of message?" Flagg asked.

Slade dropped to one knee before him, picking up the pistol that he had discarded. The man wore a bright smile, his eyes sparkling with delight. "It's fairly simple," he said, pressing the weapon into Flagg's outstretched hand.

Slade rose in one fluid motion, then ran his gaze over the pitiful excuses for human beings who took refuge beneath chairs. "A man has gun," he said, eyebrows rising. "Hey, man…Have fun."

Flagg understood.

He killed the receptionist first.

Jena emptied her stomach onto the sidewalk, bile splashing against the concrete with a horrible stench. Companion have mercy! In all her years as a Justice Keeper, she had never seen anything like *that.* The horror of it was going to be glued to the insides of her eyelids until her dying day. *Focus,* she told herself. *You have a job to do.*

This street outside a fertility clinic in downtown Cleveland had been cordoned off to prevent civilian traffic, and she could see police officers in blue uniforms manning orange barricades half a block away. They scurried about like ants, but none were willing to venture a glance in her direction. They didn't want to be reminded of what had happened to their colleagues.

Tears blurred her vision for a moment, and she could feel her Nassai recoiling in horror. *That* was a sign in and of itself. After over twenty years together, the symbiont had developed a kind of emotional toughness. Jena had honestly believed that, at this point in her career, nothing could shake her.

She had been wrong.

"Such carnage."

She turned.

Aamani Patel stood before her in a black pantsuit, her arms folded as she directed a scowl toward the pile of corpses. Jena had to give the woman credit. Somehow, she was able to maintain her composure. "Twenty officers," she murmured. "All dead. Every last one of them. Not to mention the civilians."

Doubled over with hands on her knees, Jena looked up to blink at the other woman. "Come to tell me that I'm not doing my job?" she asked. "That this is yet another example of Leyrian incompetence?"

Aamani closed her eyes, shaking her head in dismay. "Not at all," she answered, striding forward and offering one hand to Jena. "I've come to realize that there is nothing to be gained from such antagonism."

Jena took the woman's hand.

A moment later, she was standing up straight and struggling to ignore the churning in her belly. Oh, Companion have mercy! If she let herself think too deeply on it, she would be throwing up again.

Wiping her mouth with the back of one hand, Jena winced. "I wish I could tell you it's good to see you," she said, shaking her head. "But our interactions haven't been what I'd call pleasant. Why are you here anyway?"

Aamani lifted her chin, snorting with such force that her nostrils flared. "I have some contacts in the CIA," she explained. "A few friends who were more than willing to let me get a first-hand look."

The woman spun around, turning her back on Jena and standing on the curb with her fists on her hips. "Rogue Keepers affect all of us," she went on. "Not just the United States. You can understand their desire to cooperate."

Jena crossed her arms, hanging her head as a shiver went through her. "Is that why you're talking to me now?" she asked, stepping forward to stand beside the other woman. "You want to cooperate?"

Aamani cast a glance over her shoulder, her mouth a thin line, her brow lined with wrinkles. "I've had occasion to reevaluate my choices," she said. "I spoke to your young telepath, the boy named Raynar."

Jena closed her eyes, breathing deeply through her nose. "He's becoming a valued member of my team," she said with a curt nod. "Let me guess: you want access to him. There are some terrorists you need him to interrogate."

"You *really* don't trust me."

"Should I?"

A sigh was Aamani's response, and she hunched up her shoulders as if caught in a sudden chilly wind. "I suppose that's only fair," she said. "Your telepath informed me that someone has been influencing my thoughts."

"Come again?"

The other woman rounded on her with fists balled at her sides, her eyes downcast as if she were too ashamed to meet Jena's gaze. "You heard me," she said. "Someone has been influencing my thoughts, tweaking my emotions; there are telepaths on this planet, pulling the strings of who knows how many VIPs in who knows how many countries."

Covering her mouth with two fingers, Jena squinted at the other woman. "It's not possible," she said, backing away. "We thoroughly monitor all incoming traffic. Any ship that goes near the Antauran Sector is turned away."

"Then perhaps the telepaths were here before you arrived," Aamani said, voicing another possibility that Jena would have preferred not to think about. "Another layer to Slade's conspiracy. It doesn't matter. The point is we both need allies."

Jena opened her mouth to reply with another biting comment, but clamped it shut again before her tongue betrayed her. If what Aamani said was true, then she really *did* need all the help she could get. "What did you have in mind?"

"I tell you everything I know," Aamani began. "You tell me everything you know. We pool our resources, and maybe we can prevent…*this*…from happening again." A scowl twisted the other woman's features. "Think long and hard on that, Director Morane. For the first time in four years, I get the feeling that you're just as out of your depth as we are. Allies are not easily discarded in times of trouble."

Jena couldn't argue with that.

She let herself look at the crime scene one more time, really *look* at it, taking in every last detail. The urge to vomit tried to overpower her, but she kept control of herself, and her Nassai offered comforting emotions.

Two police cruisers were parked in front of the clinic, both with flashing light-bars. On the far side of the road, three officers in full tactical gear were piled one atop the other with a stop sign driven through their chests, the metal post holding them together the way a skewer holds a shish-kebab.

A severed head was sitting on the roof of one cruiser, leaking blood onto its pristine white paint job. And there were corpses strewn about the road.

One of the officers had been thrown through the windshield of his car, and now his feet protruded through the shattered glass. Still as stone. Jena wasn't sure if the impact had killed him or if he had been dead already. But that was not the worst part.

No, not the worst part by far.

The worst part was the hologram that floated on the rooftop across the street: a tall man in black pants and a red coat with long dark hair that floated in the wind. The image of Grecken Slade stared down at her, speaking the same message that had played on a loop since she had arrived. For the last five minutes, she had been tuning it out.

"This is just a taste," Slade promised. "The devastation I can unleash will be much, much worse. My demands are simple. Is Jena Morane listening? Good. You're going to stay out of my way, Jena. Your little trained minions are going to stay out of my way. From this point onward, any action that you take against me will be met with the same carnage that you see here. Think I'm bluffing? Try me. My people are everywhere, Jena. You will never be safe again."

The End of the Fourth Book of the Justice Keepers Saga.

Dear reader,

We hope you enjoyed reading *Relativity*. Please take a moment to leave a review, even if it's a short one. Your opinion is important to us.

The story continues in *Evolution*.

To read first chapter for free, head to:
https://www.nextchapter.pub/books/evolution

Discover more books by R.S. Penney at
https://www.nextchapter.pub/authors/ontario-author-rs-penney

Want to know when one of our books is free or discounted? Join the newsletter at http://eepurl.com/bqqB3H

Best regards,

R.S. Penney and the Next Chapter Team

Contact the Author

Follow me on Twitter @Rich_Penney

E-mail me at keeperssaga@gmail.com

You can check out my blog at rspenney.com

You can also visit the Justice Keepers Facebook page
https://www.facebook.com/keeperssaga
Questions, comments and theories are welcome.